THE OUTSIDE CIRCLE

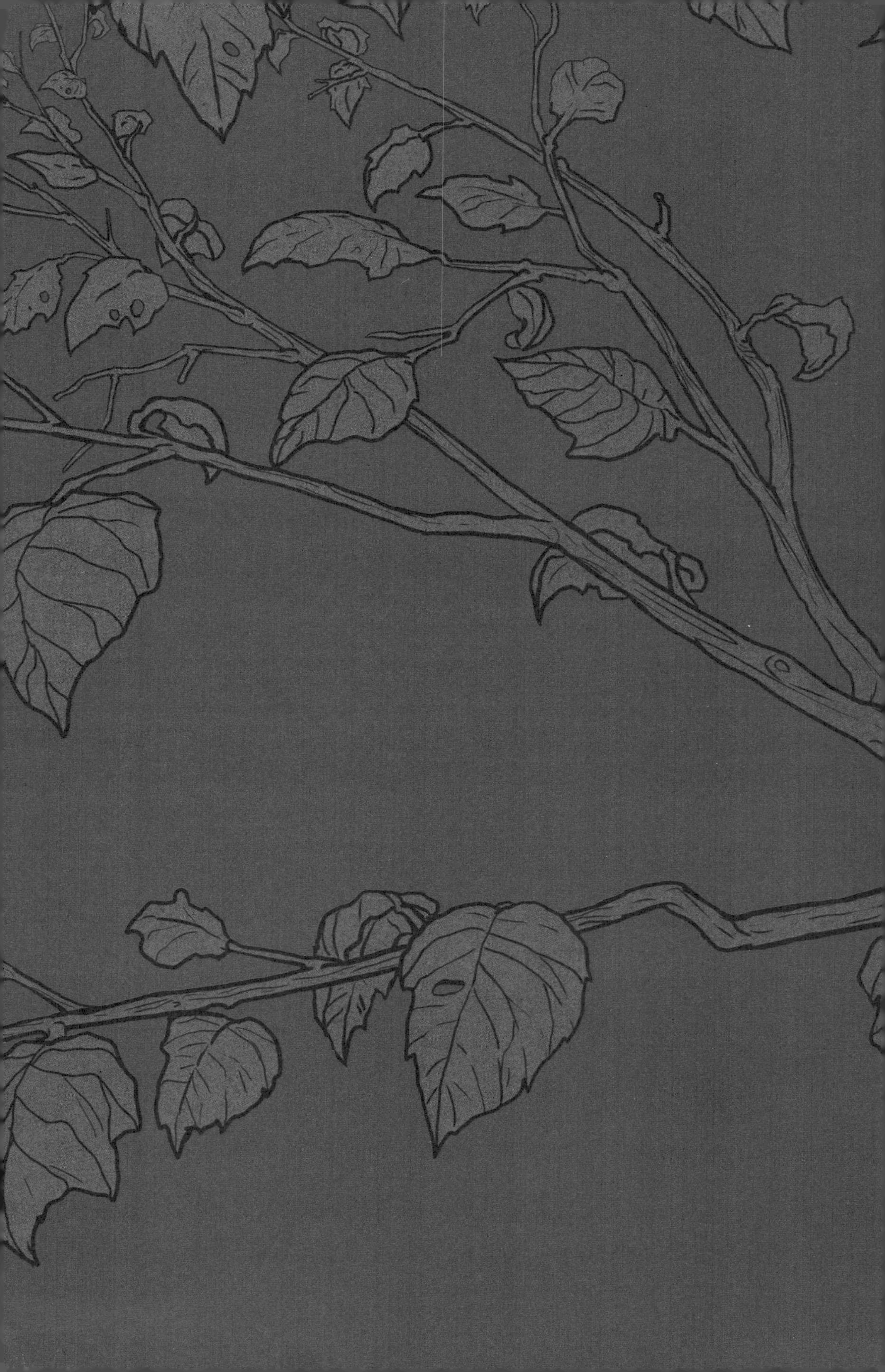

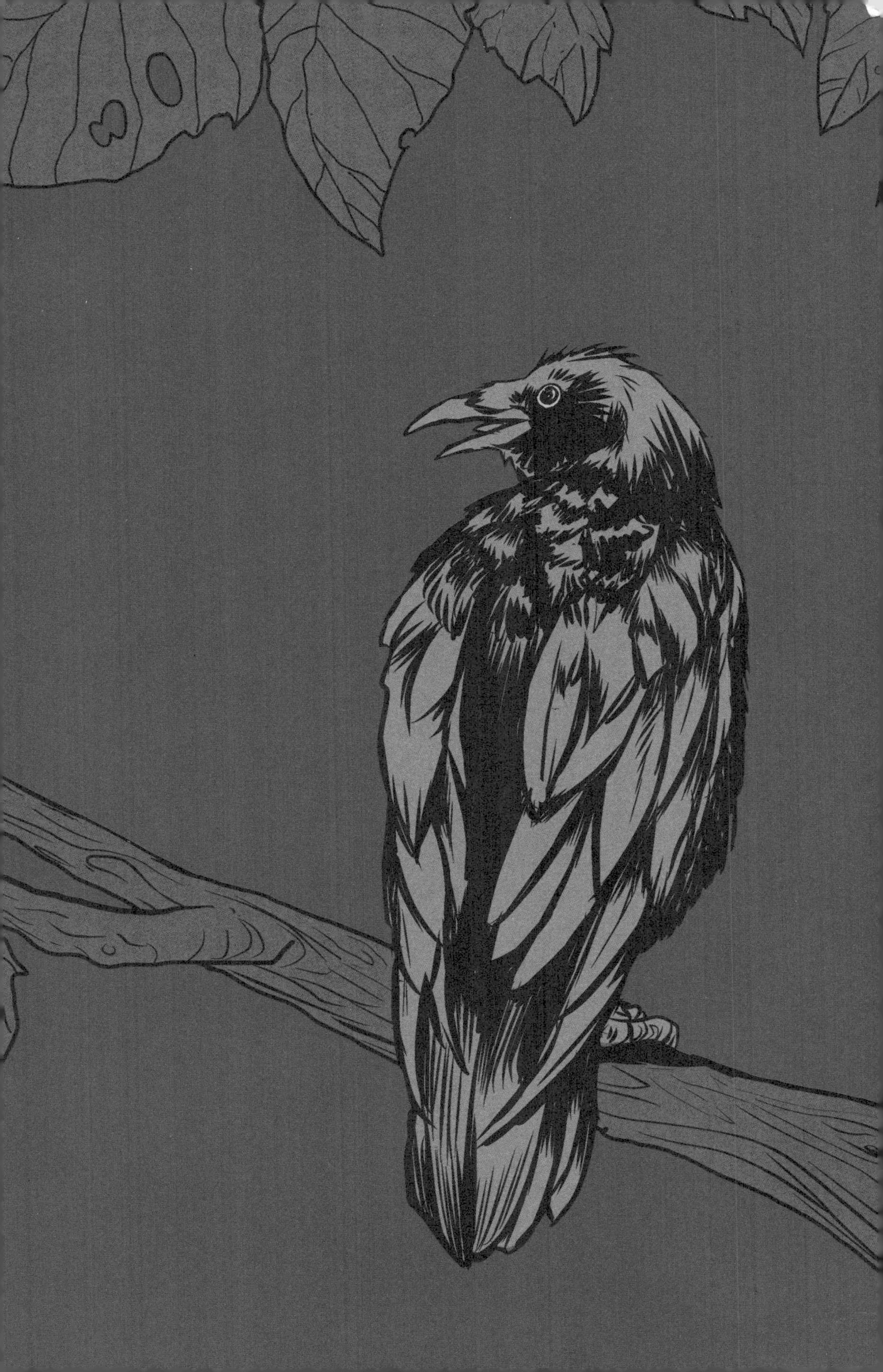

THE OUTSIDE CIRCLE

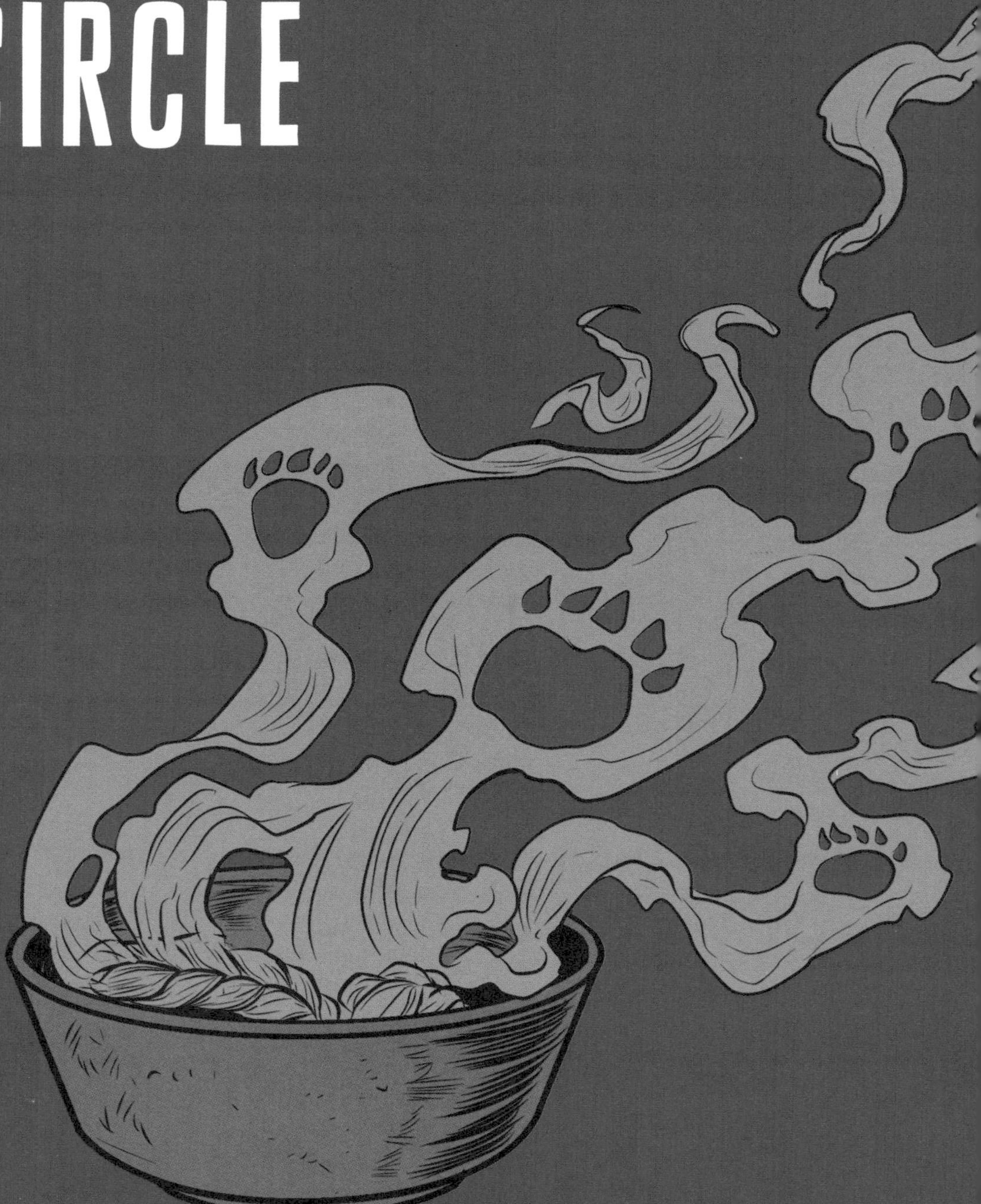

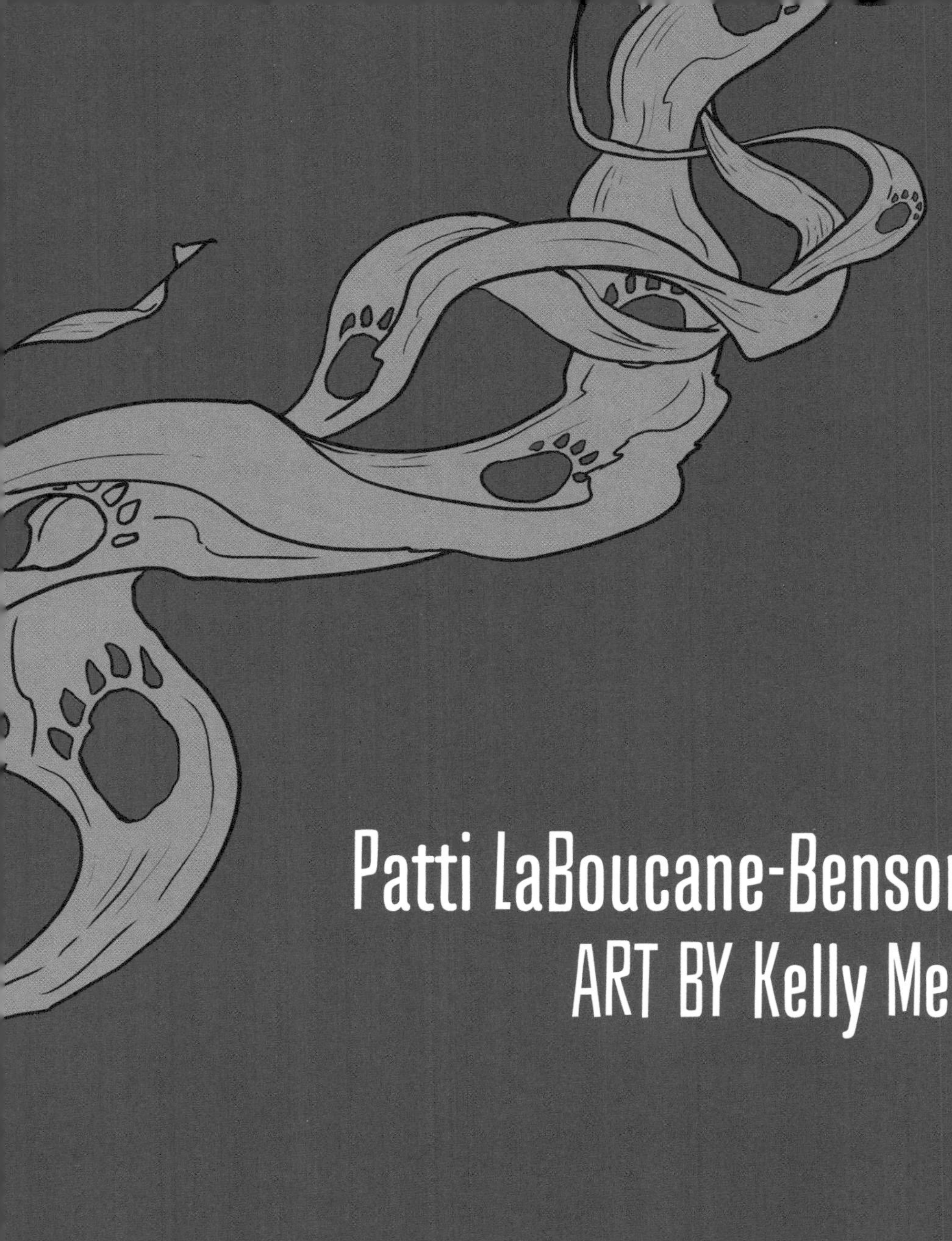

Patti LaBoucane-Benson

ART BY Kelly Mellings

FOR GABRIEL, LIVIA, JUNIPER, VIOLET, KEYANO. AND FORREST.
— Patti LaBoucane-Benson

FOR CHRISTY, VÉRITÉ, AND MINA.
— Kelly Mellings

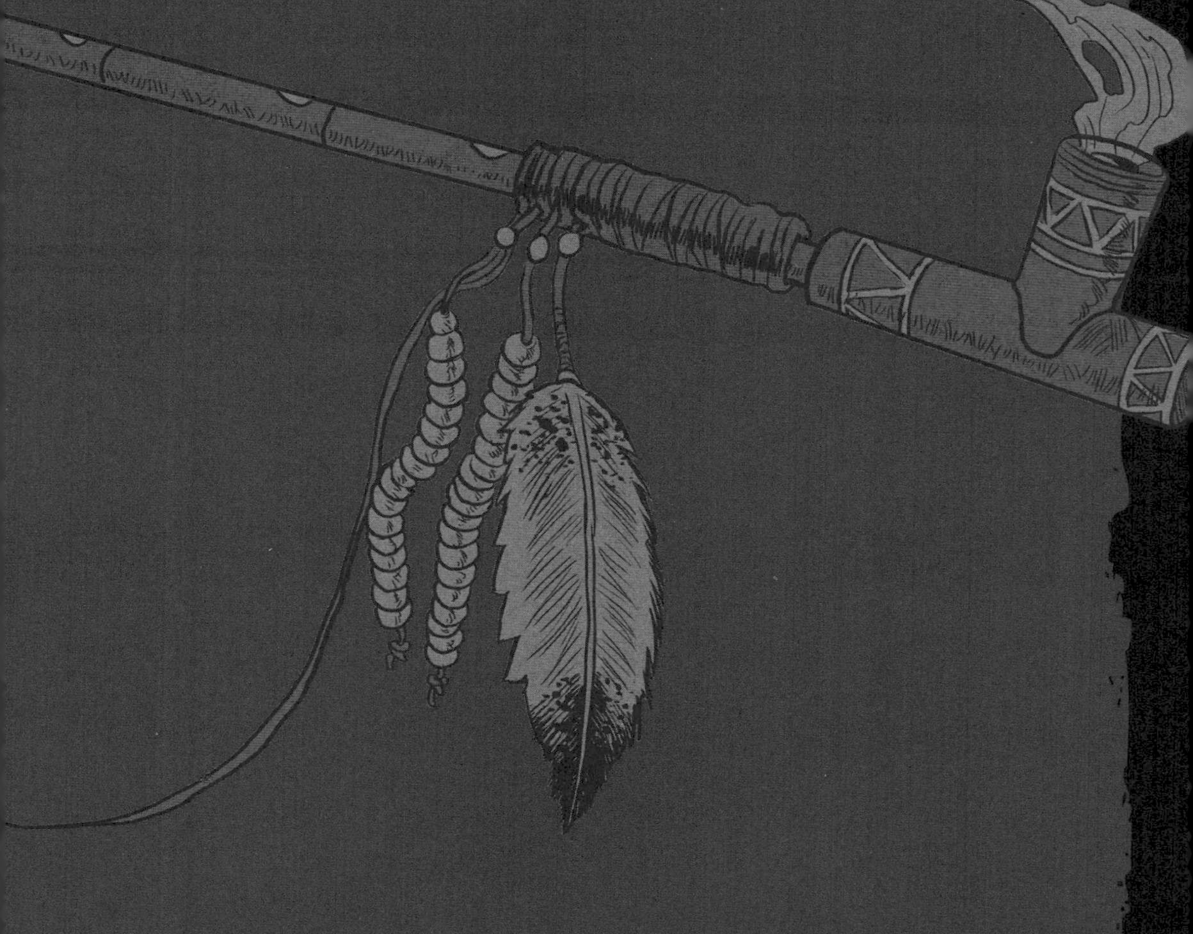

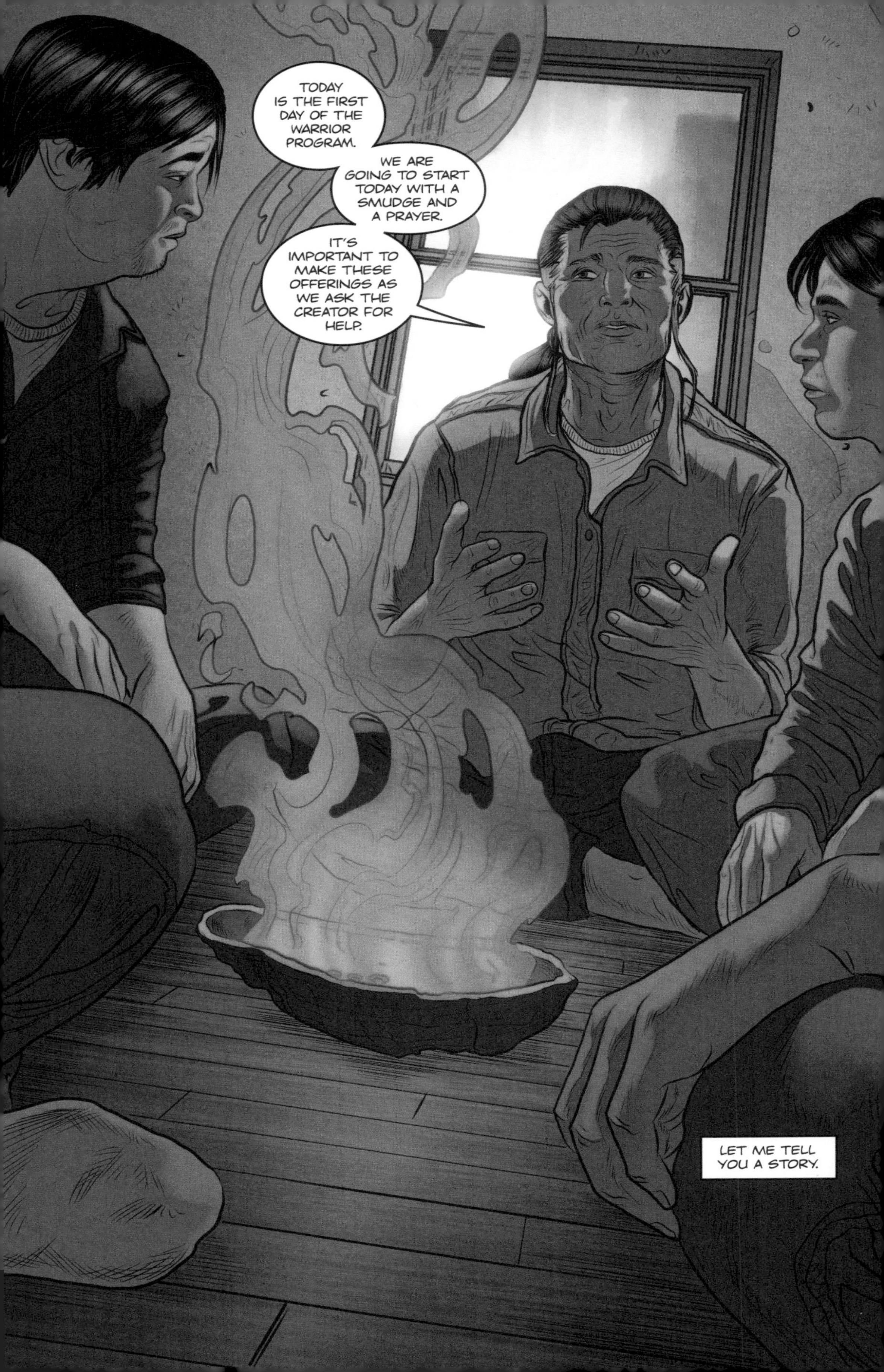
TODAY IS THE FIRST DAY OF THE WARRIOR PROGRAM.
WE ARE GOING TO START TODAY WITH A SMUDGE AND A PRAYER.
IT'S IMPORTANT TO MAKE THESE OFFERINGS AS WE ASK THE CREATOR FOR HELP.
LET ME TELL YOU A STORY.

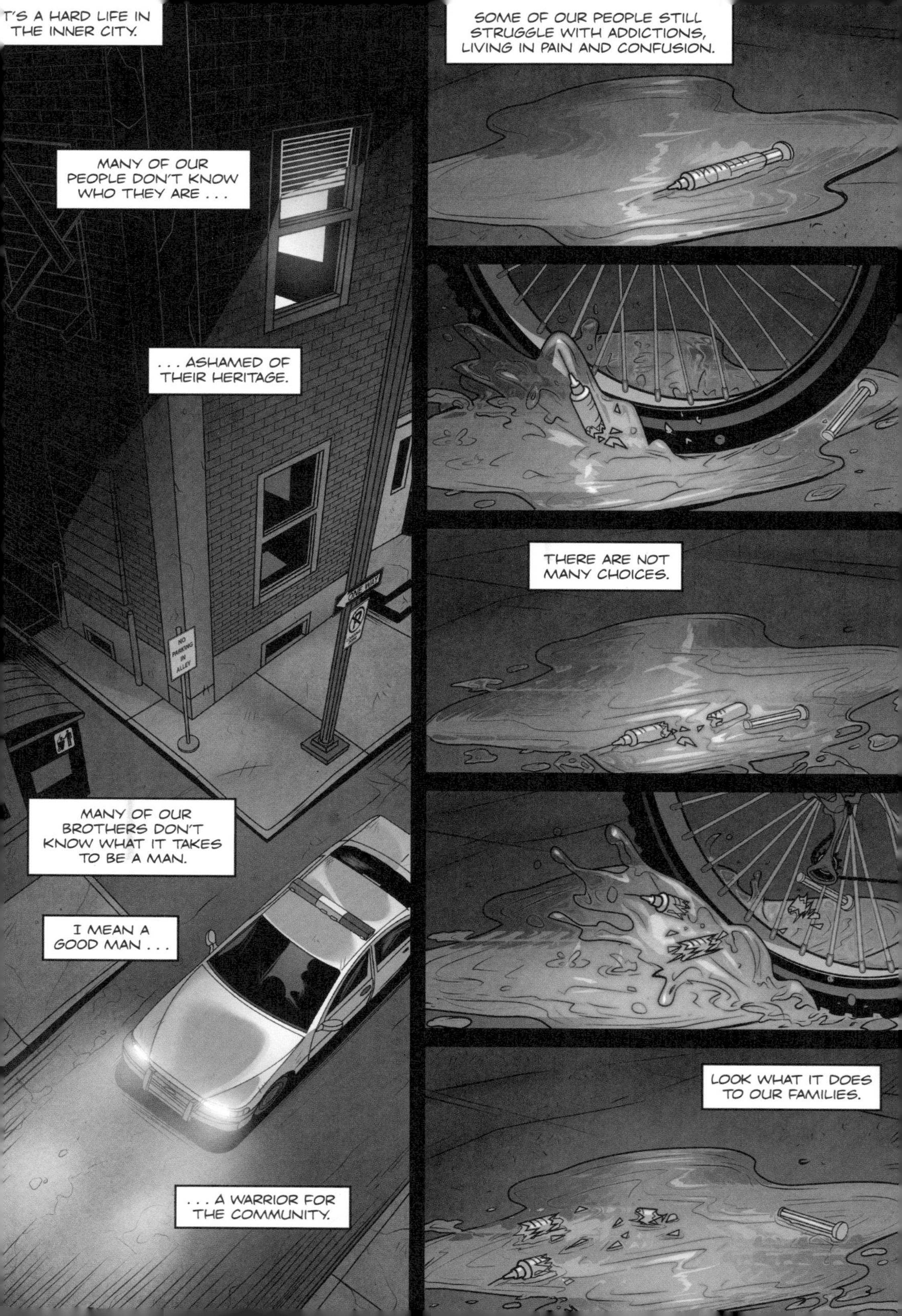
T'S A HARD LIFE IN THE INNER CITY.
MANY OF OUR PEOPLE DON'T KNOW WHO THEY ARE . . .
. . . ASHAMED OF THEIR HERITAGE.
ONE WAY
NO PARKING IN ALLEY
MANY OF OUR BROTHERS DON'T KNOW WHAT IT TAKES TO BE A MAN.
I MEAN A GOOD MAN . . .
. . . A WARRIOR FOR THE COMMUNITY.
SOME OF OUR PEOPLE STILL STRUGGLE WITH ADDICTIONS, LIVING IN PAIN AND CONFUSION.
THERE ARE NOT MANY CHOICES.
LOOK WHAT IT DOES TO OUR FAMILIES.

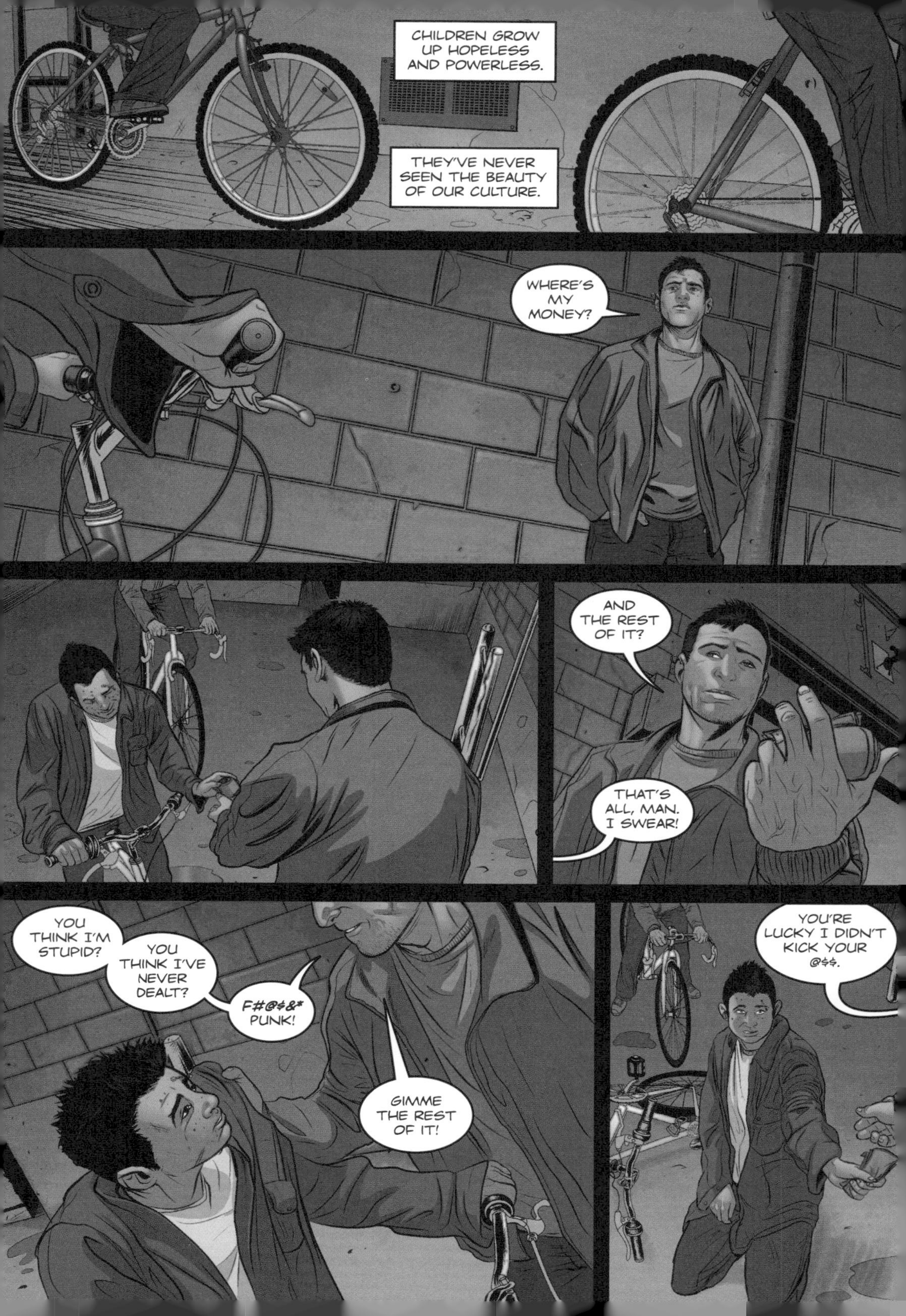
CHILDREN GROW UP HOPELESS AND POWERLESS.
THEY'VE NEVER SEEN THE BEAUTY OF OUR CULTURE.
WHERE'S MY MONEY?
AND THE REST OF IT?
THAT'S ALL, MAN. I SWEAR!
YOU THINK I'M STUPID?
YOU THINK I'VE NEVER DEALT?
F#@$&* PUNK!
GIMME THE REST OF IT!
YOU'RE LUCKY I DIDN'T KICK YOUR @$$.

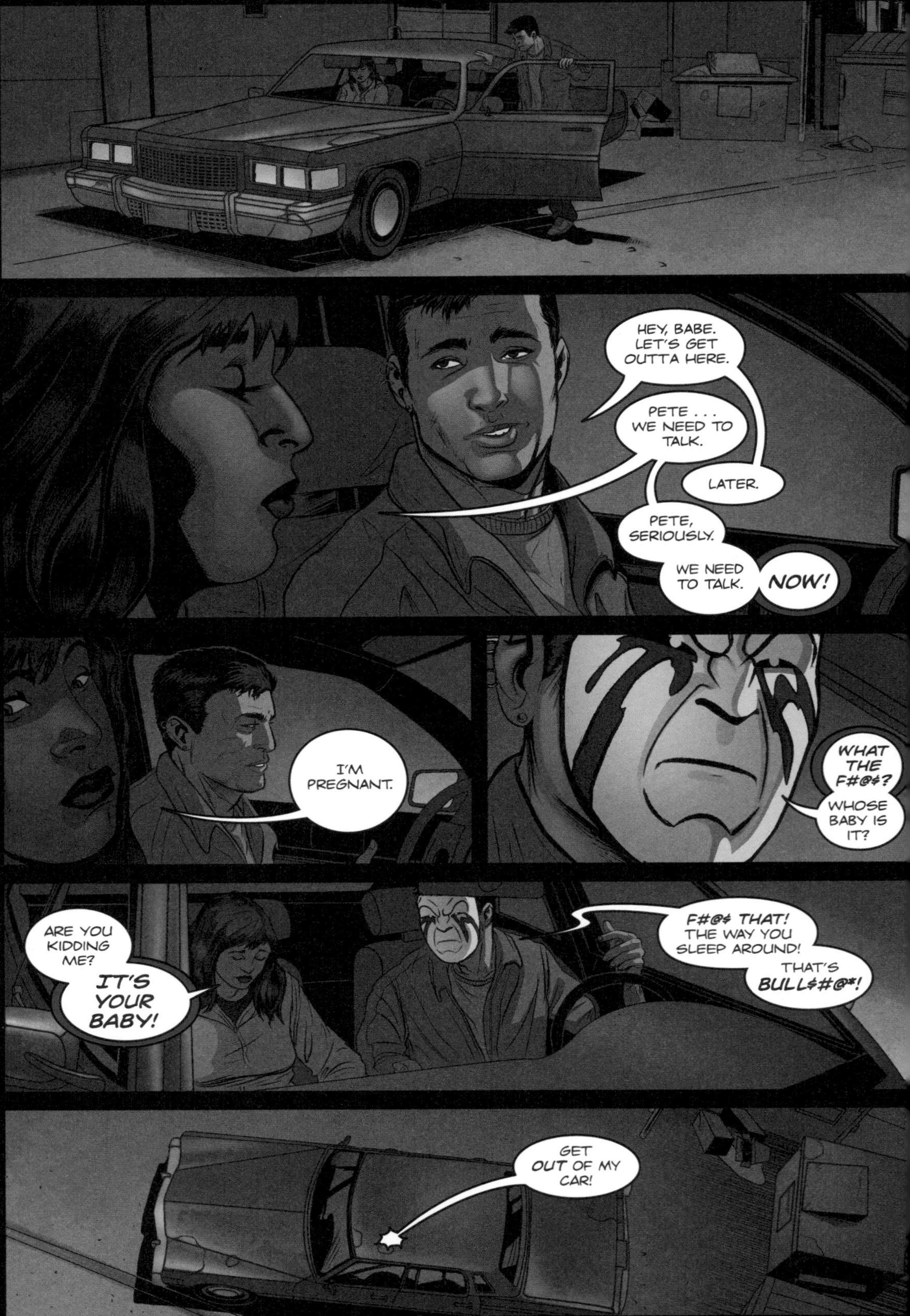
HEY, BABE. LET'S GET OUTTA HERE.
PETE . . . WE NEED TO TALK.
LATER.
PETE, SERIOUSLY.
WE NEED TO TALK.
NOW!
I'M PREGNANT.
WHAT THE F#@$?
WHOSE BABY IS IT?
ARE YOU KIDDING ME?
IT'S YOUR BABY!
F#@$ THAT! THE WAY YOU SLEEP AROUND!
THAT'S BULL$#@*!
GET OUT OF MY CAR!

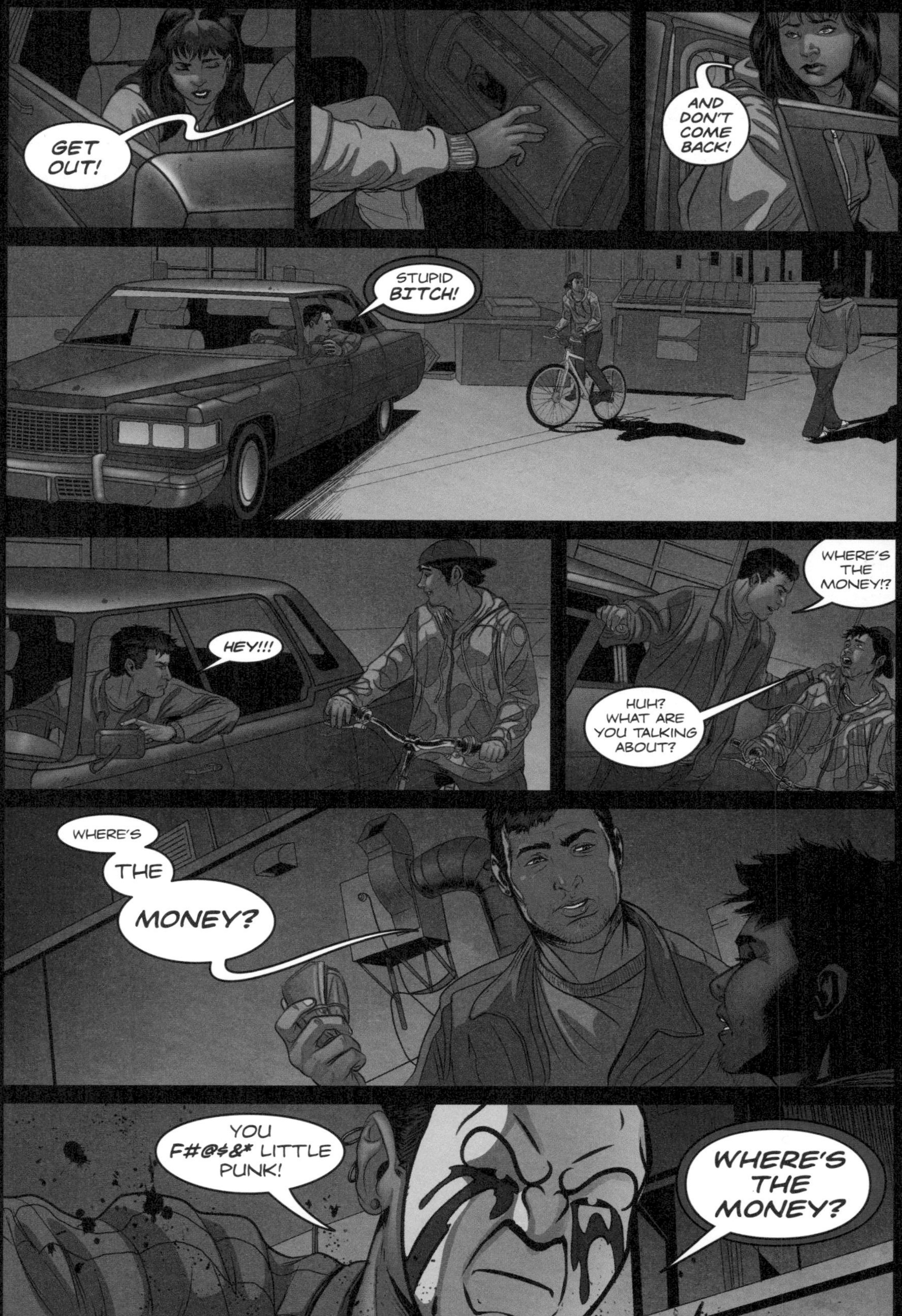
GET OUT!
AND DON'T COME BACK!
STUPID BITCH!
HEY!!!
WHERE'S THE MONEY!?
HUH? WHAT ARE YOU TALKING ABOUT?
WHERE'S THE MONEY?
YOU F#@$&* LITTLE PUNK!
WHERE'S THE MONEY?

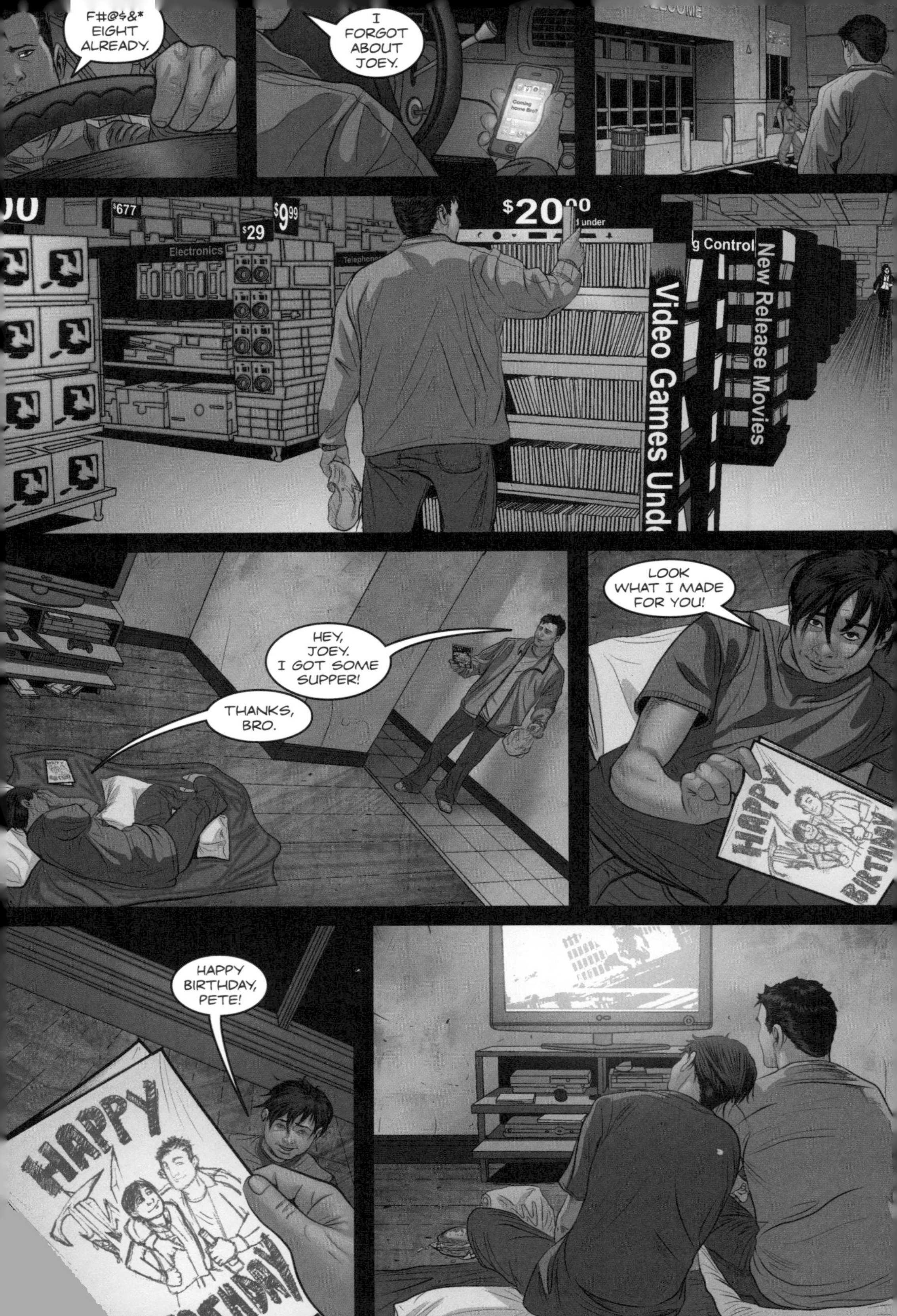
F#@$&* EIGHT ALREADY.
I FORGOT ABOUT JOEY.
Coming home Bro?
WELCOME
$677
$29
$9.99
$20.00
Electronics
Video Games Und
New Release Movies
g Control
HEY, JOEY. I GOT SOME SUPPER!
THANKS, BRO.
LOOK WHAT I MADE FOR YOU!
HAPPY BIRTHDAY
HAPPY BIRTHDAY, PETE!

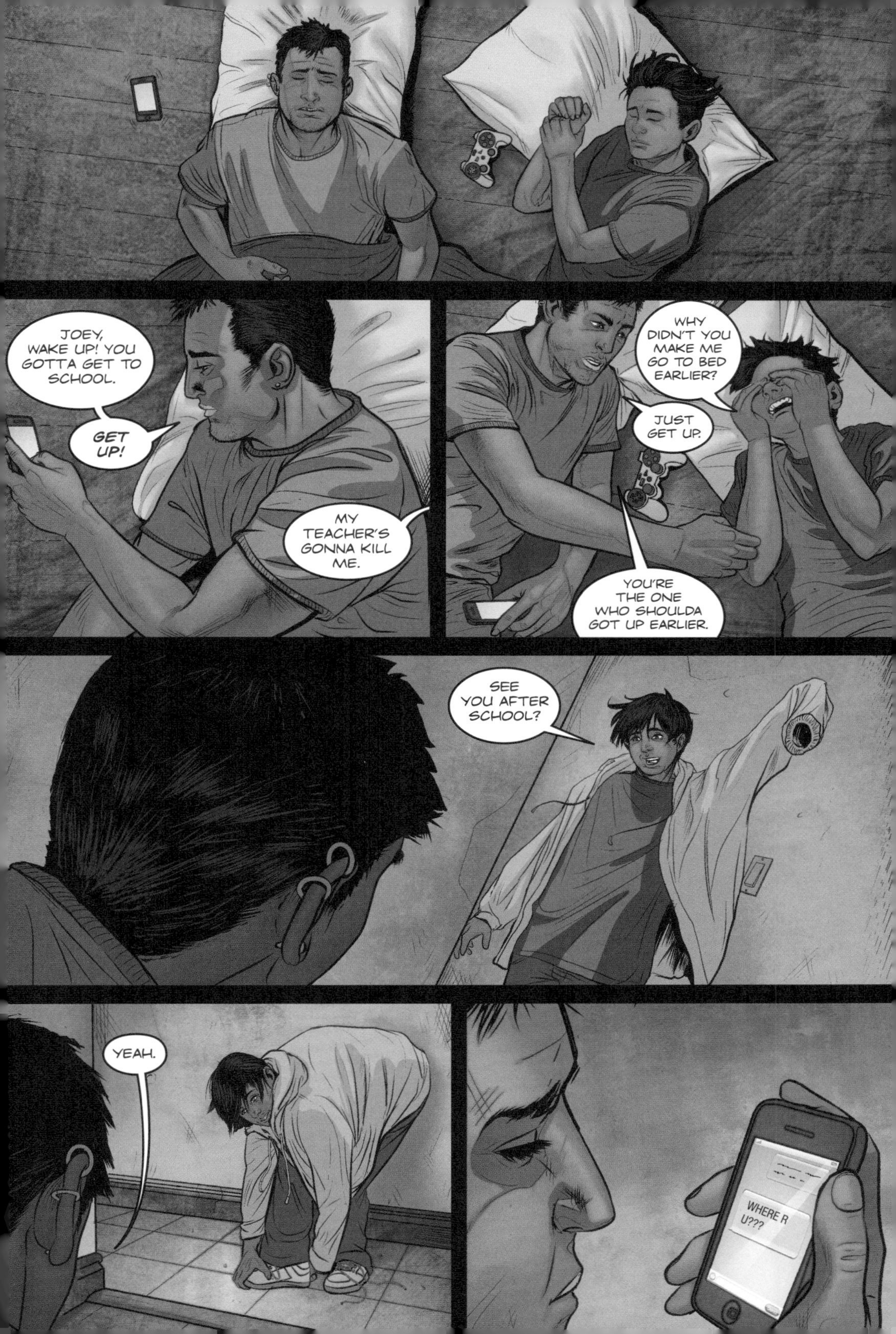
JOEY, WAKE UP! YOU GOTTA GET TO SCHOOL.
GET UP!
MY TEACHER'S GONNA KILL ME.
WHY DIDN'T YOU MAKE ME GO TO BED EARLIER?
JUST GET UP.
YOU'RE THE ONE WHO SHOULDA GOT UP EARLIER.
SEE YOU AFTER SCHOOL?
YEAH.
WHERE R U???

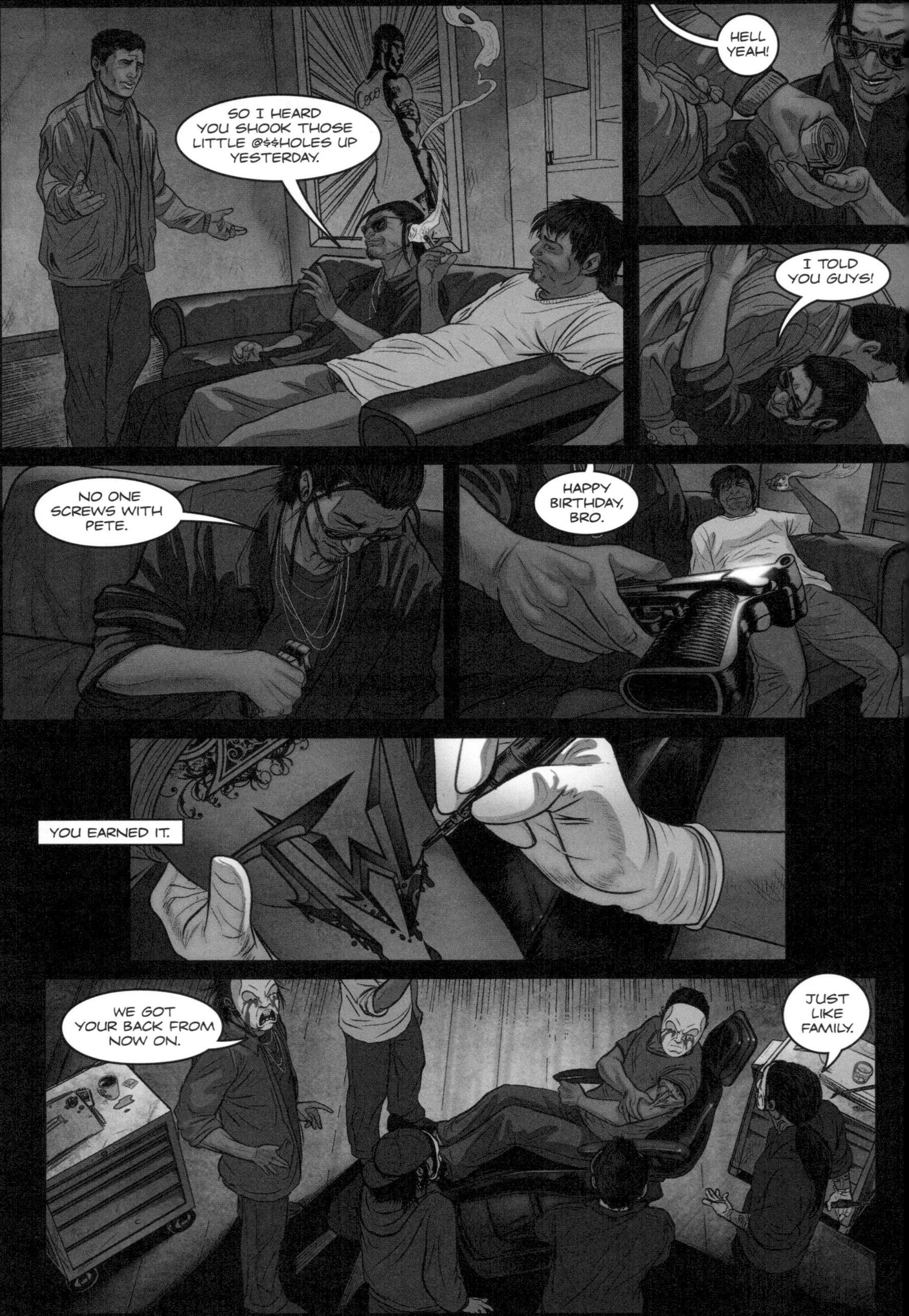
SO I HEARD YOU SHOOK THOSE LITTLE @$$HOLES UP YESTERDAY.
HELL YEAH!
I TOLD YOU GUYS!
NO ONE SCREWS WITH PETE.
HAPPY BIRTHDAY, BRO.
YOU EARNED IT.
WE GOT YOUR BACK FROM NOW ON.
JUST LIKE FAMILY.

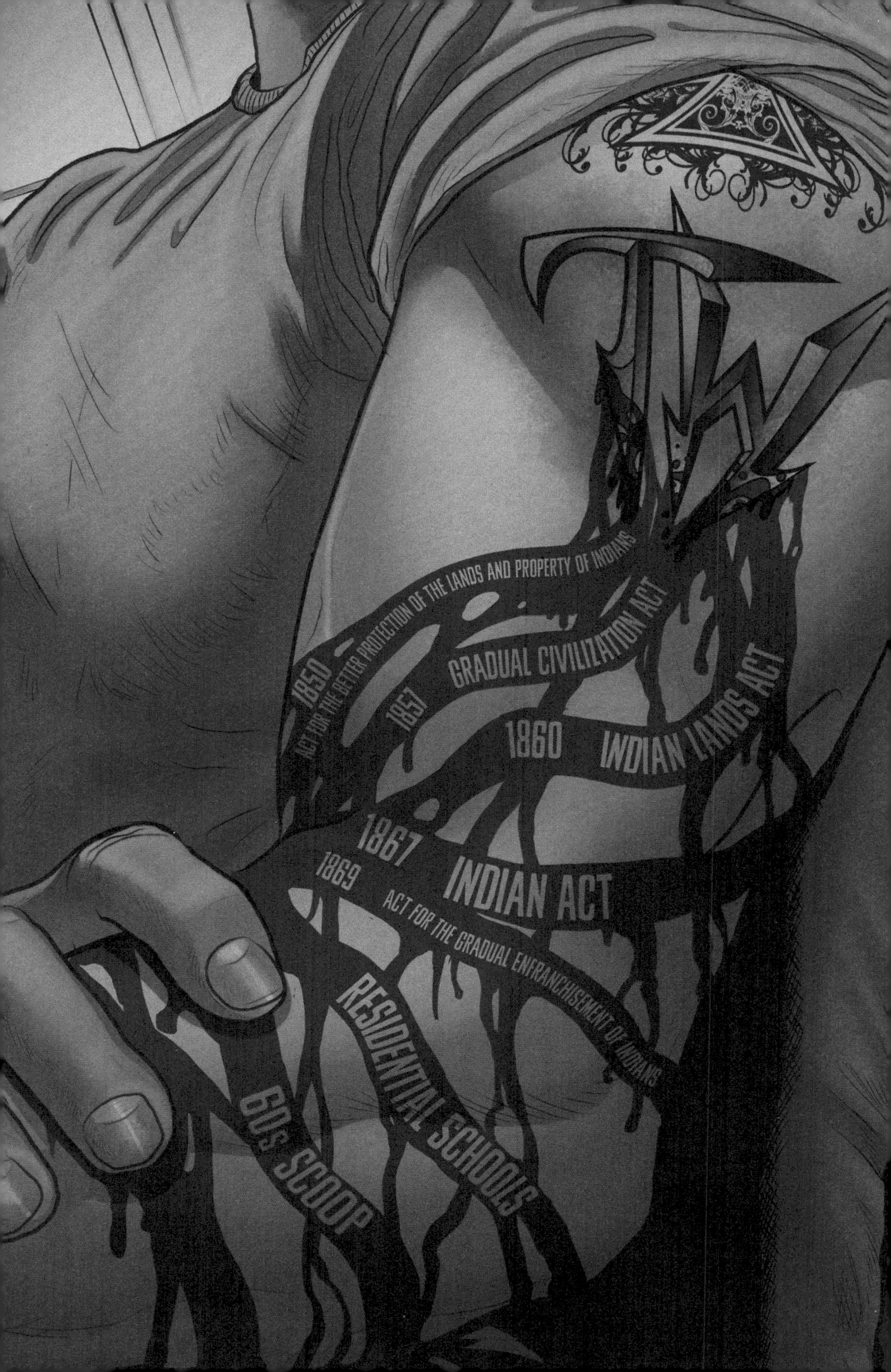
1850
ACT FOR THE BETTER PROTECTION OF THE LANDS AND PROPERTY OF INDIANS
1857
GRADUAL CIVILIZATION ACT
1860
INDIAN LANDS ACT
1867
INDIAN ACT
1869
ACT FOR THE GRADUAL ENFRANCHISEMENT OF INDIANS
RESIDENTIAL SCHOOLS
60s SCOOP

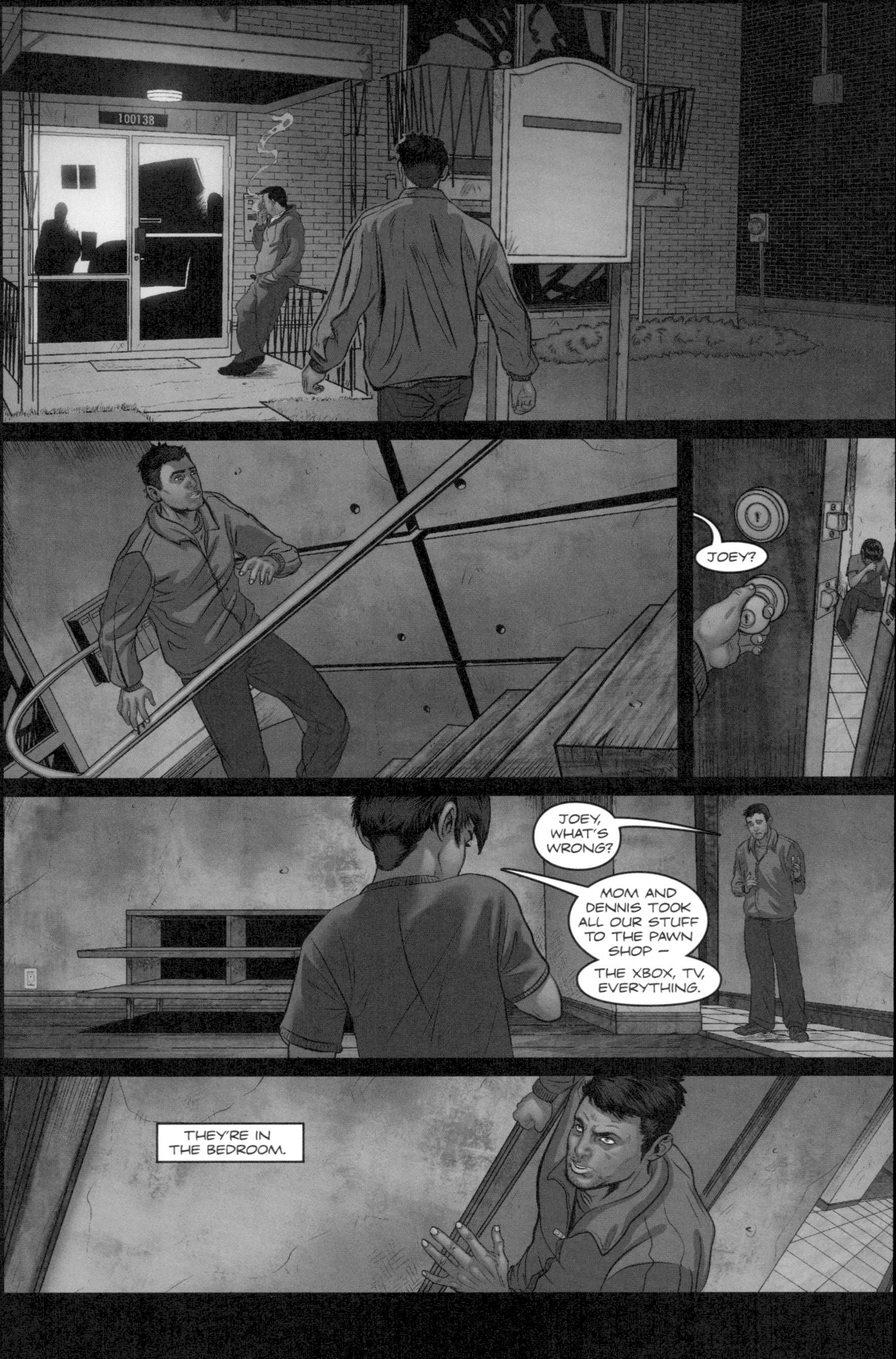
100138
JOEY?
JOEY, WHAT'S WRONG?
MOM AND DENNIS TOOK ALL OUR STUFF TO THE PAWN SHOP –
THE XBOX, TV, EVERYTHING.
THEY'RE IN THE BEDROOM.

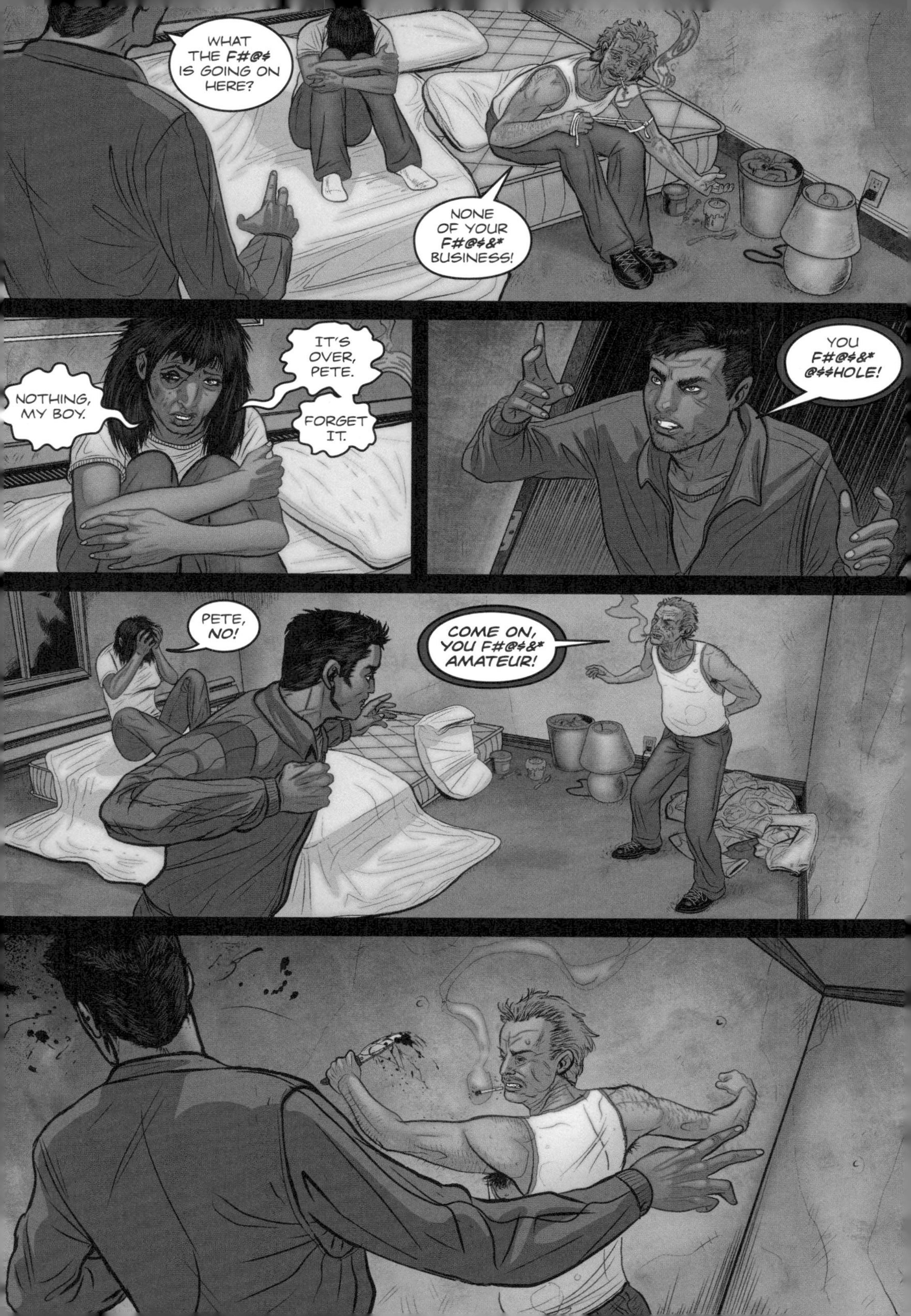
WHAT THE F#@$ IS GOING ON HERE?
NONE OF YOUR F#@$&* BUSINESS!
NOTHING, MY BOY.
IT'S OVER, PETE.
FORGET IT.
YOU F#@$&* @$$HOLE!
PETE, NO!
COME ON, YOU F#@$&* AMATEUR!

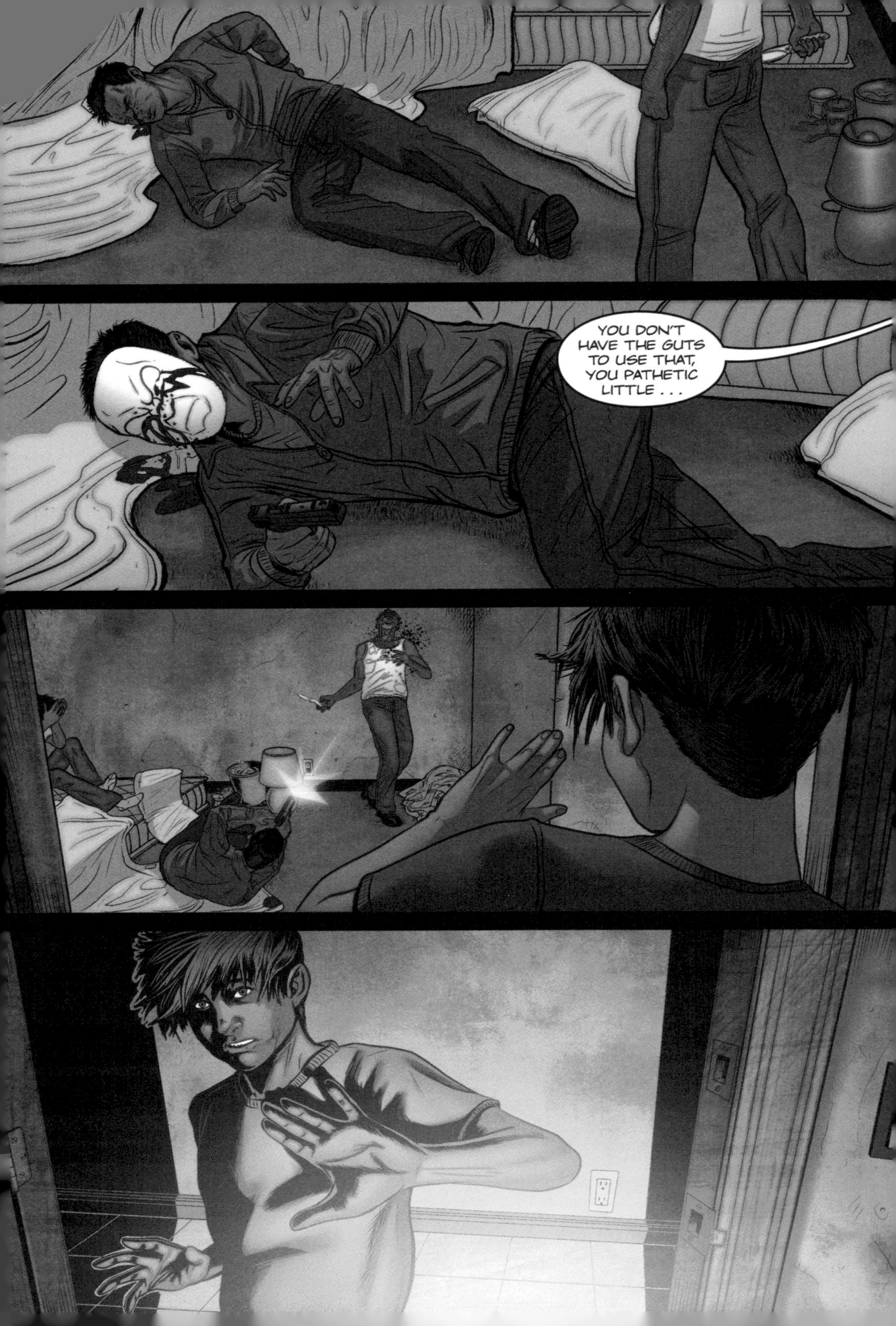
YOU DON'T HAVE THE GUTS TO USE THAT, YOU PATHETIC LITTLE . . .

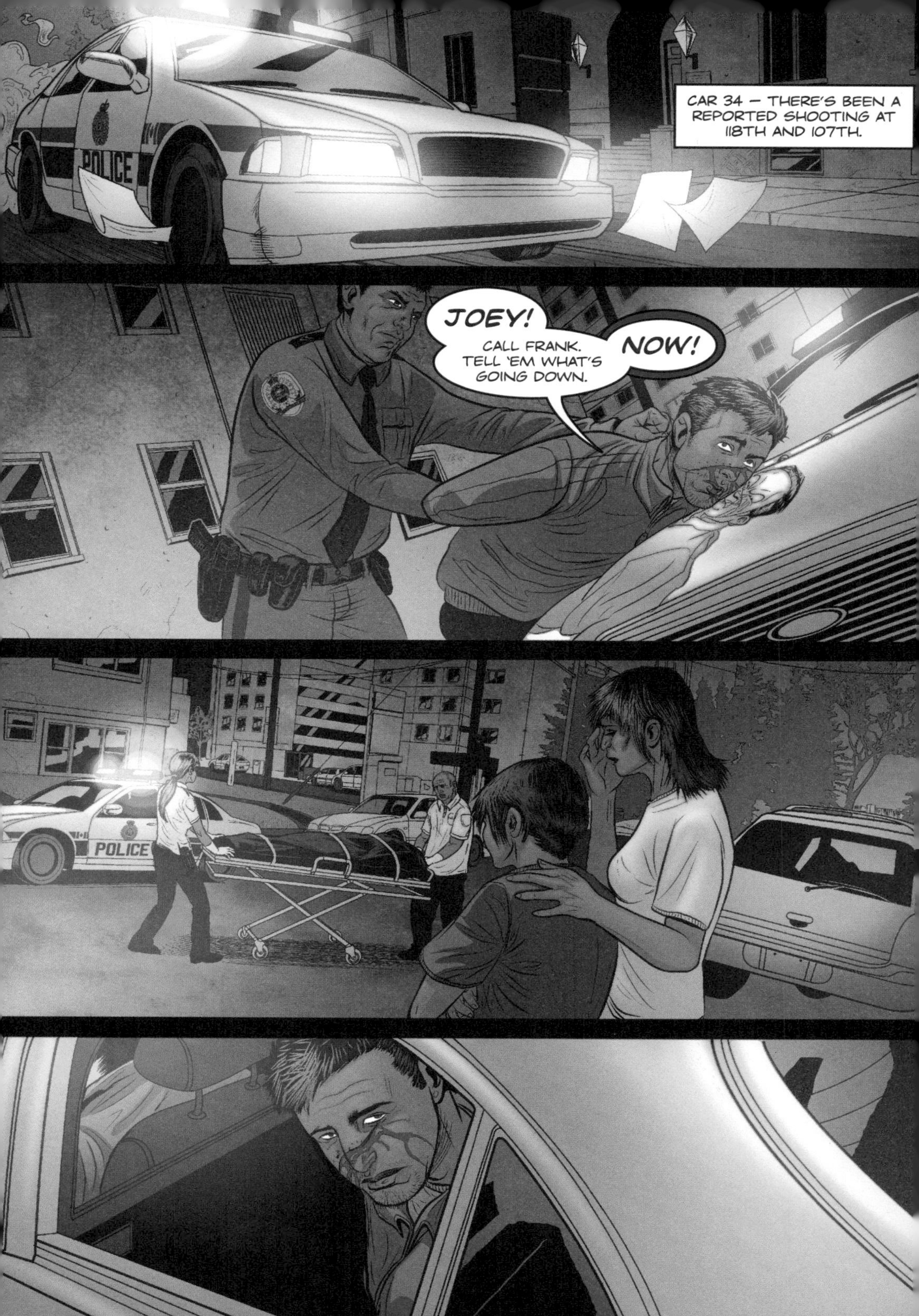

CAR 34 — THERE'S BEEN A REPORTED SHOOTING AT 118TH AND 107TH.
JOEY!
CALL FRANK. TELL 'EM WHAT'S GOING DOWN.
NOW!
POLICE
POLICE

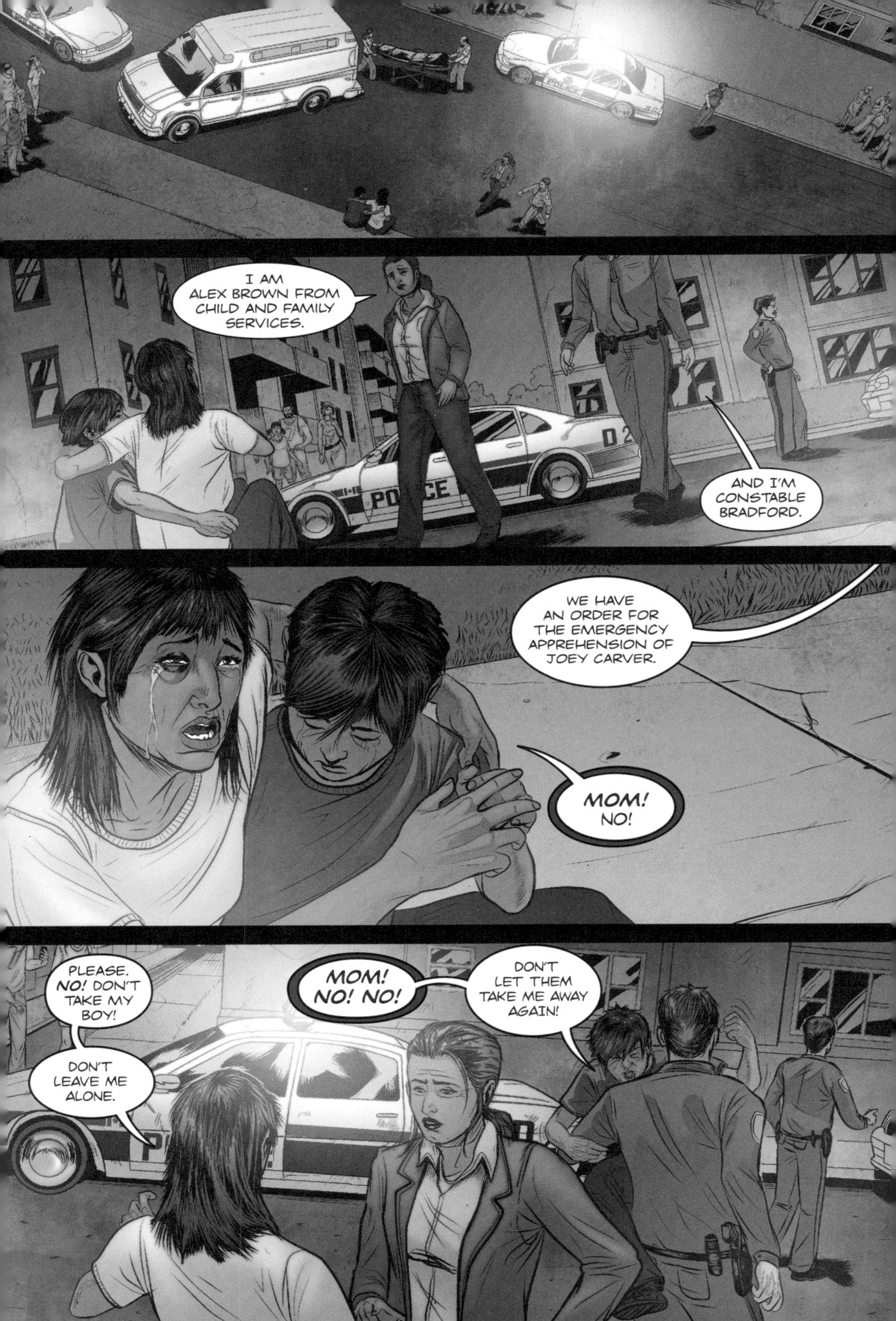
I AM ALEX BROWN FROM CHILD AND FAMILY SERVICES.
AND I'M CONSTABLE BRADFORD.
WE HAVE AN ORDER FOR THE EMERGENCY APPREHENSION OF JOEY CARVER.
MOM! NO!
PLEASE. NO! DON'T TAKE MY BOY!
DON'T LEAVE ME ALONE.
MOM! NO! NO!
DON'T LET THEM TAKE ME AWAY AGAIN!

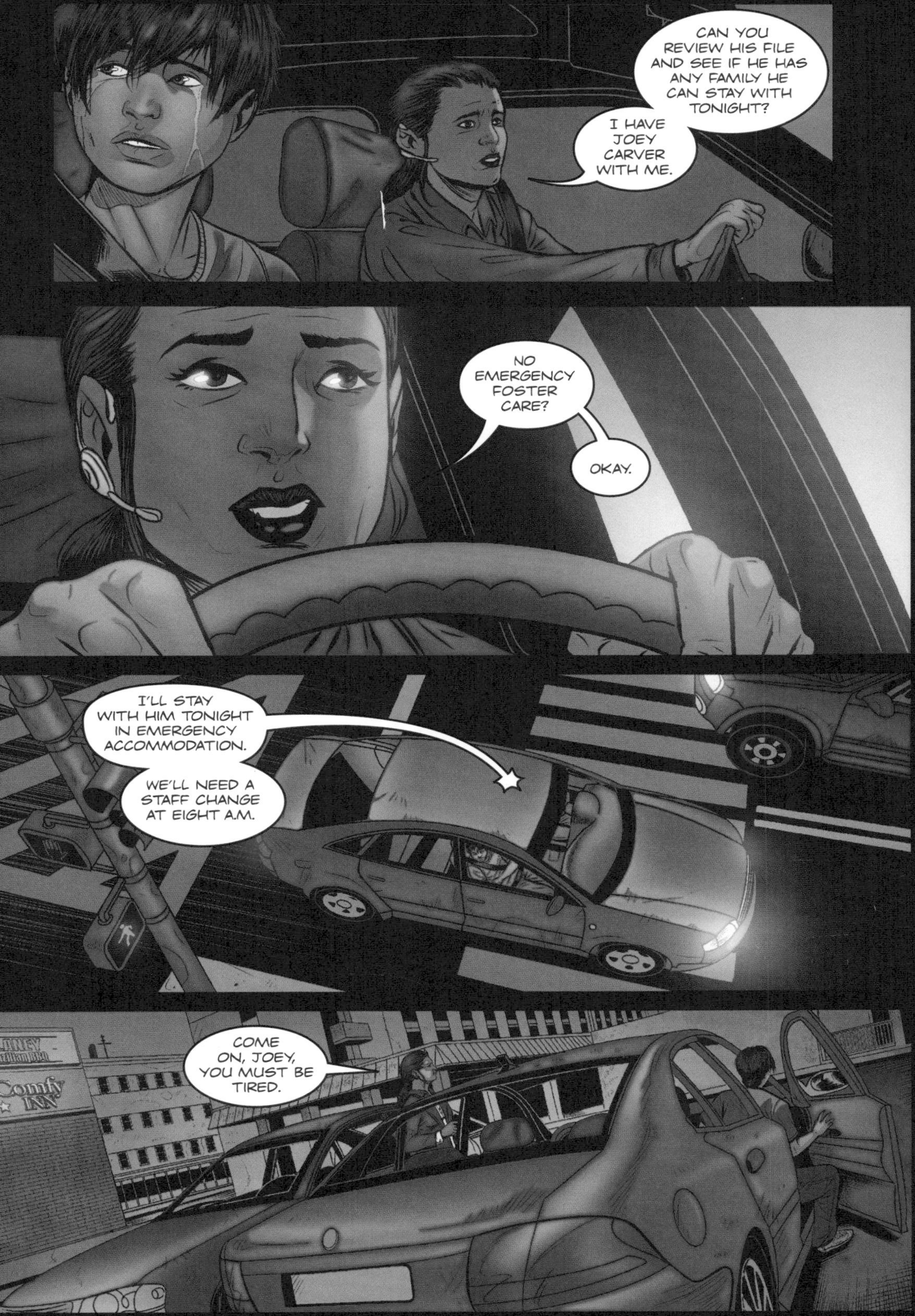

CAN YOU REVIEW HIS FILE AND SEE IF HE HAS ANY FAMILY HE CAN STAY WITH TONIGHT?
I HAVE JOEY CARVER WITH ME.
NO EMERGENCY FOSTER CARE?
OKAY.
I'LL STAY WITH HIM TONIGHT IN EMERGENCY ACCOMMODATION.
WE'LL NEED A STAFF CHANGE AT EIGHT A.M.
Comfy INN
COME ON, JOEY, YOU MUST BE TIRED.

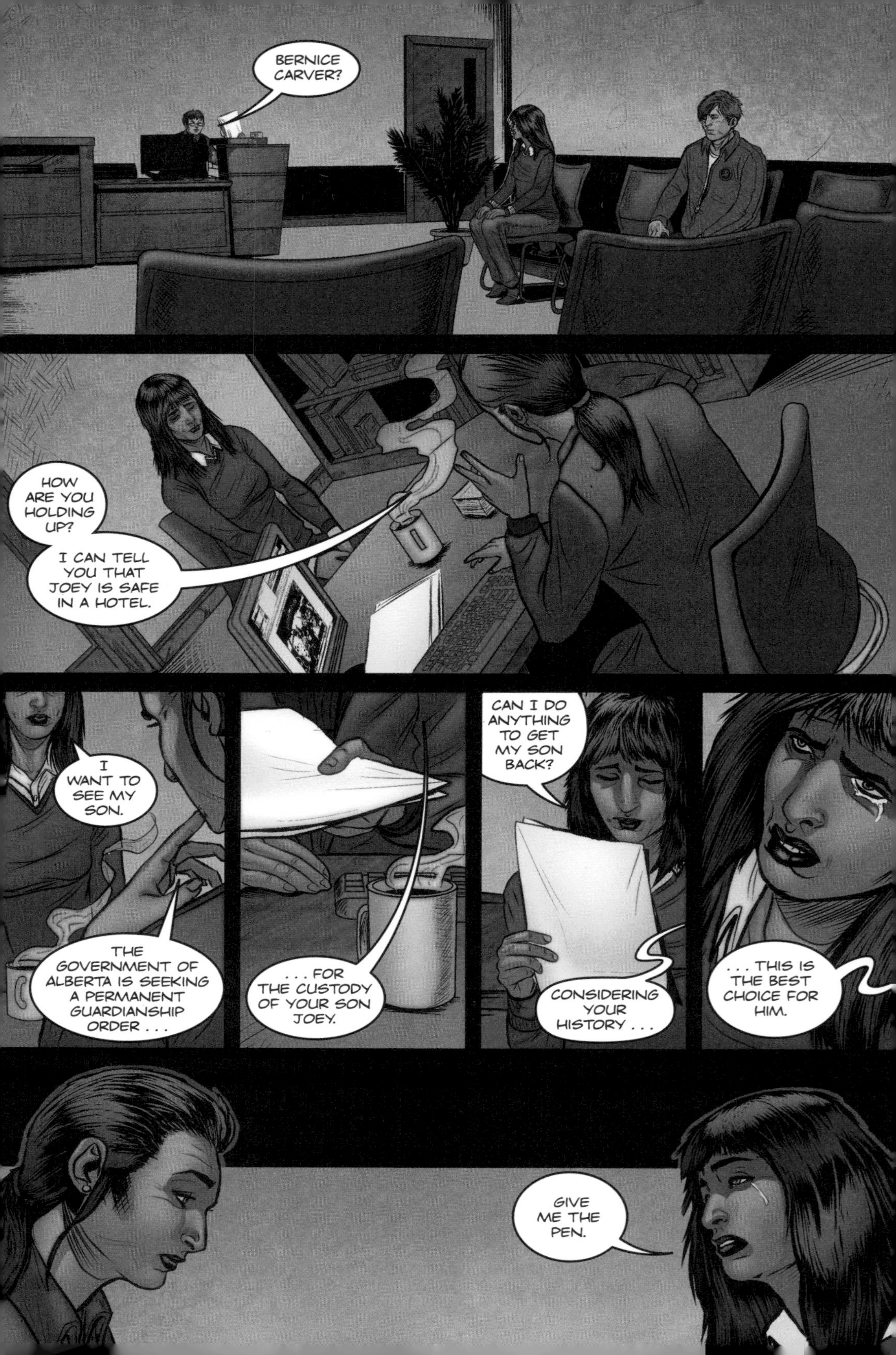
BERNICE CARVER?
HOW ARE YOU HOLDING UP?
I CAN TELL YOU THAT JOEY IS SAFE IN A HOTEL.
I WANT TO SEE MY SON.
THE GOVERNMENT OF ALBERTA IS SEEKING A PERMANENT GUARDIANSHIP ORDER . . .
. . . FOR THE CUSTODY OF YOUR SON JOEY.
CAN I DO ANYTHING TO GET MY SON BACK?
CONSIDERING YOUR HISTORY . . .
. . . THIS IS THE BEST CHOICE FOR HIM.
GIVE ME THE PEN.

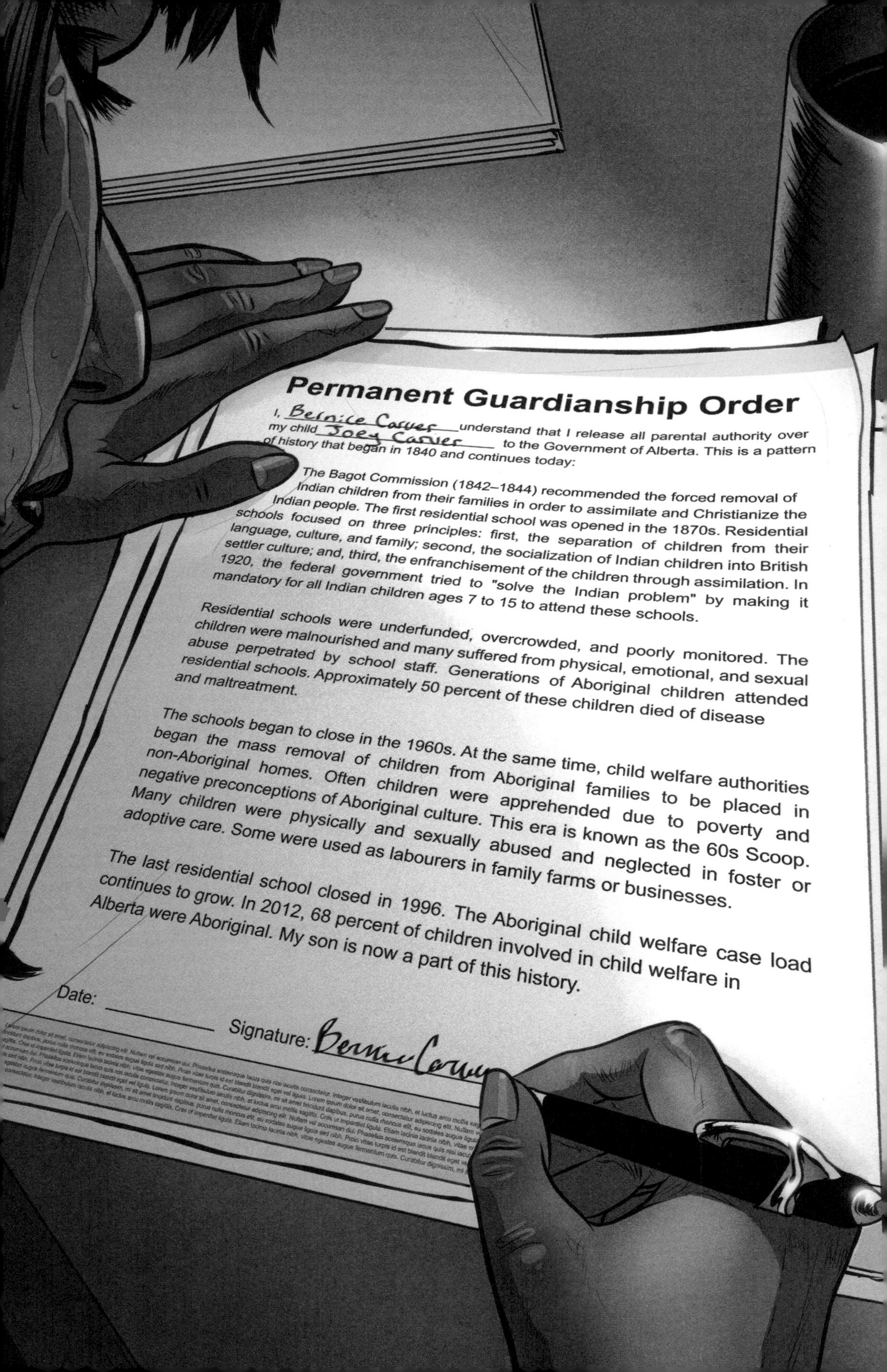

Permanent Guardianship Order
I, Bernice Carver understand that I release all parental authority over my child Joey Carver to the Government of Alberta. This is a pattern of history that began in 1840 and continues today:
The Bagot Commission (1842–1844) recommended the forced removal of Indian children from their families in order to assimilate and Christianize the Indian people. The first residential school was opened in the 1870s. Residential schools focused on three principles: first, the separation of children from their language, culture, and family; second, the socialization of Indian children into British settler culture; and, third, the enfranchisement of the children through assimilation. In 1920, the federal government tried to "solve the Indian problem" by making it mandatory for all Indian children ages 7 to 15 to attend these schools.
Residential schools were underfunded, overcrowded, and poorly monitored. The children were malnourished and many suffered from physical, emotional, and sexual abuse perpetrated by school staff. Generations of Aboriginal children attended residential schools. Approximately 50 percent of these children died of disease and maltreatment.
The schools began to close in the 1960s. At the same time, child welfare authorities began the mass removal of children from Aboriginal families to be placed in non-Aboriginal homes. Often children were apprehended due to poverty and negative preconceptions of Aboriginal culture. This era is known as the 60s Scoop. Many children were physically and sexually abused and neglected in foster or adoptive care. Some were used as labourers in family farms or businesses.
The last residential school closed in 1996. The Aboriginal child welfare case load continues to grow. In 2012, 68 percent of children involved in child welfare in Alberta were Aboriginal. My son is now a part of this history.
Date:
Signature:

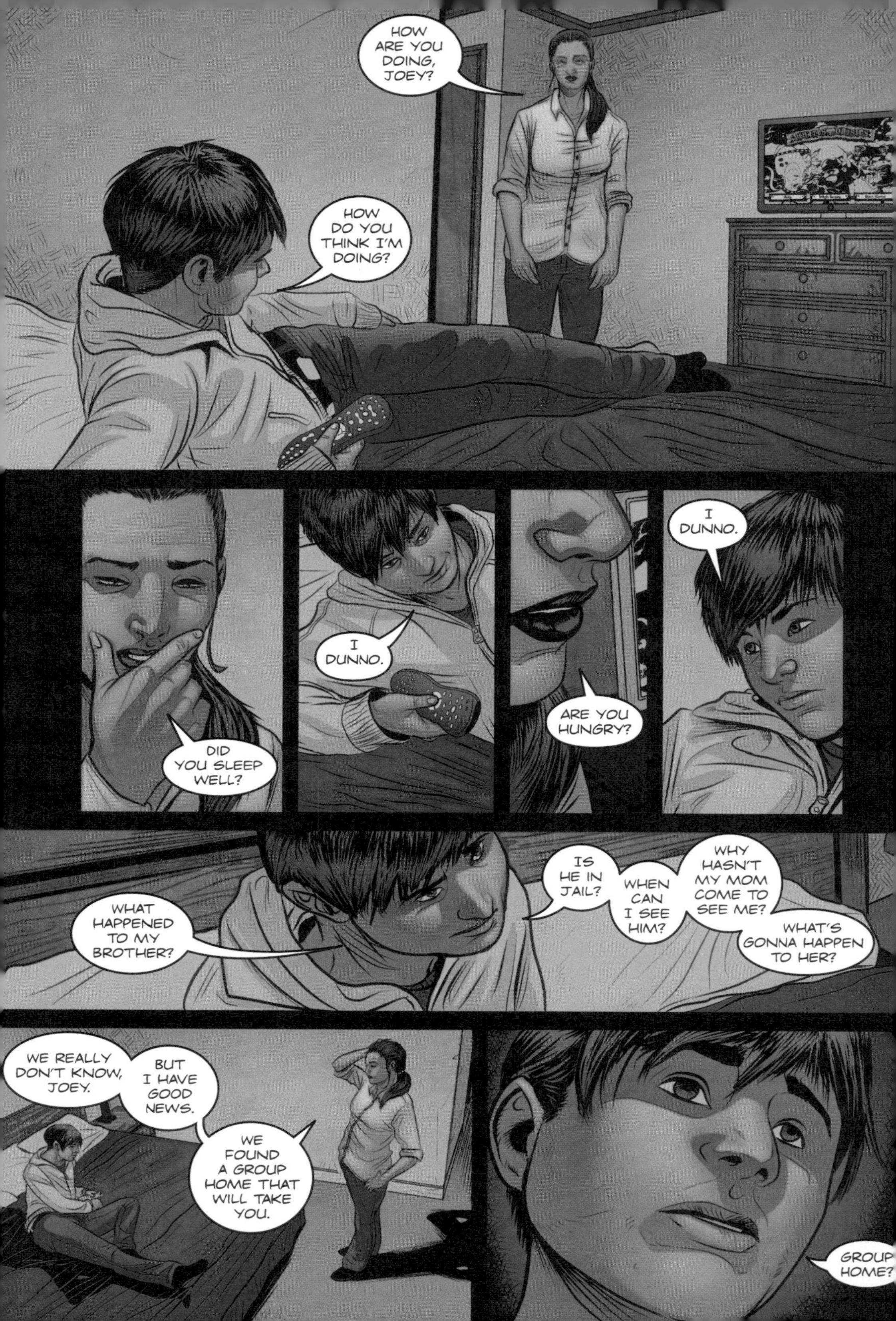
HOW ARE YOU DOING, JOEY?
HOW DO YOU THINK I'M DOING?
DID YOU SLEEP WELL?
I DUNNO.
ARE YOU HUNGRY?
I DUNNO.
WHAT HAPPENED TO MY BROTHER?
IS HE IN JAIL?
WHEN CAN I SEE HIM?
WHY HASN'T MY MOM COME TO SEE ME?
WHAT'S GONNA HAPPEN TO HER?
WE REALLY DON'T KNOW, JOEY.
BUT I HAVE GOOD NEWS.
WE FOUND A GROUP HOME THAT WILL TAKE YOU.
GROUP HOME?

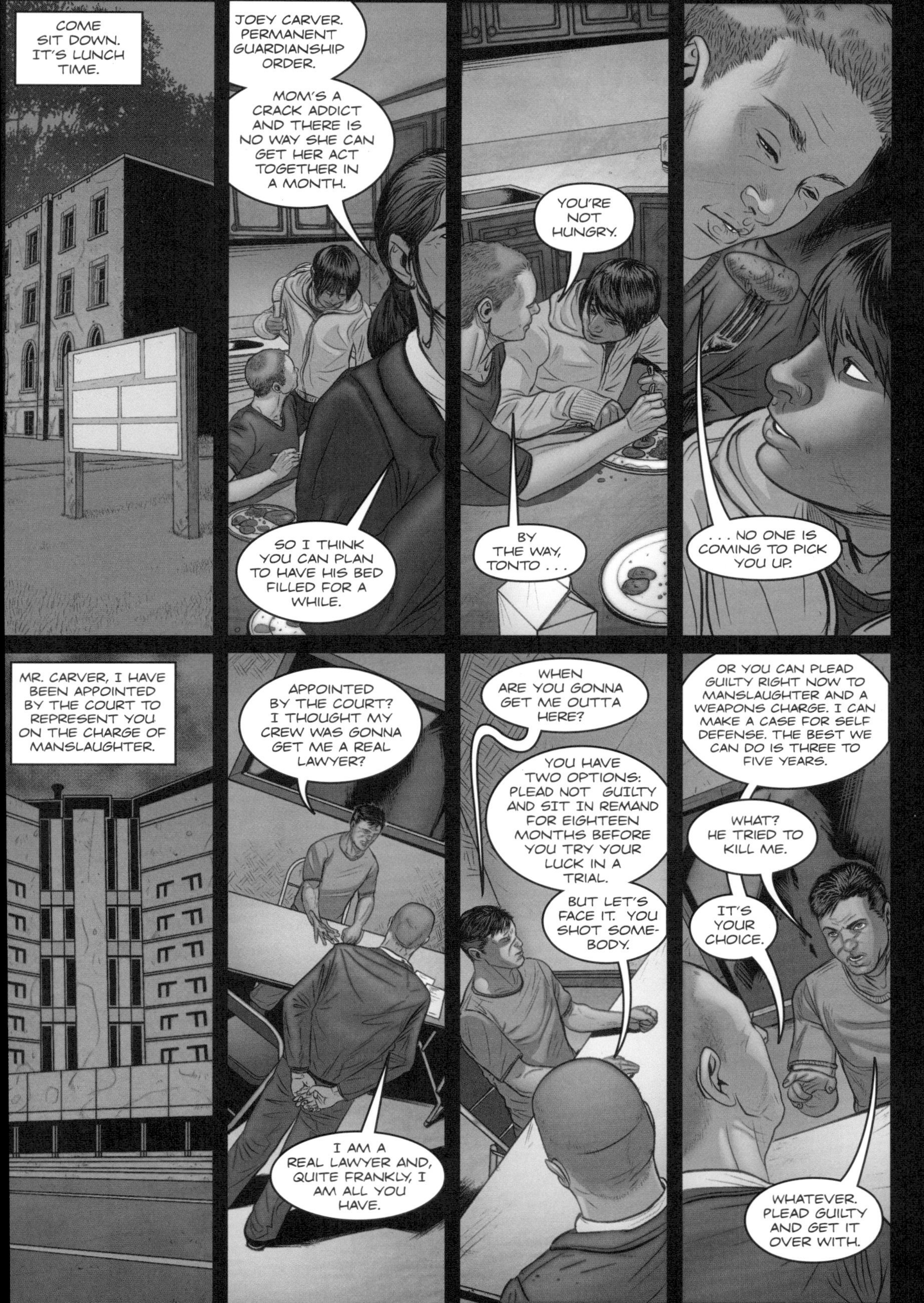
COME SIT DOWN. IT'S LUNCH TIME.
JOEY CARVER. PERMANENT GUARDIANSHIP ORDER.
MOM'S A CRACK ADDICT AND THERE IS NO WAY SHE CAN GET HER ACT TOGETHER IN A MONTH.
SO I THINK YOU CAN PLAN TO HAVE HIS BED FILLED FOR A WHILE.
YOU'RE NOT HUNGRY.
BY THE WAY, TONTO . . .
. . . NO ONE IS COMING TO PICK YOU UP.
MR. CARVER, I HAVE BEEN APPOINTED BY THE COURT TO REPRESENT YOU ON THE CHARGE OF MANSLAUGHTER.
APPOINTED BY THE COURT? I THOUGHT MY CREW WAS GONNA GET ME A REAL LAWYER?
I AM A REAL LAWYER AND, QUITE FRANKLY, I AM ALL YOU HAVE.
WHEN ARE YOU GONNA GET ME OUTTA HERE?
YOU HAVE TWO OPTIONS: PLEAD NOT GUILTY AND SIT IN REMAND FOR EIGHTEEN MONTHS BEFORE YOU TRY YOUR LUCK IN A TRIAL.
BUT LET'S FACE IT. YOU SHOT SOME-BODY.
OR YOU CAN PLEAD GUILTY RIGHT NOW TO MANSLAUGHTER AND A WEAPONS CHARGE. I CAN MAKE A CASE FOR SELF DEFENSE. THE BEST WE CAN DO IS THREE TO FIVE YEARS.
WHAT? HE TRIED TO KILL ME.
IT'S YOUR CHOICE.
WHATEVER. PLEAD GUILTY AND GET IT OVER WITH.

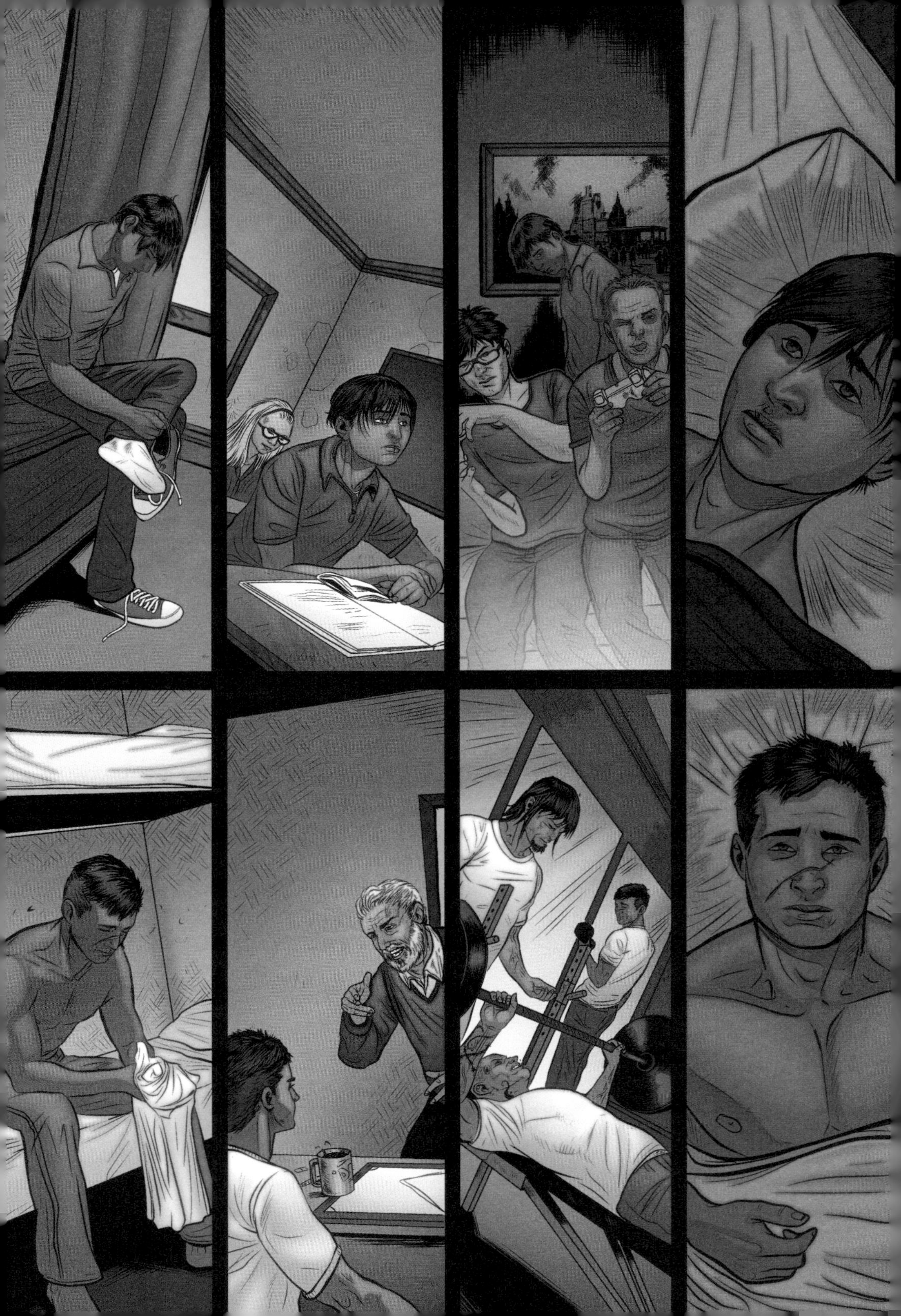

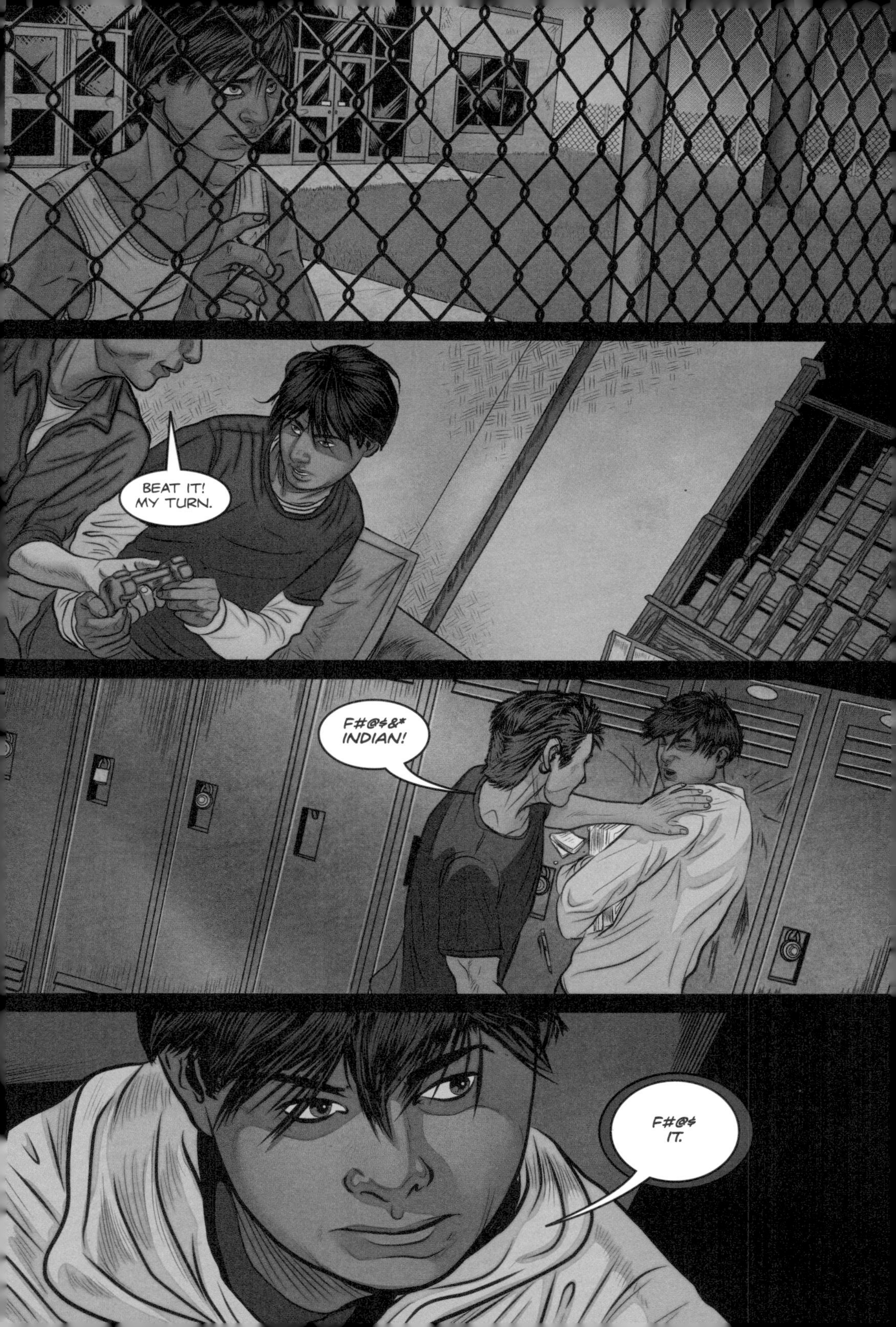
BEAT IT! MY TURN.
F#@$&* INDIAN!
F#@$ IT.

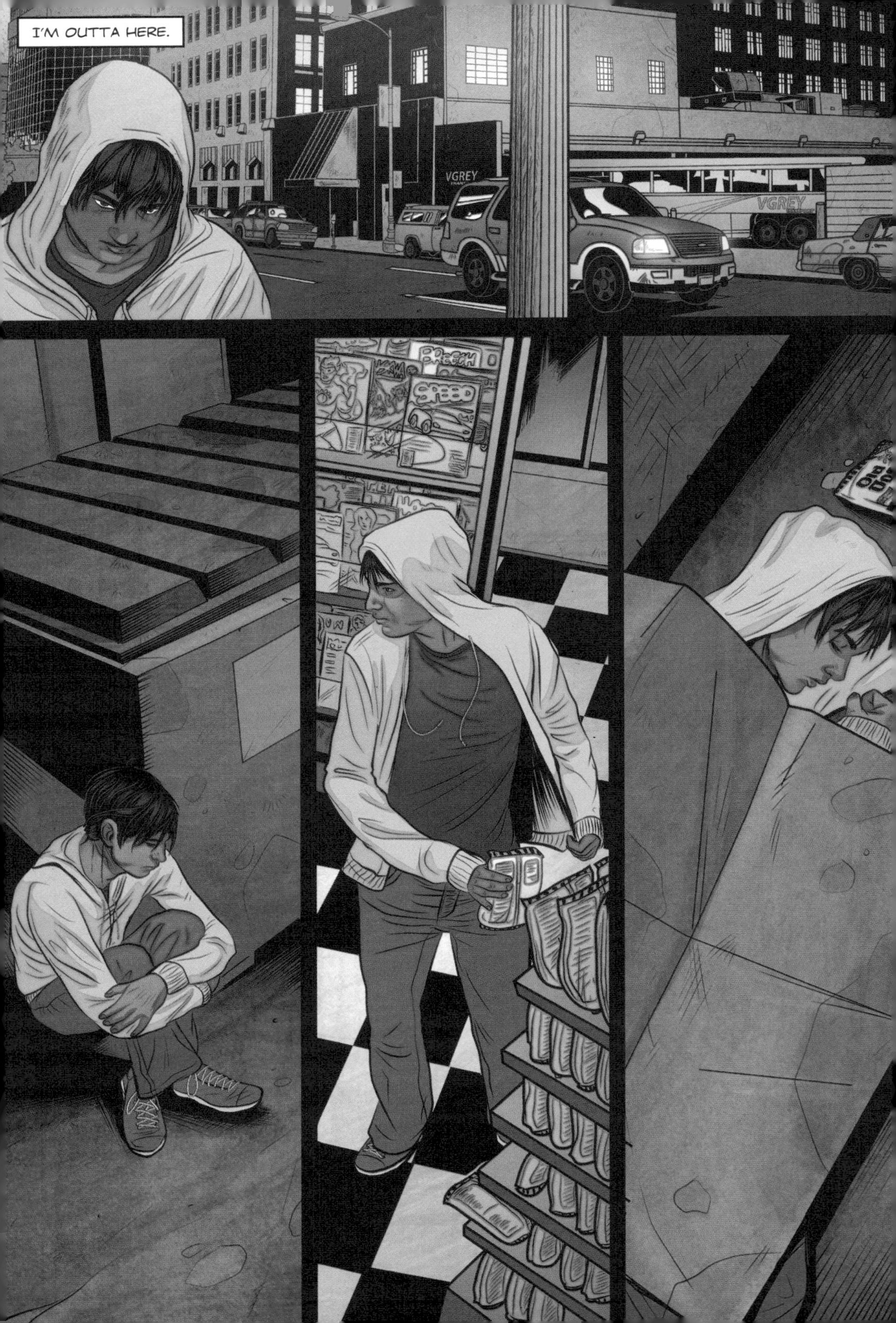
I'M OUTTA HERE.
VGREY

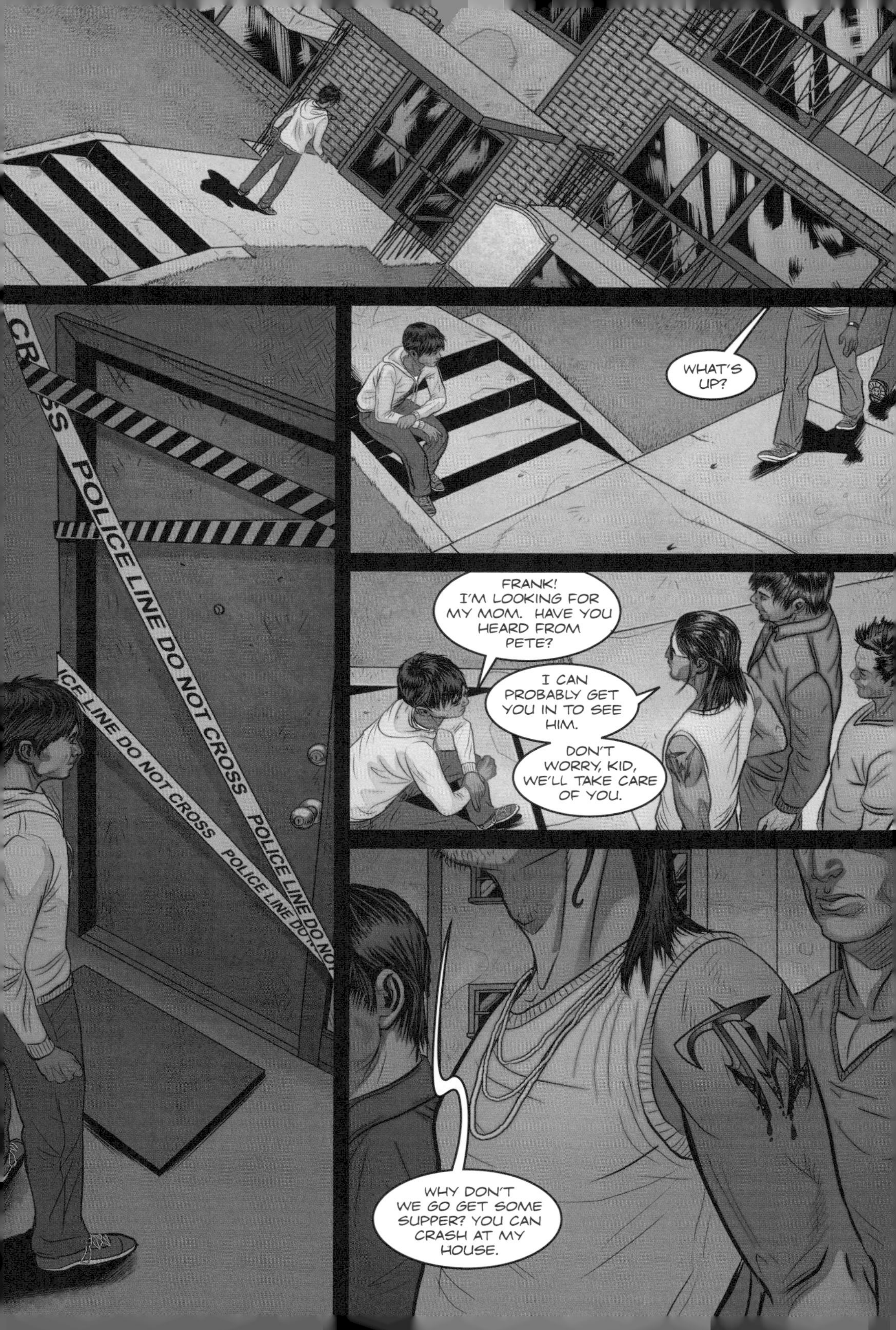
POLICE LINE DO NOT CROSS
POLICE LINE DO NOT CROSS
WHAT'S UP?
FRANK! I'M LOOKING FOR MY MOM. HAVE YOU HEARD FROM PETE?
I CAN PROBABLY GET YOU IN TO SEE HIM.
DON'T WORRY, KID, WE'LL TAKE CARE OF YOU.
WHY DON'T WE GO GET SOME SUPPER? YOU CAN CRASH AT MY HOUSE.

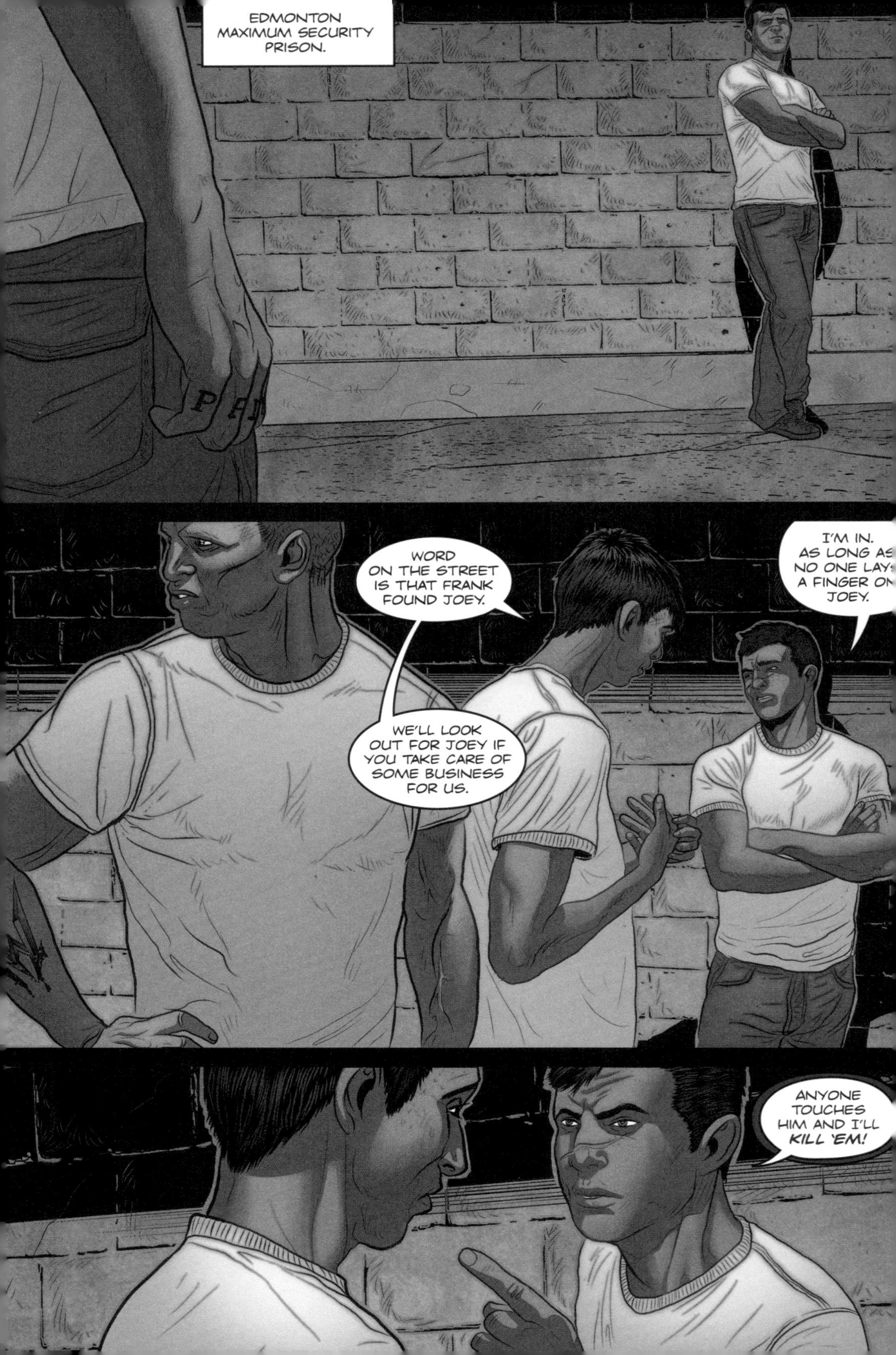
EDMONTON MAXIMUM SECURITY PRISON.
WORD ON THE STREET IS THAT FRANK FOUND JOEY.
WE'LL LOOK OUT FOR JOEY IF YOU TAKE CARE OF SOME BUSINESS FOR US.
I'M IN. AS LONG AS NO ONE LAYS A FINGER ON JOEY.
ANYONE TOUCHES HIM AND I'LL *KILL 'EM!*

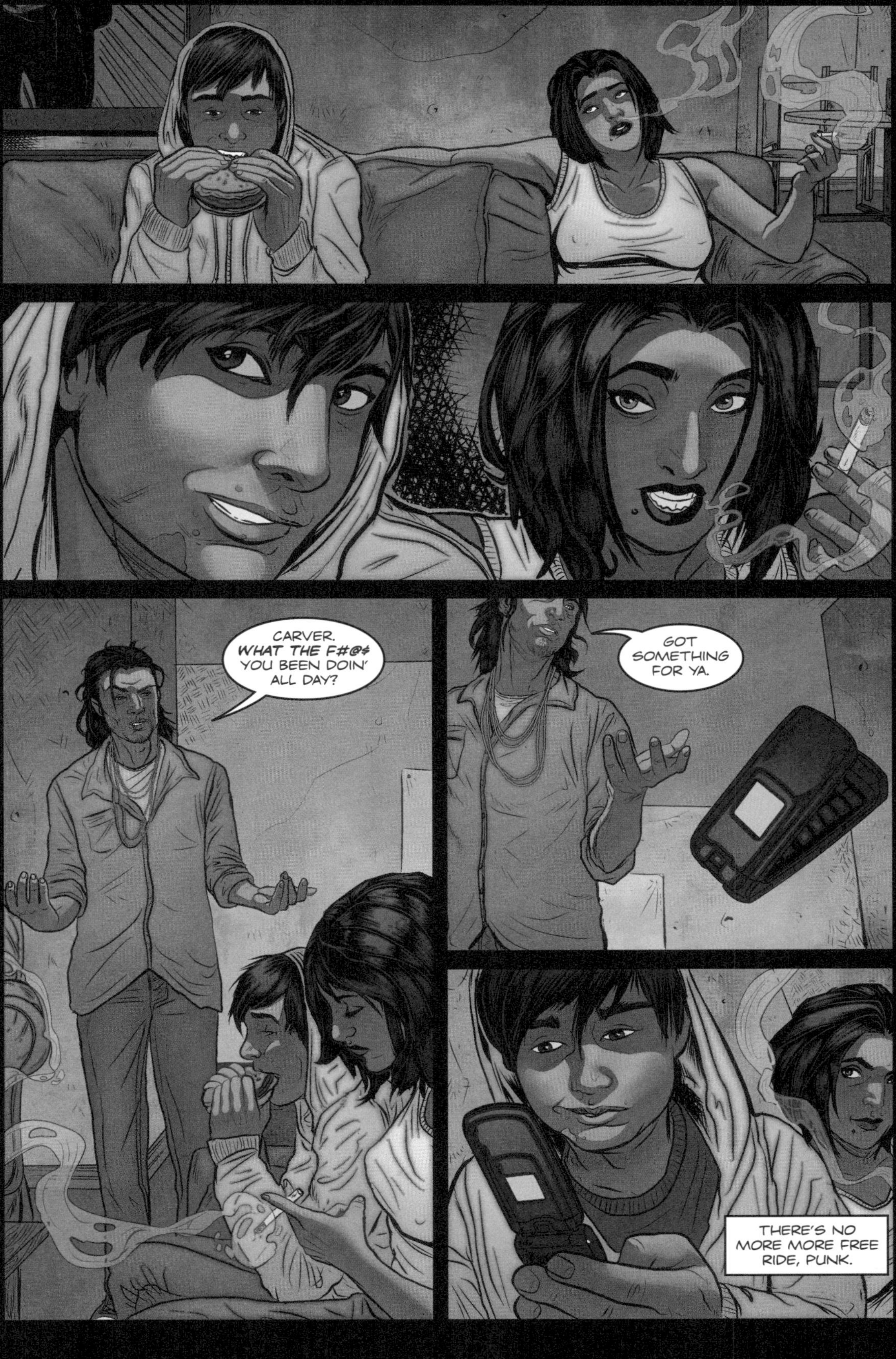
CARVER. WHAT THE F#@$ YOU BEEN DOIN' ALL DAY?
GOT SOMETHING FOR YA.
THERE'S NO MORE MORE FREE RIDE, PUNK.

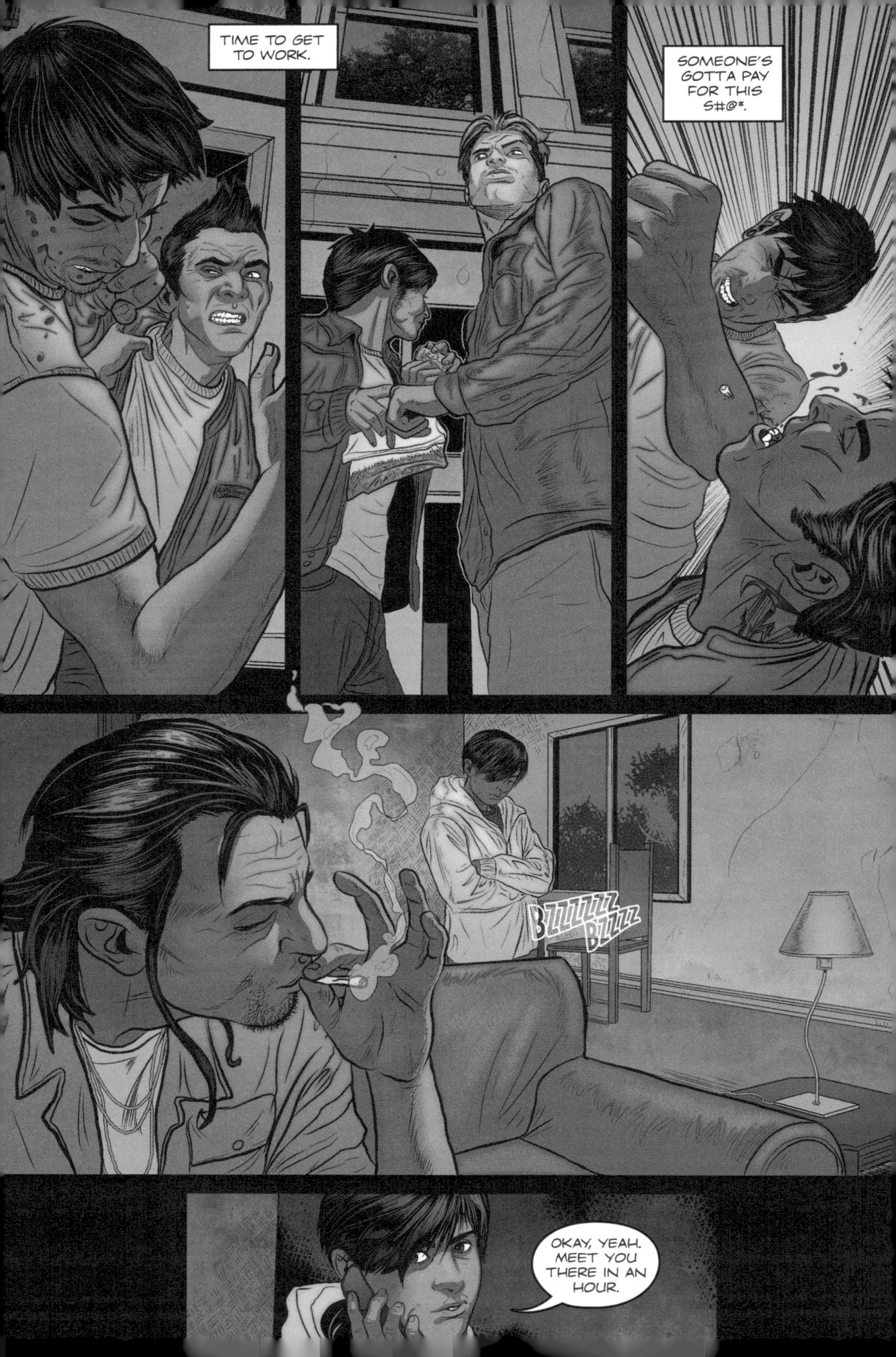
TIME TO GET TO WORK.
SOMEONE'S GOTTA PAY FOR THIS S#@*.
BZZZZZZZ BZZZZZ
OKAY, YEAH. MEET YOU THERE IN AN HOUR.

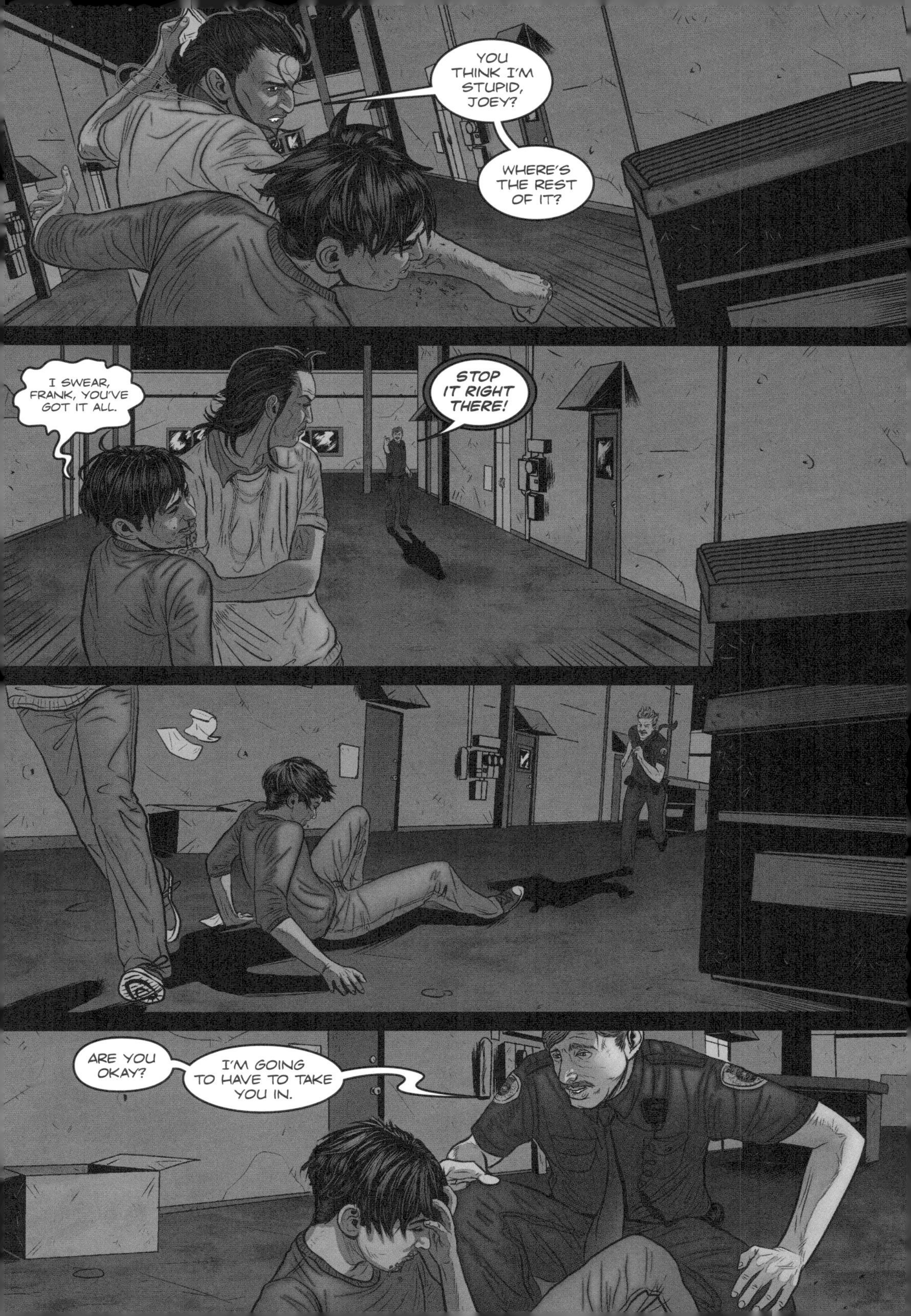
YOU THINK I'M STUPID, JOEY?
WHERE'S THE REST OF IT?
I SWEAR, FRANK, YOU'VE GOT IT ALL.
STOP IT RIGHT THERE!
ARE YOU OKAY?
I'M GOING TO HAVE TO TAKE YOU IN.

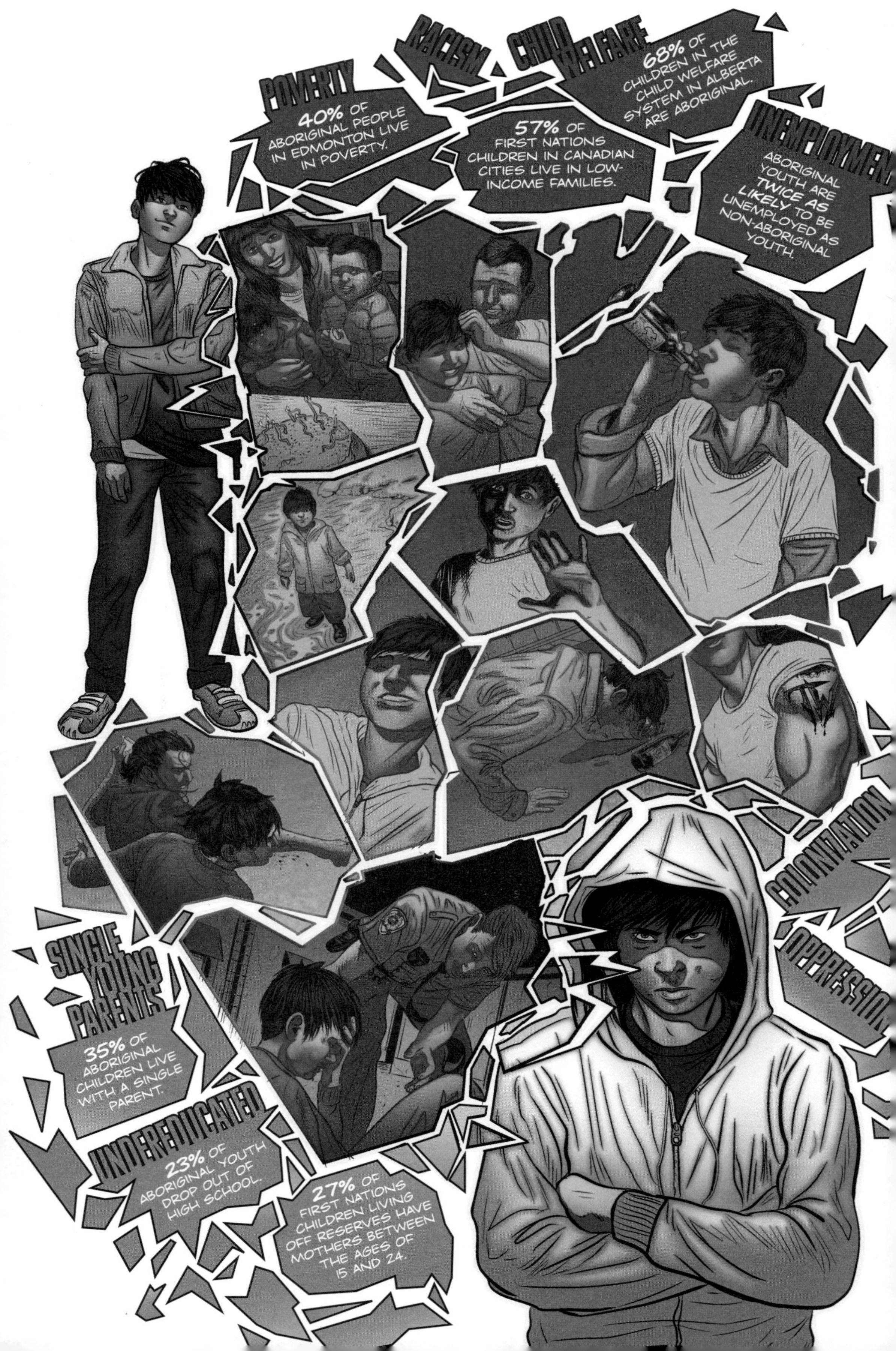
POVERTY
40% OF ABORIGINAL PEOPLE IN EDMONTON LIVE IN POVERTY.
RACISM
CHILD WELFARE
68% OF CHILDREN IN THE CHILD WELFARE SYSTEM IN ALBERTA ARE ABORIGINAL.
57% OF FIRST NATIONS CHILDREN IN CANADIAN CITIES LIVE IN LOW-INCOME FAMILIES.
UNEMPLOYMENT
ABORIGINAL YOUTH ARE TWICE AS LIKELY TO BE UNEMPLOYED AS NON-ABORIGINAL YOUTH.
COLONIZATION
OPPRESSION
SINGLE YOUNG PARENTS
35% OF ABORIGINAL CHILDREN LIVE WITH A SINGLE PARENT.
UNDEREDUCATED
23% OF ABORIGINAL YOUTH DROP OUT OF HIGH SCHOOL.
27% OF FIRST NATIONS CHILDREN LIVING OFF RESERVES HAVE MOTHERS BETWEEN THE AGES OF 15 AND 24.

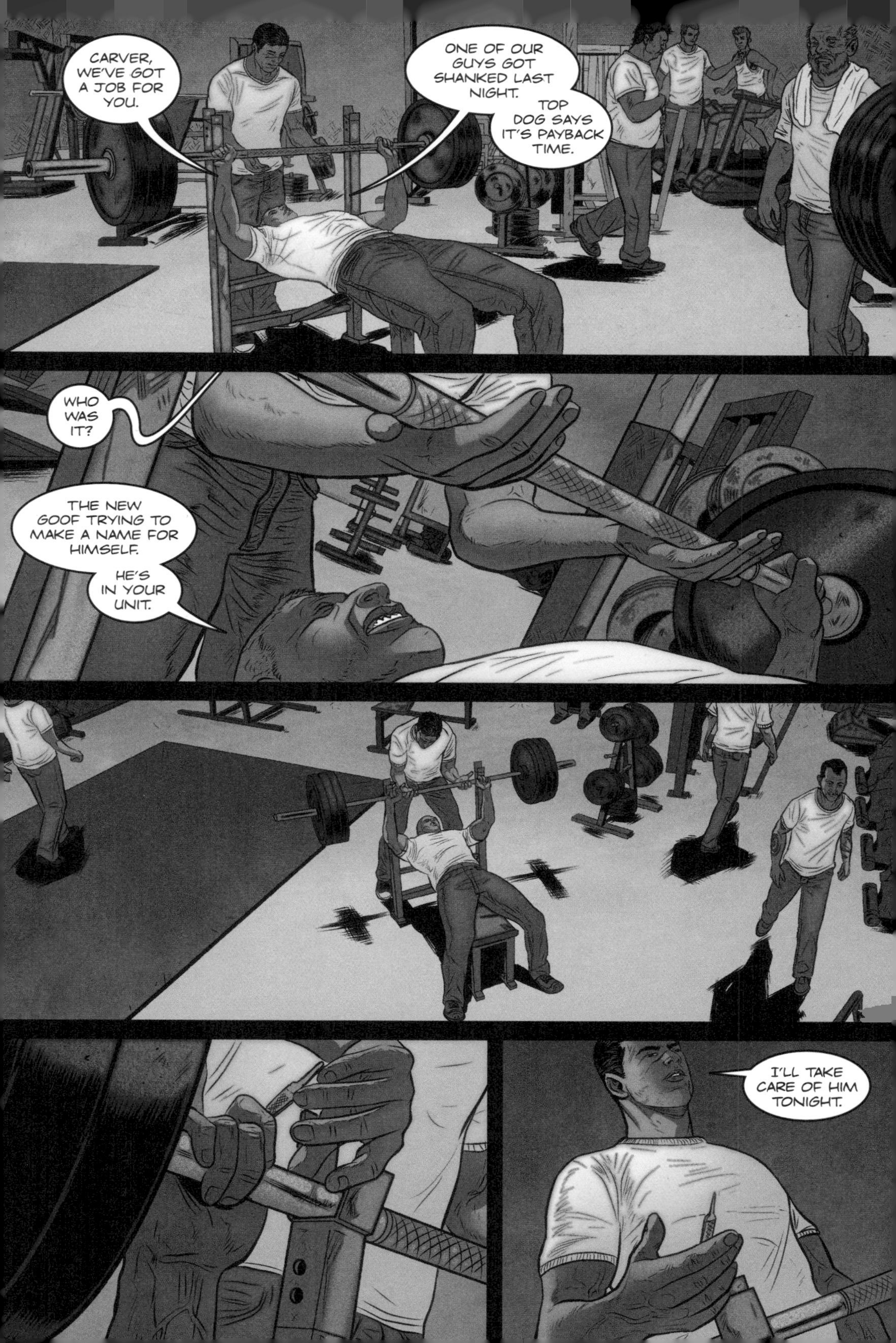
CARVER, WE'VE GOT A JOB FOR YOU.
ONE OF OUR GUYS GOT SHANKED LAST NIGHT.
TOP DOG SAYS IT'S PAYBACK TIME.
WHO WAS IT?
THE NEW GOOF TRYING TO MAKE A NAME FOR HIMSELF.
HE'S IN YOUR UNIT.
I'LL TAKE CARE OF HIM TONIGHT.

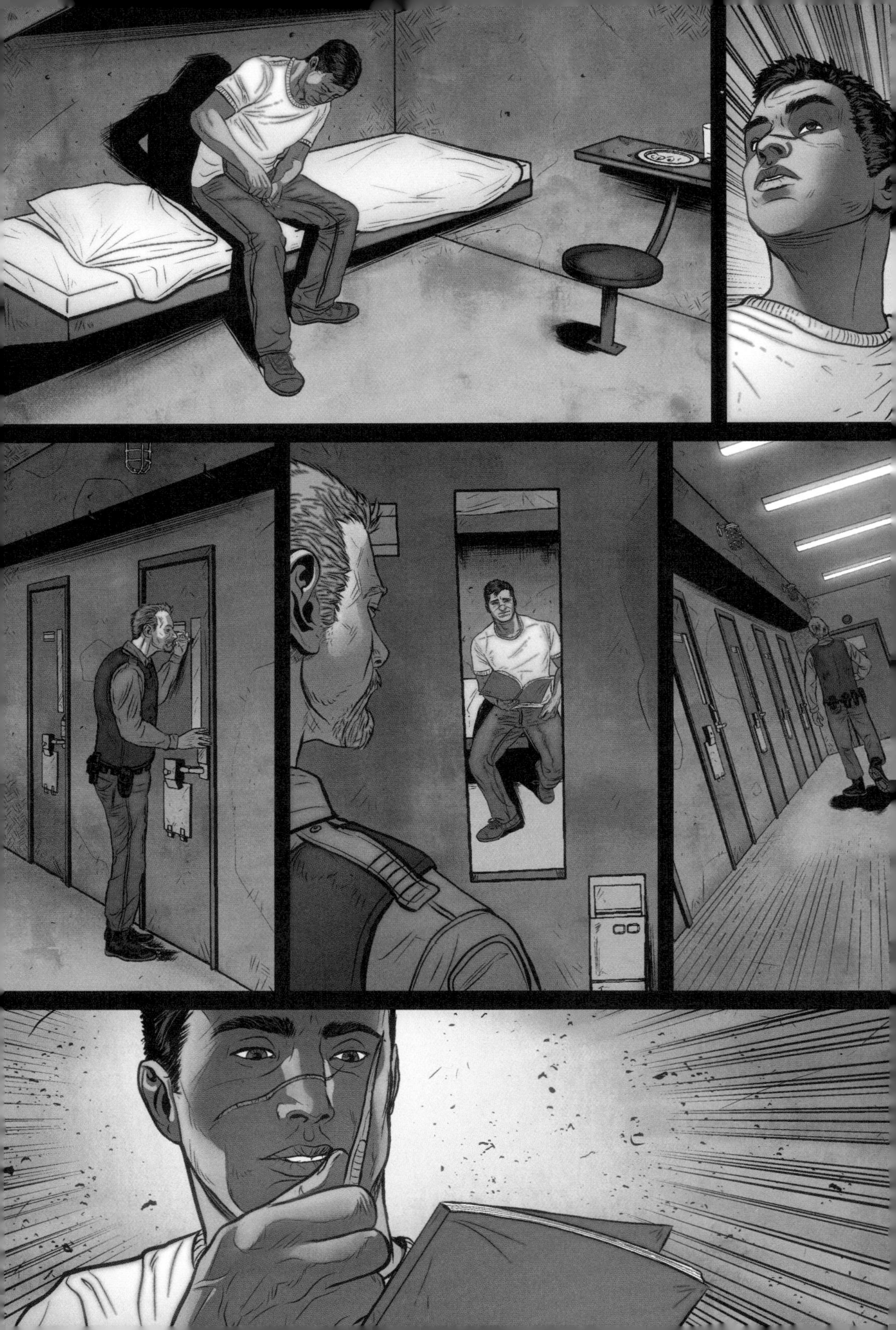

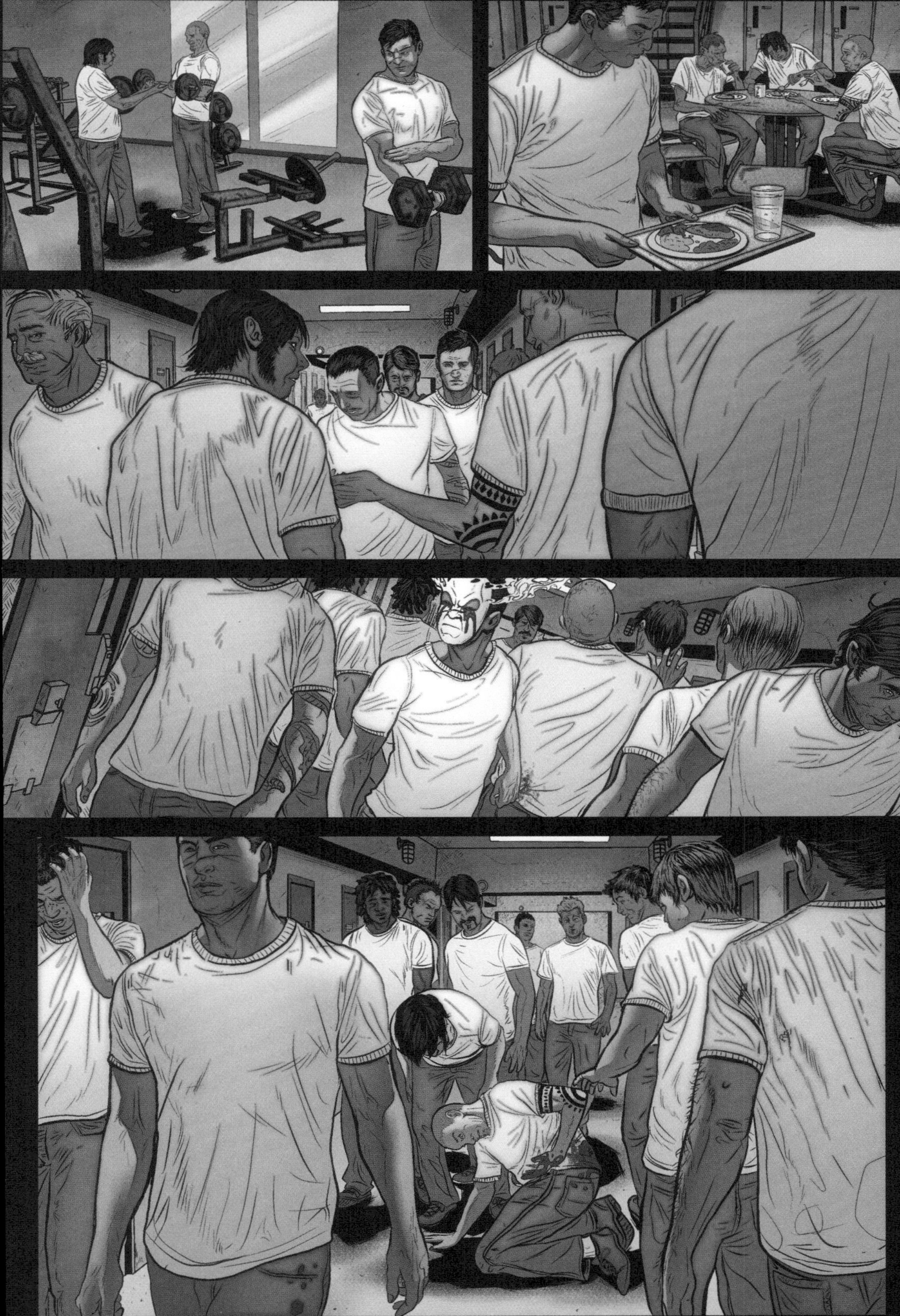

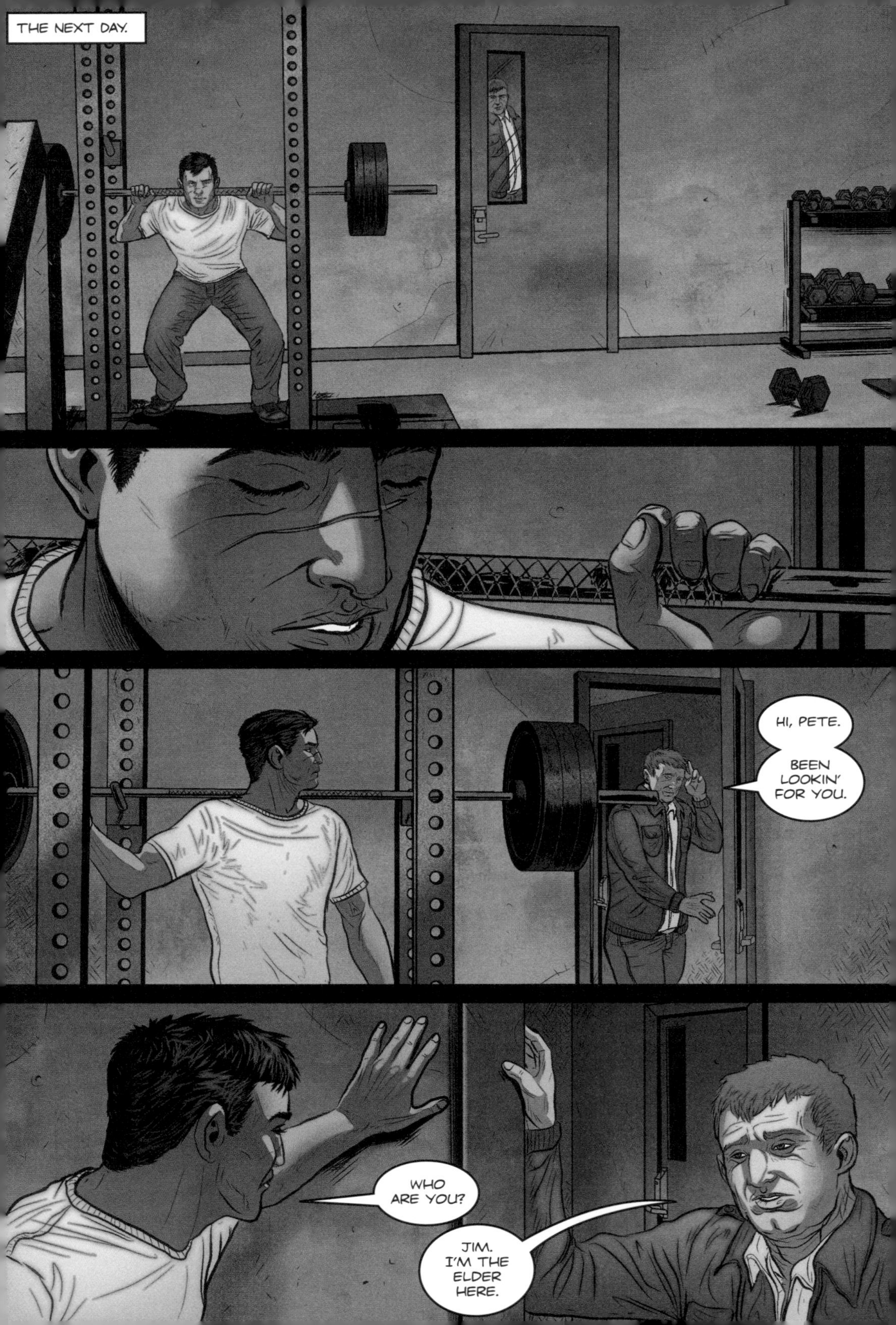
THE NEXT DAY.
HI, PETE.
BEEN LOOKIN' FOR YOU.
WHO ARE YOU?
JIM. I'M THE ELDER HERE.

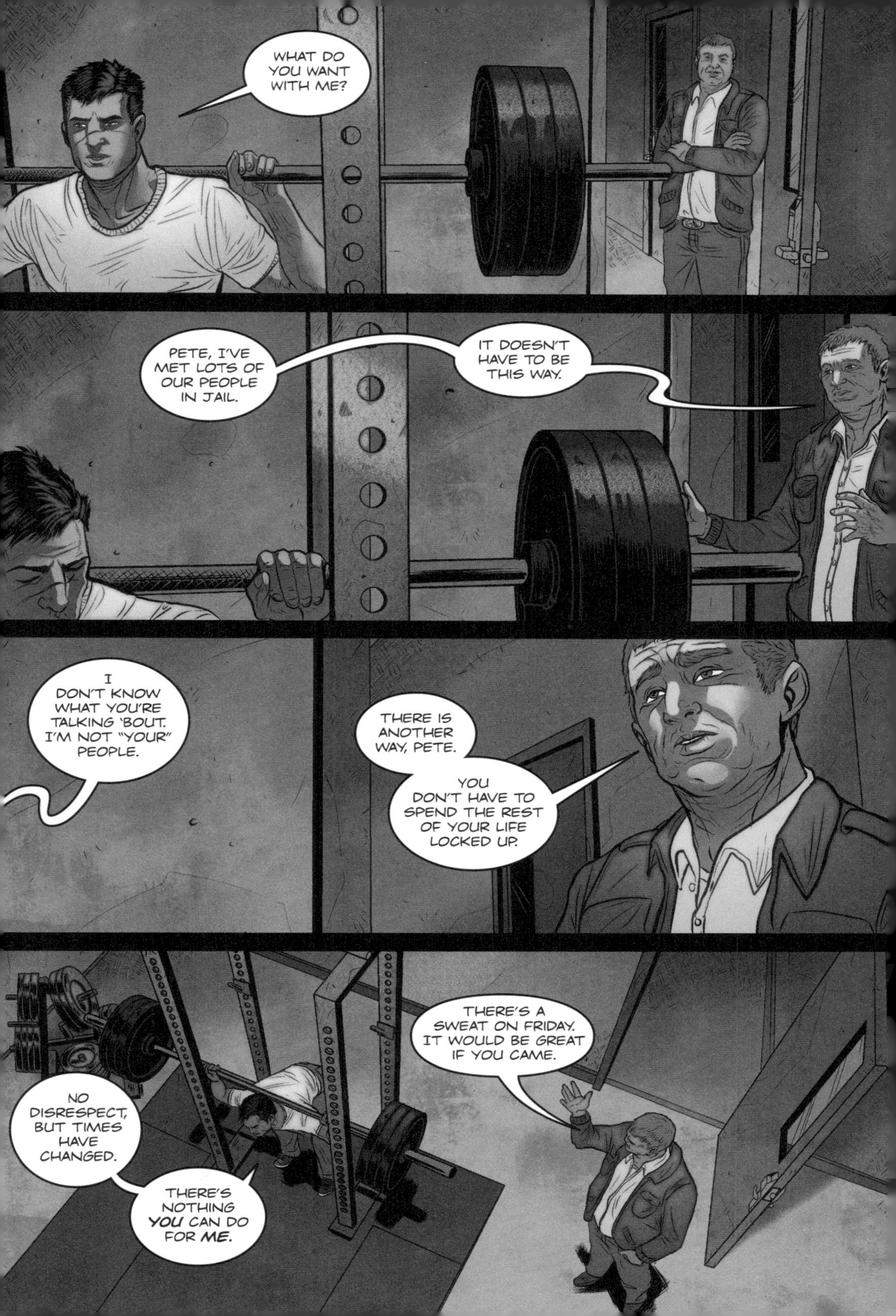
WHAT DO YOU WANT WITH ME?
PETE, I'VE MET LOTS OF OUR PEOPLE IN JAIL.
IT DOESN'T HAVE TO BE THIS WAY.
I DON'T KNOW WHAT YOU'RE TALKING 'BOUT. I'M NOT "YOUR" PEOPLE.
THERE IS ANOTHER WAY, PETE.
YOU DON'T HAVE TO SPEND THE REST OF YOUR LIFE LOCKED UP.
THERE'S A SWEAT ON FRIDAY. IT WOULD BE GREAT IF YOU CAME.
NO DISRESPECT, BUT TIMES HAVE CHANGED.
THERE'S NOTHING **YOU** CAN DO FOR **ME**.

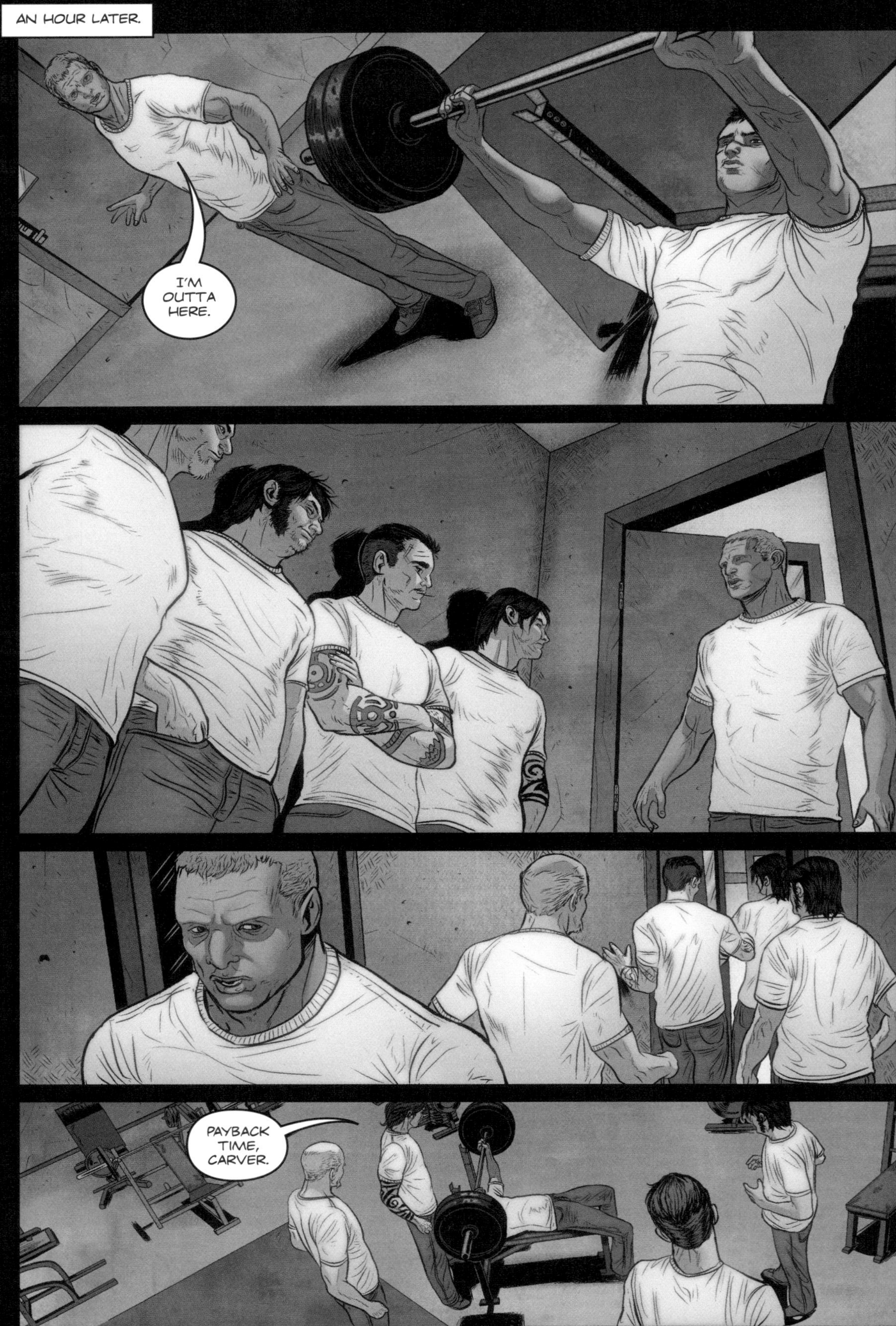
AN HOUR LATER.
I'M OUTTA HERE.
PAYBACK TIME, CARVER.

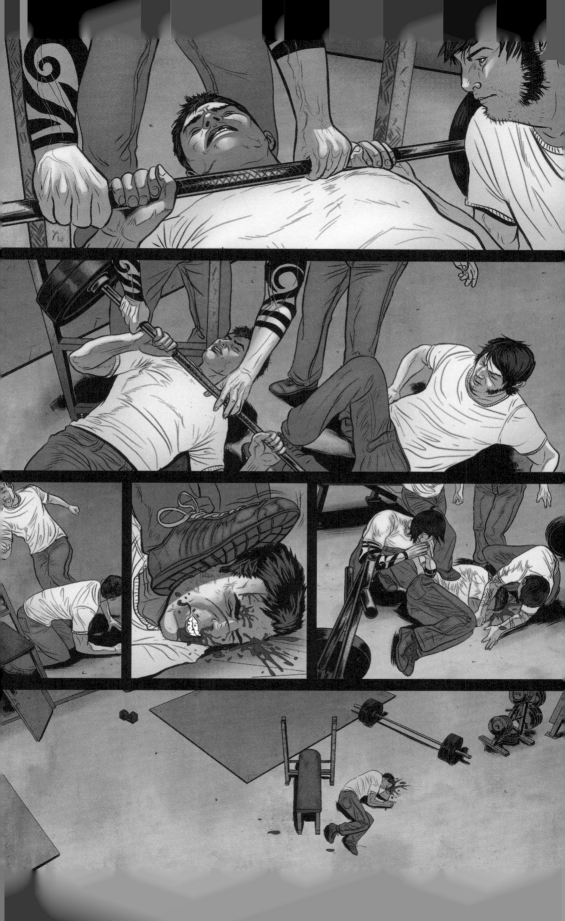

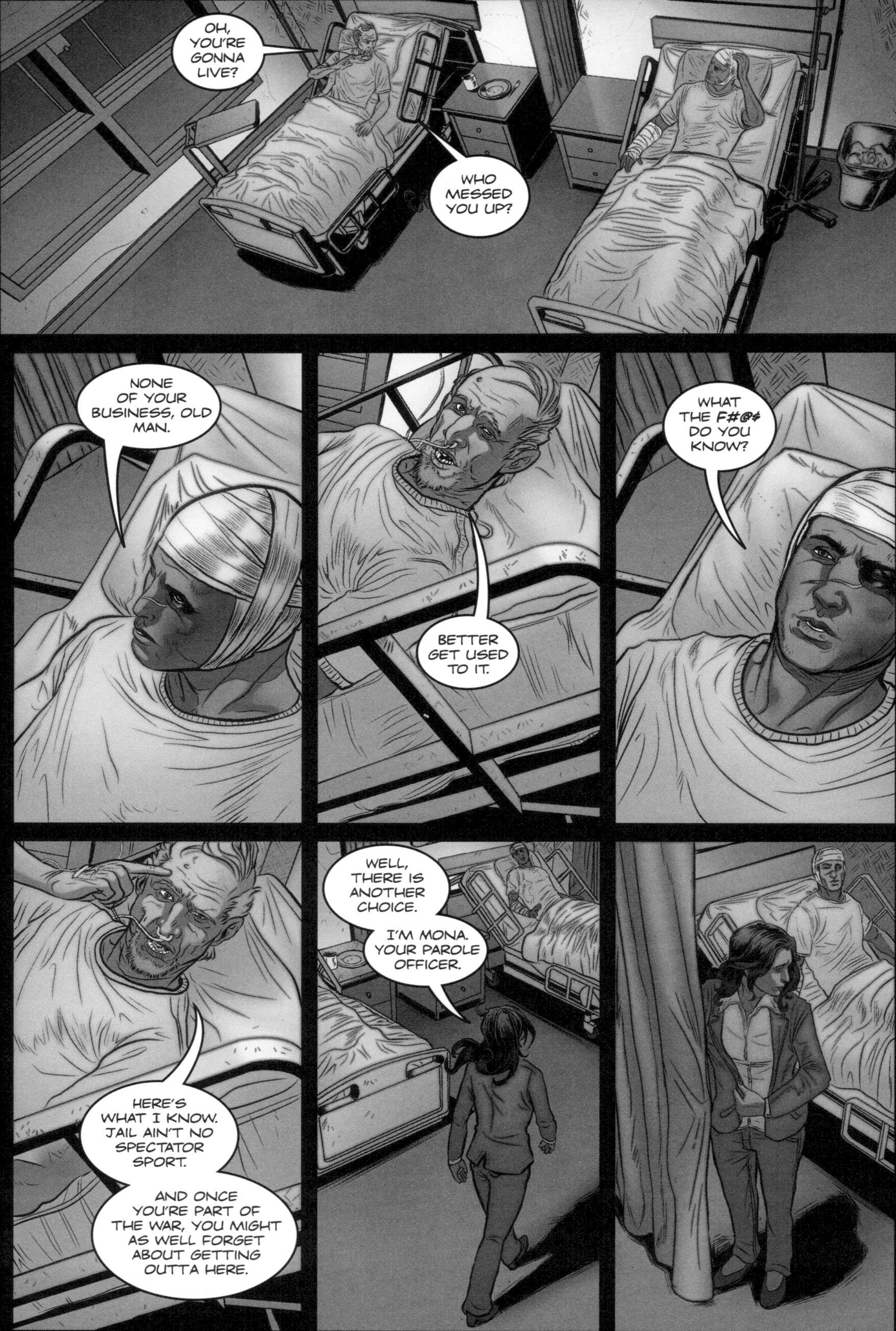
OH, YOU'RE GONNA LIVE?
WHO MESSED YOU UP?
NONE OF YOUR BUSINESS, OLD MAN.
BETTER GET USED TO IT.
WHAT THE F#@$ DO YOU KNOW?
HERE'S WHAT I KNOW. JAIL AIN'T NO SPECTATOR SPORT.
AND ONCE YOU'RE PART OF THE WAR, YOU MIGHT AS WELL FORGET ABOUT GETTING OUTTA HERE.
WELL, THERE IS ANOTHER CHOICE.
I'M MONA. YOUR PAROLE OFFICER.

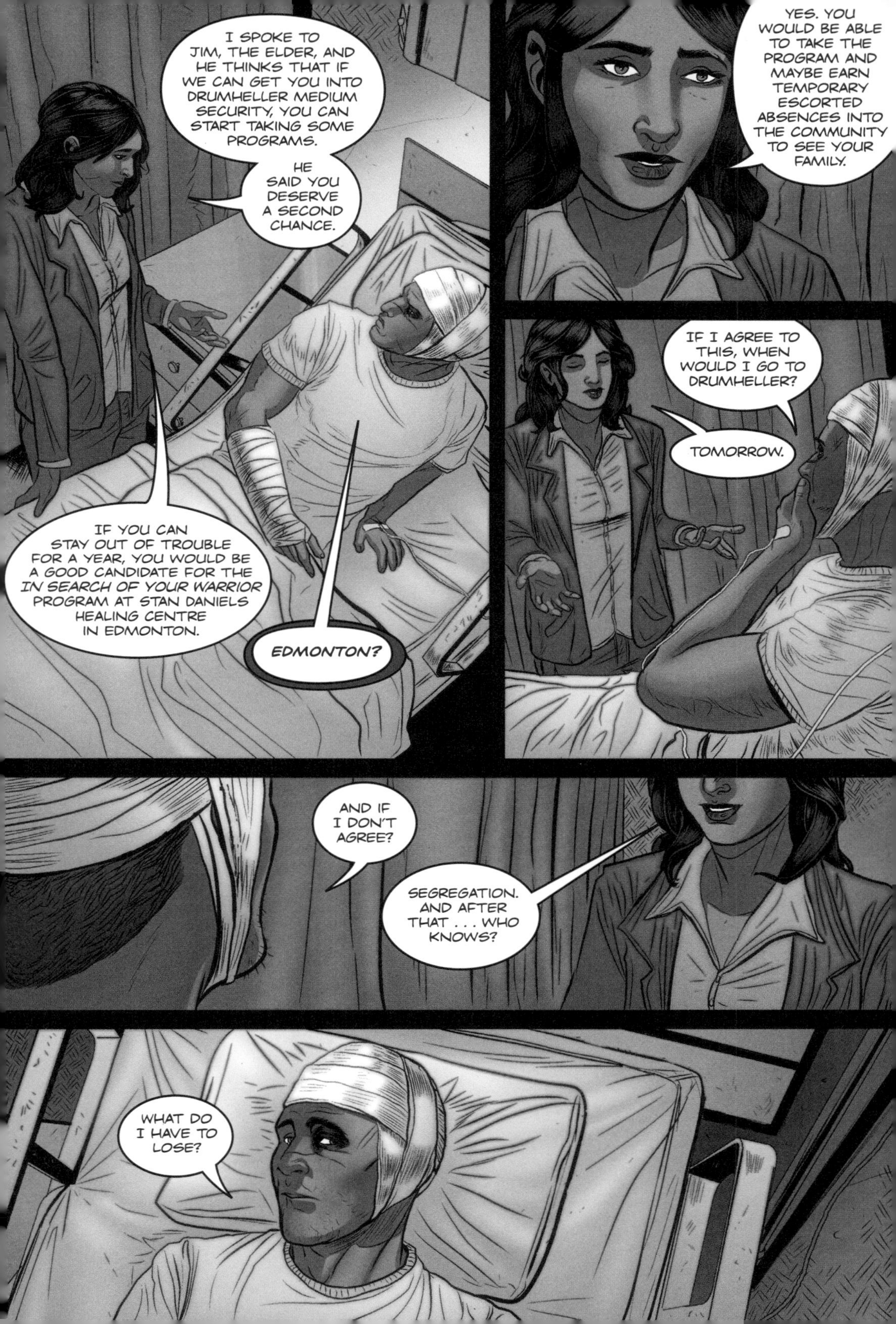
I SPOKE TO JIM, THE ELDER, AND HE THINKS THAT IF WE CAN GET YOU INTO DRUMHELLER MEDIUM SECURITY, YOU CAN START TAKING SOME PROGRAMS.
HE SAID YOU DESERVE A SECOND CHANCE.
IF YOU CAN STAY OUT OF TROUBLE FOR A YEAR, YOU WOULD BE A GOOD CANDIDATE FOR THE *IN SEARCH OF YOUR WARRIOR* PROGRAM AT STAN DANIELS HEALING CENTRE IN EDMONTON.
EDMONTON?
YES. YOU WOULD BE ABLE TO TAKE THE PROGRAM AND MAYBE EARN TEMPORARY ESCORTED ABSENCES INTO THE COMMUNITY TO SEE YOUR FAMILY.
IF I AGREE TO THIS, WHEN WOULD I GO TO DRUMHELLER?
TOMORROW.
AND IF I DON'T AGREE?
SEGREGATION. AND AFTER THAT . . . WHO KNOWS?
WHAT DO I HAVE TO LOSE?

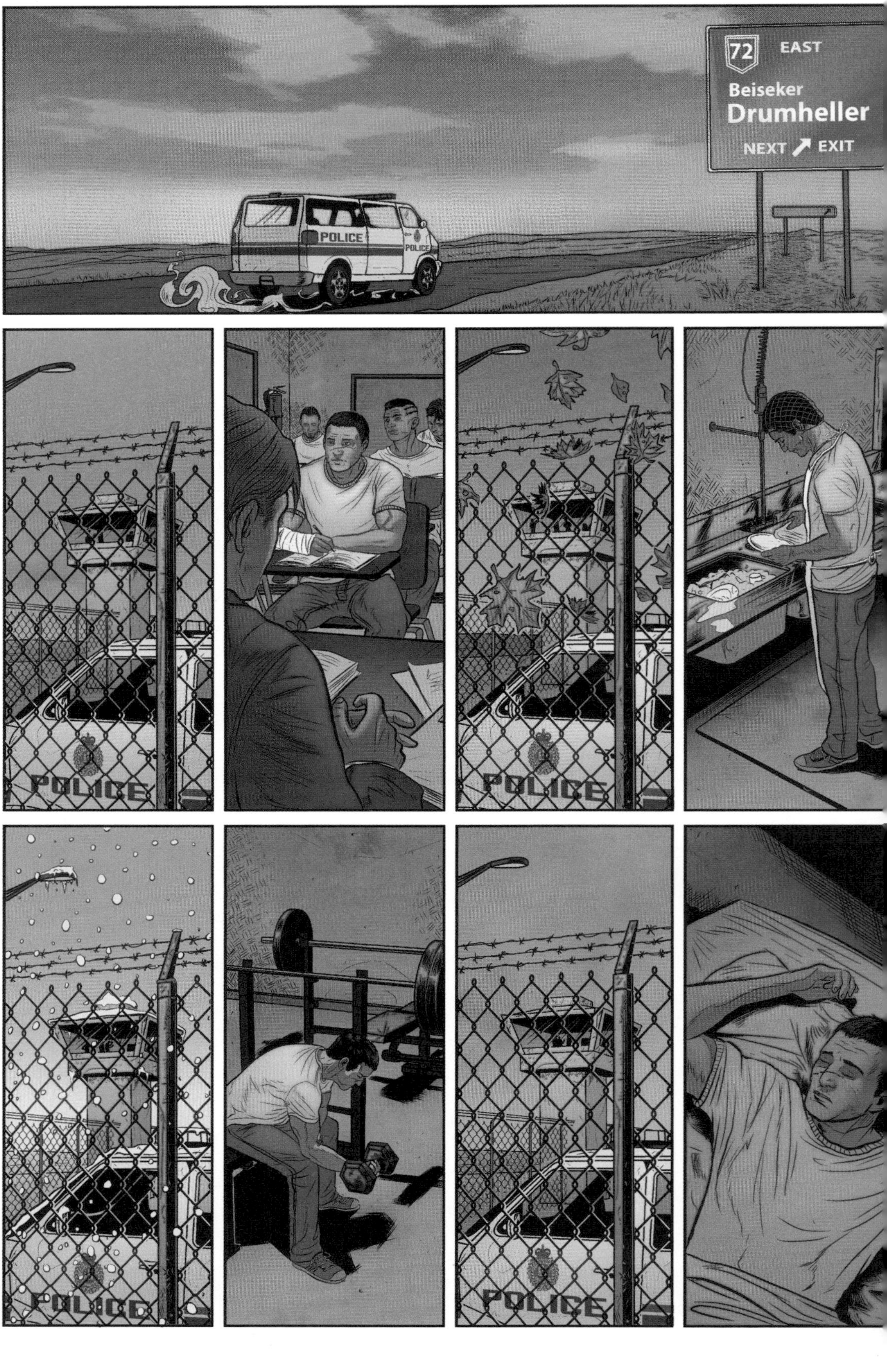
72 EAST
Beiseker
Drumheller
NEXT EXIT
POLICE
POLICE
POLICE
POLICE
POLICE
POLICE

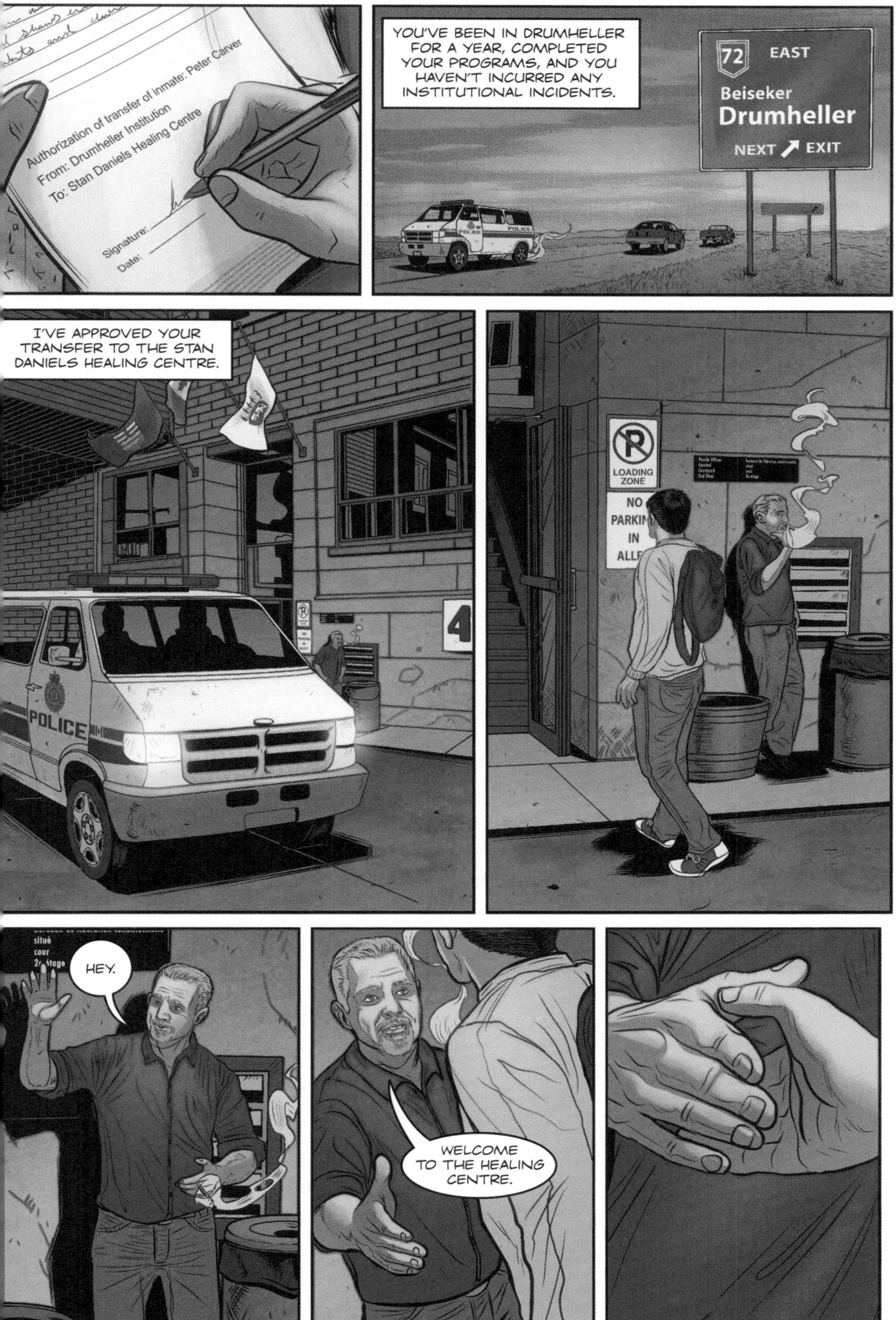
Authorization of transfer of inmate: Peter Carver
From: Drumheller Institution
To: Stan Daniels Healing Centre
Signature:
Date:
YOU'VE BEEN IN DRUMHELLER FOR A YEAR, COMPLETED YOUR PROGRAMS, AND YOU HAVEN'T INCURRED ANY INSTITUTIONAL INCIDENTS.
72 EAST
Beiseker
Drumheller
NEXT EXIT
POLICE
I'VE APPROVED YOUR TRANSFER TO THE STAN DANIELS HEALING CENTRE.
POLICE
LOADING ZONE
NO PARKIN IN ALLE
HEY.
WELCOME TO THE HEALING CENTRE.

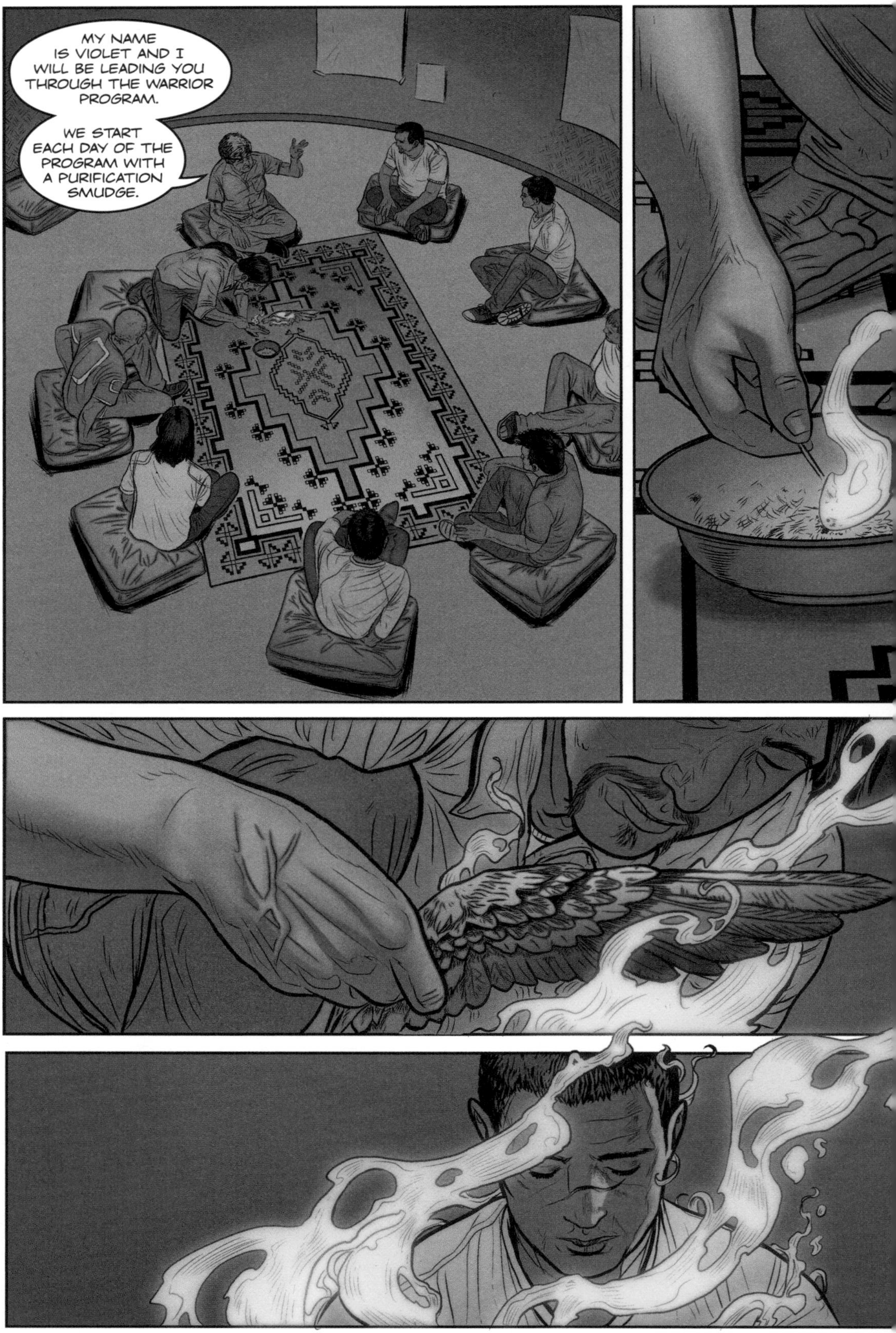
MY NAME IS VIOLET AND I WILL BE LEADING YOU THROUGH THE WARRIOR PROGRAM.
WE START EACH DAY OF THE PROGRAM WITH A PURIFICATION SMUDGE.

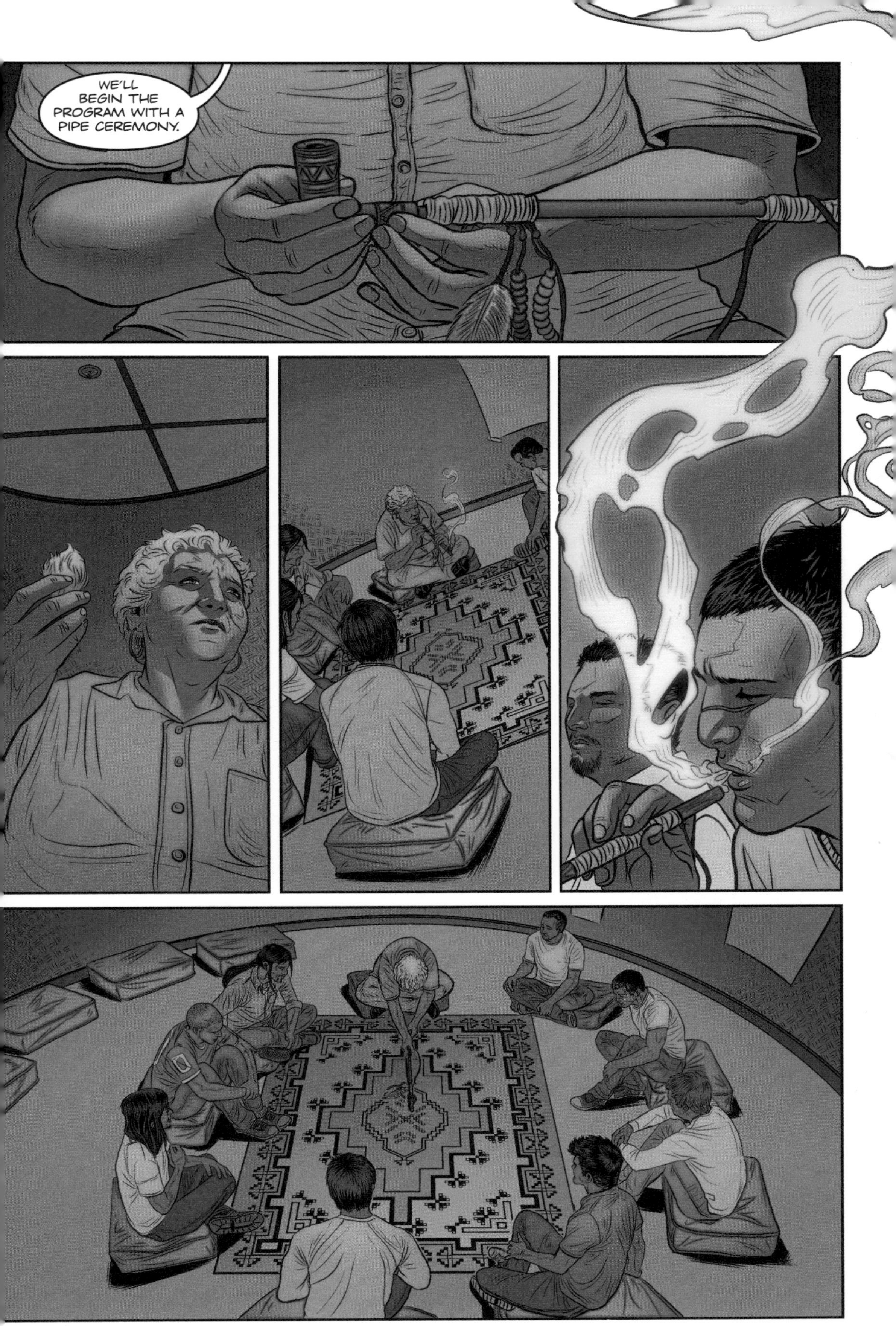
WE'LL BEGIN THE PROGRAM WITH A PIPE CEREMONY.

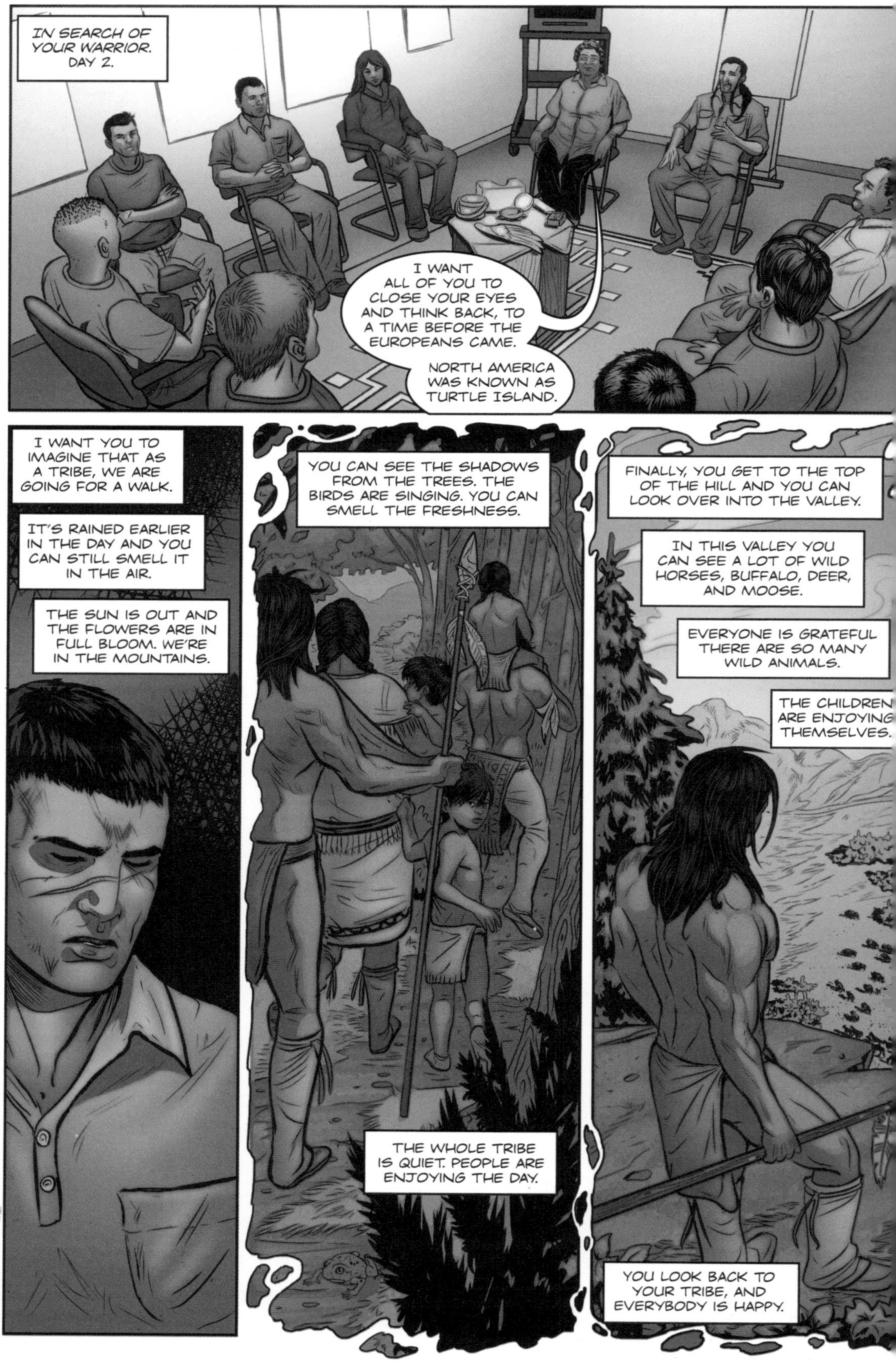
IN SEARCH OF YOUR WARRIOR. DAY 2.
I WANT ALL OF YOU TO CLOSE YOUR EYES AND THINK BACK, TO A TIME BEFORE THE EUROPEANS CAME.
NORTH AMERICA WAS KNOWN AS TURTLE ISLAND.
I WANT YOU TO IMAGINE THAT AS A TRIBE, WE ARE GOING FOR A WALK.
IT'S RAINED EARLIER IN THE DAY AND YOU CAN STILL SMELL IT IN THE AIR.
THE SUN IS OUT AND THE FLOWERS ARE IN FULL BLOOM. WE'RE IN THE MOUNTAINS.
YOU CAN SEE THE SHADOWS FROM THE TREES. THE BIRDS ARE SINGING. YOU CAN SMELL THE FRESHNESS.
THE WHOLE TRIBE IS QUIET. PEOPLE ARE ENJOYING THE DAY.
FINALLY, YOU GET TO THE TOP OF THE HILL AND YOU CAN LOOK OVER INTO THE VALLEY.
IN THIS VALLEY YOU CAN SEE A LOT OF WILD HORSES, BUFFALO, DEER, AND MOOSE.
EVERYONE IS GRATEFUL THERE ARE SO MANY WILD ANIMALS.
THE CHILDREN ARE ENJOYING THEMSELVES.
YOU LOOK BACK TO YOUR TRIBE, AND EVERYBODY IS HAPPY.

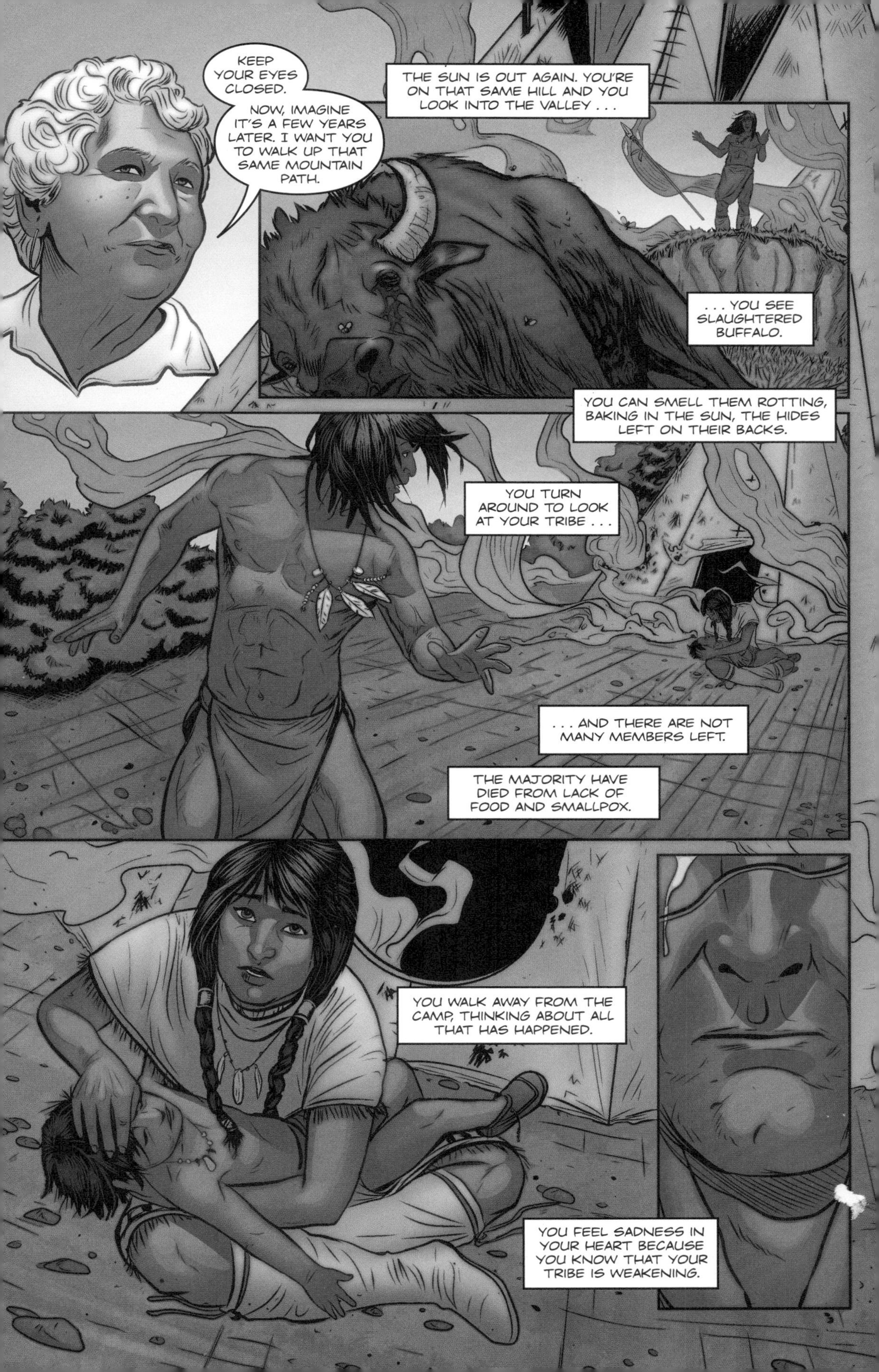
KEEP YOUR EYES CLOSED.
NOW, IMAGINE IT'S A FEW YEARS LATER. I WANT YOU TO WALK UP THAT SAME MOUNTAIN PATH.
THE SUN IS OUT AGAIN. YOU'RE ON THAT SAME HILL AND YOU LOOK INTO THE VALLEY . . .
. . . YOU SEE SLAUGHTERED BUFFALO.
YOU CAN SMELL THEM ROTTING, BAKING IN THE SUN, THE HIDES LEFT ON THEIR BACKS.
YOU TURN AROUND TO LOOK AT YOUR TRIBE . . .
. . . AND THERE ARE NOT MANY MEMBERS LEFT.
THE MAJORITY HAVE DIED FROM LACK OF FOOD AND SMALLPOX.
YOU WALK AWAY FROM THE CAMP, THINKING ABOUT ALL THAT HAS HAPPENED.
YOU FEEL SADNESS IN YOUR HEART BECAUSE YOU KNOW THAT YOUR TRIBE IS WEAKENING.

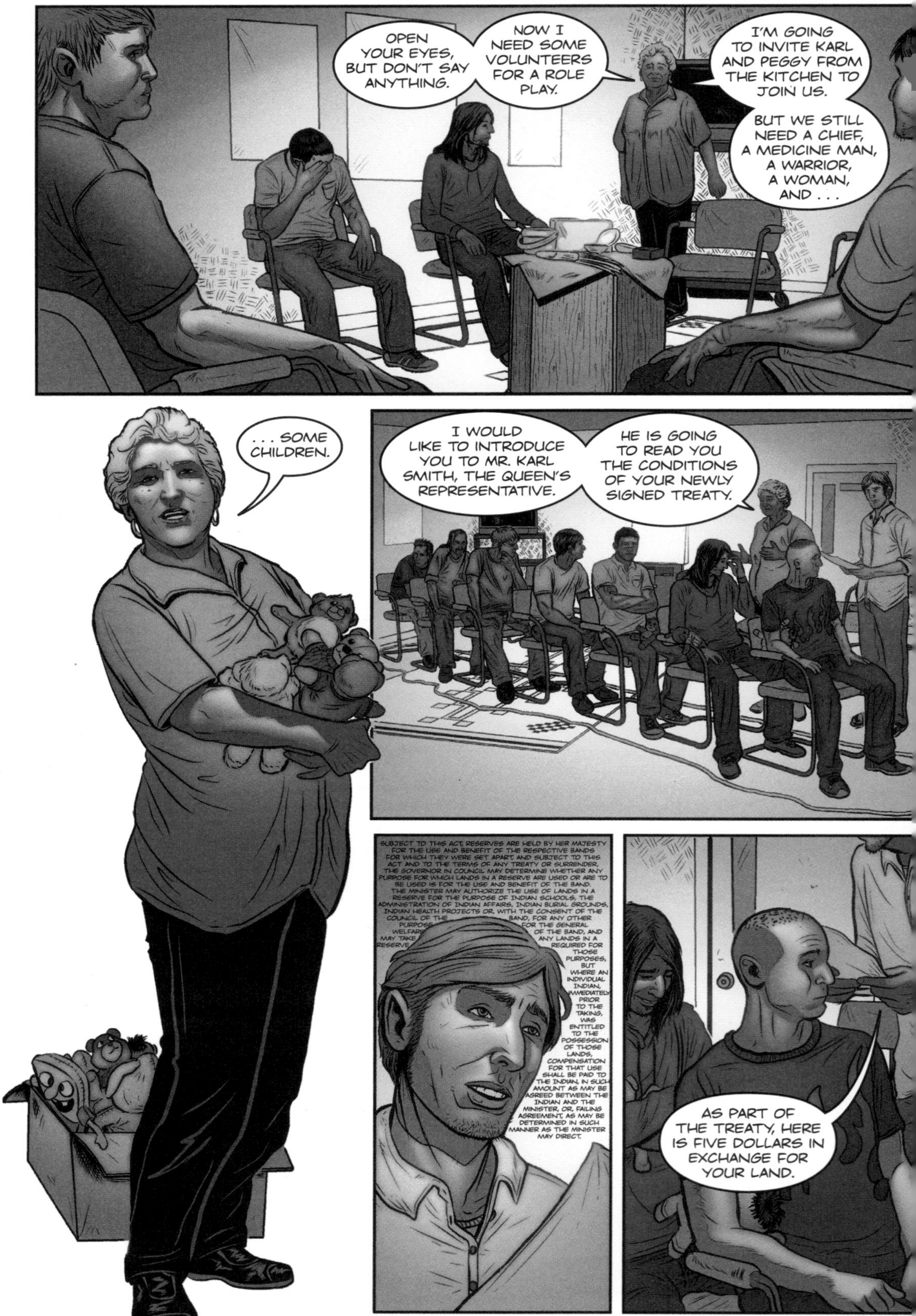
OPEN YOUR EYES, BUT DON'T SAY ANYTHING.
NOW I NEED SOME VOLUNTEERS FOR A ROLE PLAY.
I'M GOING TO INVITE KARL AND PEGGY FROM THE KITCHEN TO JOIN US.
BUT WE STILL NEED A CHIEF, A MEDICINE MAN, A WARRIOR, A WOMAN, AND . . .
. . . SOME CHILDREN.
I WOULD LIKE TO INTRODUCE YOU TO MR. KARL SMITH, THE QUEEN'S REPRESENTATIVE.
HE IS GOING TO READ YOU THE CONDITIONS OF YOUR NEWLY SIGNED TREATY.
SUBJECT TO THIS ACT, RESERVES ARE HELD BY HER MAJESTY FOR THE USE AND BENEFIT OF THE RESPECTIVE BANDS FOR WHICH THEY WERE SET APART, AND SUBJECT TO THIS ACT AND TO THE TERMS OF ANY TREATY OR SURRENDER, THE GOVERNOR IN COUNCIL MAY DETERMINE WHETHER ANY PURPOSE FOR WHICH LANDS IN A RESERVE ARE USED OR ARE TO BE USED IS FOR THE USE AND BENEFIT OF THE BAND. THE MINISTER MAY AUTHORIZE THE USE OF LANDS IN A RESERVE FOR THE PURPOSE OF INDIAN SCHOOLS, THE ADMINISTRATION OF INDIAN AFFAIRS, INDIAN BURIAL GROUNDS, INDIAN HEALTH PROJECTS OR, WITH THE CONSENT OF THE COUNCIL OF THE BAND, FOR ANY OTHER PURPOSE FOR THE GENERAL WELFARE OF THE BAND, AND MAY TAKE ANY LANDS IN A RESERVE REQUIRED FOR THOSE PURPOSES, BUT WHERE AN INDIVIDUAL INDIAN, IMMEDIATELY PRIOR TO THE TAKING, WAS ENTITLED TO THE POSSESSION OF THOSE LANDS, COMPENSATION FOR THAT USE SHALL BE PAID TO THE INDIAN, IN SUCH AMOUNT AS MAY BE AGREED BETWEEN THE INDIAN AND THE MINISTER, OR, FAILING AGREEMENT, AS MAY BE DETERMINED IN SUCH MANNER AS THE MINISTER MAY DIRECT.
AS PART OF THE TREATY, HERE IS FIVE DOLLARS IN EXCHANGE FOR YOUR LAND.

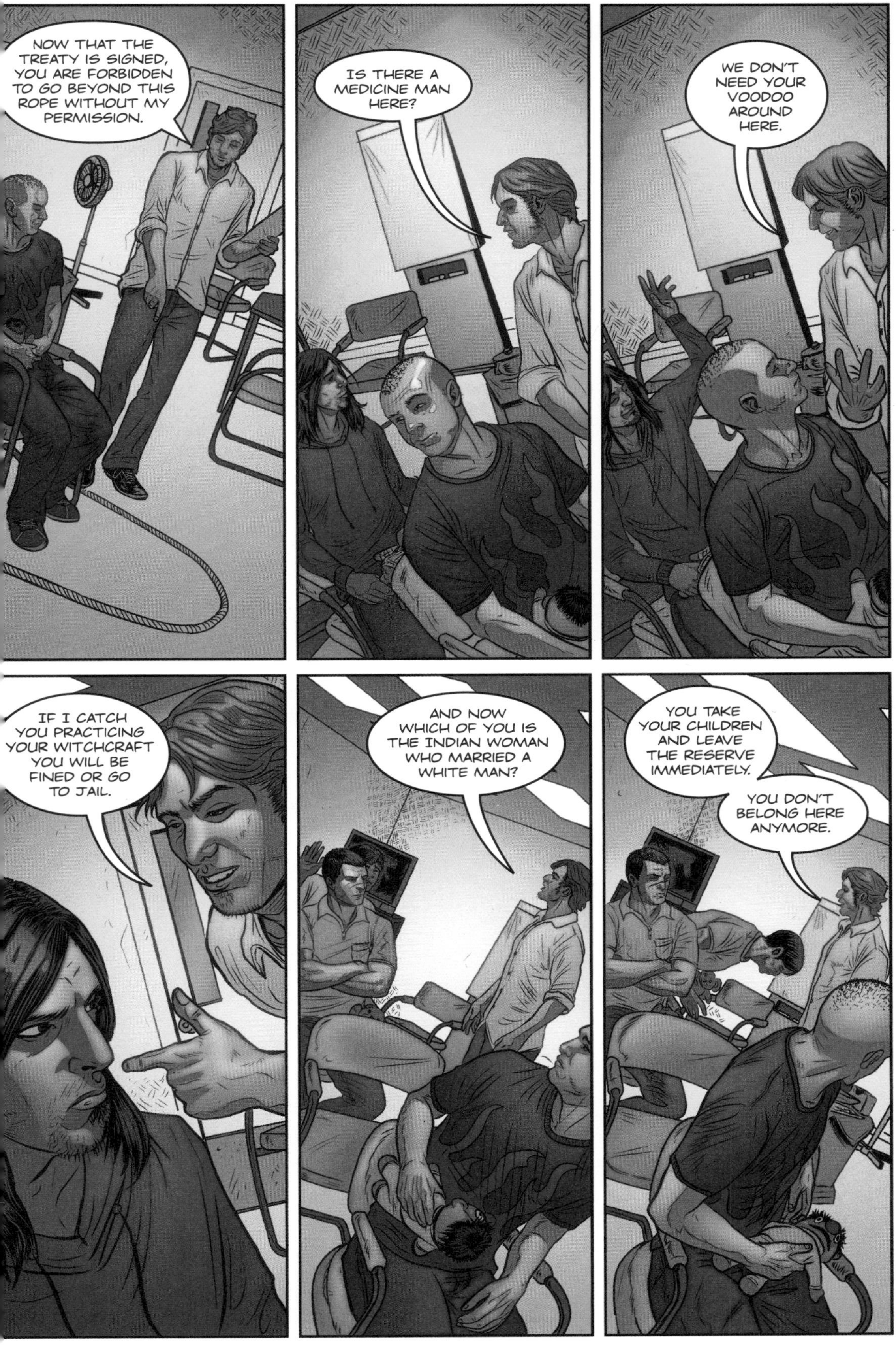
NOW THAT THE TREATY IS SIGNED, YOU ARE FORBIDDEN TO GO BEYOND THIS ROPE WITHOUT MY PERMISSION.
IS THERE A MEDICINE MAN HERE?
WE DON'T NEED YOUR VOODOO AROUND HERE.
IF I CATCH YOU PRACTICING YOUR WITCHCRAFT YOU WILL BE FINED OR GO TO JAIL.
AND NOW WHICH OF YOU IS THE INDIAN WOMAN WHO MARRIED A WHITE MAN?
YOU TAKE YOUR CHILDREN AND LEAVE THE RESERVE IMMEDIATELY.
YOU DON'T BELONG HERE ANYMORE.

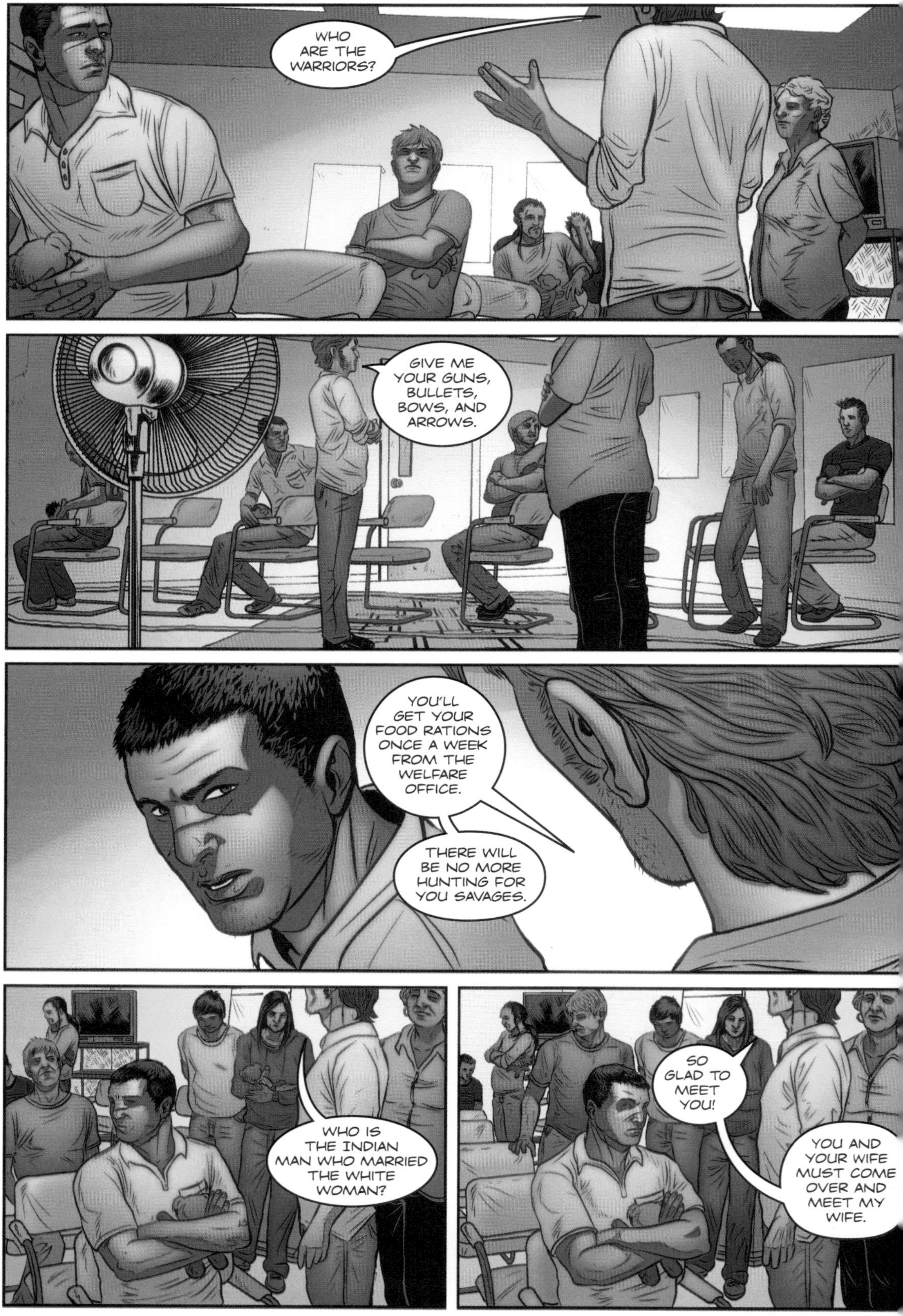
WHO ARE THE WARRIORS?
GIVE ME YOUR GUNS, BULLETS, BOWS, AND ARROWS.
YOU'LL GET YOUR FOOD RATIONS ONCE A WEEK FROM THE WELFARE OFFICE.
THERE WILL BE NO MORE HUNTING FOR YOU SAVAGES.
WHO IS THE INDIAN MAN WHO MARRIED THE WHITE WOMAN?
SO GLAD TO MEET YOU!
YOU AND YOUR WIFE MUST COME OVER AND MEET MY WIFE.

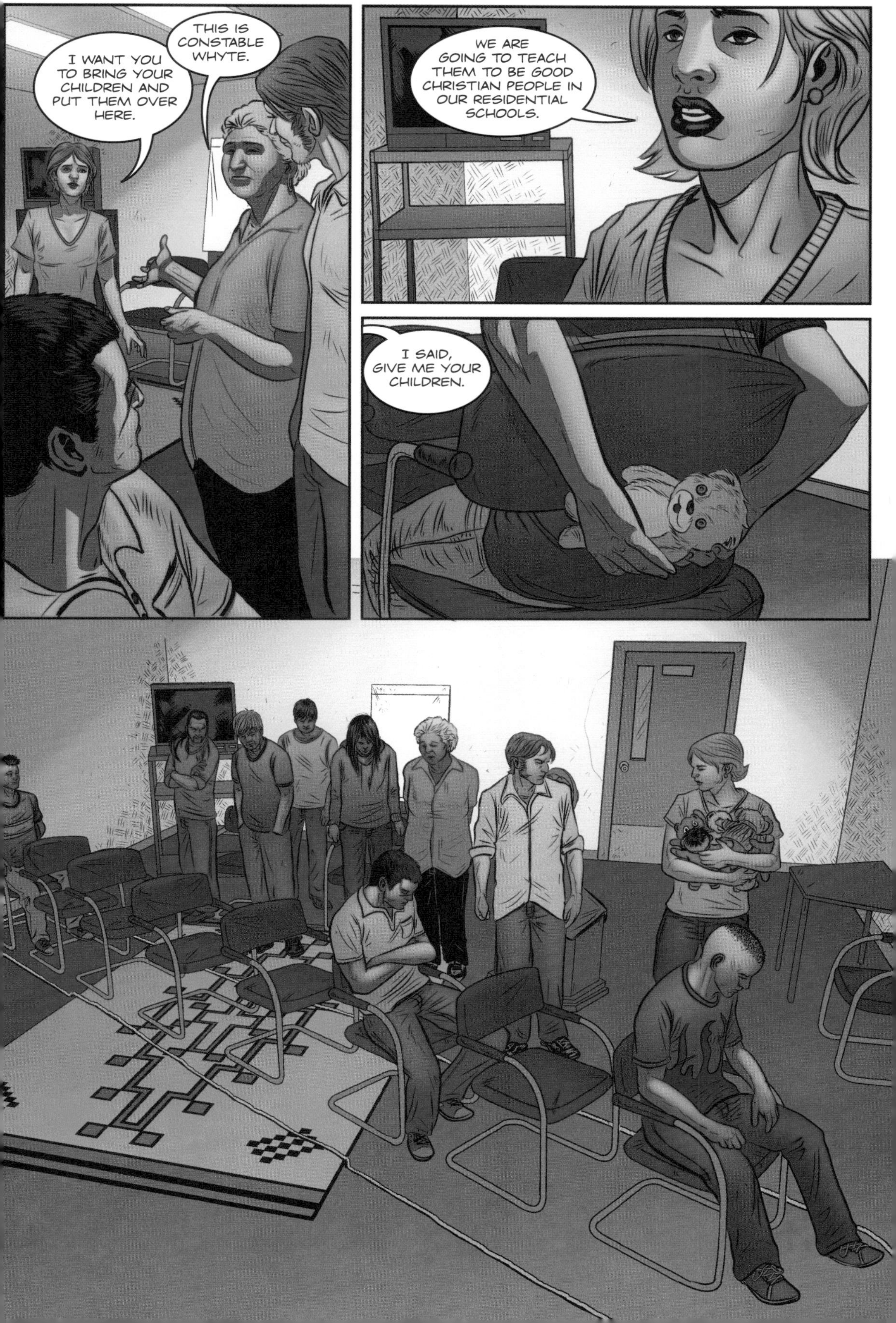
I WANT YOU TO BRING YOUR CHILDREN AND PUT THEM OVER HERE.
THIS IS CONSTABLE WHYTE.
WE ARE GOING TO TEACH THEM TO BE GOOD CHRISTIAN PEOPLE IN OUR RESIDENTIAL SCHOOLS.
I SAID, GIVE ME YOUR CHILDREN.

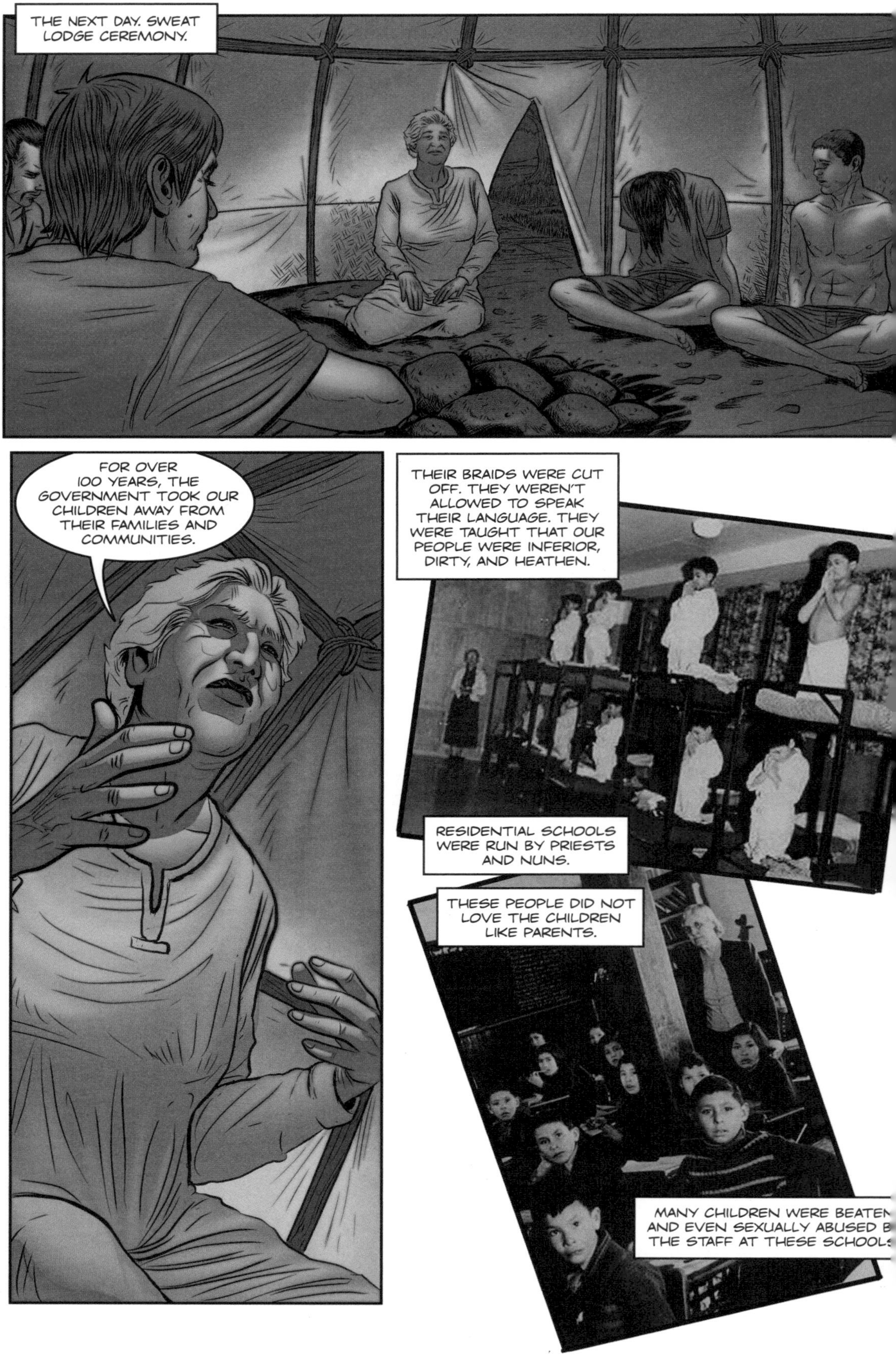
THE NEXT DAY. SWEAT LODGE CEREMONY.
FOR OVER 100 YEARS, THE GOVERNMENT TOOK OUR CHILDREN AWAY FROM THEIR FAMILIES AND COMMUNITIES.
THEIR BRAIDS WERE CUT OFF. THEY WEREN'T ALLOWED TO SPEAK THEIR LANGUAGE. THEY WERE TAUGHT THAT OUR PEOPLE WERE INFERIOR, DIRTY, AND HEATHEN.
RESIDENTIAL SCHOOLS WERE RUN BY PRIESTS AND NUNS.
THESE PEOPLE DID NOT LOVE THE CHILDREN LIKE PARENTS.
MANY CHILDREN WERE BEATEN AND EVEN SEXUALLY ABUSED BY THE STAFF AT THESE SCHOOLS.

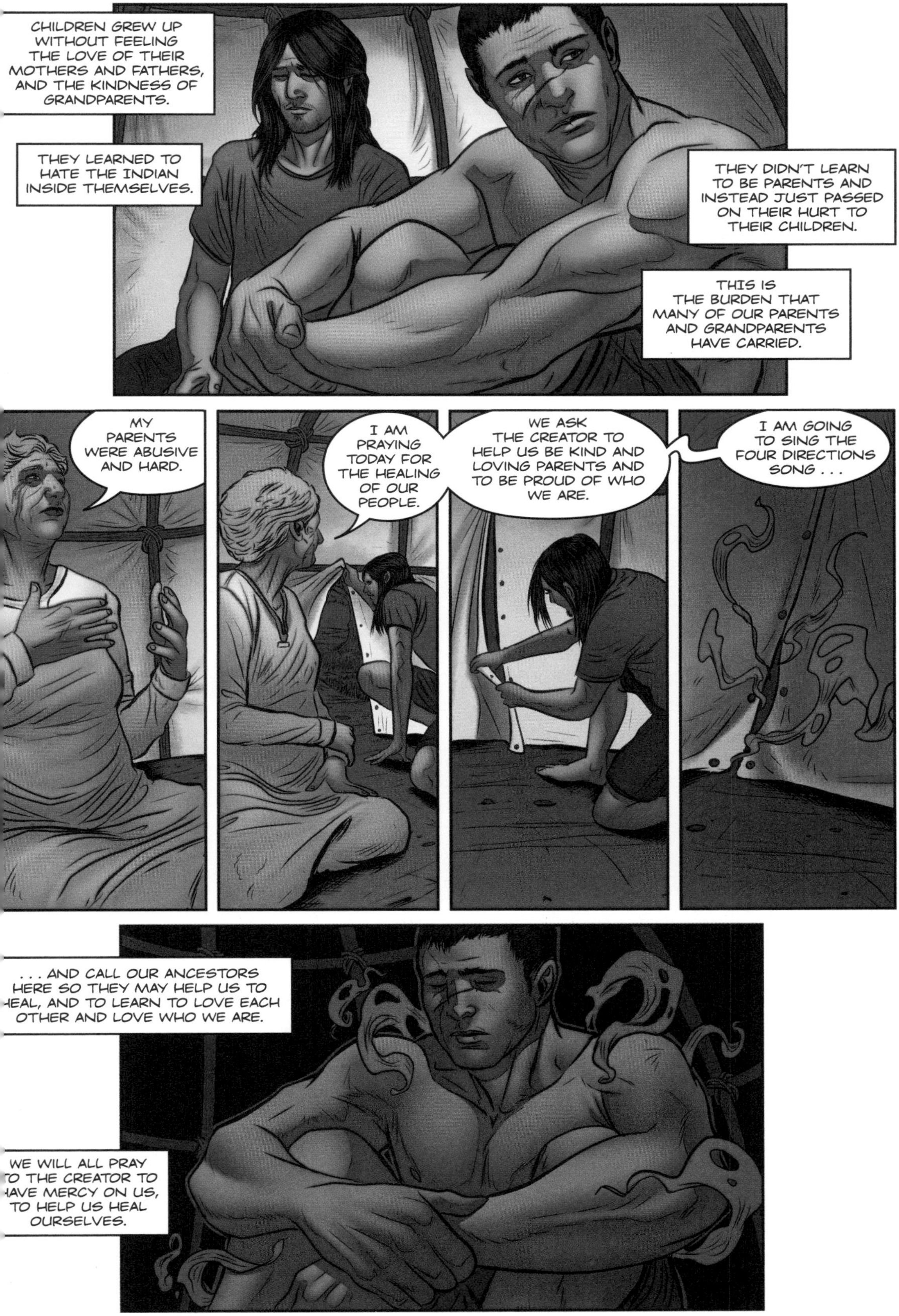
CHILDREN GREW UP WITHOUT FEELING THE LOVE OF THEIR MOTHERS AND FATHERS, AND THE KINDNESS OF GRANDPARENTS.
THEY LEARNED TO HATE THE INDIAN INSIDE THEMSELVES.
THEY DIDN'T LEARN TO BE PARENTS AND INSTEAD JUST PASSED ON THEIR HURT TO THEIR CHILDREN.
THIS IS THE BURDEN THAT MANY OF OUR PARENTS AND GRANDPARENTS HAVE CARRIED.
MY PARENTS WERE ABUSIVE AND HARD.
I AM PRAYING TODAY FOR THE HEALING OF OUR PEOPLE.
WE ASK THE CREATOR TO HELP US BE KIND AND LOVING PARENTS AND TO BE PROUD OF WHO WE ARE.
I AM GOING TO SING THE FOUR DIRECTIONS SONG . . .
. . . AND CALL OUR ANCESTORS HERE SO THEY MAY HELP US TO EAL, AND TO LEARN TO LOVE EACH OTHER AND LOVE WHO WE ARE.
WE WILL ALL PRAY O THE CREATOR TO AVE MERCY ON US, TO HELP US HEAL OURSELVES.

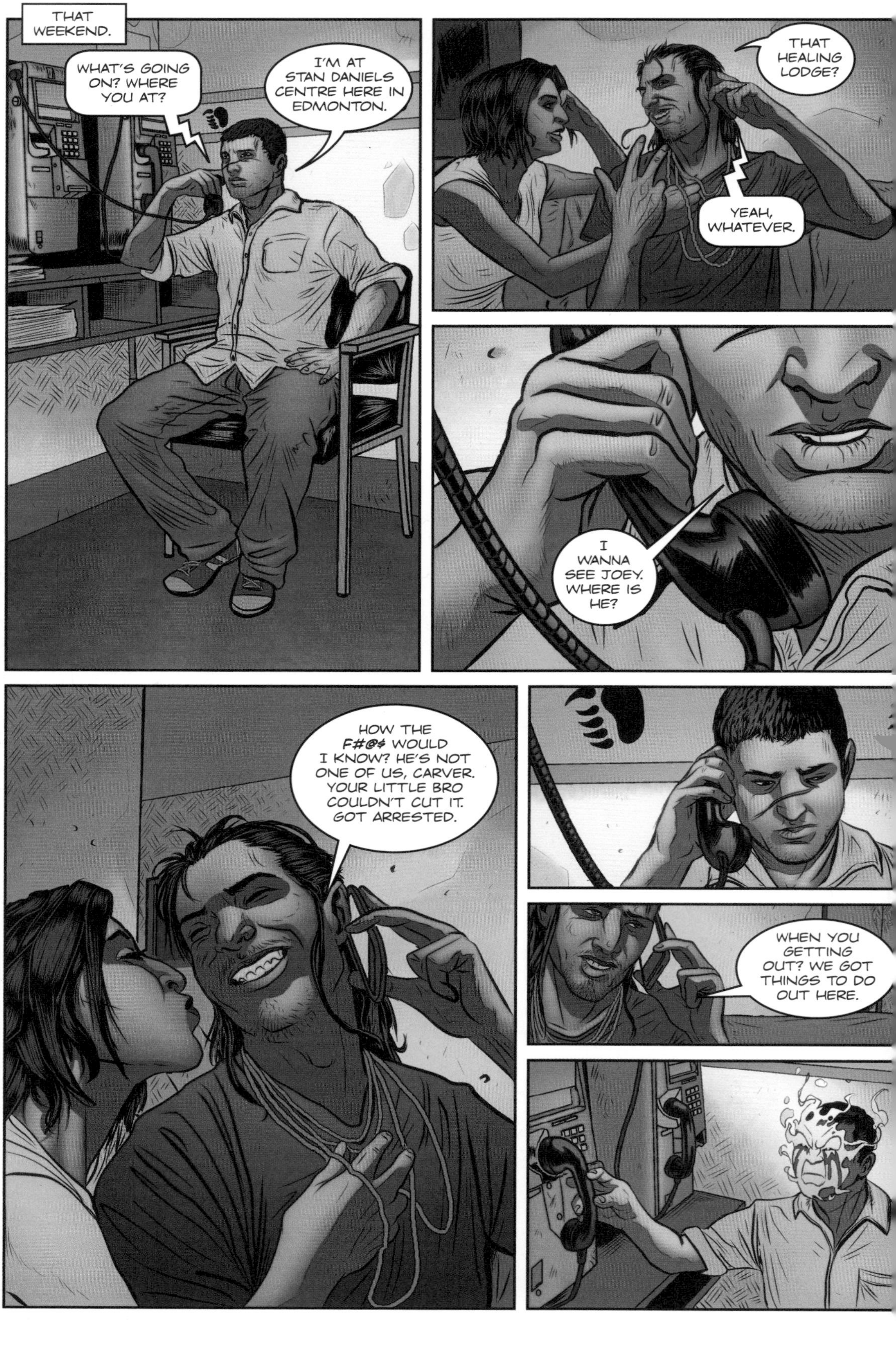
THAT WEEKEND.
WHAT'S GOING ON? WHERE YOU AT?
I'M AT STAN DANIELS CENTRE HERE IN EDMONTON.
THAT HEALING LODGE?
YEAH, WHATEVER.
I WANNA SEE JOEY. WHERE IS HE?
HOW THE F#@$ WOULD I KNOW? HE'S NOT ONE OF US, CARVER. YOUR LITTLE BRO COULDN'T CUT IT. GOT ARRESTED.
WHEN YOU GETTING OUT? WE GOT THINGS TO DO OUT HERE.

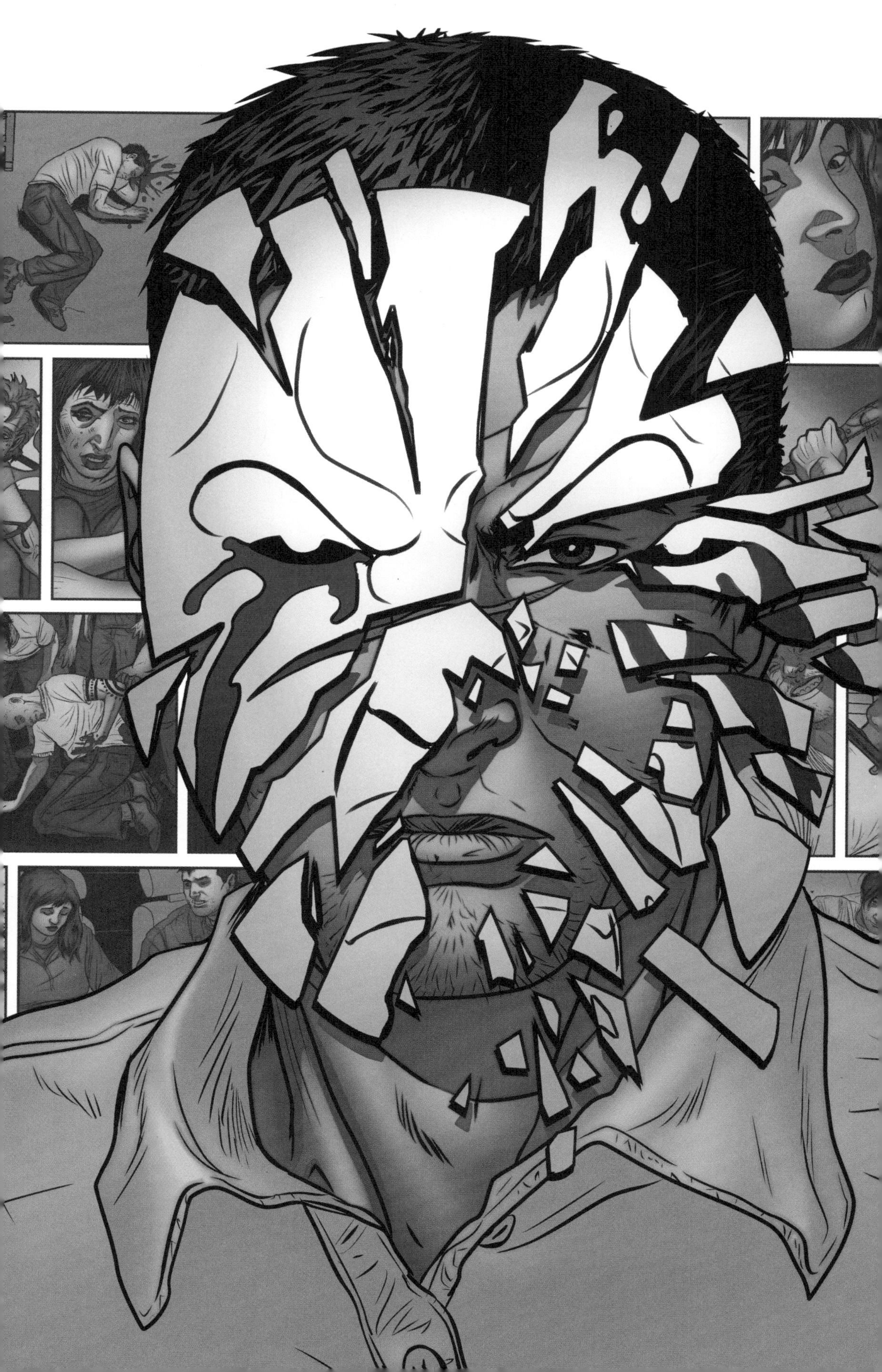

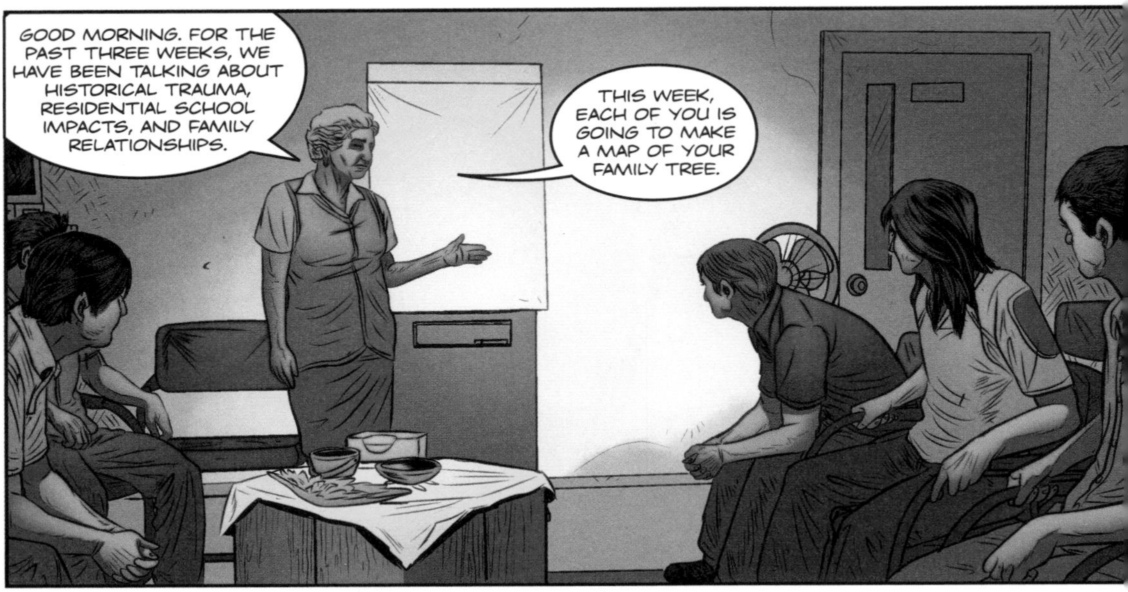
GOOD MORNING. FOR THE PAST THREE WEEKS, WE HAVE BEEN TALKING ABOUT HISTORICAL TRAUMA, RESIDENTIAL SCHOOL IMPACTS, AND FAMILY RELATIONSHIPS.
THIS WEEK, EACH OF YOU IS GOING TO MAKE A MAP OF YOUR FAMILY TREE.

AS CHILDREN, WE ARE INFLUENCED BY OUR FAMILY MEMBERS AND THEIR PATTERNS.

FOR EXAMPLE, MANY FORMS OF ABUSE AND VIOLENCE HAVE BEEN SHOWN TO BE PASSED FROM ONE GENERATION TO THE NEXT.

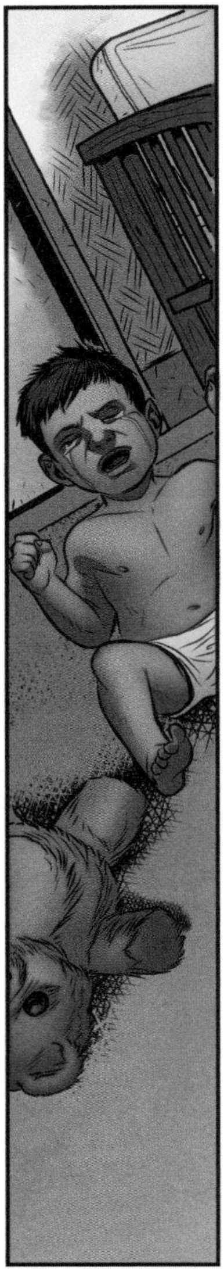

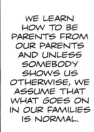

WE LEARN HOW TO BE PARENTS FROM OUR PARENTS AND UNLESS SOMEBODY SHOWS US OTHERWISE, WE ASSUME THAT WHAT GOES ON IN OUR FAMILIES IS NORMAL.

IN ORDER TO UNDERSTAND HOW OUR FAMILIES HAVE AFFECTED US, WE EACH NEED TO UNDERSTAND THE WHOLE PICTURE OF THE FAMILY WE WERE RAISED IN.

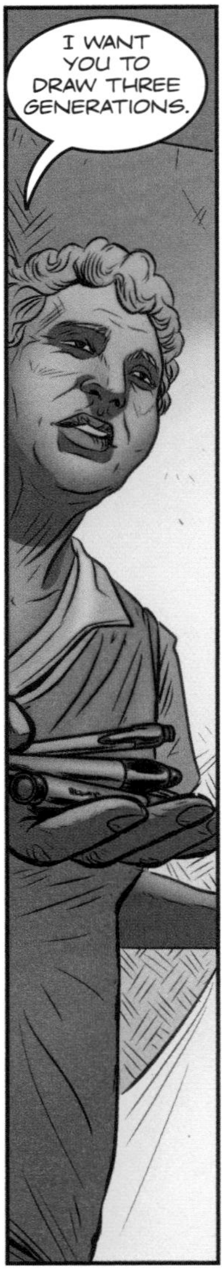
I WANT YOU TO DRAW THREE GENERATIONS.

INCLUDE PARENTS, GRANDPARENTS, SIBLINGS, AUNTIES, UNCLES, FOSTER FAMILIES, EXTENDED FAMILY MEMBERS, AND ALL THE PEOPLE WHO HAVE HAD A ROLE IN YOUR FAMILY, EVEN IF THEY AREN'T BLOOD RELATIVES.

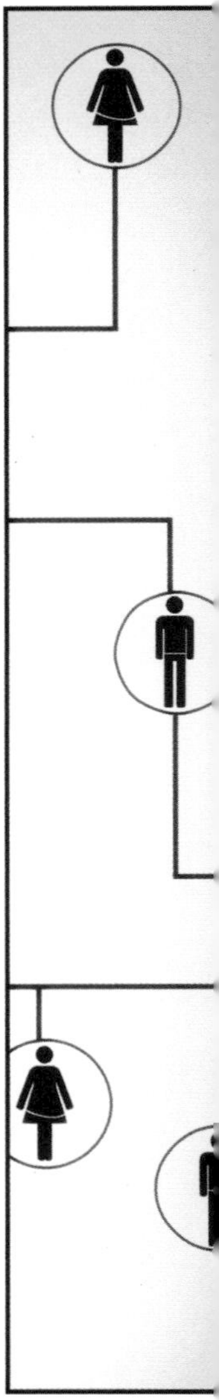

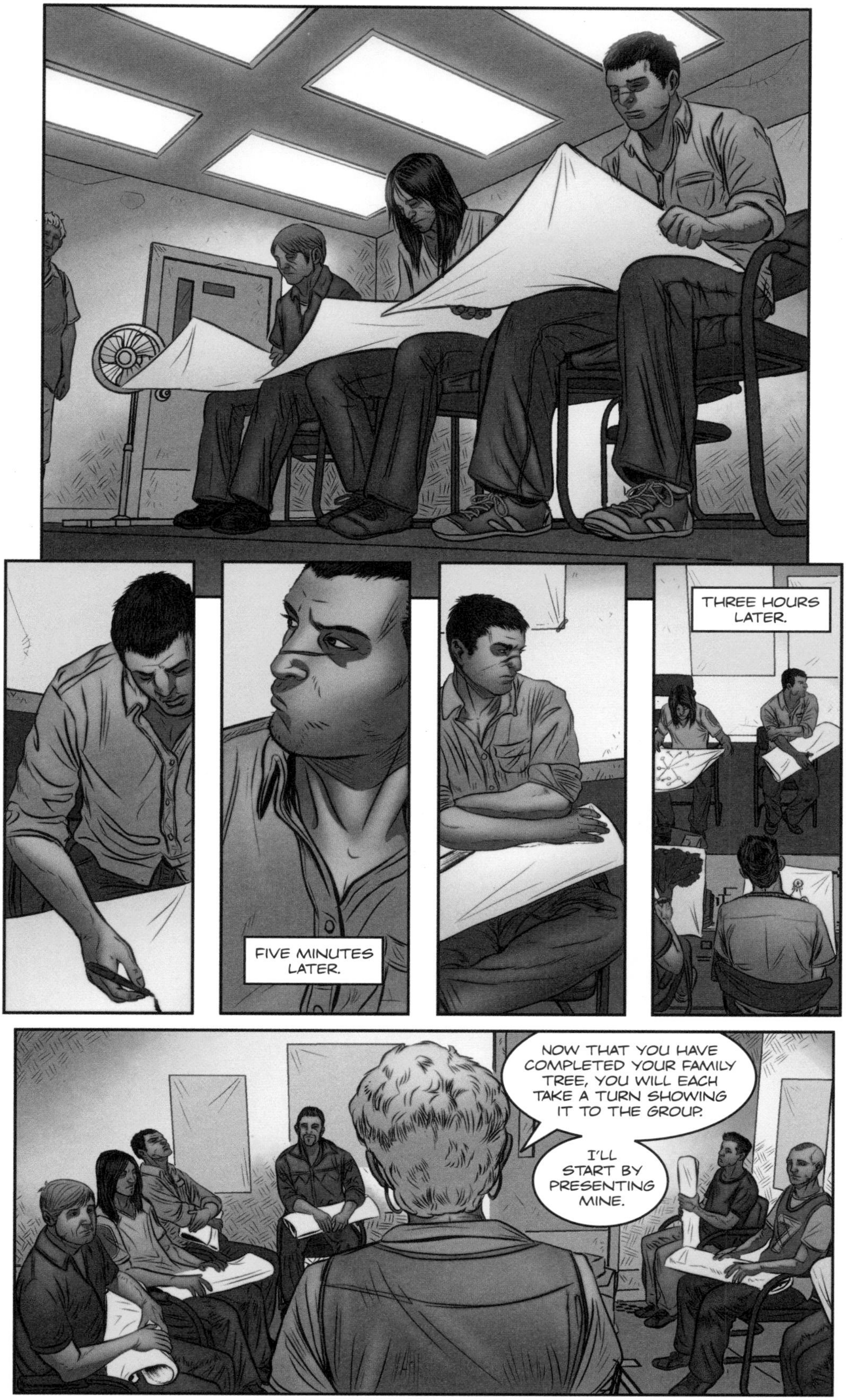
FIVE MINUTES LATER.
THREE HOURS LATER.
NOW THAT YOU HAVE COMPLETED YOUR FAMILY TREE, YOU WILL EACH TAKE A TURN SHOWING IT TO THE GROUP.
I'LL START BY PRESENTING MINE.

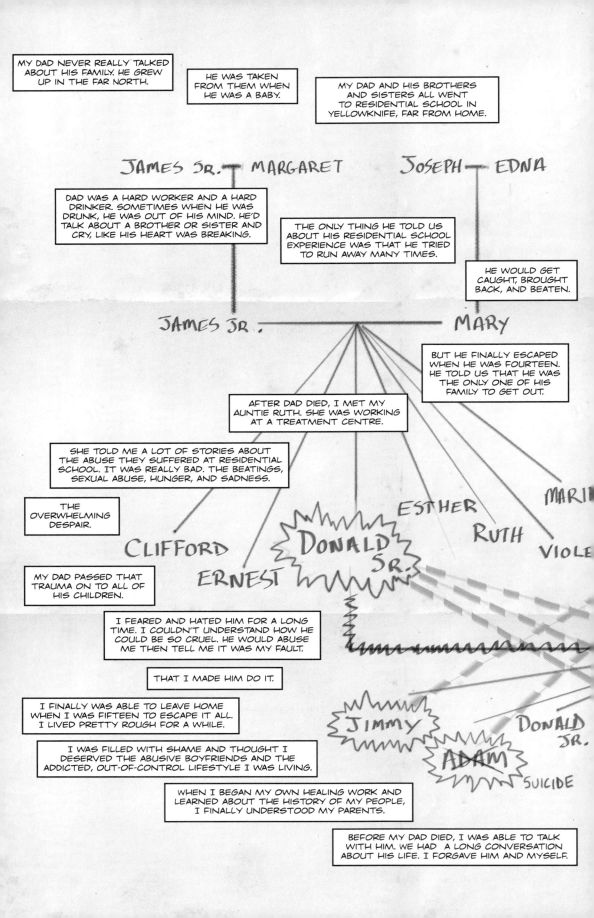

MY DAD NEVER REALLY TALKED ABOUT HIS FAMILY. HE GREW UP IN THE FAR NORTH.

HE WAS TAKEN FROM THEM WHEN HE WAS A BABY.

MY DAD AND HIS BROTHERS AND SISTERS ALL WENT TO RESIDENTIAL SCHOOL IN YELLOWKNIFE, FAR FROM HOME.

JAMES SR. ⎯ MARGARET   JOSEPH ⎯ EDNA

DAD WAS A HARD WORKER AND A HARD DRINKER. SOMETIMES WHEN HE WAS DRUNK, HE WAS OUT OF HIS MIND. HE'D TALK ABOUT A BROTHER OR SISTER AND CRY, LIKE HIS HEART WAS BREAKING.

THE ONLY THING HE TOLD US ABOUT HIS RESIDENTIAL SCHOOL EXPERIENCE WAS THAT HE TRIED TO RUN AWAY MANY TIMES.

HE WOULD GET CAUGHT, BROUGHT BACK, AND BEATEN.

JAMES JR. ⎯⎯⎯⎯⎯⎯⎯⎯⎯⎯ MARY

BUT HE FINALLY ESCAPED WHEN HE WAS FOURTEEN. HE TOLD US THAT HE WAS THE ONLY ONE OF HIS FAMILY TO GET OUT.

AFTER DAD DIED, I MET MY AUNTIE RUTH. SHE WAS WORKING AT A TREATMENT CENTRE.

SHE TOLD ME A LOT OF STORIES ABOUT THE ABUSE THEY SUFFERED AT RESIDENTIAL SCHOOL. IT WAS REALLY BAD. THE BEATINGS, SEXUAL ABUSE, HUNGER, AND SADNESS.

THE OVERWHELMING DESPAIR.

ESTHER   MARI

RUTH

CLIFFORD   DONALD SR.

VIOLE

ERNEST

MY DAD PASSED THAT TRAUMA ON TO ALL OF HIS CHILDREN.

I FEARED AND HATED HIM FOR A LONG TIME. I COULDN'T UNDERSTAND HOW HE COULD BE SO CRUEL. HE WOULD ABUSE ME THEN TELL ME IT WAS MY FAULT.

THAT I MADE HIM DO IT.

I FINALLY WAS ABLE TO LEAVE HOME WHEN I WAS FIFTEEN TO ESCAPE IT ALL. I LIVED PRETTY ROUGH FOR A WHILE.

JIMMY   DONALD JR.

I WAS FILLED WITH SHAME AND THOUGHT I DESERVED THE ABUSIVE BOYFRIENDS AND THE ADDICTED, OUT-OF-CONTROL LIFESTYLE I WAS LIVING.

ADAM

SUICIDE

WHEN I BEGAN MY OWN HEALING WORK AND LEARNED ABOUT THE HISTORY OF MY PEOPLE, I FINALLY UNDERSTOOD MY PARENTS.

BEFORE MY DAD DIED, I WAS ABLE TO TALK WITH HIM. WE HAD A LONG CONVERSATION ABOUT HIS LIFE. I FORGAVE HIM AND MYSELF.

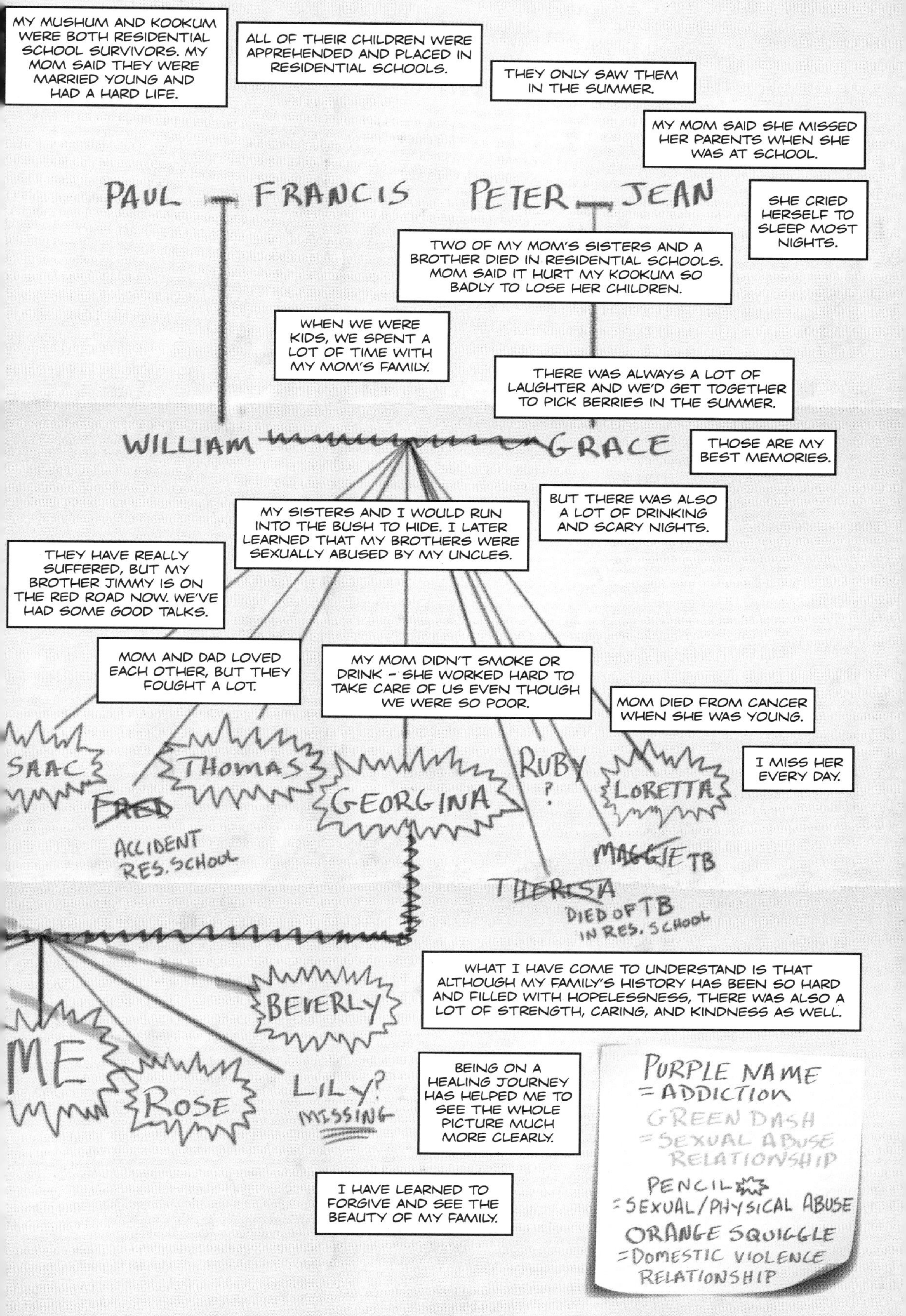
MY MUSHUM AND KOOKUM WERE BOTH RESIDENTIAL SCHOOL SURVIVORS. MY MOM SAID THEY WERE MARRIED YOUNG AND HAD A HARD LIFE.
ALL OF THEIR CHILDREN WERE APPREHENDED AND PLACED IN RESIDENTIAL SCHOOLS.
THEY ONLY SAW THEM IN THE SUMMER.
MY MOM SAID SHE MISSED HER PARENTS WHEN SHE WAS AT SCHOOL.
SHE CRIED HERSELF TO SLEEP MOST NIGHTS.
PAUL
FRANCIS
PETER
JEAN
TWO OF MY MOM'S SISTERS AND A BROTHER DIED IN RESIDENTIAL SCHOOLS. MOM SAID IT HURT MY KOOKUM SO BADLY TO LOSE HER CHILDREN.
WHEN WE WERE KIDS, WE SPENT A LOT OF TIME WITH MY MOM'S FAMILY.
THERE WAS ALWAYS A LOT OF LAUGHTER AND WE'D GET TOGETHER TO PICK BERRIES IN THE SUMMER.
WILLIAM
GRACE
THOSE ARE MY BEST MEMORIES.
BUT THERE WAS ALSO A LOT OF DRINKING AND SCARY NIGHTS.
MY SISTERS AND I WOULD RUN INTO THE BUSH TO HIDE. I LATER LEARNED THAT MY BROTHERS WERE SEXUALLY ABUSED BY MY UNCLES.
THEY HAVE REALLY SUFFERED, BUT MY BROTHER JIMMY IS ON THE RED ROAD NOW. WE'VE HAD SOME GOOD TALKS.
MOM AND DAD LOVED EACH OTHER, BUT THEY FOUGHT A LOT.
MY MOM DIDN'T SMOKE OR DRINK – SHE WORKED HARD TO TAKE CARE OF US EVEN THOUGH WE WERE SO POOR.
MOM DIED FROM CANCER WHEN SHE WAS YOUNG.
I MISS HER EVERY DAY.
SAAC
THOMAS
FRED
ACCIDENT RES. SCHOOL
GEORGINA
RUBY ?
LORETTA
MAGGIE TB
THERESA
DIED OF TB IN RES. SCHOOL
BEVERLY
WHAT I HAVE COME TO UNDERSTAND IS THAT ALTHOUGH MY FAMILY'S HISTORY HAS BEEN SO HARD AND FILLED WITH HOPELESSNESS, THERE WAS ALSO A LOT OF STRENGTH, CARING, AND KINDNESS AS WELL.
ME
ROSE
LILY? MISSING
BEING ON A HEALING JOURNEY HAS HELPED ME TO SEE THE WHOLE PICTURE MUCH MORE CLEARLY.
I HAVE LEARNED TO FORGIVE AND SEE THE BEAUTY OF MY FAMILY.
PURPLE NAME = ADDICTION
GREEN DASH = SEXUAL ABUSE RELATIONSHIP
PENCIL = SEXUAL/PHYSICAL ABUSE
ORANGE SQUIGGLE = DOMESTIC VIOLENCE RELATIONSHIP

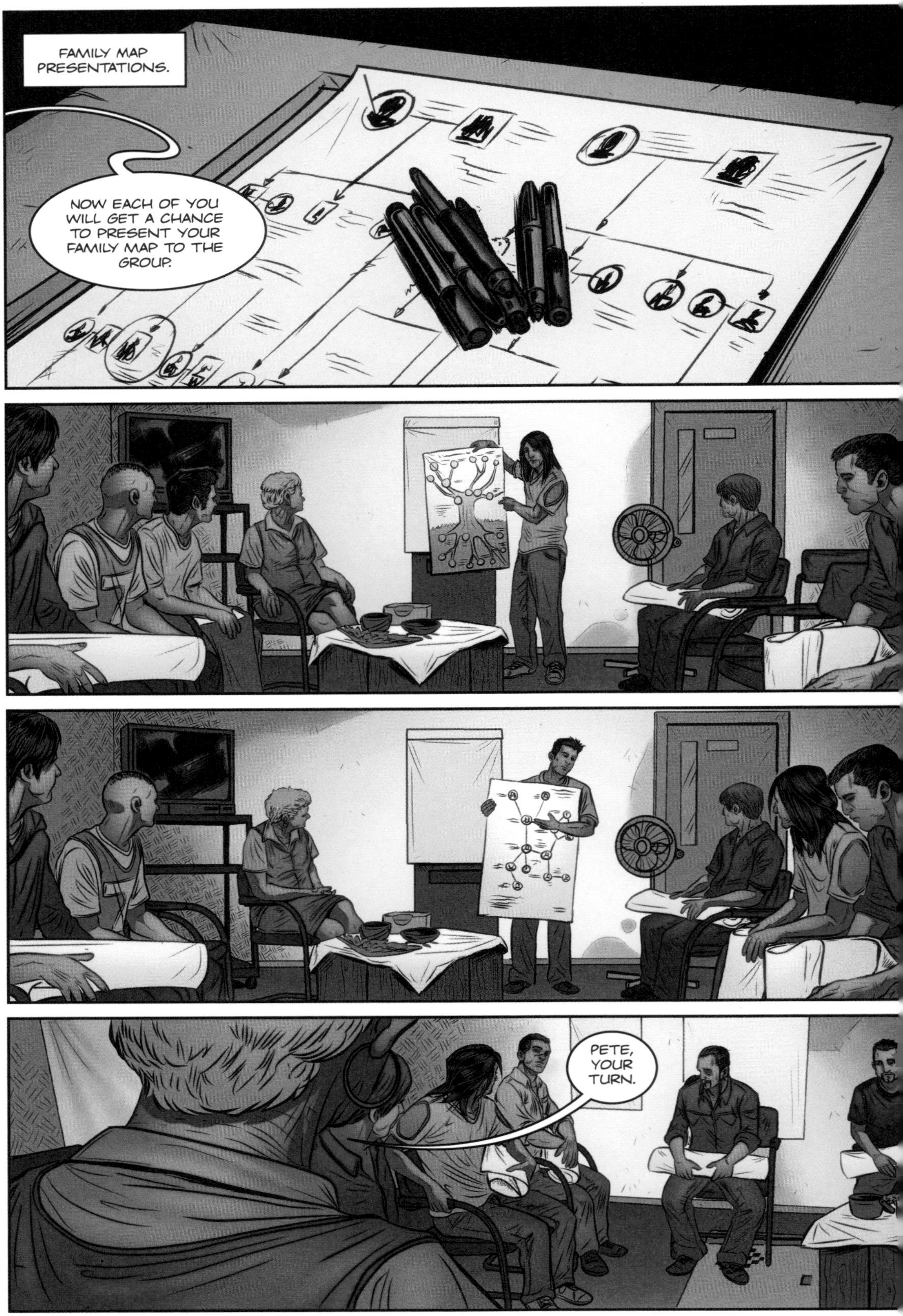
FAMILY MAP PRESENTATIONS.
NOW EACH OF YOU WILL GET A CHANCE TO PRESENT YOUR FAMILY MAP TO THE GROUP.
PETE, YOUR TURN.

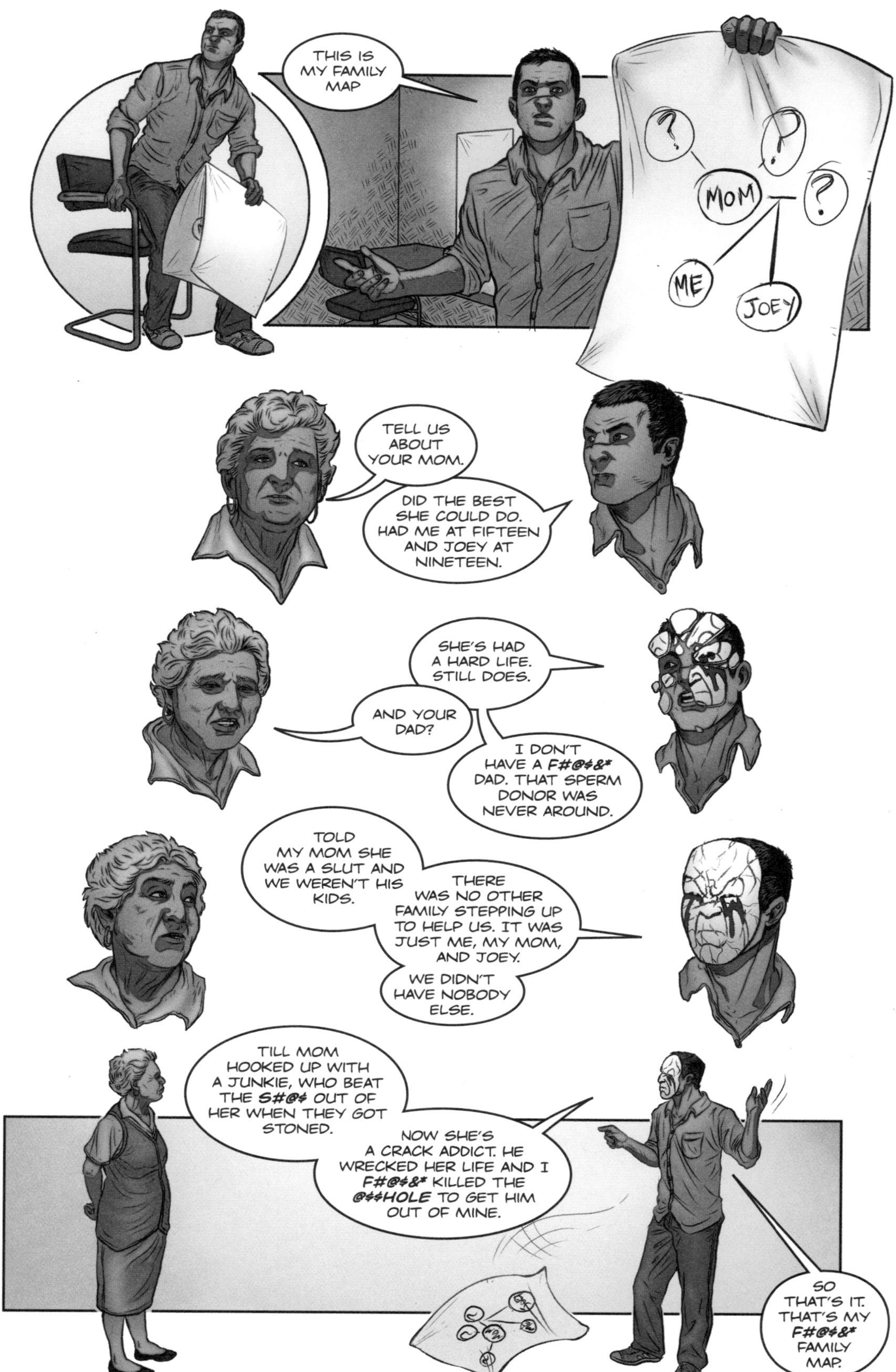

THIS IS MY FAMILY MAP
?
?
MOM
?
ME
JOEY
TELL US ABOUT YOUR MOM.
DID THE BEST SHE COULD DO. HAD ME AT FIFTEEN AND JOEY AT NINETEEN.
SHE'S HAD A HARD LIFE. STILL DOES.
AND YOUR DAD?
I DON'T HAVE A F#@$&* DAD. THAT SPERM DONOR WAS NEVER AROUND.
TOLD MY MOM SHE WAS A SLUT AND WE WEREN'T HIS KIDS.
THERE WAS NO OTHER FAMILY STEPPING UP TO HELP US. IT WAS JUST ME, MY MOM, AND JOEY.
WE DIDN'T HAVE NOBODY ELSE.
TILL MOM HOOKED UP WITH A JUNKIE, WHO BEAT THE S#@$ OUT OF HER WHEN THEY GOT STONED.
NOW SHE'S A CRACK ADDICT. HE WRECKED HER LIFE AND I F#@$&* KILLED THE @$$HOLE TO GET HIM OUT OF MINE.
SO THAT'S IT. THAT'S MY F#@$&* FAMILY MAP.

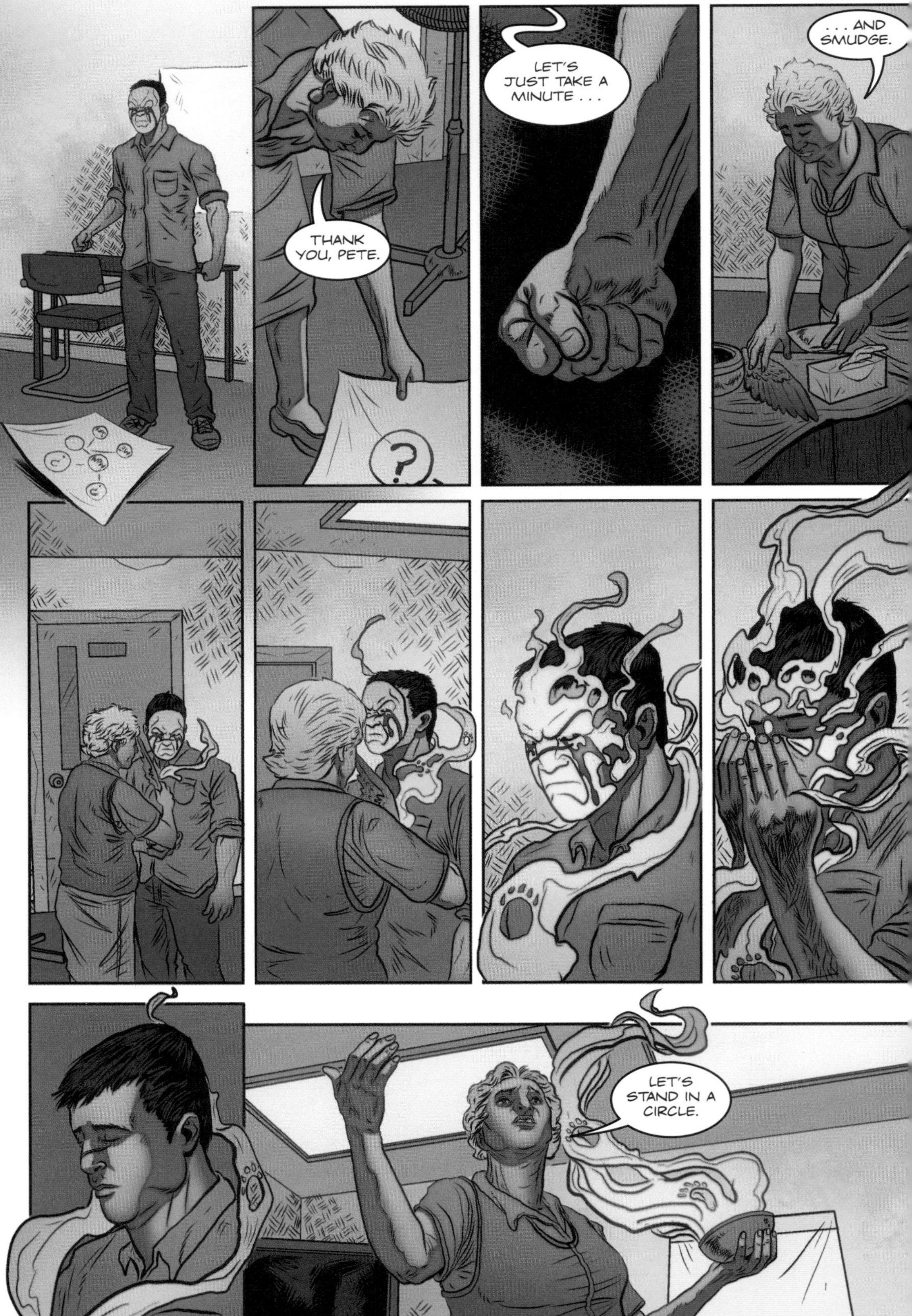
THANK YOU, PETE.
LET'S JUST TAKE A MINUTE . . .
. . . AND SMUDGE.
LET'S STAND IN A CIRCLE.

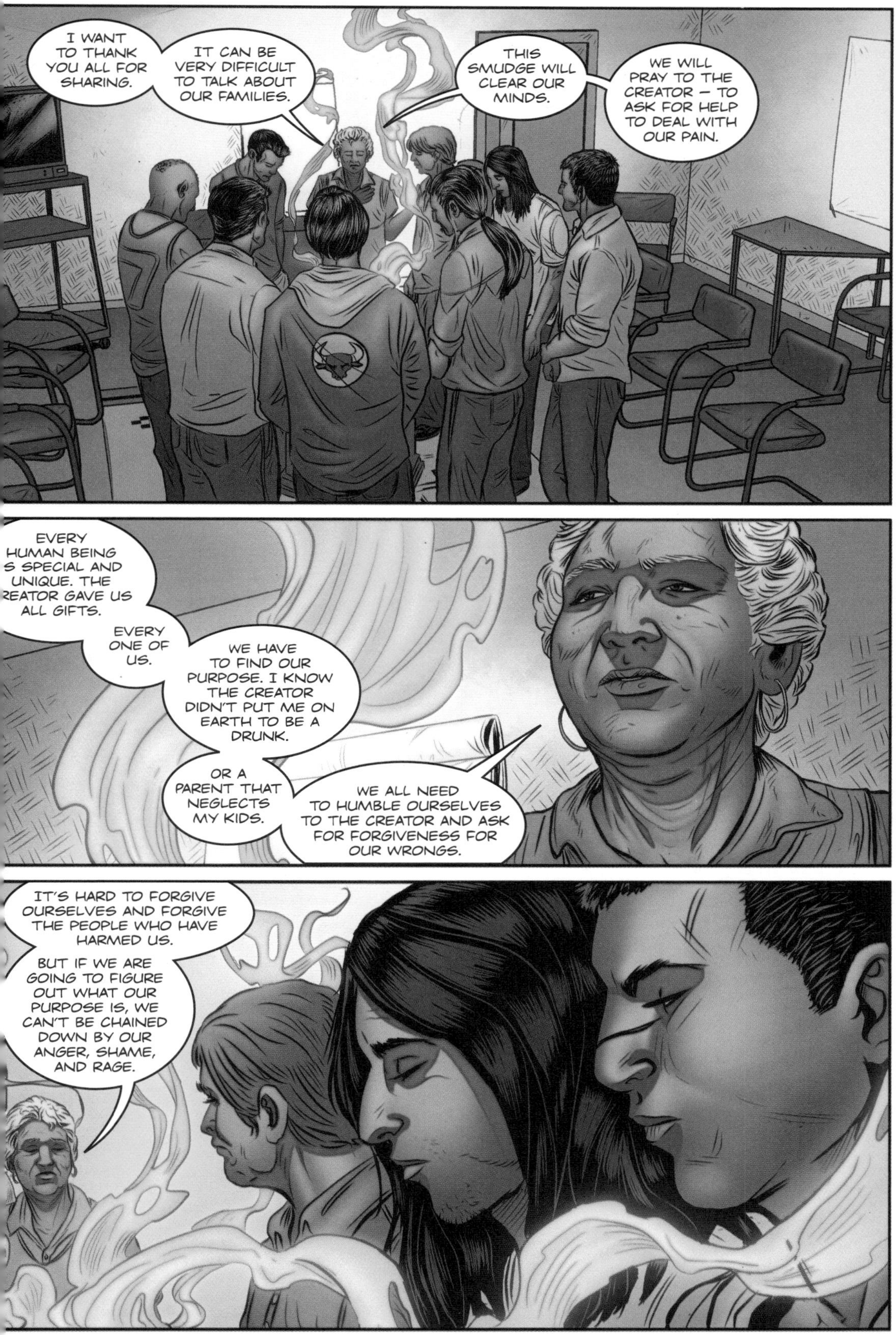
I WANT TO THANK YOU ALL FOR SHARING.
IT CAN BE VERY DIFFICULT TO TALK ABOUT OUR FAMILIES.
THIS SMUDGE WILL CLEAR OUR MINDS.
WE WILL PRAY TO THE CREATOR — TO ASK FOR HELP TO DEAL WITH OUR PAIN.
EVERY HUMAN BEING S SPECIAL AND UNIQUE. THE REATOR GAVE US ALL GIFTS.
EVERY ONE OF US.
WE HAVE TO FIND OUR PURPOSE. I KNOW THE CREATOR DIDN'T PUT ME ON EARTH TO BE A DRUNK.
OR A PARENT THAT NEGLECTS MY KIDS.
WE ALL NEED TO HUMBLE OURSELVES TO THE CREATOR AND ASK FOR FORGIVENESS FOR OUR WRONGS.
IT'S HARD TO FORGIVE OURSELVES AND FORGIVE THE PEOPLE WHO HAVE HARMED US.
BUT IF WE ARE GOING TO FIGURE OUT WHAT OUR PURPOSE IS, WE CAN'T BE CHAINED DOWN BY OUR ANGER, SHAME, AND RAGE.

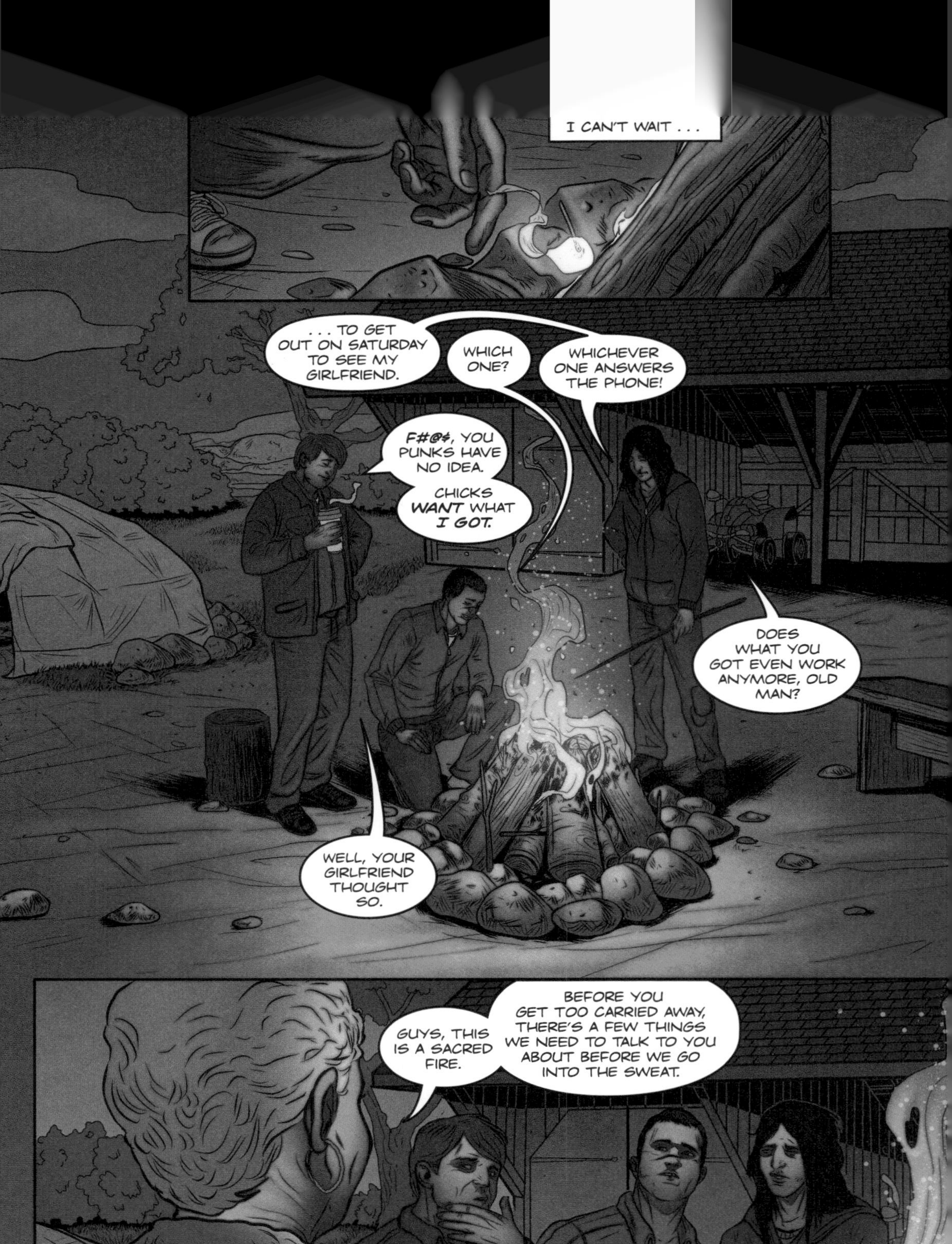
I CAN'T WAIT . . .
. . . TO GET OUT ON SATURDAY TO SEE MY GIRLFRIEND.
WHICH ONE?
WHICHEVER ONE ANSWERS THE PHONE!
F#@$, YOU PUNKS HAVE NO IDEA.
CHICKS WANT WHAT I GOT.
DOES WHAT YOU GOT EVEN WORK ANYMORE, OLD MAN?
WELL, YOUR GIRLFRIEND THOUGHT SO.
GUYS, THIS IS A SACRED FIRE.
BEFORE YOU GET TOO CARRIED AWAY, THERE'S A FEW THINGS WE NEED TO TALK TO YOU ABOUT BEFORE WE GO INTO THE SWEAT.

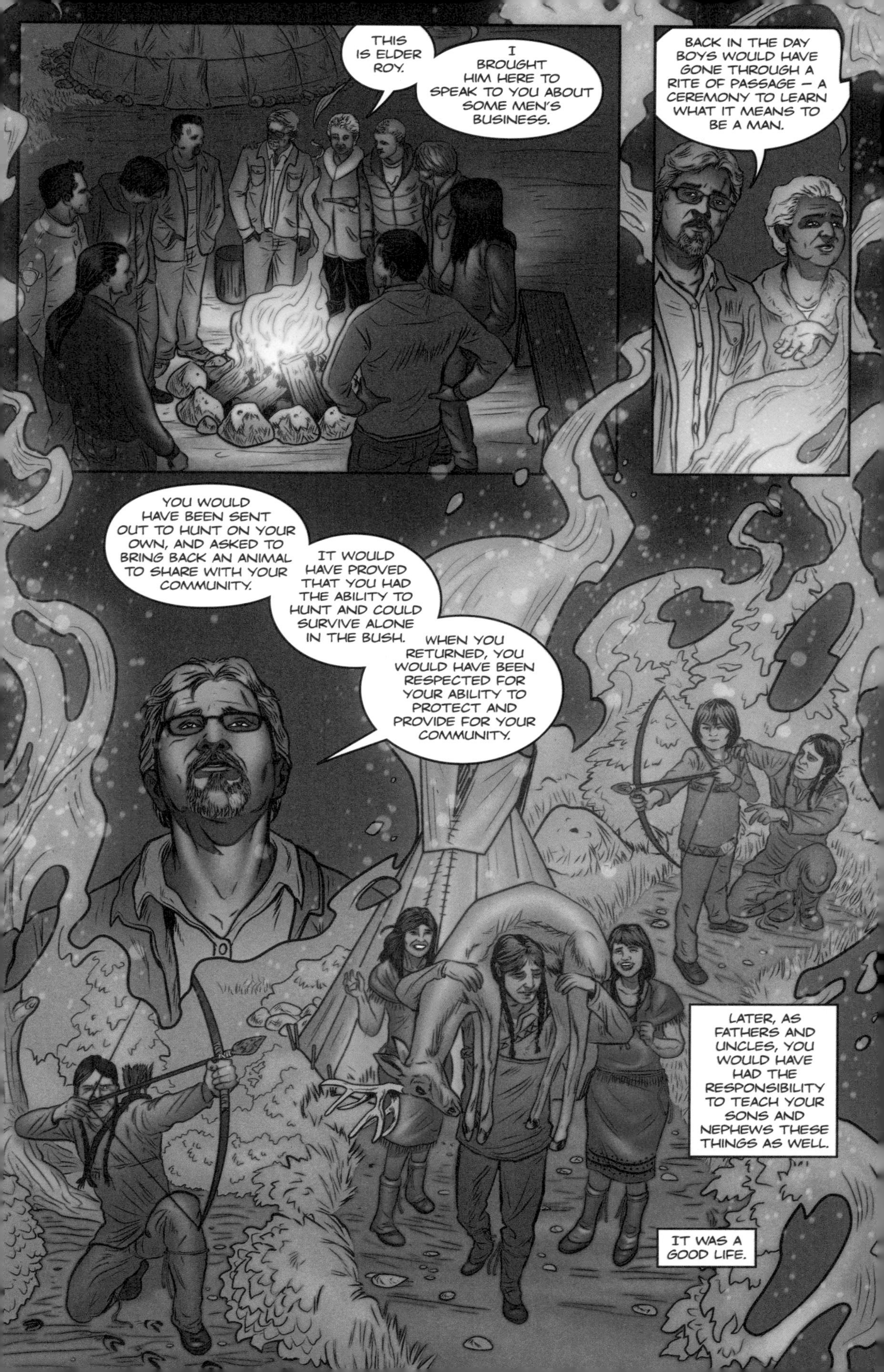
THIS IS ELDER ROY.
I BROUGHT HIM HERE TO SPEAK TO YOU ABOUT SOME MEN'S BUSINESS.
BACK IN THE DAY BOYS WOULD HAVE GONE THROUGH A RITE OF PASSAGE — A CEREMONY TO LEARN WHAT IT MEANS TO BE A MAN.
YOU WOULD HAVE BEEN SENT OUT TO HUNT ON YOUR OWN, AND ASKED TO BRING BACK AN ANIMAL TO SHARE WITH YOUR COMMUNITY.
IT WOULD HAVE PROVED THAT YOU HAD THE ABILITY TO HUNT AND COULD SURVIVE ALONE IN THE BUSH.
WHEN YOU RETURNED, YOU WOULD HAVE BEEN RESPECTED FOR YOUR ABILITY TO PROTECT AND PROVIDE FOR YOUR COMMUNITY.
LATER, AS FATHERS AND UNCLES, YOU WOULD HAVE HAD THE RESPONSIBILITY TO TEACH YOUR SONS AND NEPHEWS THESE THINGS AS WELL.
IT WAS A GOOD LIFE.

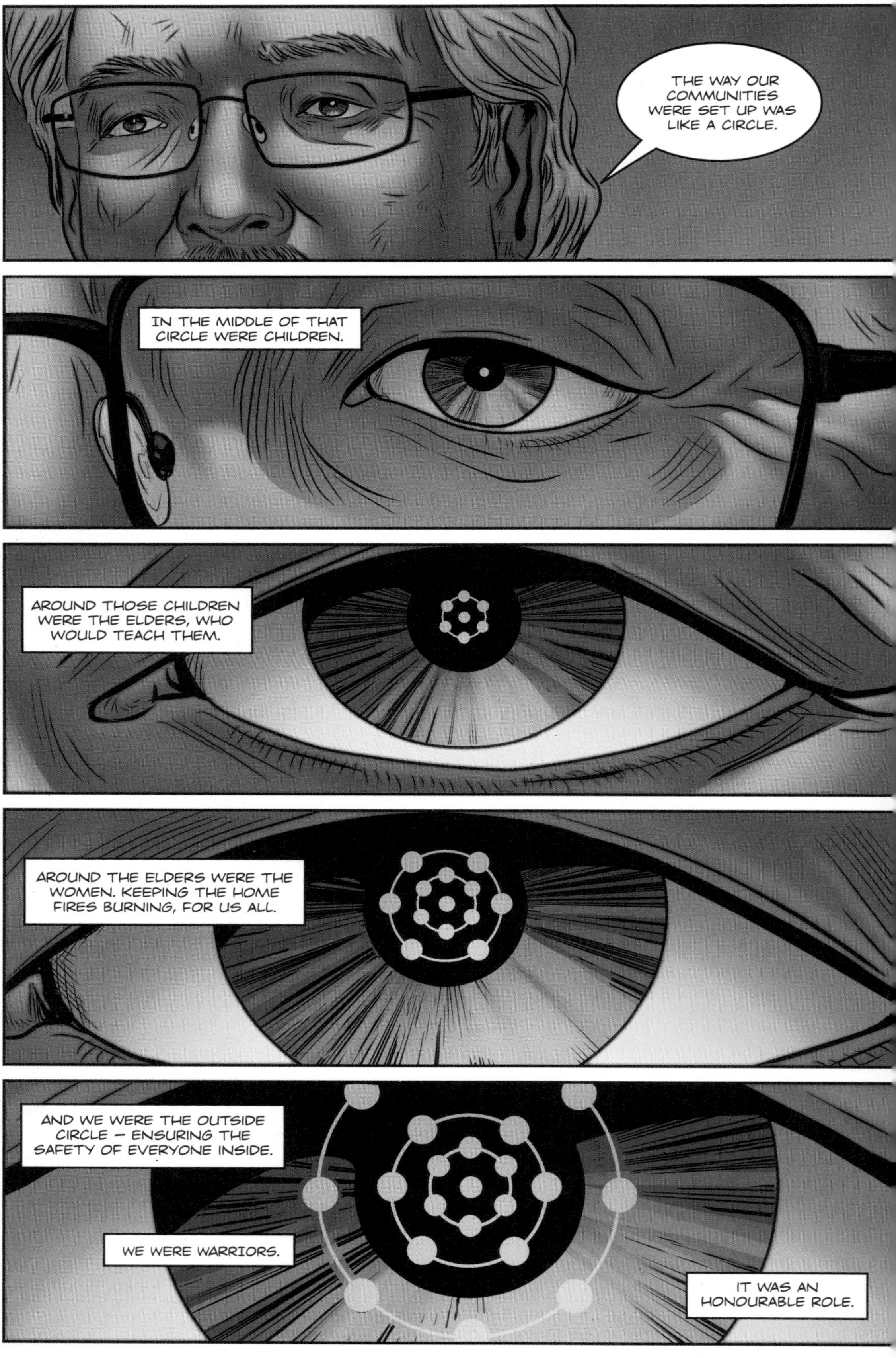
THE WAY OUR COMMUNITIES WERE SET UP WAS LIKE A CIRCLE.
IN THE MIDDLE OF THAT CIRCLE WERE CHILDREN.
AROUND THOSE CHILDREN WERE THE ELDERS, WHO WOULD TEACH THEM.
AROUND THE ELDERS WERE THE WOMEN. KEEPING THE HOME FIRES BURNING, FOR US ALL.
AND WE WERE THE OUTSIDE CIRCLE — ENSURING THE SAFETY OF EVERYONE INSIDE.
WE WERE WARRIORS.
IT WAS AN HONOURABLE ROLE.

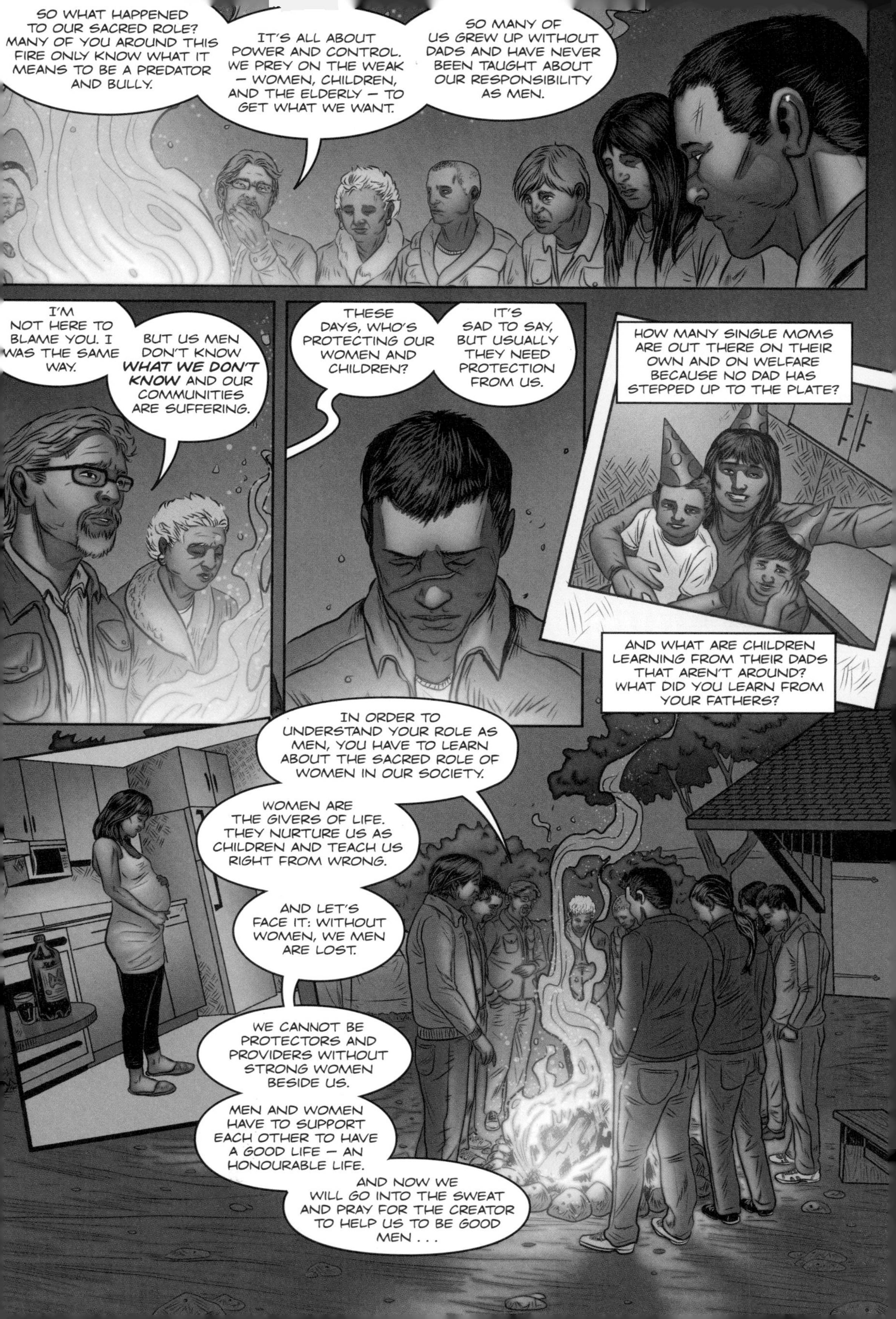
SO WHAT HAPPENED TO OUR SACRED ROLE? MANY OF YOU AROUND THIS FIRE ONLY KNOW WHAT IT MEANS TO BE A PREDATOR AND BULLY.
IT'S ALL ABOUT POWER AND CONTROL. WE PREY ON THE WEAK — WOMEN, CHILDREN, AND THE ELDERLY — TO GET WHAT WE WANT.
SO MANY OF US GREW UP WITHOUT DADS AND HAVE NEVER BEEN TAUGHT ABOUT OUR RESPONSIBILITY AS MEN.
I'M NOT HERE TO BLAME YOU. I WAS THE SAME WAY.
BUT US MEN DON'T KNOW WHAT WE DON'T KNOW AND OUR COMMUNITIES ARE SUFFERING.
THESE DAYS, WHO'S PROTECTING OUR WOMEN AND CHILDREN?
IT'S SAD TO SAY, BUT USUALLY THEY NEED PROTECTION FROM US.
HOW MANY SINGLE MOMS ARE OUT THERE ON THEIR OWN AND ON WELFARE BECAUSE NO DAD HAS STEPPED UP TO THE PLATE?
AND WHAT ARE CHILDREN LEARNING FROM THEIR DADS THAT AREN'T AROUND? WHAT DID YOU LEARN FROM YOUR FATHERS?
IN ORDER TO UNDERSTAND YOUR ROLE AS MEN, YOU HAVE TO LEARN ABOUT THE SACRED ROLE OF WOMEN IN OUR SOCIETY.
WOMEN ARE THE GIVERS OF LIFE. THEY NURTURE US AS CHILDREN AND TEACH US RIGHT FROM WRONG.
AND LET'S FACE IT: WITHOUT WOMEN, WE MEN ARE LOST.
WE CANNOT BE PROTECTORS AND PROVIDERS WITHOUT STRONG WOMEN BESIDE US.
MEN AND WOMEN HAVE TO SUPPORT EACH OTHER TO HAVE A GOOD LIFE — AN HONOURABLE LIFE.
AND NOW WE WILL GO INTO THE SWEAT AND PRAY FOR THE CREATOR TO HELP US TO BE GOOD MEN . . .

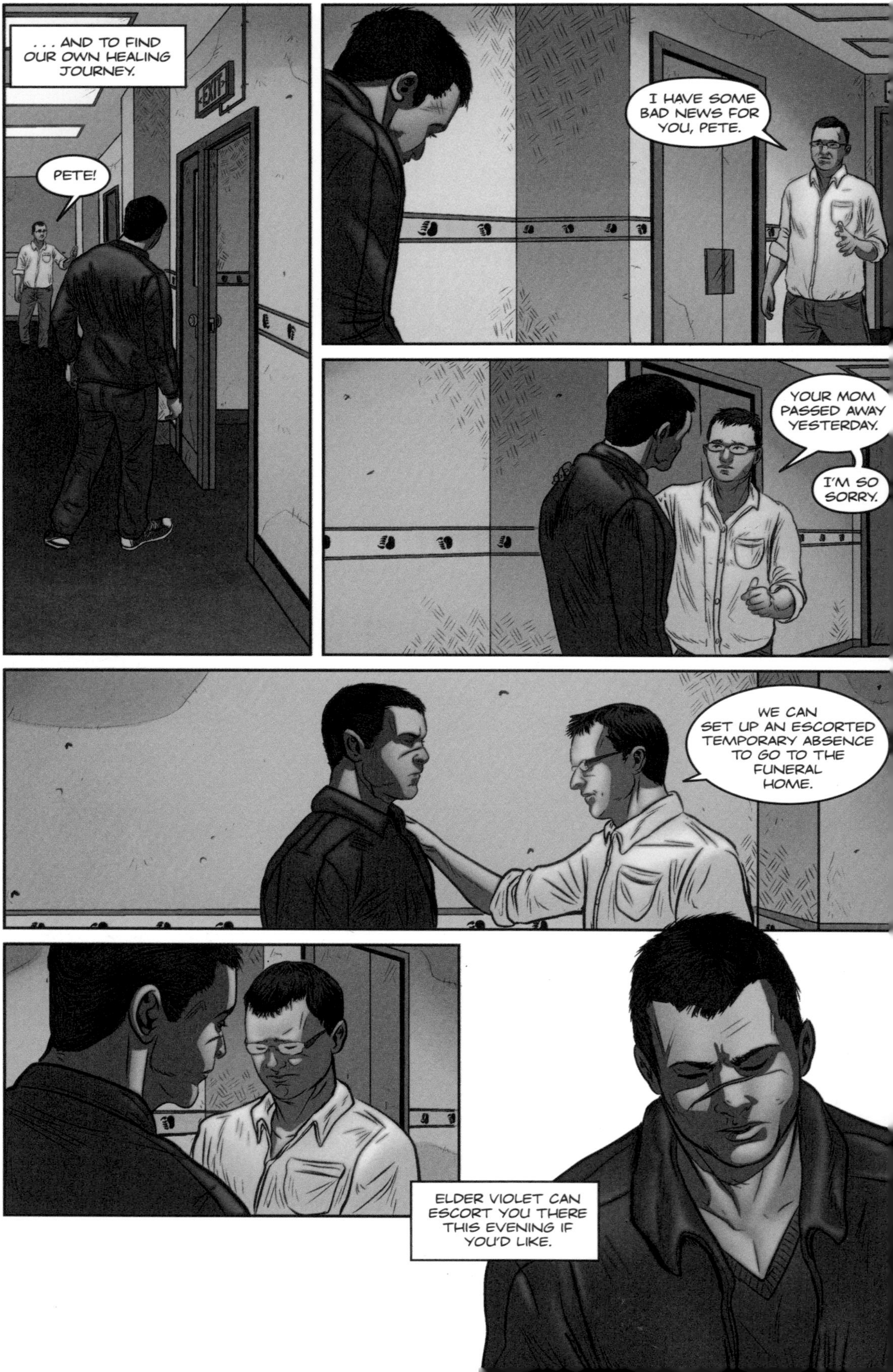
. . . AND TO FIND OUR OWN HEALING JOURNEY.
EXIT
PETE!
I HAVE SOME BAD NEWS FOR YOU, PETE.
YOUR MOM PASSED AWAY YESTERDAY.
I'M SO SORRY.
WE CAN SET UP AN ESCORTED TEMPORARY ABSENCE TO GO TO THE FUNERAL HOME.
ELDER VIOLET CAN ESCORT YOU THERE THIS EVENING IF YOU'D LIKE.

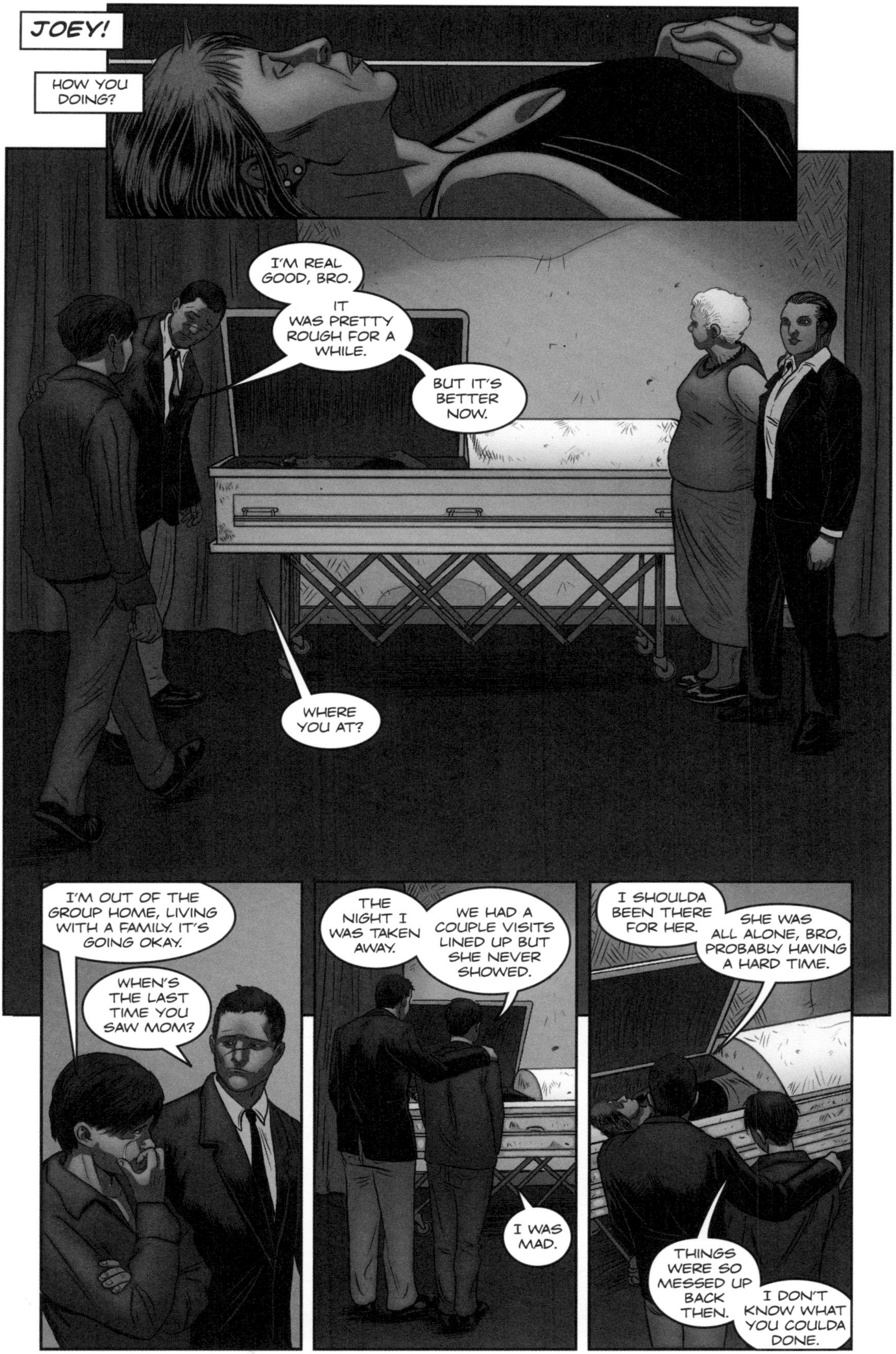
JOEY!
HOW YOU DOING?
I'M REAL GOOD, BRO.
IT WAS PRETTY ROUGH FOR A WHILE.
BUT IT'S BETTER NOW.
WHERE YOU AT?
I'M OUT OF THE GROUP HOME, LIVING WITH A FAMILY. IT'S GOING OKAY.
WHEN'S THE LAST TIME YOU SAW MOM?
THE NIGHT I WAS TAKEN AWAY.
WE HAD A COUPLE VISITS LINED UP BUT SHE NEVER SHOWED.
I WAS MAD.
I SHOULDA BEEN THERE FOR HER.
SHE WAS ALL ALONE, BRO, PROBABLY HAVING A HARD TIME.
THINGS WERE SO MESSED UP BACK THEN.
I DON'T KNOW WHAT YOU COULDA DONE.

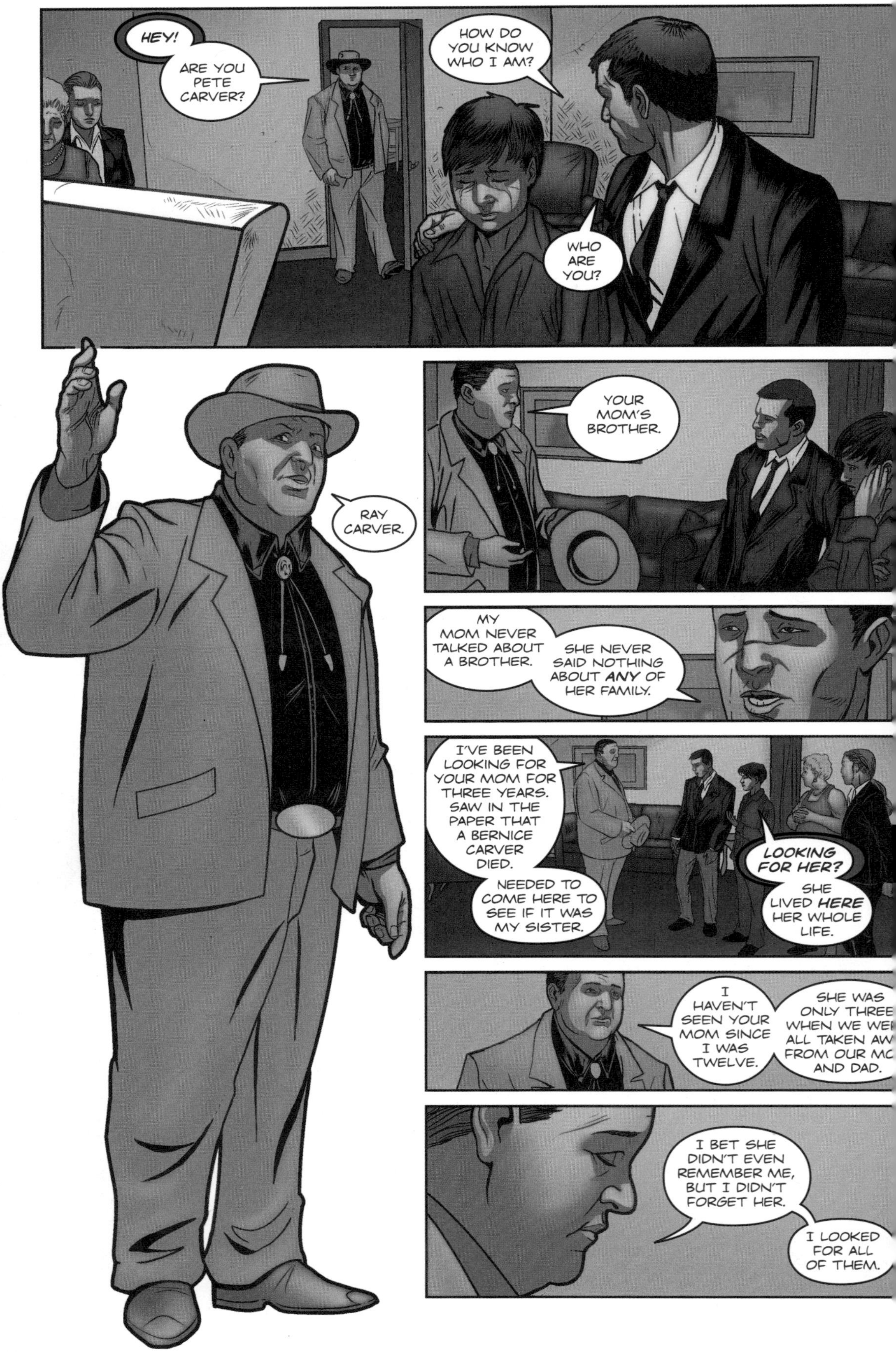
HEY!
ARE YOU PETE CARVER?
HOW DO YOU KNOW WHO I AM?
WHO ARE YOU?
RAY CARVER.
YOUR MOM'S BROTHER.
MY MOM NEVER TALKED ABOUT A BROTHER.
SHE NEVER SAID NOTHING ABOUT ANY OF HER FAMILY.
I'VE BEEN LOOKING FOR YOUR MOM FOR THREE YEARS. SAW IN THE PAPER THAT A BERNICE CARVER DIED.
NEEDED TO COME HERE TO SEE IF IT WAS MY SISTER.
LOOKING FOR HER?
SHE LIVED HERE HER WHOLE LIFE.
I HAVEN'T SEEN YOUR MOM SINCE I WAS TWELVE.
SHE WAS ONLY THREE WHEN WE WE ALL TAKEN AW FROM OUR MO AND DAD.
I BET SHE DIDN'T EVEN REMEMBER ME, BUT I DIDN'T FORGET HER.
I LOOKED FOR ALL OF THEM.

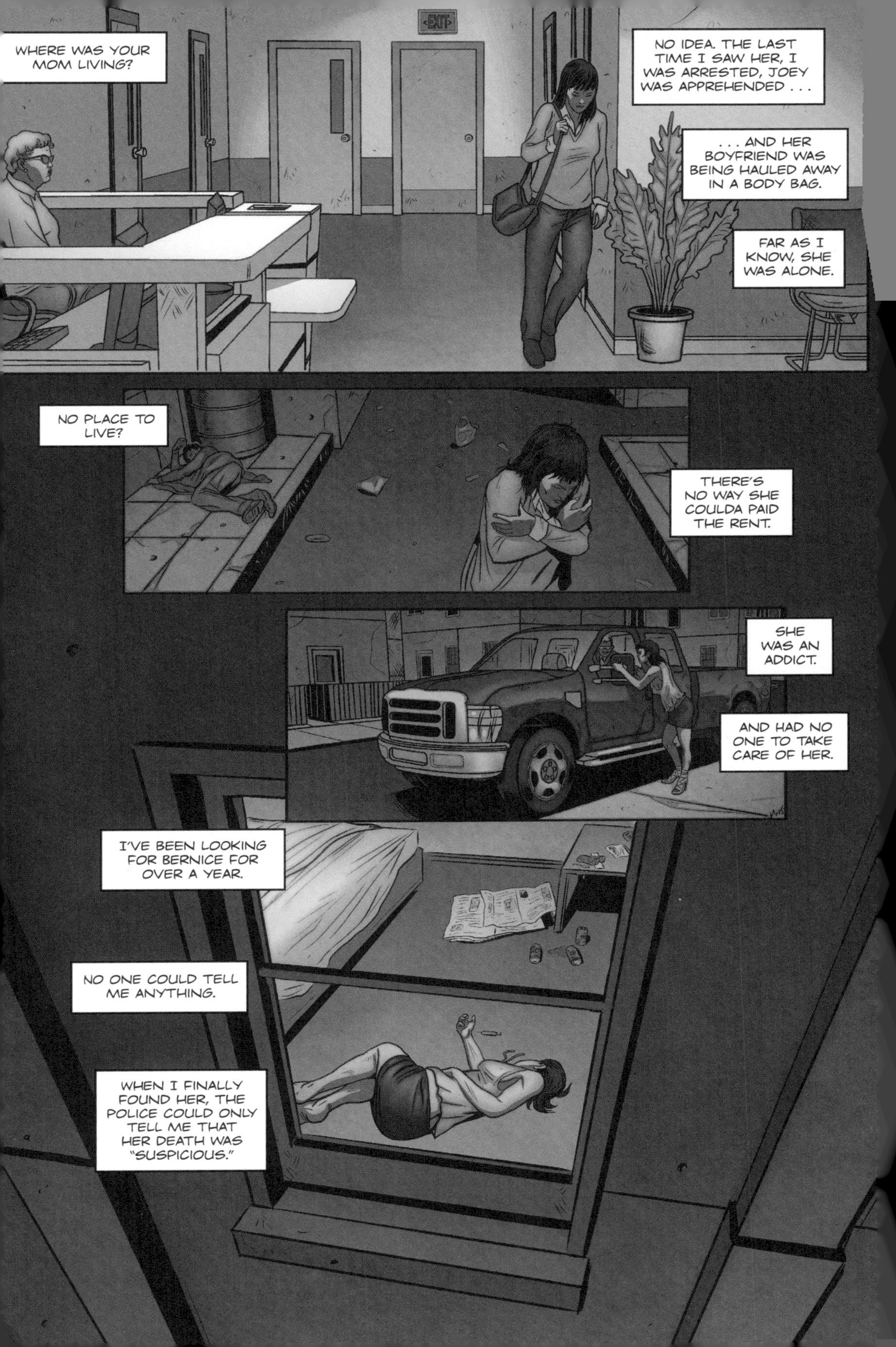
WHERE WAS YOUR MOM LIVING?
NO IDEA. THE LAST TIME I SAW HER, I WAS ARRESTED, JOEY WAS APPREHENDED . . .
. . . AND HER BOYFRIEND WAS BEING HAULED AWAY IN A BODY BAG.
FAR AS I KNOW, SHE WAS ALONE.
NO PLACE TO LIVE?
THERE'S NO WAY SHE COULDA PAID THE RENT.
SHE WAS AN ADDICT.
AND HAD NO ONE TO TAKE CARE OF HER.
I'VE BEEN LOOKING FOR BERNICE FOR OVER A YEAR.
NO ONE COULD TELL ME ANYTHING.
WHEN I FINALLY FOUND HER, THE POLICE COULD ONLY TELL ME THAT HER DEATH WAS "SUSPICIOUS."

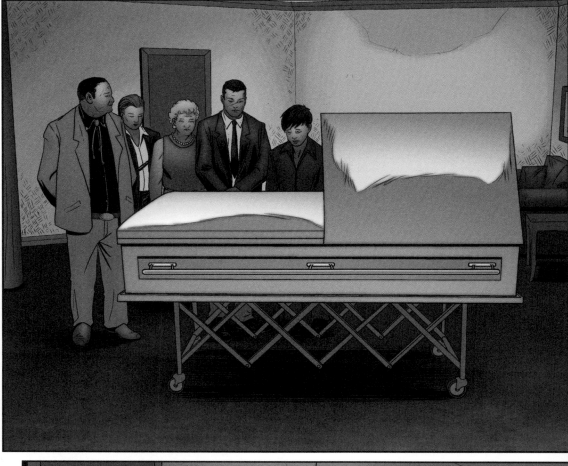

WE'RE HAVING A SWEAT TOMORROW.

I THINK IT WOULD BE GOOD IF YOU WERE THERE.

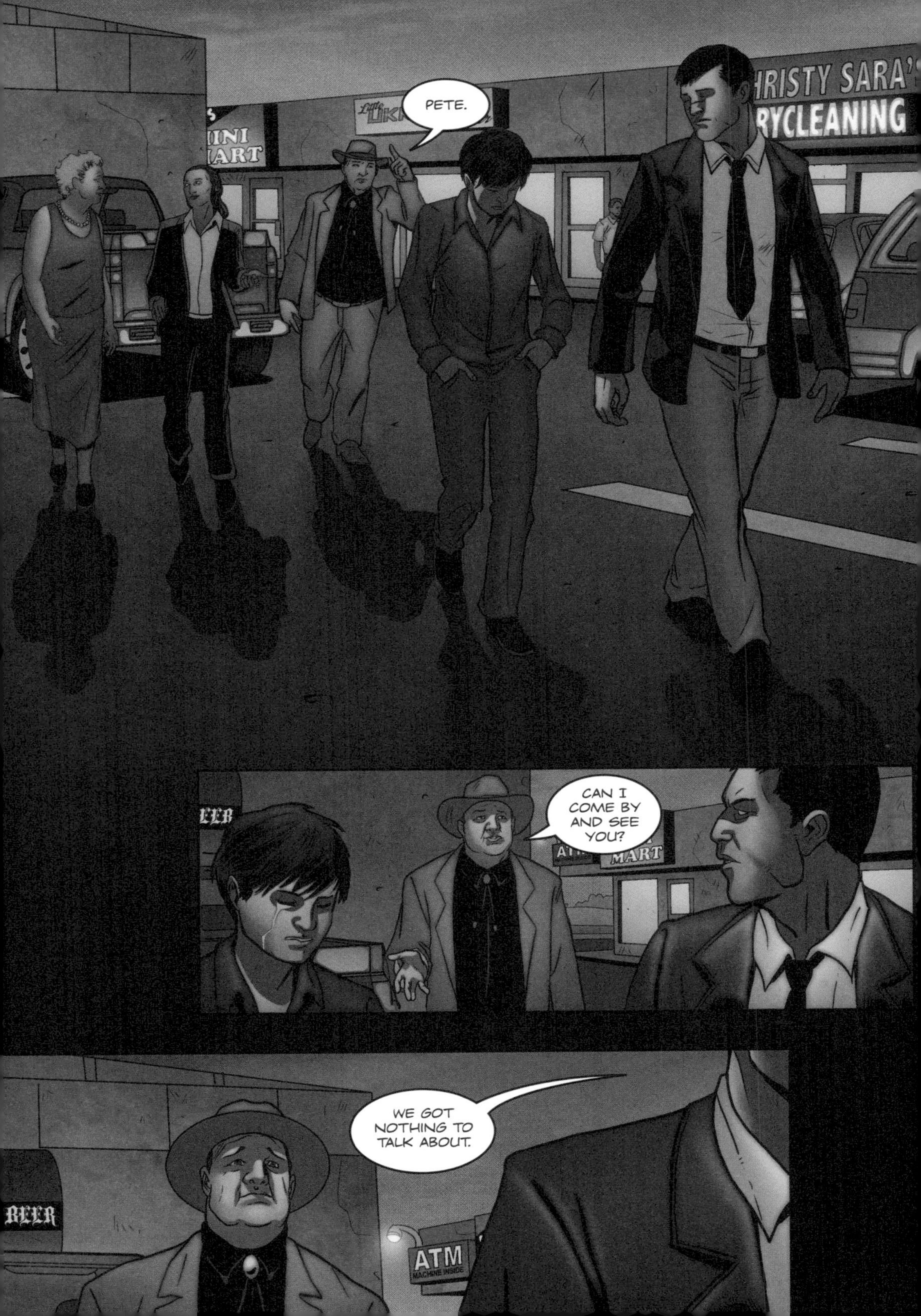
PETE.
CAN I COME BY AND SEE YOU?
WE GOT NOTHING TO TALK ABOUT.
BEER
ATM
MACHINE INSIDE

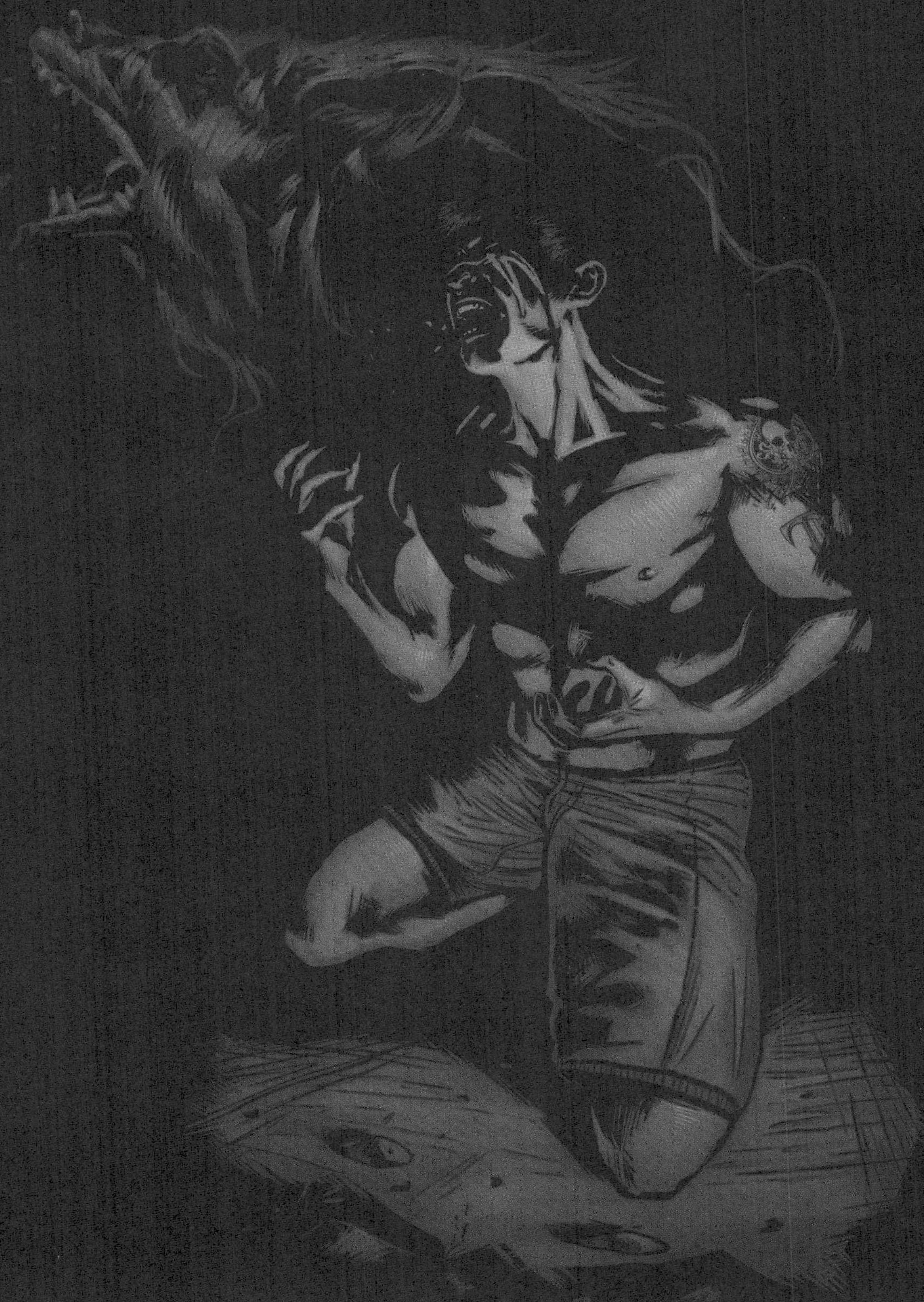

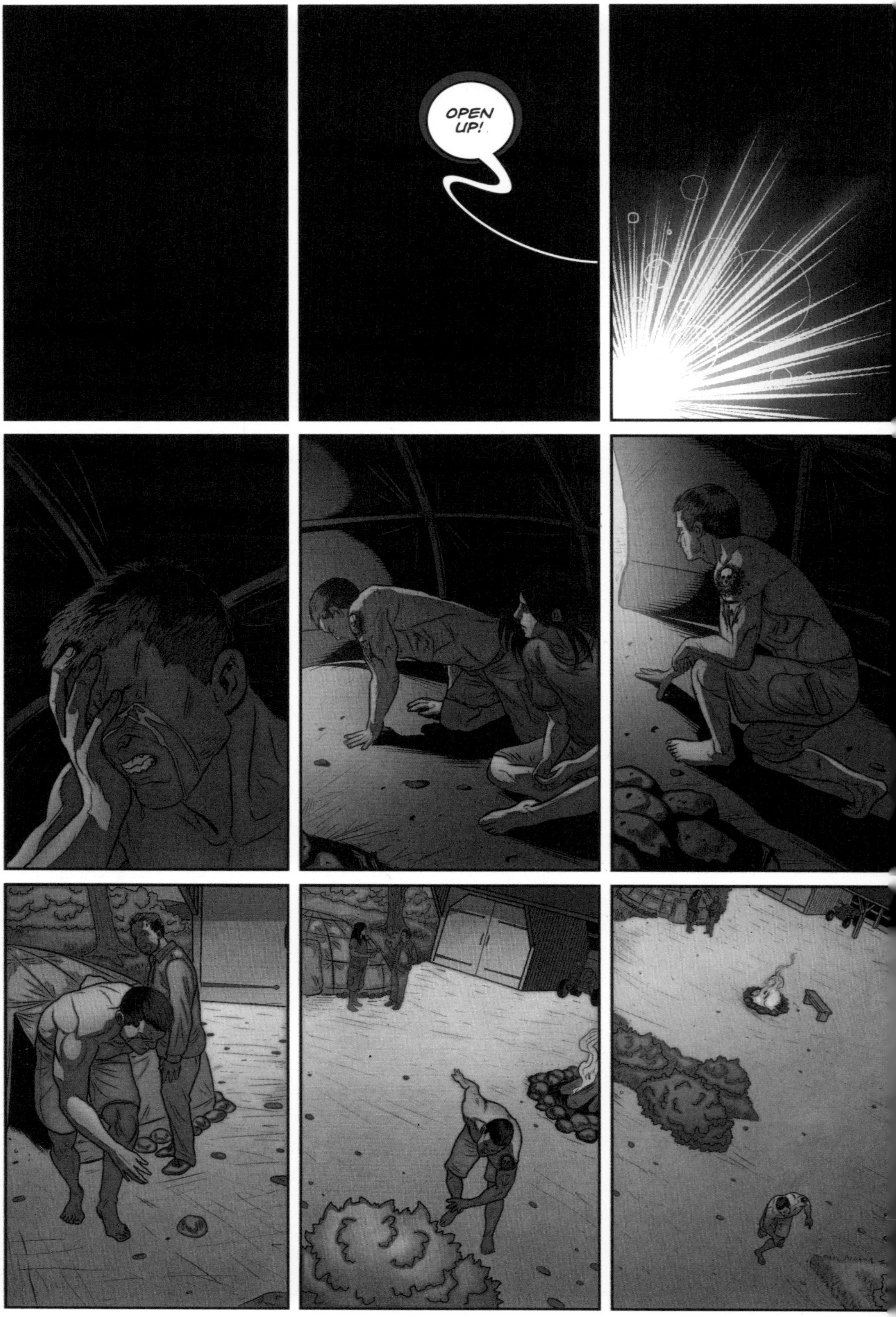
OPEN UP!

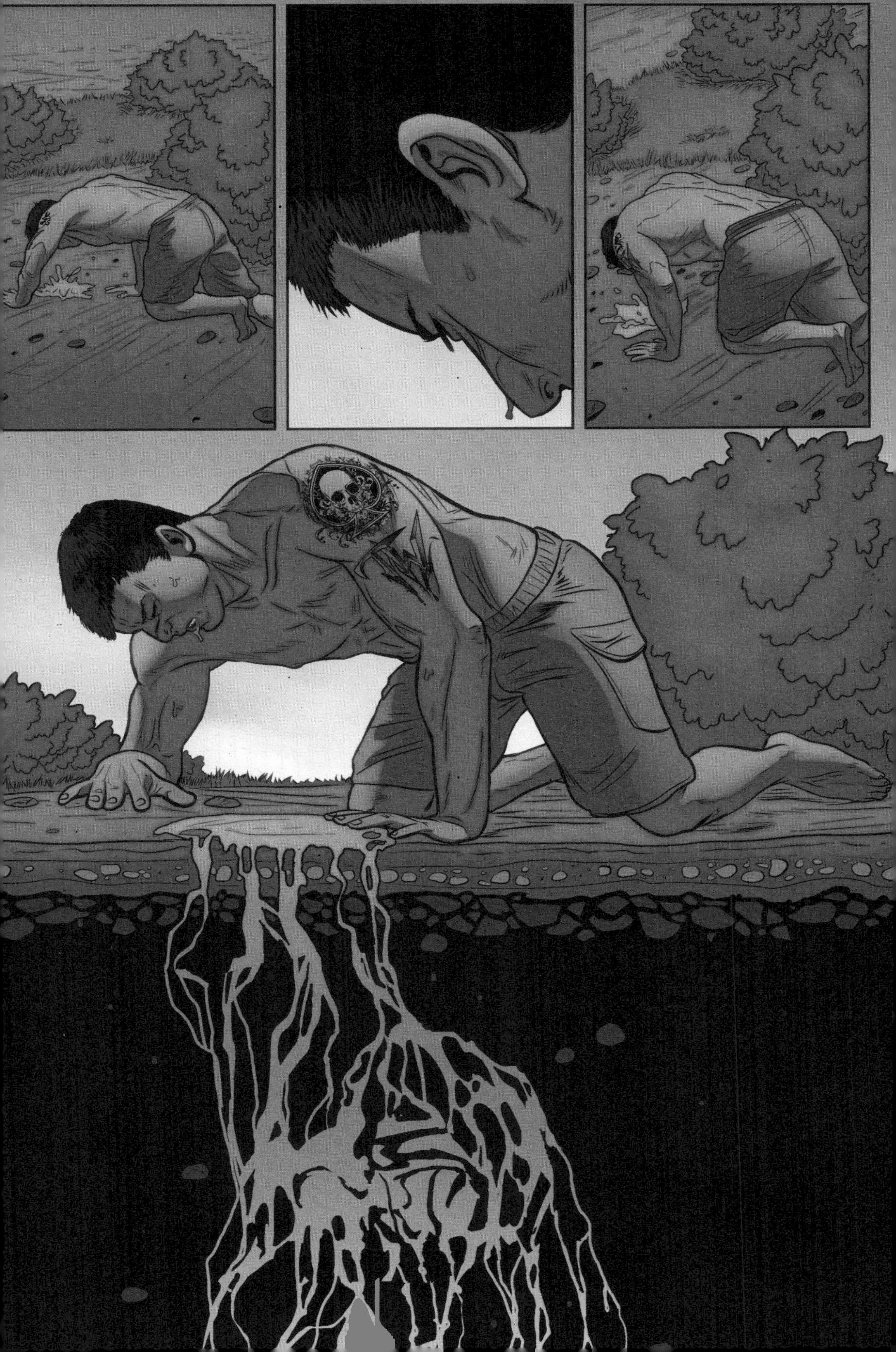

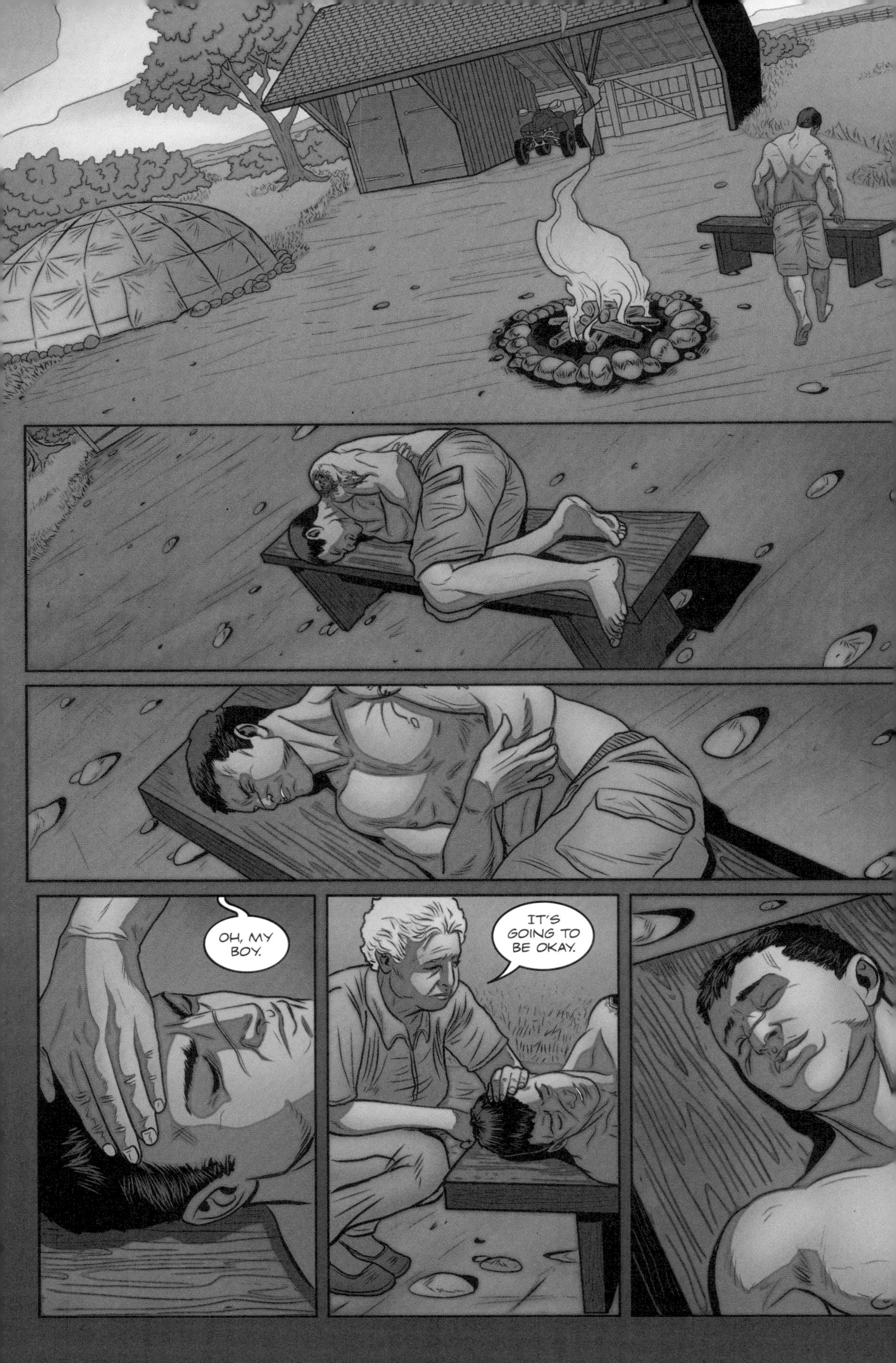
OH, MY BOY.
IT'S GOING TO BE OKAY.

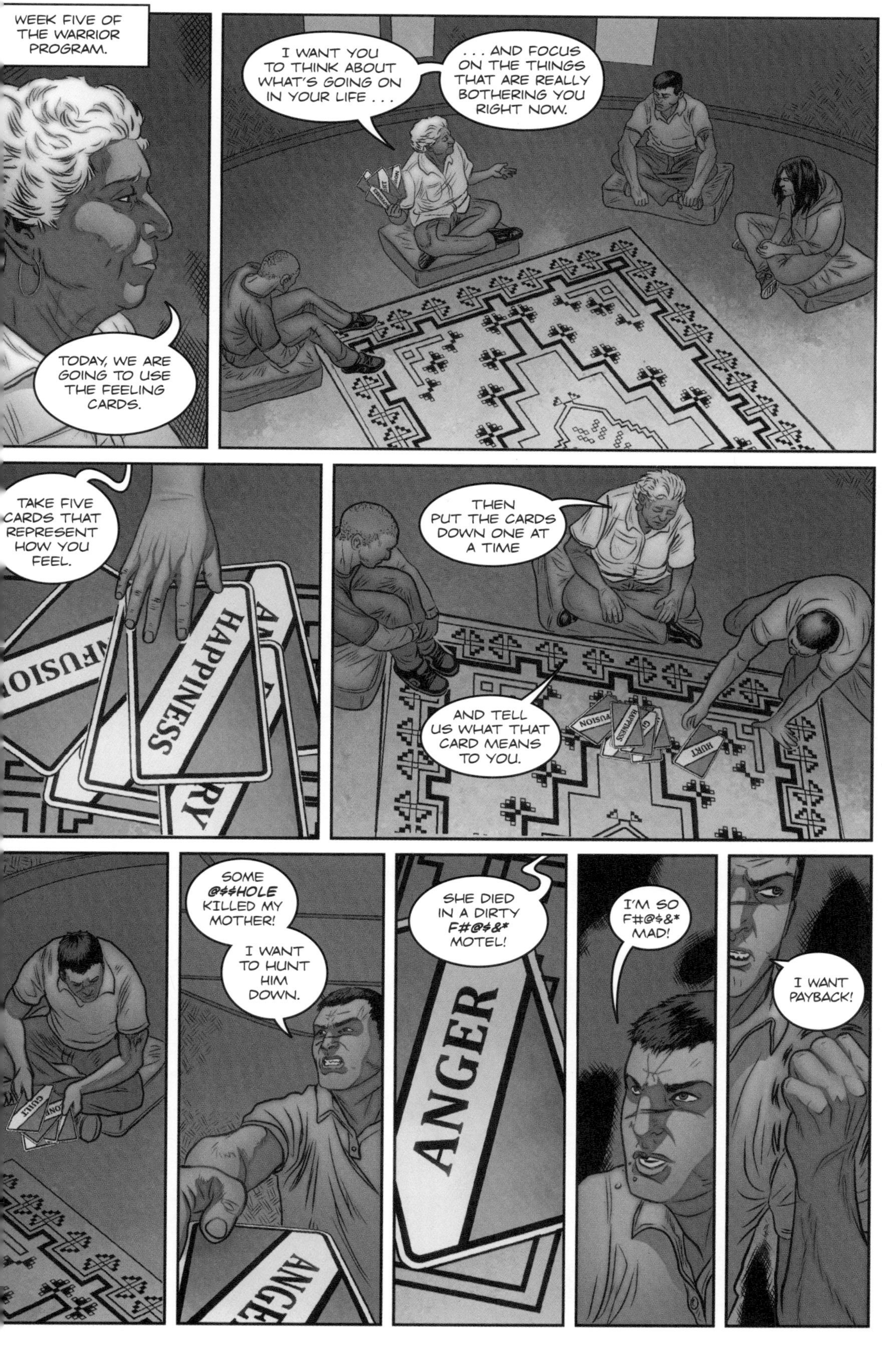
WEEK FIVE OF THE WARRIOR PROGRAM.
TODAY, WE ARE GOING TO USE THE FEELING CARDS.
I WANT YOU TO THINK ABOUT WHAT'S GOING ON IN YOUR LIFE . . .
. . . AND FOCUS ON THE THINGS THAT ARE REALLY BOTHERING YOU RIGHT NOW.
TAKE FIVE CARDS THAT REPRESENT HOW YOU FEEL.
HAPPINESS
THEN PUT THE CARDS DOWN ONE AT A TIME
AND TELL US WHAT THAT CARD MEANS TO YOU.
HURT
SOME @$$HOLE KILLED MY MOTHER!
I WANT TO HUNT HIM DOWN.
SHE DIED IN A DIRTY F#@$&* MOTEL!
ANGER
I'M SO F#@$&* MAD!
I WANT PAYBACK!

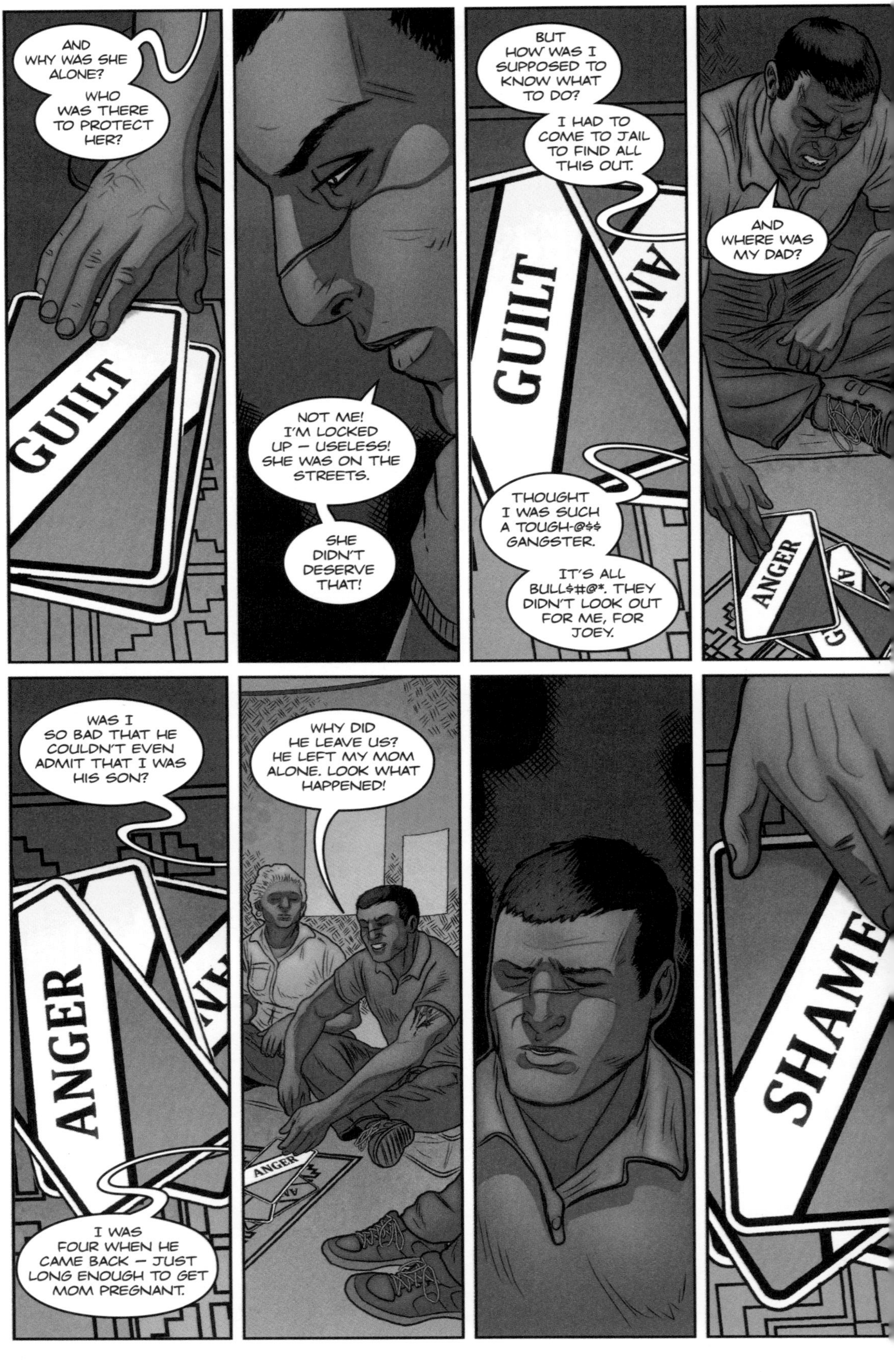

AND WHY WAS SHE ALONE?
WHO WAS THERE TO PROTECT HER?
GUILT
NOT ME! I'M LOCKED UP — USELESS! SHE WAS ON THE STREETS.
SHE DIDN'T DESERVE THAT!
BUT HOW WAS I SUPPOSED TO KNOW WHAT TO DO?
I HAD TO COME TO JAIL TO FIND ALL THIS OUT.
GUILT
THOUGHT I WAS SUCH A TOUGH-@$$ GANGSTER.
IT'S ALL BULL$#@*. THEY DIDN'T LOOK OUT FOR ME, FOR JOEY.
AND WHERE WAS MY DAD?
ANGER
WAS I SO BAD THAT HE COULDN'T EVEN ADMIT THAT I WAS HIS SON?
ANGER
I WAS FOUR WHEN HE CAME BACK — JUST LONG ENOUGH TO GET MOM PREGNANT.
WHY DID HE LEAVE US? HE LEFT MY MOM ALONE. LOOK WHAT HAPPENED!
ANGER
SHAME

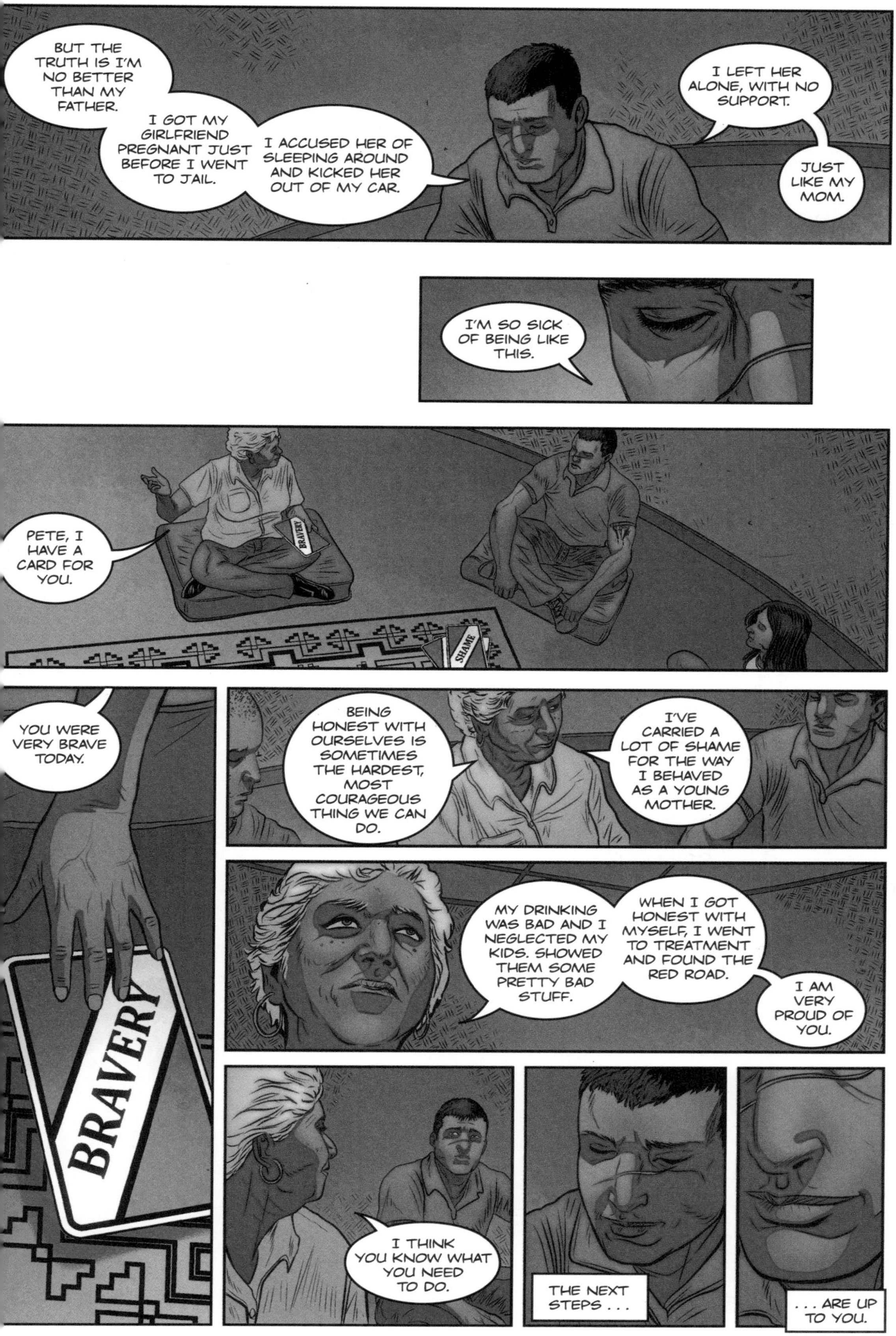

BUT THE TRUTH IS I'M NO BETTER THAN MY FATHER.
I GOT MY GIRLFRIEND PREGNANT JUST BEFORE I WENT TO JAIL.
I ACCUSED HER OF SLEEPING AROUND AND KICKED HER OUT OF MY CAR.
I LEFT HER ALONE, WITH NO SUPPORT.
JUST LIKE MY MOM.
I'M SO SICK OF BEING LIKE THIS.
PETE, I HAVE A CARD FOR YOU.
BRAVERY
SHAME
YOU WERE VERY BRAVE TODAY.
BEING HONEST WITH OURSELVES IS SOMETIMES THE HARDEST, MOST COURAGEOUS THING WE CAN DO.
I'VE CARRIED A LOT OF SHAME FOR THE WAY I BEHAVED AS A YOUNG MOTHER.
MY DRINKING WAS BAD AND I NEGLECTED MY KIDS. SHOWED THEM SOME PRETTY BAD STUFF.
WHEN I GOT HONEST WITH MYSELF, I WENT TO TREATMENT AND FOUND THE RED ROAD.
I AM VERY PROUD OF YOU.
BRAVERY
I THINK YOU KNOW WHAT YOU NEED TO DO.
THE NEXT STEPS . . .
. . . ARE UP TO YOU.

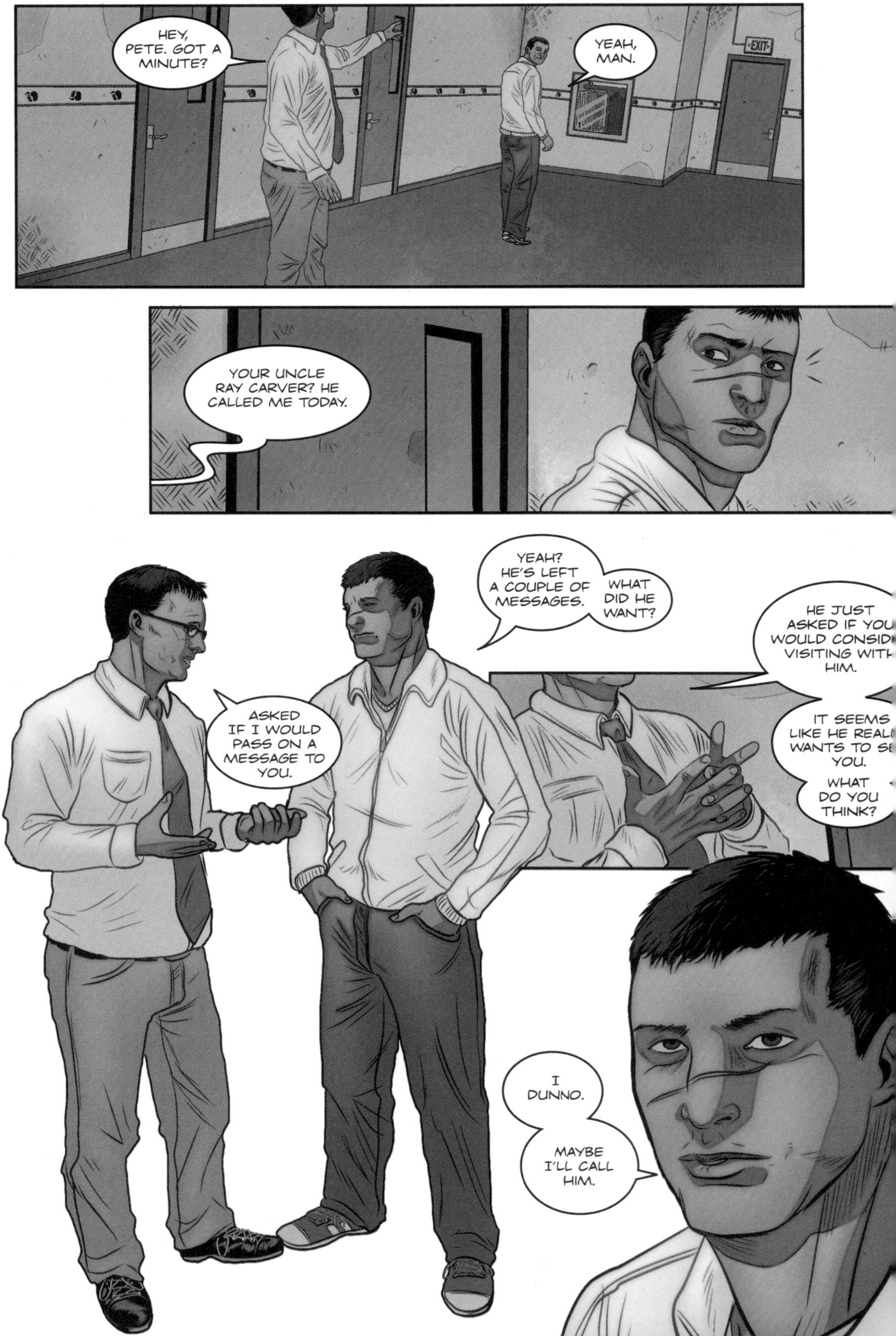
HEY, PETE. GOT A MINUTE?
YEAH, MAN.
EXIT
YOUR UNCLE RAY CARVER? HE CALLED ME TODAY.
YEAH? HE'S LEFT A COUPLE OF MESSAGES.
WHAT DID HE WANT?
ASKED IF I WOULD PASS ON A MESSAGE TO YOU.
HE JUST ASKED IF YOU WOULD CONSID VISITING WITH HIM.
IT SEEMS LIKE HE REAL WANTS TO S YOU.
WHAT DO YOU THINK?
I DUNNO.
MAYBE I'LL CALL HIM.

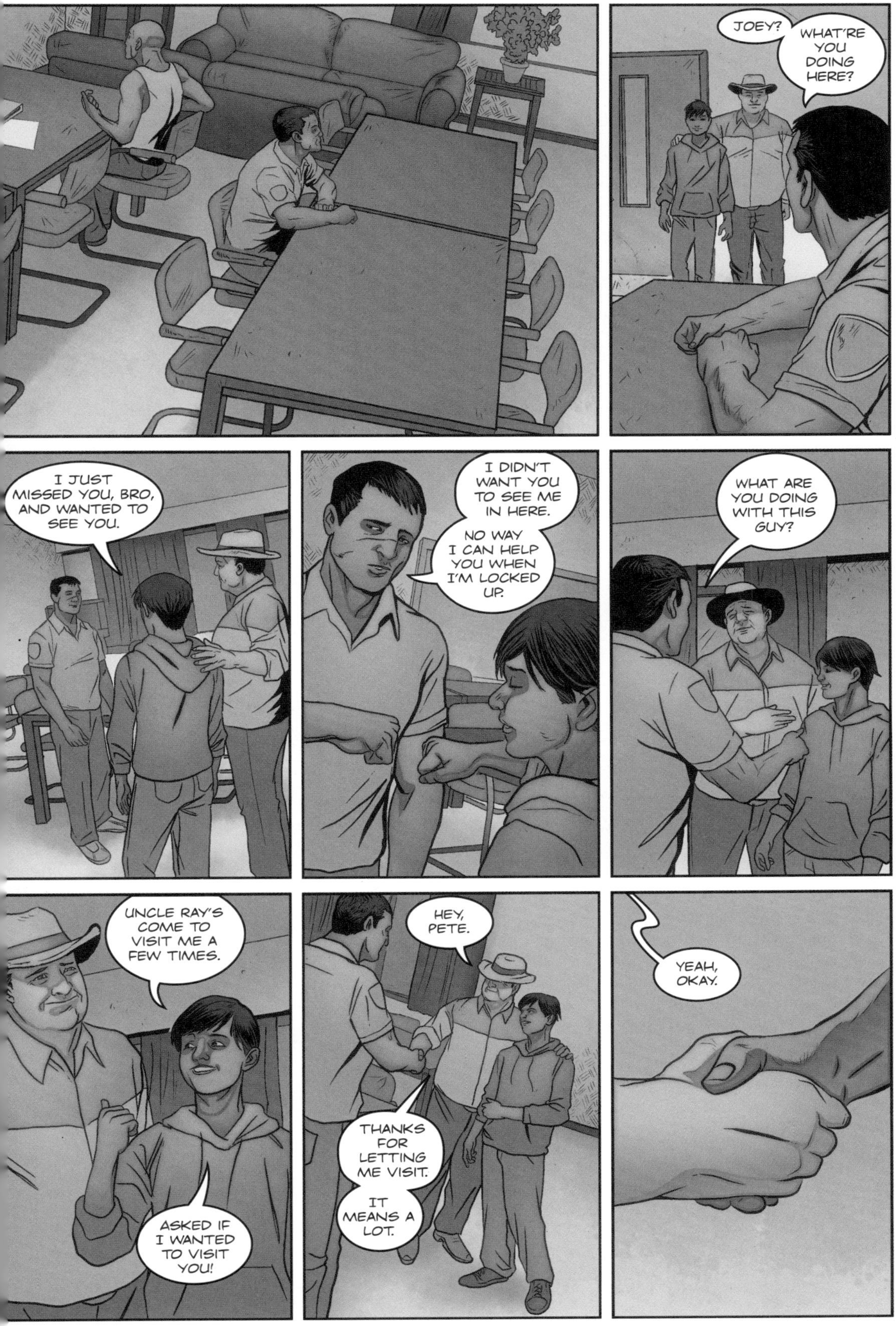
JOEY?
WHAT'RE YOU DOING HERE?
I JUST MISSED YOU, BRO, AND WANTED TO SEE YOU.
I DIDN'T WANT YOU TO SEE ME IN HERE.
NO WAY I CAN HELP YOU WHEN I'M LOCKED UP.
WHAT ARE YOU DOING WITH THIS GUY?
UNCLE RAY'S COME TO VISIT ME A FEW TIMES.
ASKED IF I WANTED TO VISIT YOU!
HEY, PETE.
THANKS FOR LETTING ME VISIT.
IT MEANS A LOT.
YEAH, OKAY.

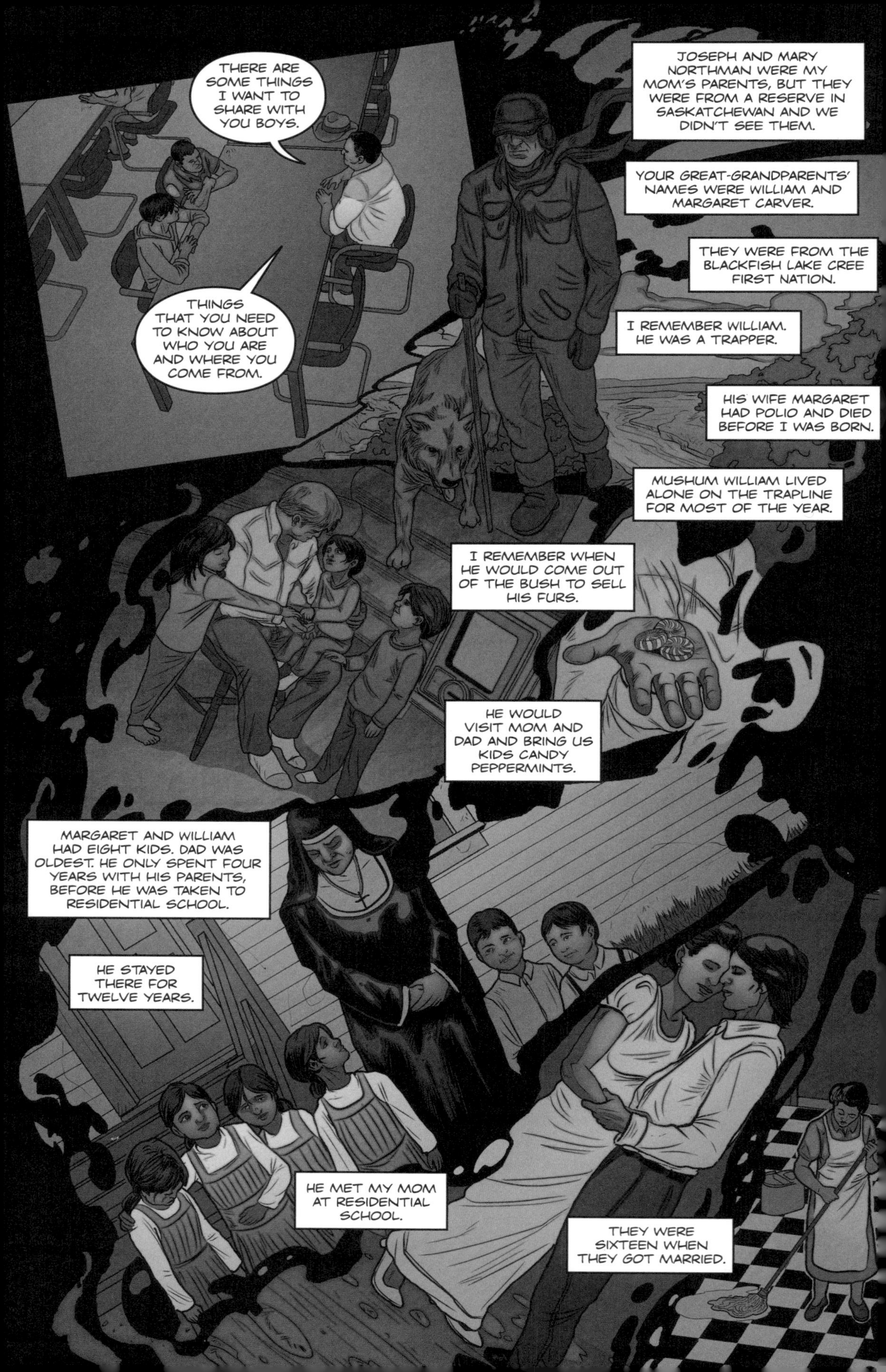
THERE ARE SOME THINGS I WANT TO SHARE WITH YOU BOYS.
THINGS THAT YOU NEED TO KNOW ABOUT WHO YOU ARE AND WHERE YOU COME FROM.
JOSEPH AND MARY NORTHMAN WERE MY MOM'S PARENTS, BUT THEY WERE FROM A RESERVE IN SASKATCHEWAN AND WE DIDN'T SEE THEM.
YOUR GREAT-GRANDPARENTS' NAMES WERE WILLIAM AND MARGARET CARVER.
THEY WERE FROM THE BLACKFISH LAKE CREE FIRST NATION.
I REMEMBER WILLIAM. HE WAS A TRAPPER.
HIS WIFE MARGARET HAD POLIO AND DIED BEFORE I WAS BORN.
MUSHUM WILLIAM LIVED ALONE ON THE TRAPLINE FOR MOST OF THE YEAR.
I REMEMBER WHEN HE WOULD COME OUT OF THE BUSH TO SELL HIS FURS.
HE WOULD VISIT MOM AND DAD AND BRING US KIDS CANDY PEPPERMINTS.
MARGARET AND WILLIAM HAD EIGHT KIDS. DAD WAS OLDEST. HE ONLY SPENT FOUR YEARS WITH HIS PARENTS, BEFORE HE WAS TAKEN TO RESIDENTIAL SCHOOL.
HE STAYED THERE FOR TWELVE YEARS.
HE MET MY MOM AT RESIDENTIAL SCHOOL.
THEY WERE SIXTEEN WHEN THEY GOT MARRIED.

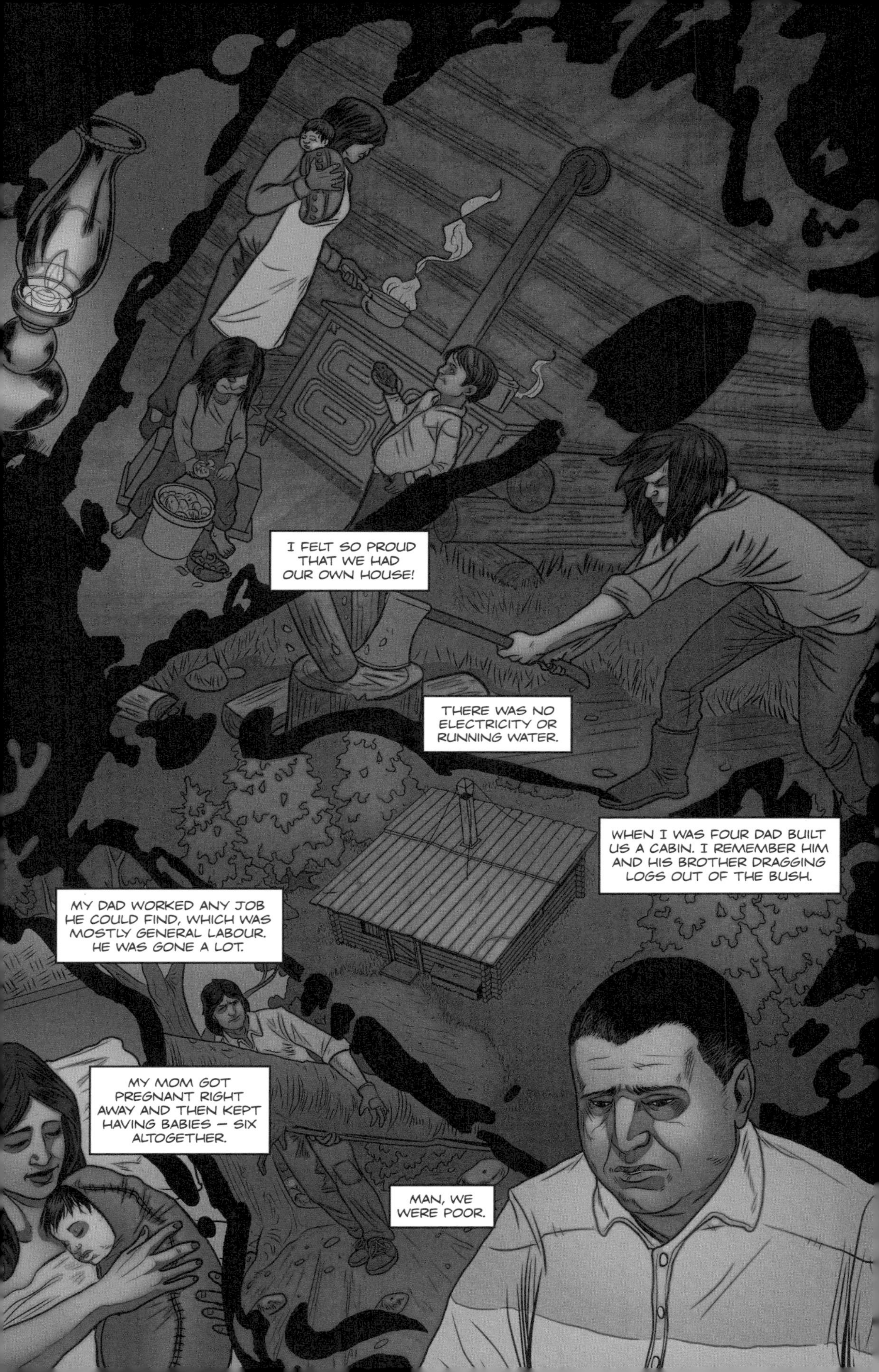
I FELT SO PROUD THAT WE HAD OUR OWN HOUSE!
THERE WAS NO ELECTRICITY OR RUNNING WATER.
WHEN I WAS FOUR DAD BUILT US A CABIN. I REMEMBER HIM AND HIS BROTHER DRAGGING LOGS OUT OF THE BUSH.
MY DAD WORKED ANY JOB HE COULD FIND, WHICH WAS MOSTLY GENERAL LABOUR. HE WAS GONE A LOT.
MY MOM GOT PREGNANT RIGHT AWAY AND THEN KEPT HAVING BABIES — SIX ALTOGETHER.
MAN, WE WERE POOR.

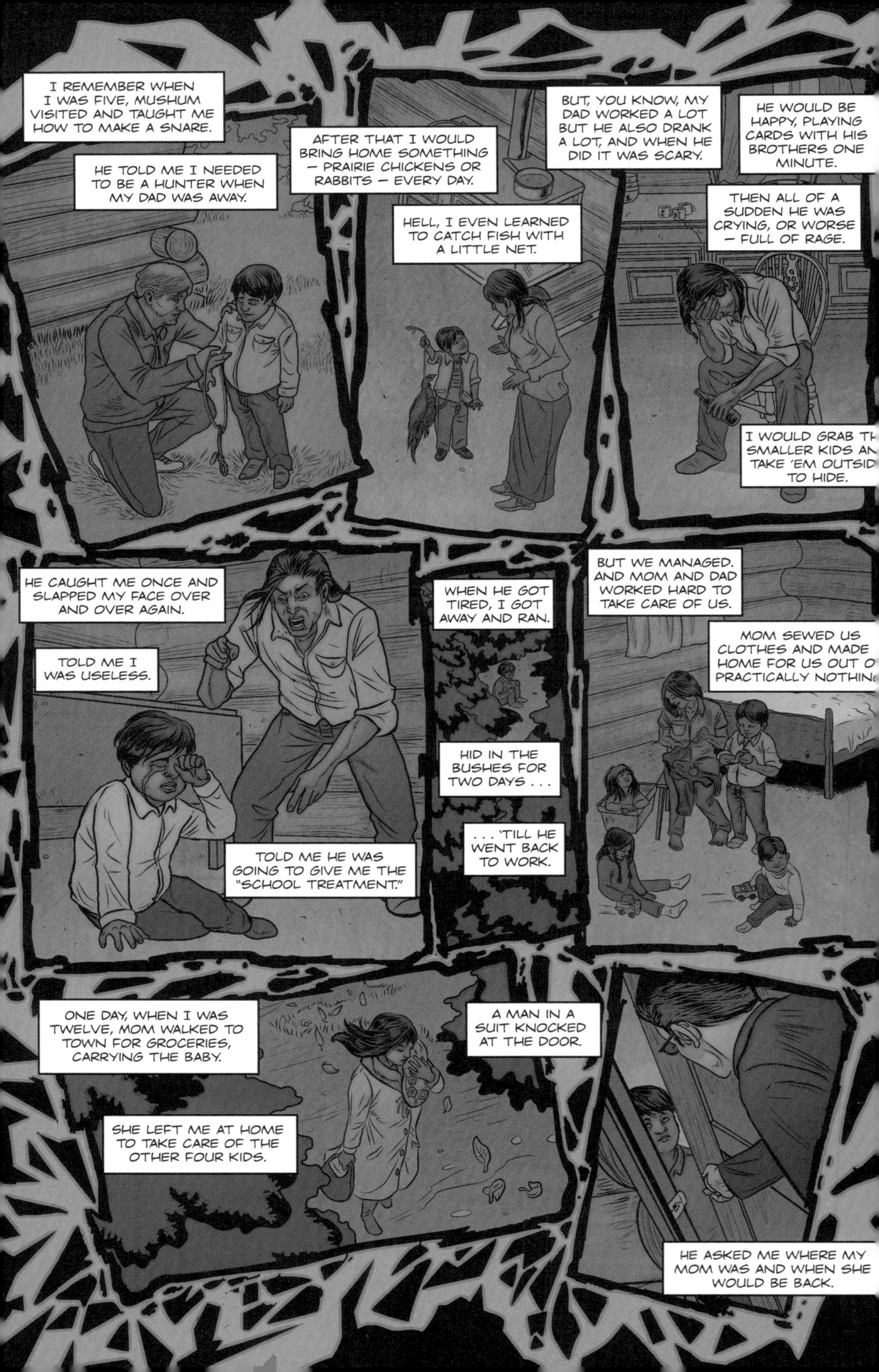
I REMEMBER WHEN I WAS FIVE, MUSHUM VISITED AND TAUGHT ME HOW TO MAKE A SNARE.
HE TOLD ME I NEEDED TO BE A HUNTER WHEN MY DAD WAS AWAY.
AFTER THAT I WOULD BRING HOME SOMETHING — PRAIRIE CHICKENS OR RABBITS — EVERY DAY.
HELL, I EVEN LEARNED TO CATCH FISH WITH A LITTLE NET.
BUT, YOU KNOW, MY DAD WORKED A LOT BUT HE ALSO DRANK A LOT, AND WHEN HE DID IT WAS SCARY.
HE WOULD BE HAPPY, PLAYING CARDS WITH HIS BROTHERS ONE MINUTE.
THEN ALL OF A SUDDEN HE WAS CRYING, OR WORSE — FULL OF RAGE.
I WOULD GRAB TH SMALLER KIDS AN TAKE 'EM OUTSID TO HIDE.
HE CAUGHT ME ONCE AND SLAPPED MY FACE OVER AND OVER AGAIN.
TOLD ME I WAS USELESS.
TOLD ME HE WAS GOING TO GIVE ME THE "SCHOOL TREATMENT."
WHEN HE GOT TIRED, I GOT AWAY AND RAN.
HID IN THE BUSHES FOR TWO DAYS . . .
. . . 'TILL HE WENT BACK TO WORK.
BUT WE MANAGED. AND MOM AND DAD WORKED HARD TO TAKE CARE OF US.
MOM SEWED US CLOTHES AND MADE HOME FOR US OUT O PRACTICALLY NOTHIN
ONE DAY, WHEN I WAS TWELVE, MOM WALKED TO TOWN FOR GROCERIES, CARRYING THE BABY.
SHE LEFT ME AT HOME TO TAKE CARE OF THE OTHER FOUR KIDS.
A MAN IN A SUIT KNOCKED AT THE DOOR.
HE ASKED ME WHERE MY MOM WAS AND WHEN SHE WOULD BE BACK.

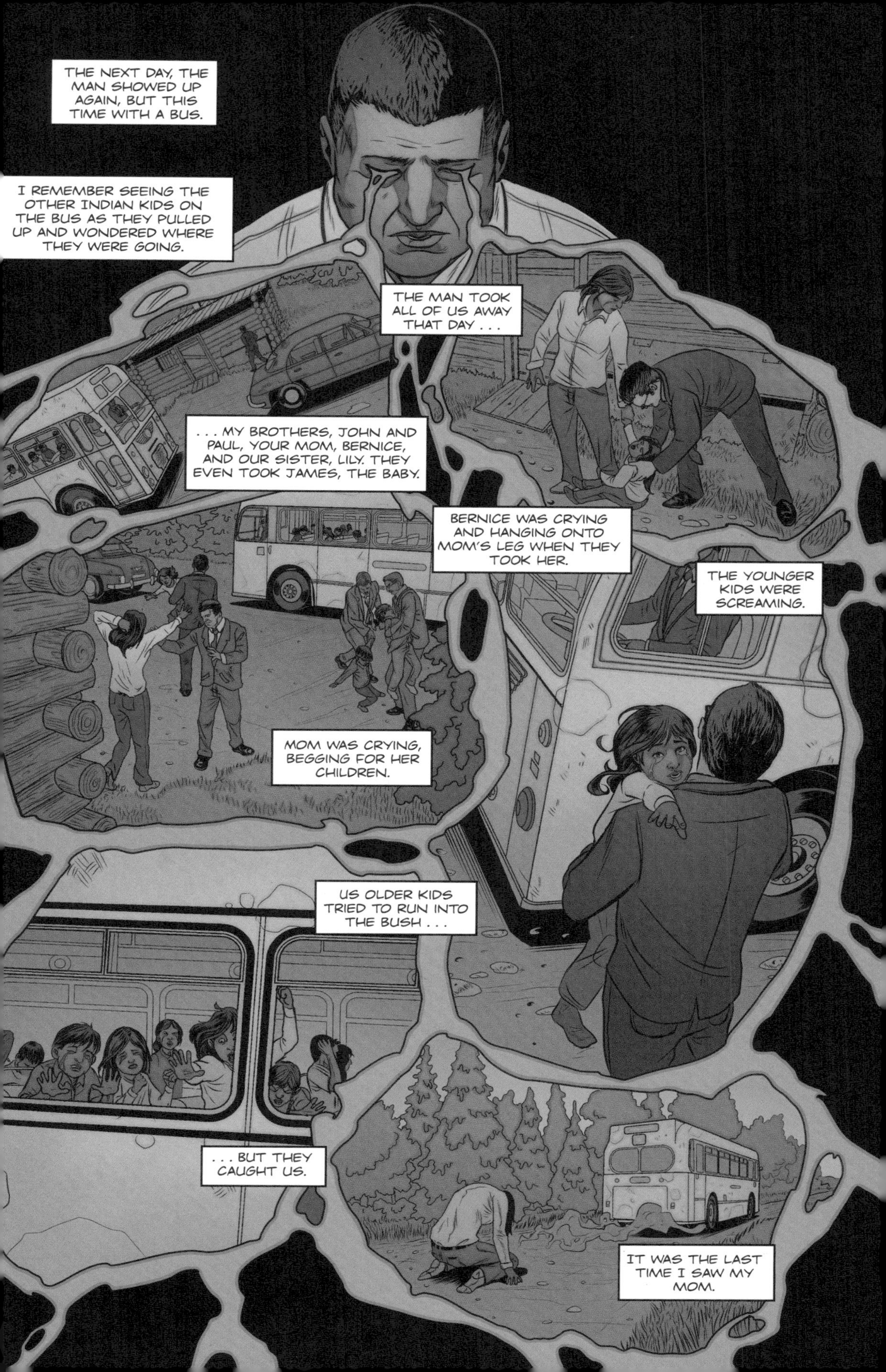
THE NEXT DAY, THE MAN SHOWED UP AGAIN, BUT THIS TIME WITH A BUS.
I REMEMBER SEEING THE OTHER INDIAN KIDS ON THE BUS AS THEY PULLED UP AND WONDERED WHERE THEY WERE GOING.
THE MAN TOOK ALL OF US AWAY THAT DAY . . .
. . . MY BROTHERS, JOHN AND PAUL, YOUR MOM, BERNICE, AND OUR SISTER, LILY. THEY EVEN TOOK JAMES, THE BABY.
BERNICE WAS CRYING AND HANGING ONTO MOM'S LEG WHEN THEY TOOK HER.
THE YOUNGER KIDS WERE SCREAMING.
MOM WAS CRYING, BEGGING FOR HER CHILDREN.
US OLDER KIDS TRIED TO RUN INTO THE BUSH . . .
. . . BUT THEY CAUGHT US.
IT WAS THE LAST TIME I SAW MY MOM.

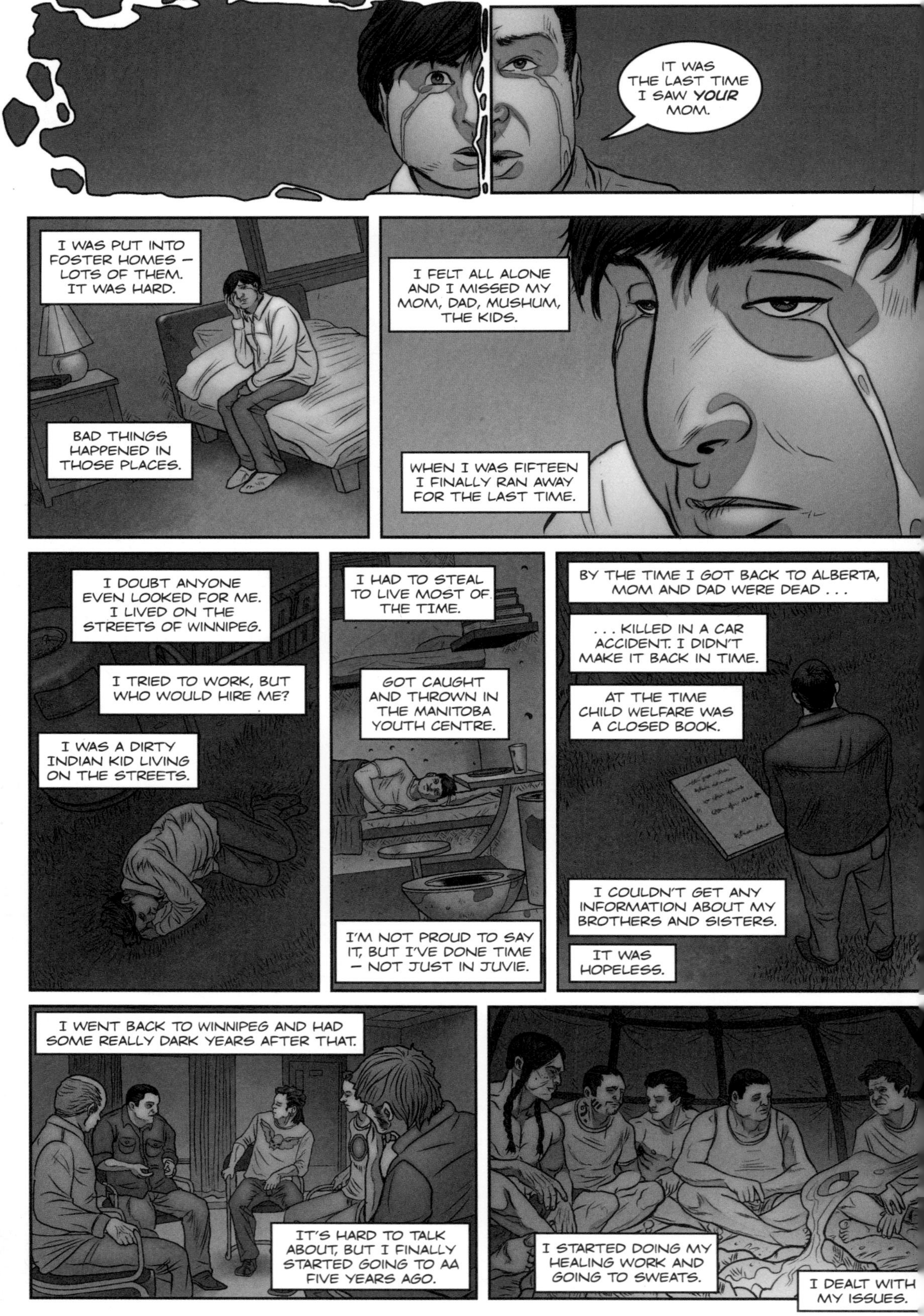
IT WAS THE LAST TIME I SAW YOUR MOM.
I WAS PUT INTO FOSTER HOMES — LOTS OF THEM. IT WAS HARD.
BAD THINGS HAPPENED IN THOSE PLACES.
I FELT ALL ALONE AND I MISSED MY MOM, DAD, MUSHUM, THE KIDS.
WHEN I WAS FIFTEEN I FINALLY RAN AWAY FOR THE LAST TIME.
I DOUBT ANYONE EVEN LOOKED FOR ME. I LIVED ON THE STREETS OF WINNIPEG.
I TRIED TO WORK, BUT WHO WOULD HIRE ME?
I WAS A DIRTY INDIAN KID LIVING ON THE STREETS.
I HAD TO STEAL TO LIVE MOST OF THE TIME.
GOT CAUGHT AND THROWN IN THE MANITOBA YOUTH CENTRE.
I'M NOT PROUD TO SAY IT, BUT I'VE DONE TIME — NOT JUST IN JUVIE.
BY THE TIME I GOT BACK TO ALBERTA, MOM AND DAD WERE DEAD . . .
. . . KILLED IN A CAR ACCIDENT. I DIDN'T MAKE IT BACK IN TIME.
AT THE TIME CHILD WELFARE WAS A CLOSED BOOK.
I COULDN'T GET ANY INFORMATION ABOUT MY BROTHERS AND SISTERS.
IT WAS HOPELESS.
I WENT BACK TO WINNIPEG AND HAD SOME REALLY DARK YEARS AFTER THAT.
IT'S HARD TO TALK ABOUT, BUT I FINALLY STARTED GOING TO AA FIVE YEARS AGO.
I STARTED DOING MY HEALING WORK AND GOING TO SWEATS.
I DEALT WITH MY ISSUES.

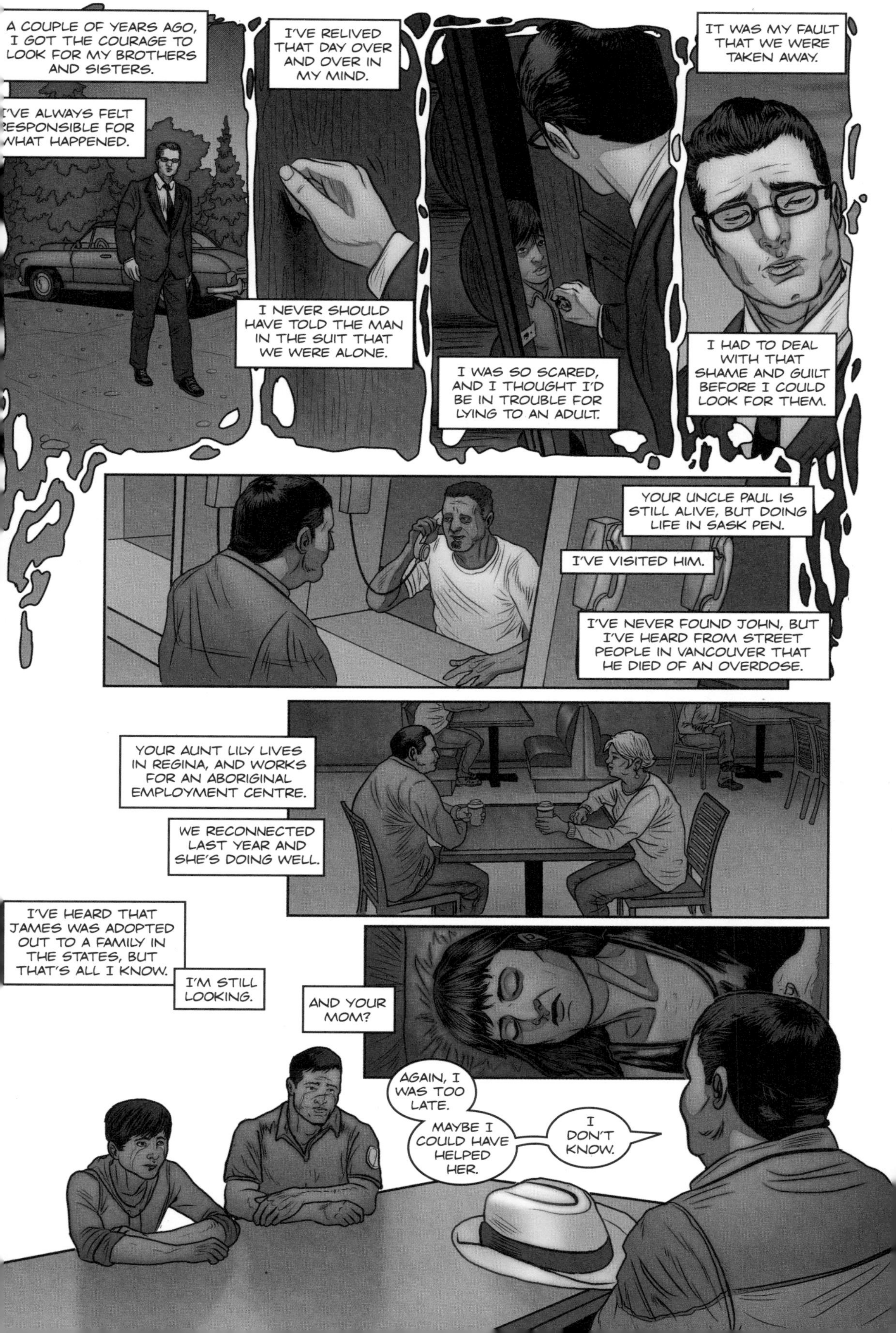
A COUPLE OF YEARS AGO, I GOT THE COURAGE TO LOOK FOR MY BROTHERS AND SISTERS.
I'VE ALWAYS FELT RESPONSIBLE FOR WHAT HAPPENED.
I'VE RELIVED THAT DAY OVER AND OVER IN MY MIND.
I NEVER SHOULD HAVE TOLD THE MAN IN THE SUIT THAT WE WERE ALONE.
I WAS SO SCARED, AND I THOUGHT I'D BE IN TROUBLE FOR LYING TO AN ADULT.
IT WAS MY FAULT THAT WE WERE TAKEN AWAY.
I HAD TO DEAL WITH THAT SHAME AND GUILT BEFORE I COULD LOOK FOR THEM.
YOUR UNCLE PAUL IS STILL ALIVE, BUT DOING LIFE IN SASK PEN.
I'VE VISITED HIM.
I'VE NEVER FOUND JOHN, BUT I'VE HEARD FROM STREET PEOPLE IN VANCOUVER THAT HE DIED OF AN OVERDOSE.
YOUR AUNT LILY LIVES IN REGINA, AND WORKS FOR AN ABORIGINAL EMPLOYMENT CENTRE.
WE RECONNECTED LAST YEAR AND SHE'S DOING WELL.
I'VE HEARD THAT JAMES WAS ADOPTED OUT TO A FAMILY IN THE STATES, BUT THAT'S ALL I KNOW.
I'M STILL LOOKING.
AND YOUR MOM?
AGAIN, I WAS TOO LATE.
MAYBE I COULD HAVE HELPED HER.
I DON'T KNOW.

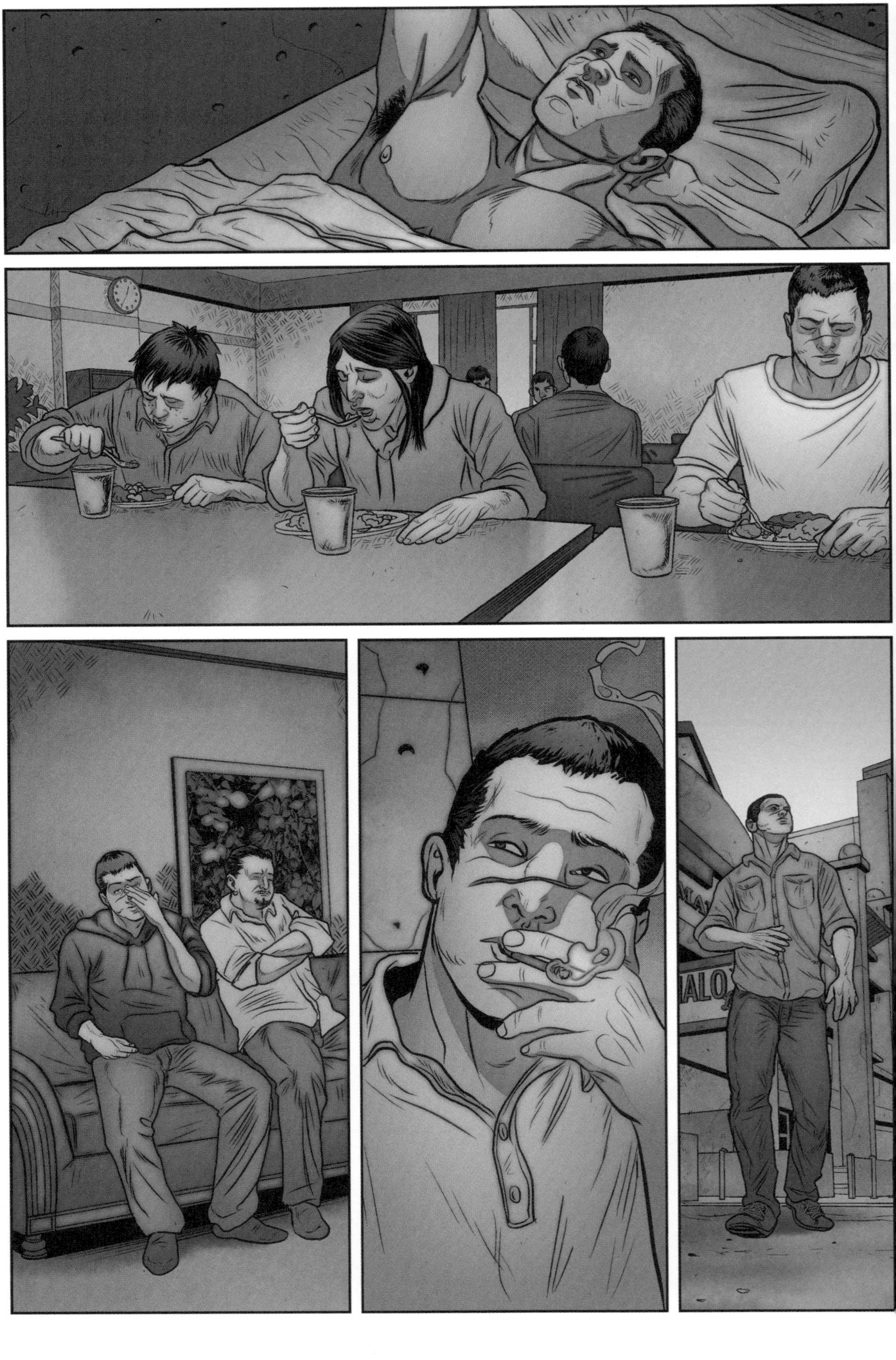

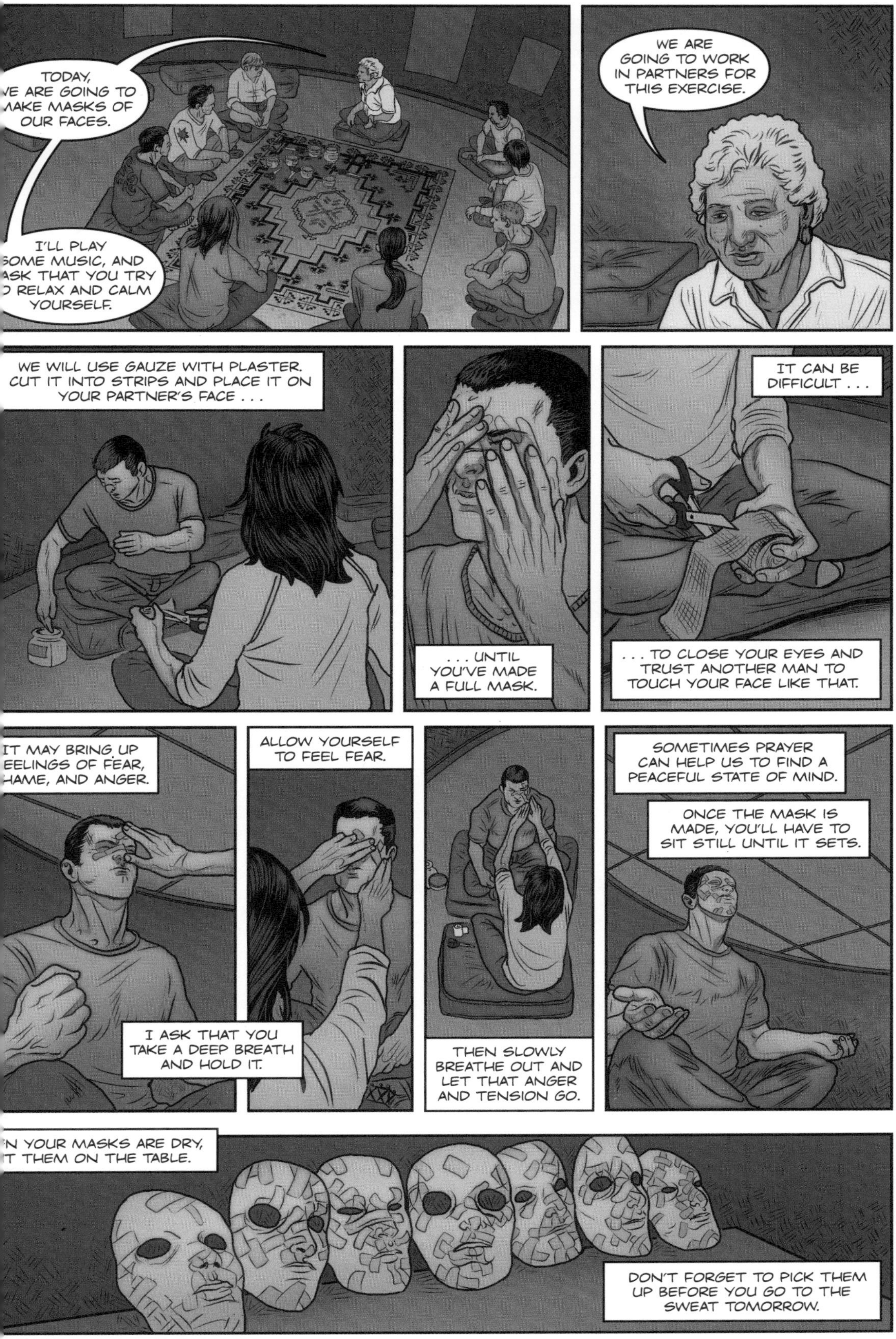
TODAY, WE ARE GOING TO MAKE MASKS OF OUR FACES.
I'LL PLAY SOME MUSIC, AND ASK THAT YOU TRY TO RELAX AND CALM YOURSELF.
WE ARE GOING TO WORK IN PARTNERS FOR THIS EXERCISE.
WE WILL USE GAUZE WITH PLASTER. CUT IT INTO STRIPS AND PLACE IT ON YOUR PARTNER'S FACE . . .
. . . UNTIL YOU'VE MADE A FULL MASK.
IT CAN BE DIFFICULT . . .
. . . TO CLOSE YOUR EYES AND TRUST ANOTHER MAN TO TOUCH YOUR FACE LIKE THAT.
IT MAY BRING UP FEELINGS OF FEAR, SHAME, AND ANGER.
I ASK THAT YOU TAKE A DEEP BREATH AND HOLD IT.
ALLOW YOURSELF TO FEEL FEAR.
THEN SLOWLY BREATHE OUT AND LET THAT ANGER AND TENSION GO.
SOMETIMES PRAYER CAN HELP US TO FIND A PEACEFUL STATE OF MIND.
ONCE THE MASK IS MADE, YOU'LL HAVE TO SIT STILL UNTIL IT SETS.
WHEN YOUR MASKS ARE DRY, PUT THEM ON THE TABLE.
DON'T FORGET TO PICK THEM UP BEFORE YOU GO TO THE SWEAT TOMORROW.

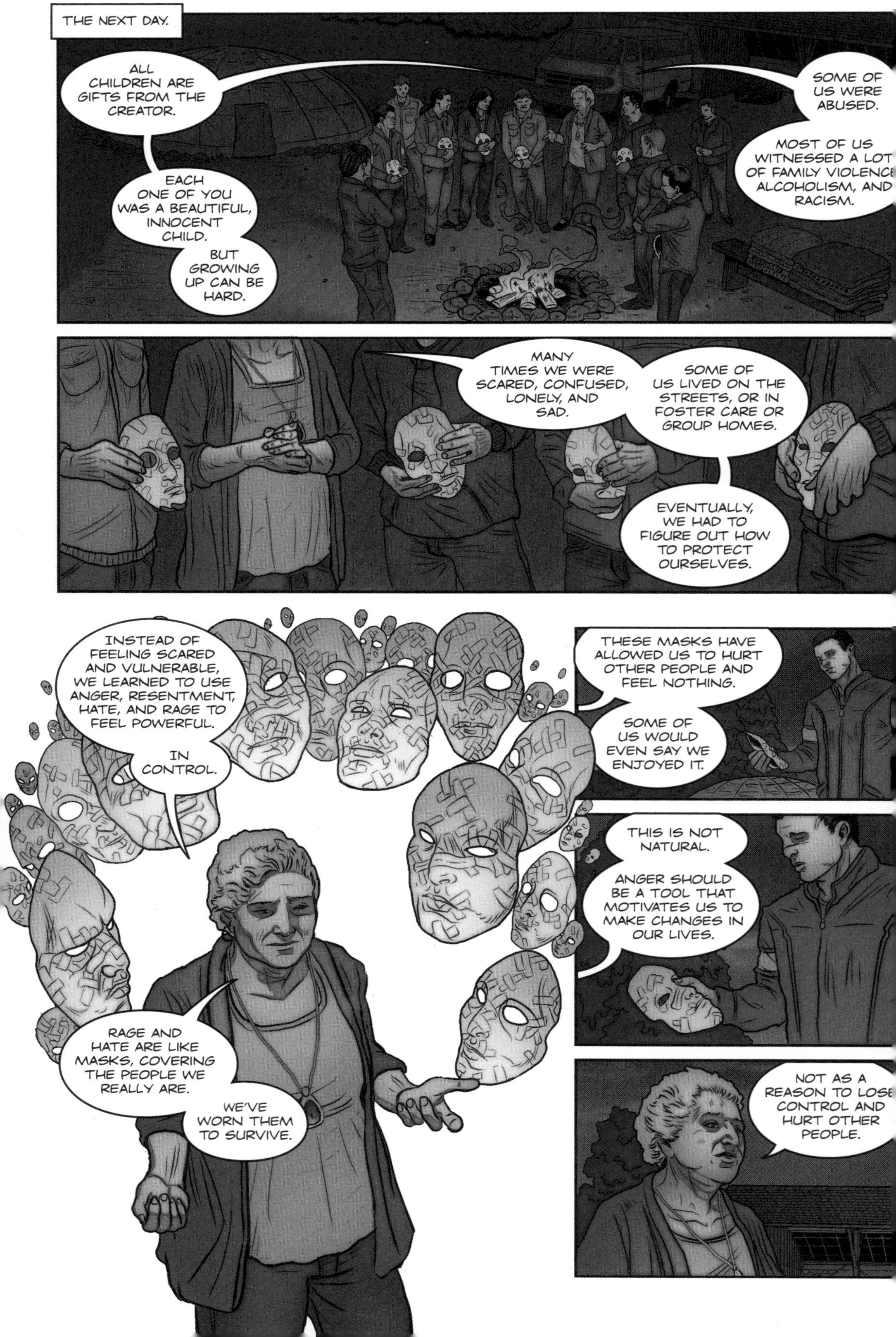
THE NEXT DAY.
ALL CHILDREN ARE GIFTS FROM THE CREATOR.
EACH ONE OF YOU WAS A BEAUTIFUL, INNOCENT CHILD.
BUT GROWING UP CAN BE HARD.
SOME OF US WERE ABUSED.
MOST OF US WITNESSED A LOT OF FAMILY VIOLENCE, ALCOHOLISM, AND RACISM.
MANY TIMES WE WERE SCARED, CONFUSED, LONELY, AND SAD.
SOME OF US LIVED ON THE STREETS, OR IN FOSTER CARE OR GROUP HOMES.
EVENTUALLY, WE HAD TO FIGURE OUT HOW TO PROTECT OURSELVES.
INSTEAD OF FEELING SCARED AND VULNERABLE, WE LEARNED TO USE ANGER, RESENTMENT, HATE, AND RAGE TO FEEL POWERFUL.
IN CONTROL.
RAGE AND HATE ARE LIKE MASKS, COVERING THE PEOPLE WE REALLY ARE.
WE'VE WORN THEM TO SURVIVE.
THESE MASKS HAVE ALLOWED US TO HURT OTHER PEOPLE AND FEEL NOTHING.
SOME OF US WOULD EVEN SAY WE ENJOYED IT.
THIS IS NOT NATURAL.
ANGER SHOULD BE A TOOL THAT MOTIVATES US TO MAKE CHANGES IN OUR LIVES.
NOT AS A REASON TO LOSE CONTROL AND HURT OTHER PEOPLE.

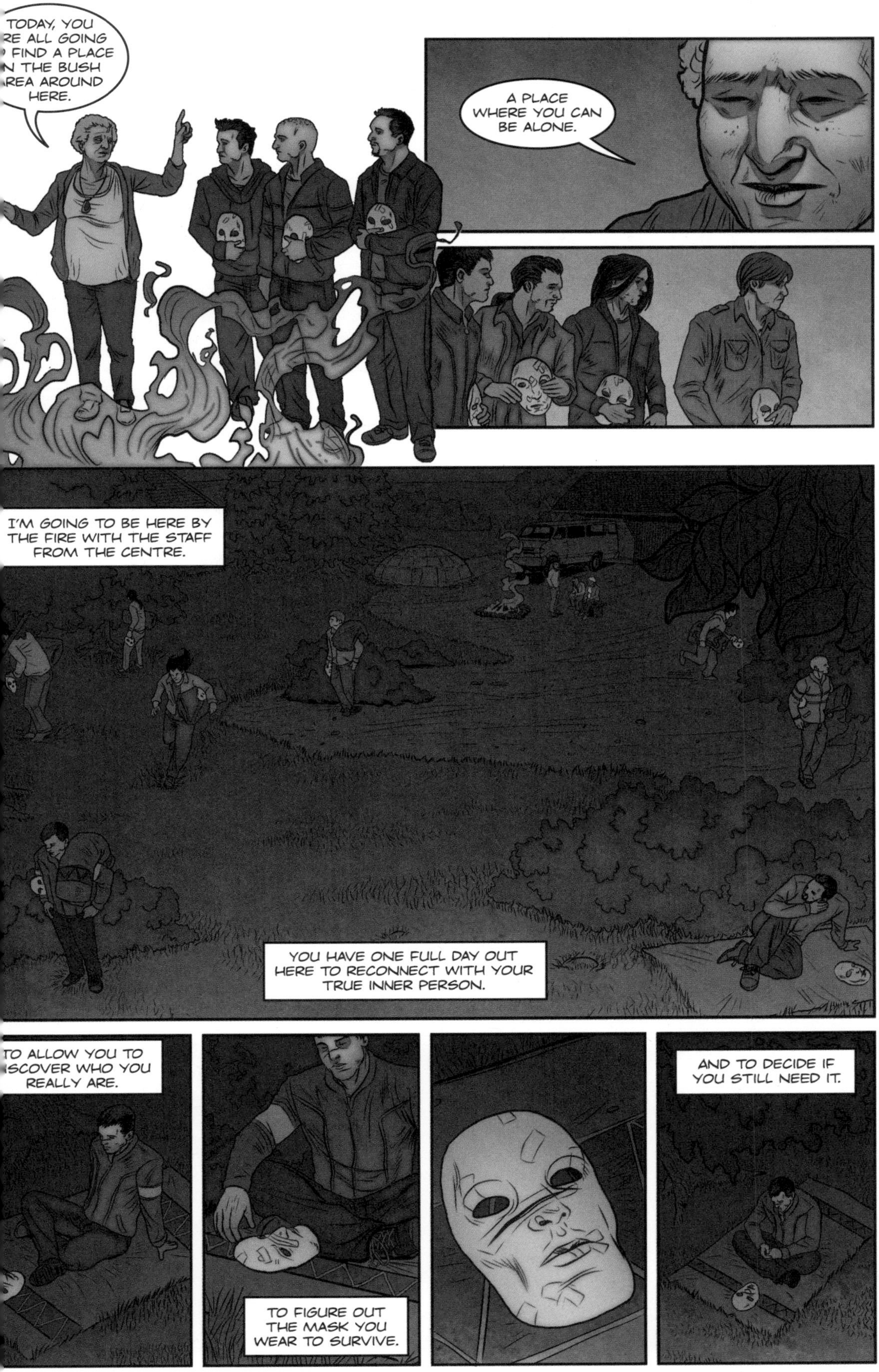
TODAY, YOU
RE ALL GOING
FIND A PLACE
N THE BUSH
REA AROUND
HERE.
A PLACE WHERE YOU CAN BE ALONE.
I'M GOING TO BE HERE BY THE FIRE WITH THE STAFF FROM THE CENTRE.
YOU HAVE ONE FULL DAY OUT HERE TO RECONNECT WITH YOUR TRUE INNER PERSON.
TO ALLOW YOU TO
SCOVER WHO YOU
REALLY ARE.
TO FIGURE OUT THE MASK YOU WEAR TO SURVIVE.
AND TO DECIDE IF YOU STILL NEED IT.

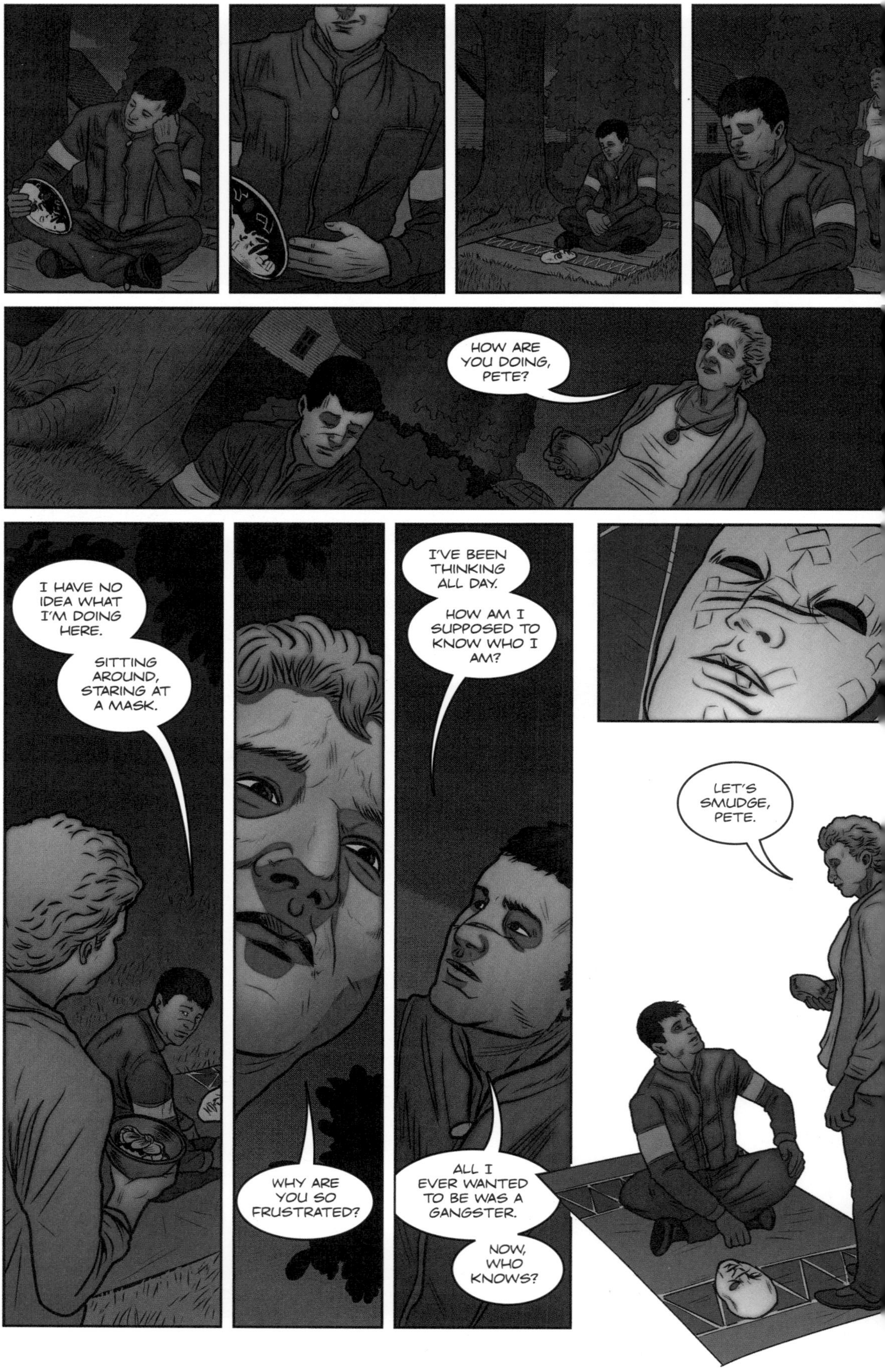
HOW ARE YOU DOING, PETE?
I HAVE NO IDEA WHAT I'M DOING HERE.
SITTING AROUND, STARING AT A MASK.
WHY ARE YOU SO FRUSTRATED?
I'VE BEEN THINKING ALL DAY.
HOW AM I SUPPOSED TO KNOW WHO I AM?
ALL I EVER WANTED TO BE WAS A GANGSTER.
NOW, WHO KNOWS?
LET'S SMUDGE, PETE.

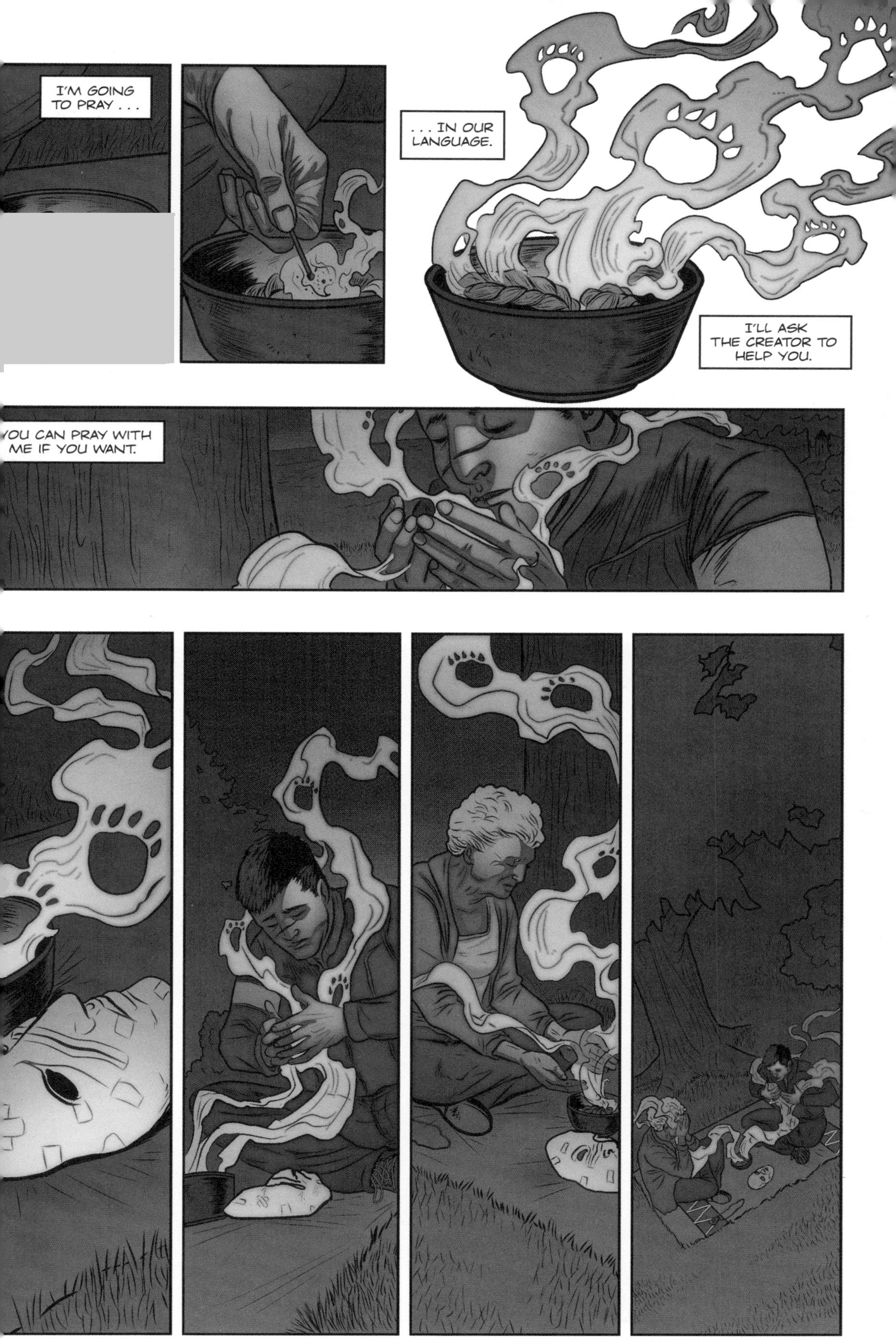
I'M GOING TO PRAY . . .
. . . IN OUR LANGUAGE.
I'LL ASK THE CREATOR TO HELP YOU.
YOU CAN PRAY WITH ME IF YOU WANT.

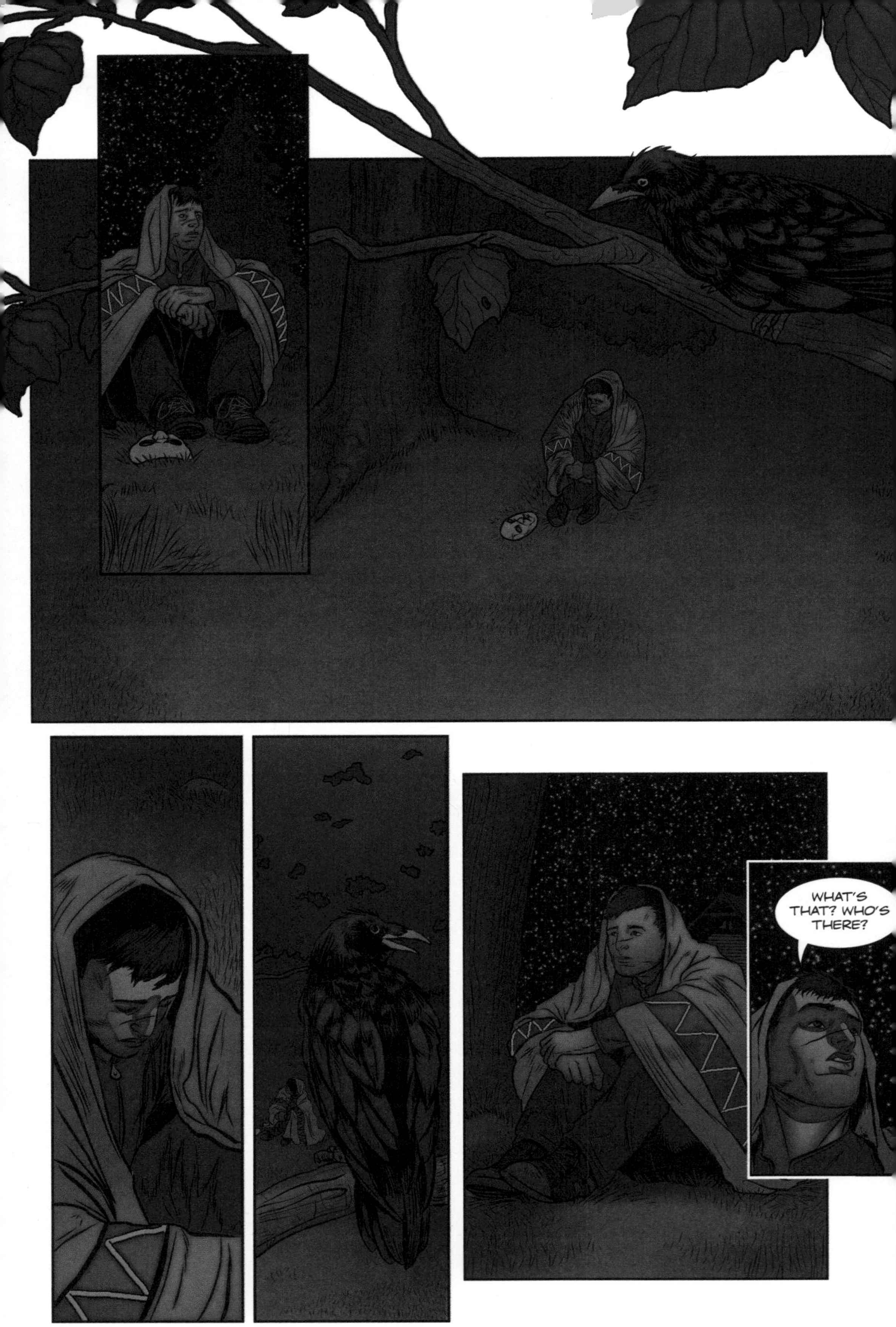
WHAT'S THAT? WHO'S THERE?

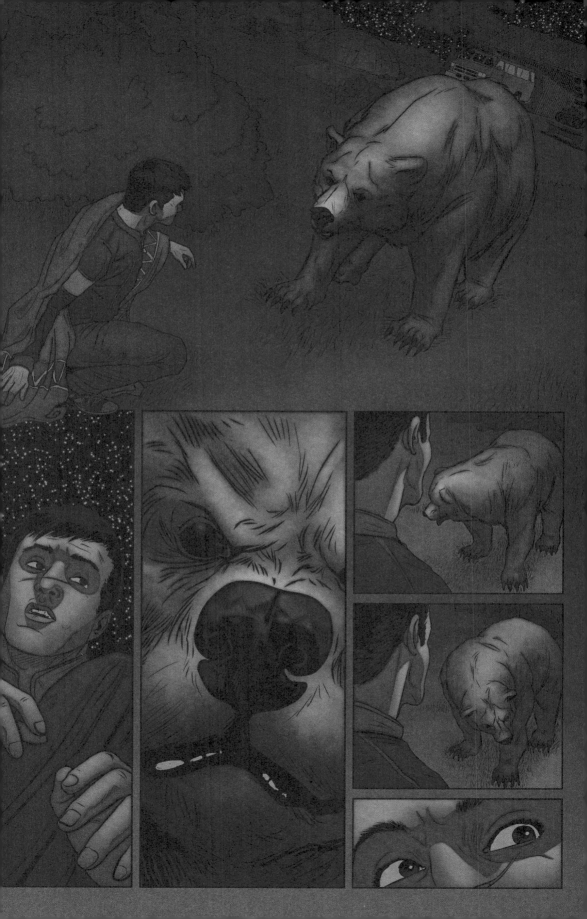

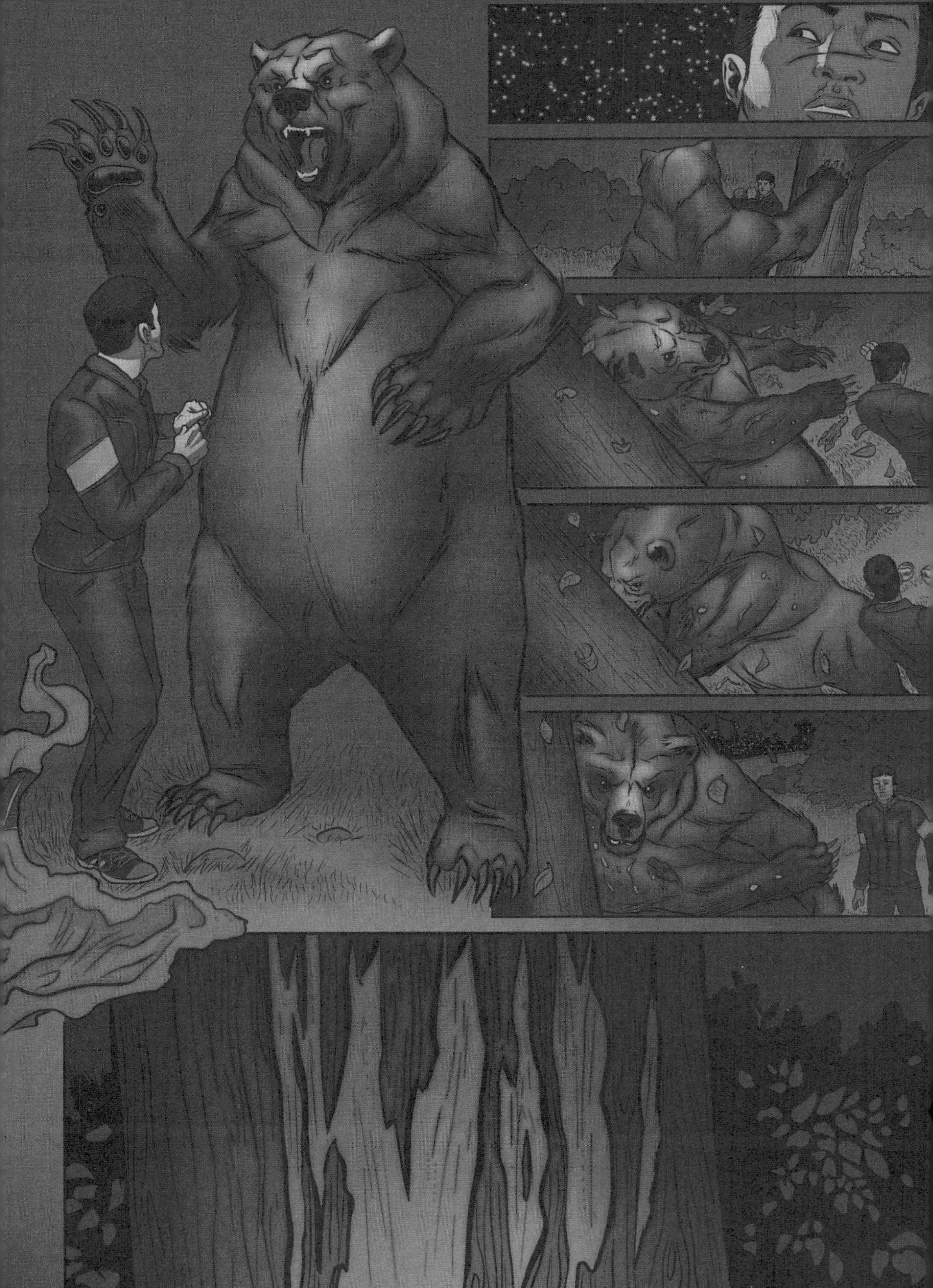

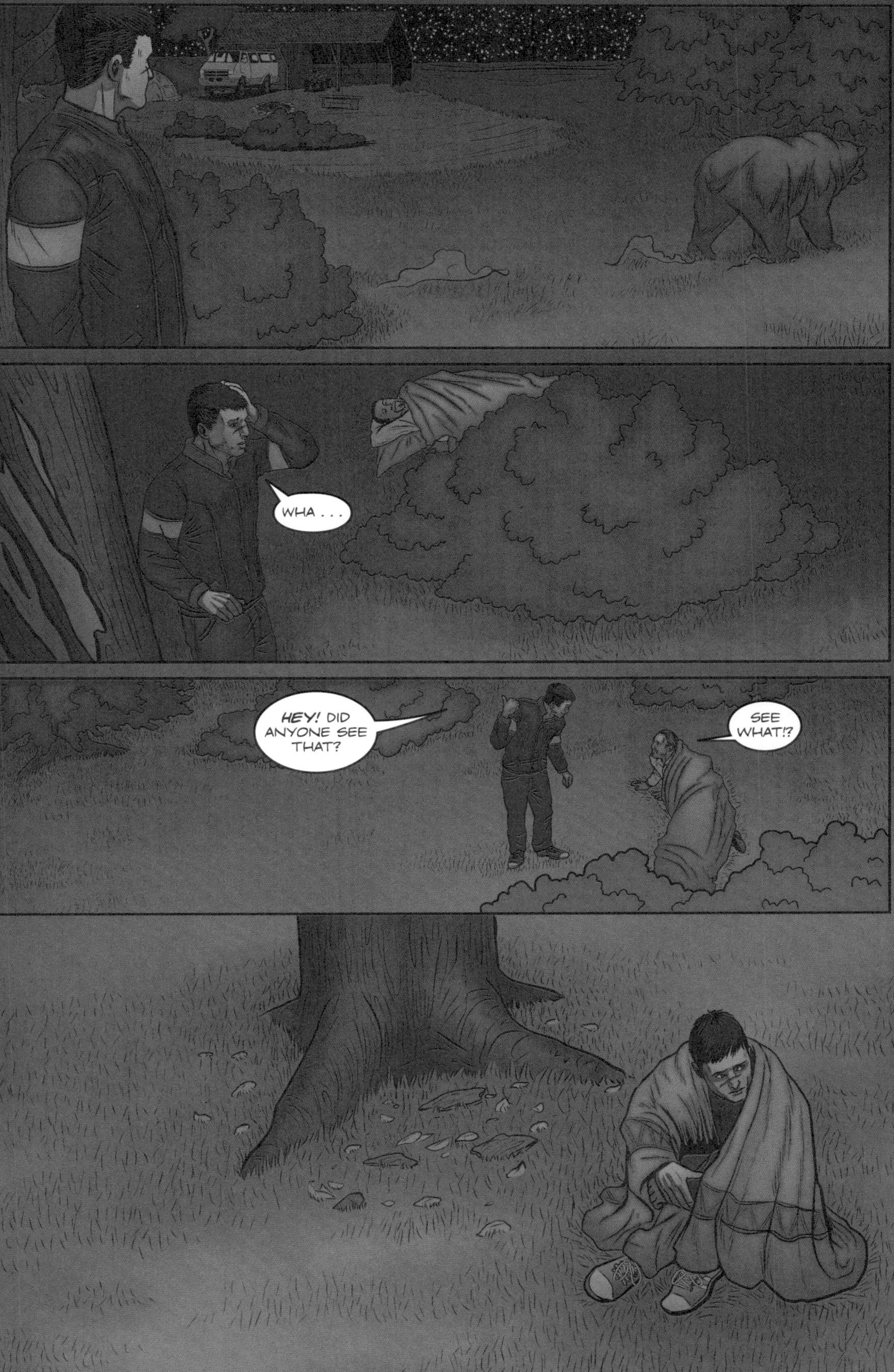
WHA . . .
HEY! DID ANYONE SEE THAT?
SEE WHAT!?

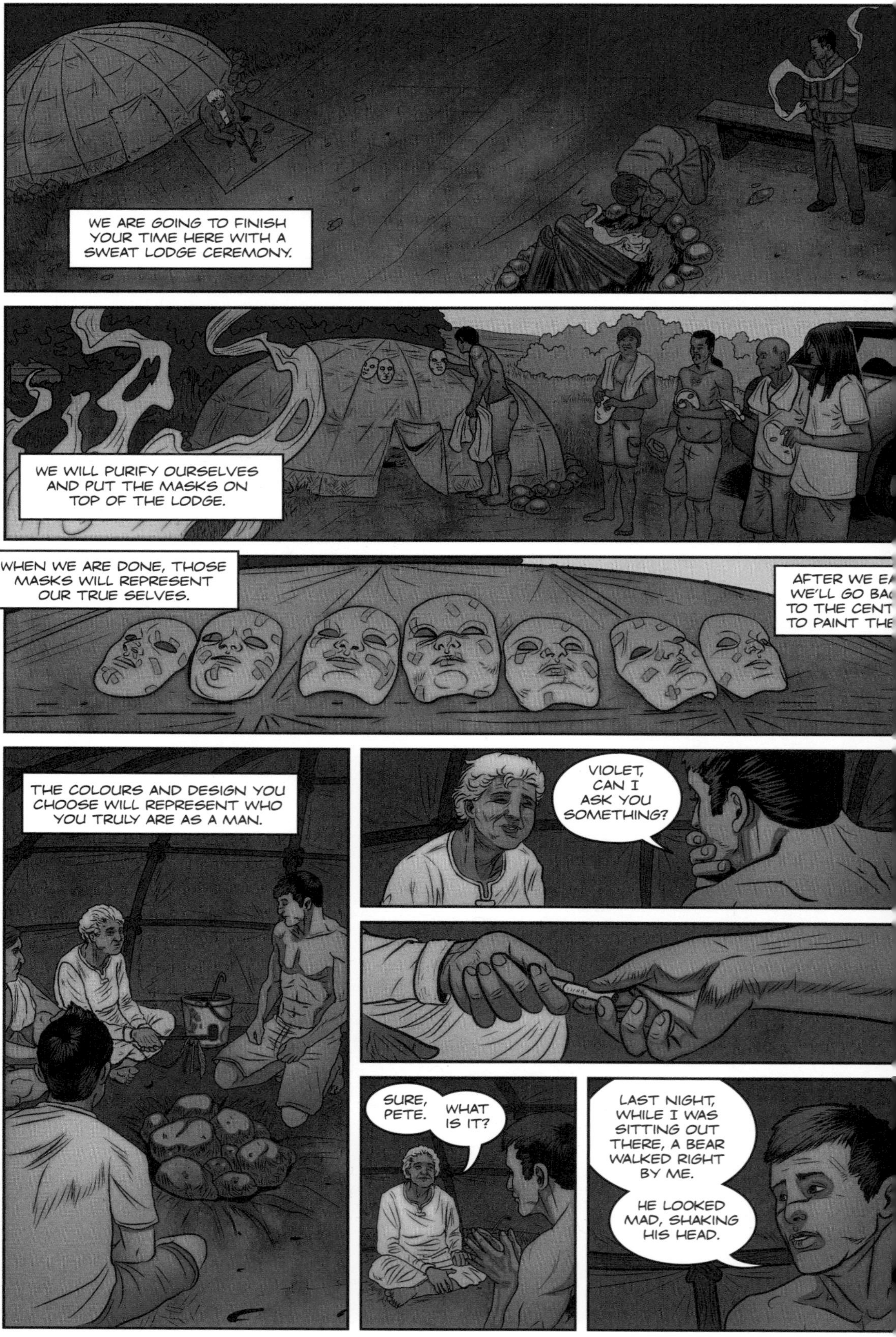
WE ARE GOING TO FINISH YOUR TIME HERE WITH A SWEAT LODGE CEREMONY.
WE WILL PURIFY OURSELVES AND PUT THE MASKS ON TOP OF THE LODGE.
WHEN WE ARE DONE, THOSE MASKS WILL REPRESENT OUR TRUE SELVES.
AFTER WE EA
WE'LL GO BA
TO THE CENT
TO PAINT THE
THE COLOURS AND DESIGN YOU CHOOSE WILL REPRESENT WHO YOU TRULY ARE AS A MAN.
VIOLET, CAN I ASK YOU SOMETHING?
SURE, PETE.
WHAT IS IT?
LAST NIGHT, WHILE I WAS SITTING OUT THERE, A BEAR WALKED RIGHT BY ME.
HE LOOKED MAD, SHAKING HIS HEAD.

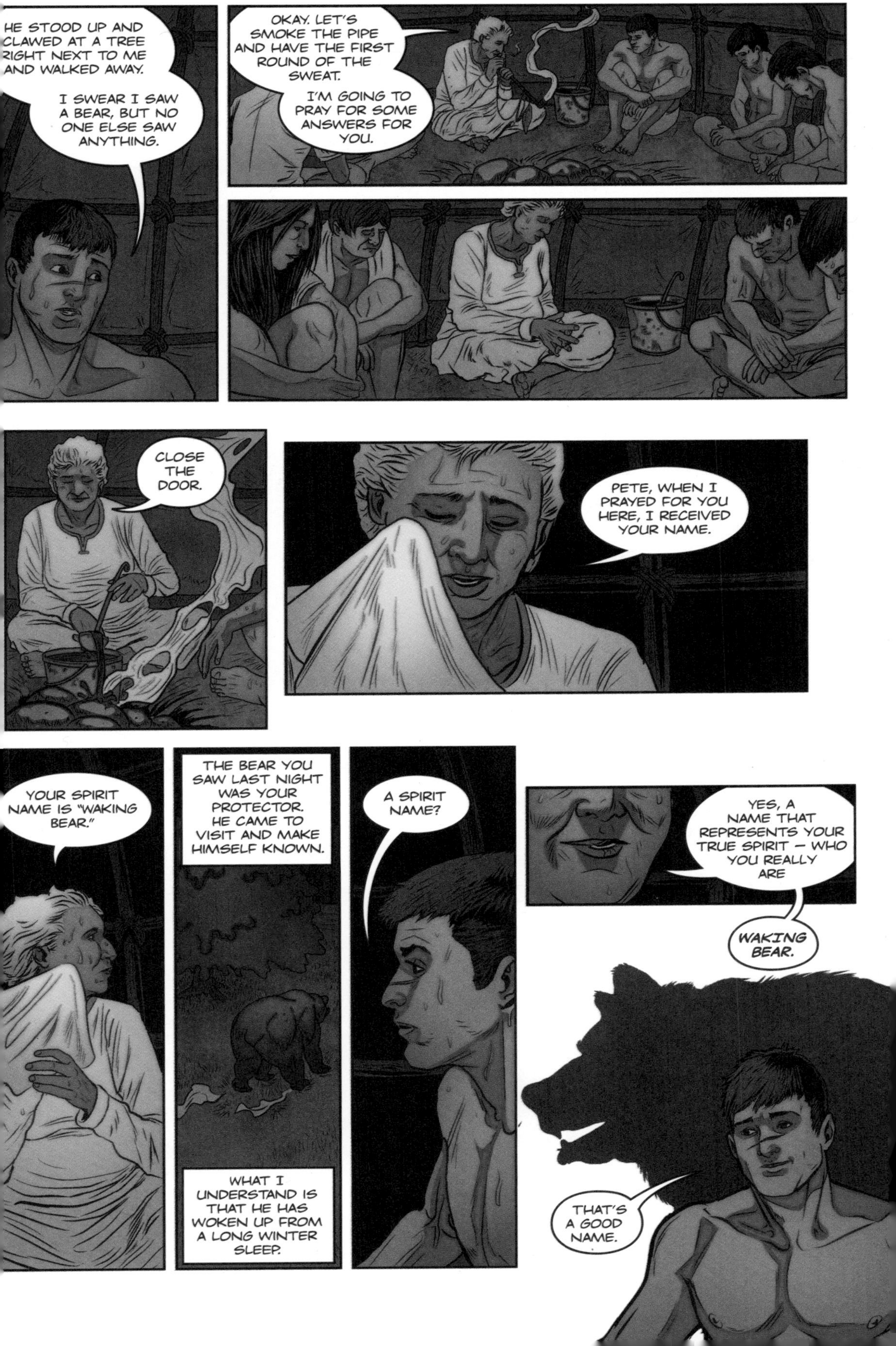
HE STOOD UP AND CLAWED AT A TREE RIGHT NEXT TO ME AND WALKED AWAY.
I SWEAR I SAW A BEAR, BUT NO ONE ELSE SAW ANYTHING.
OKAY. LET'S SMOKE THE PIPE AND HAVE THE FIRST ROUND OF THE SWEAT.
I'M GOING TO PRAY FOR SOME ANSWERS FOR YOU.
CLOSE THE DOOR.
PETE, WHEN I PRAYED FOR YOU HERE, I RECEIVED YOUR NAME.
YOUR SPIRIT NAME IS "WAKING BEAR."
THE BEAR YOU SAW LAST NIGHT WAS YOUR PROTECTOR. HE CAME TO VISIT AND MAKE HIMSELF KNOWN.
WHAT I UNDERSTAND IS THAT HE HAS WOKEN UP FROM A LONG WINTER SLEEP.
A SPIRIT NAME?
YES, A NAME THAT REPRESENTS YOUR TRUE SPIRIT — WHO YOU REALLY ARE
WAKING BEAR.
THAT'S A GOOD NAME.

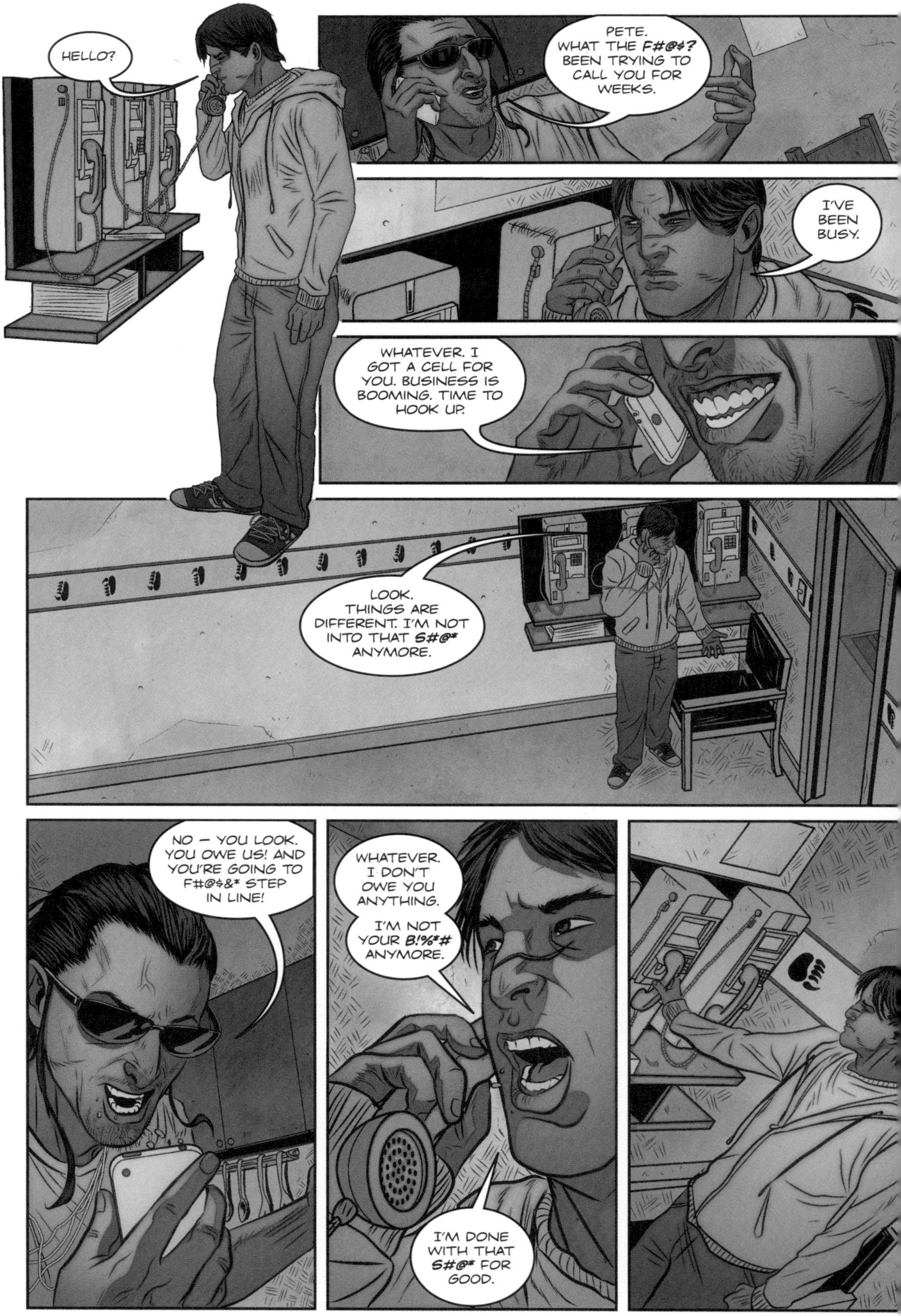
HELLO?
PETE. WHAT THE F#@$? BEEN TRYING TO CALL YOU FOR WEEKS.
I'VE BEEN BUSY.
WHATEVER. I GOT A CELL FOR YOU. BUSINESS IS BOOMING. TIME TO HOOK UP.
LOOK. THINGS ARE DIFFERENT. I'M NOT INTO THAT S#@* ANYMORE.
NO — YOU LOOK. YOU OWE US! AND YOU'RE GOING TO F#@$&* STEP IN LINE!
WHATEVER. I DON'T OWE YOU ANYTHING.
I'M NOT YOUR B!%*# ANYMORE.
I'M DONE WITH THAT S#@* FOR GOOD.

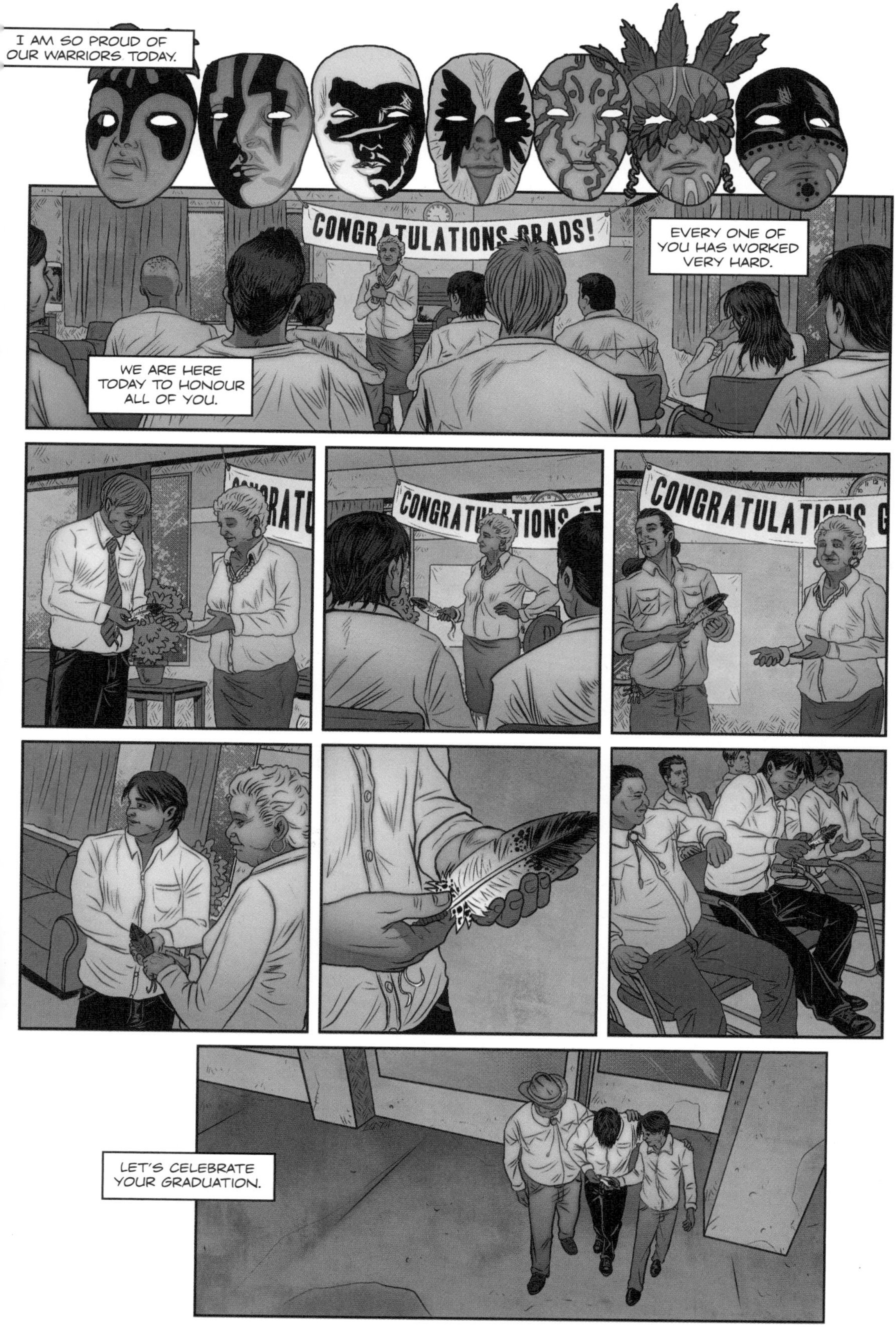
I AM SO PROUD OF OUR WARRIORS TODAY.
CONGRATULATIONS GRADS!
EVERY ONE OF YOU HAS WORKED VERY HARD.
WE ARE HERE TODAY TO HONOUR ALL OF YOU.
CONGRATU
CONGRATULATIONS G
CONGRATULATIONS G
LET'S CELEBRATE YOUR GRADUATION.

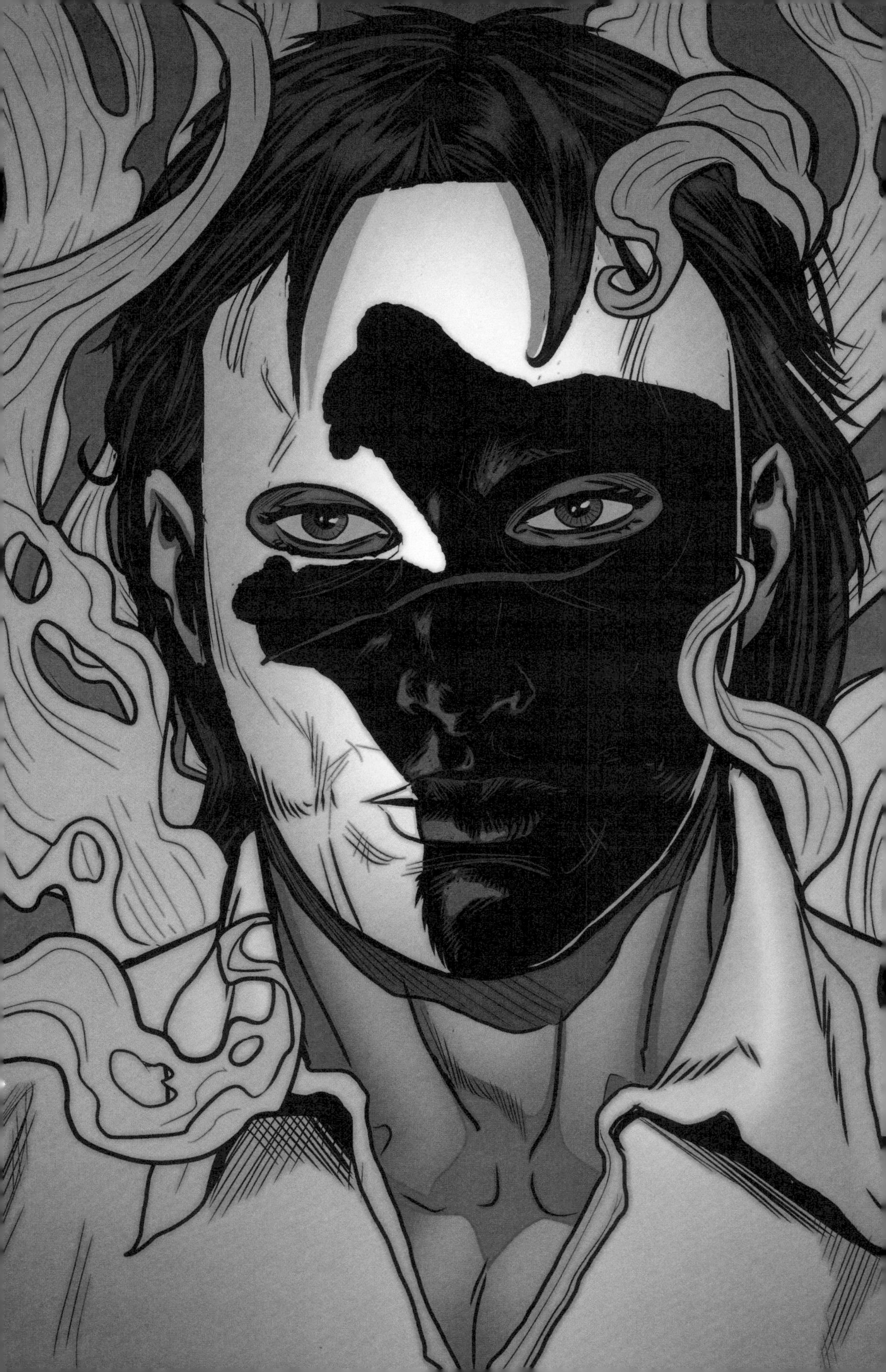

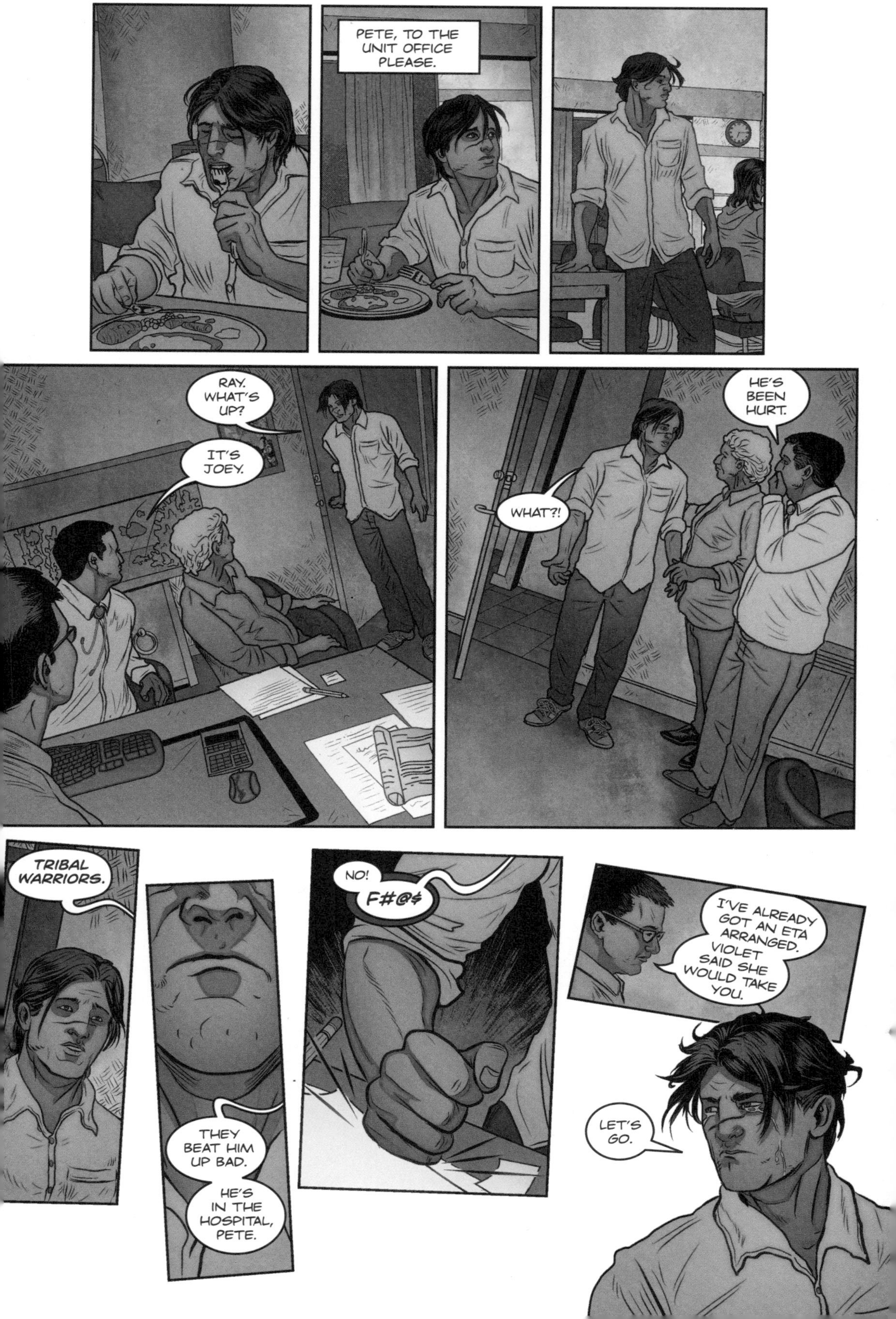
PETE, TO THE UNIT OFFICE PLEASE.
RAY. WHAT'S UP?
IT'S JOEY.
HE'S BEEN HURT.
WHAT?!
TRIBAL WARRIORS.
THEY BEAT HIM UP BAD.
HE'S IN THE HOSPITAL, PETE.
NO!
F#@$
I'VE ALREADY GOT AN ETA ARRANGED. VIOLET SAID SHE WOULD TAKE YOU.
LET'S GO.

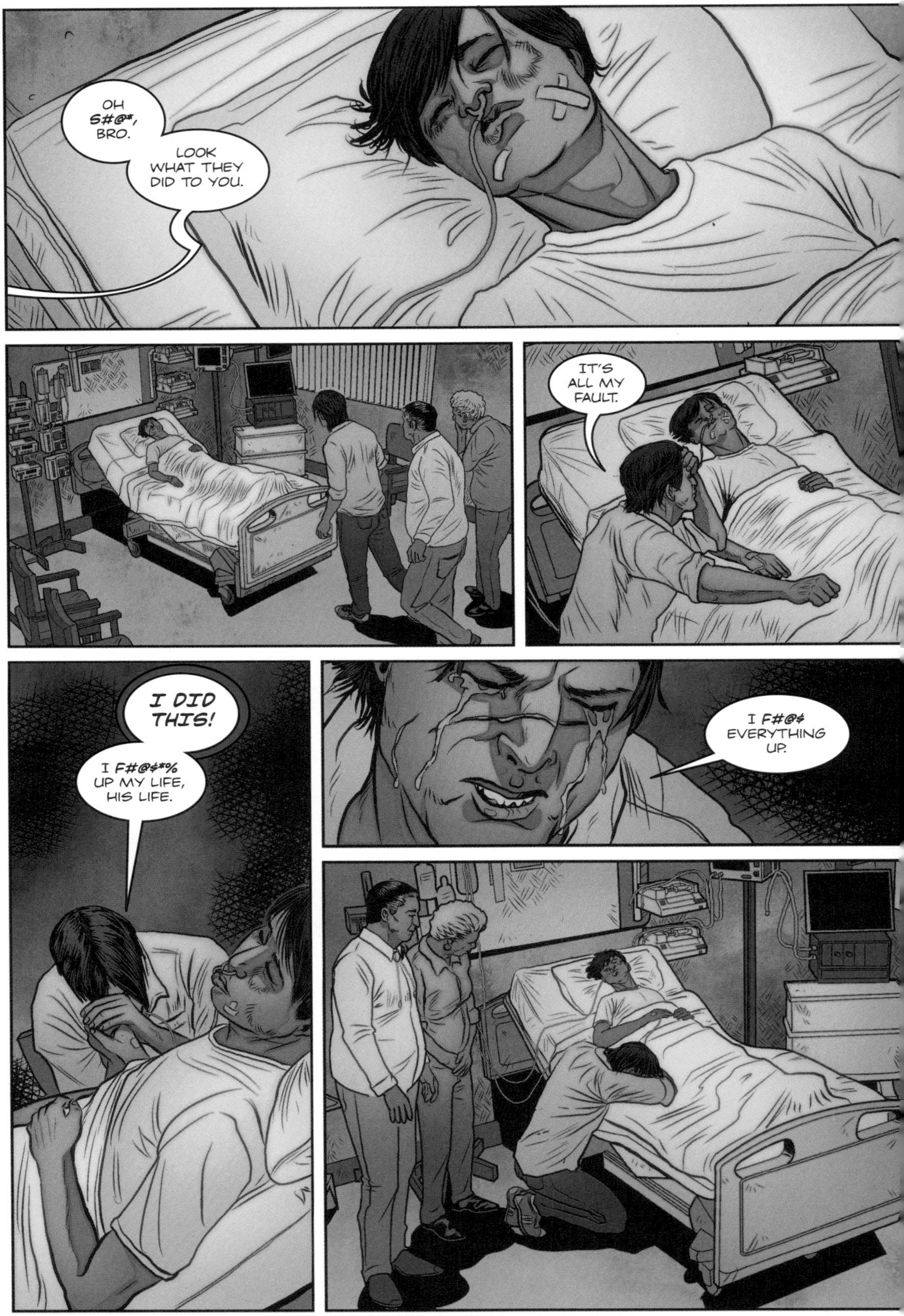
OH S#@*, BRO.
LOOK WHAT THEY DID TO YOU.
IT'S ALL MY FAULT.
I DID THIS!
I F#@$*% UP MY LIFE, HIS LIFE.
I F#@$ EVERYTHING UP.

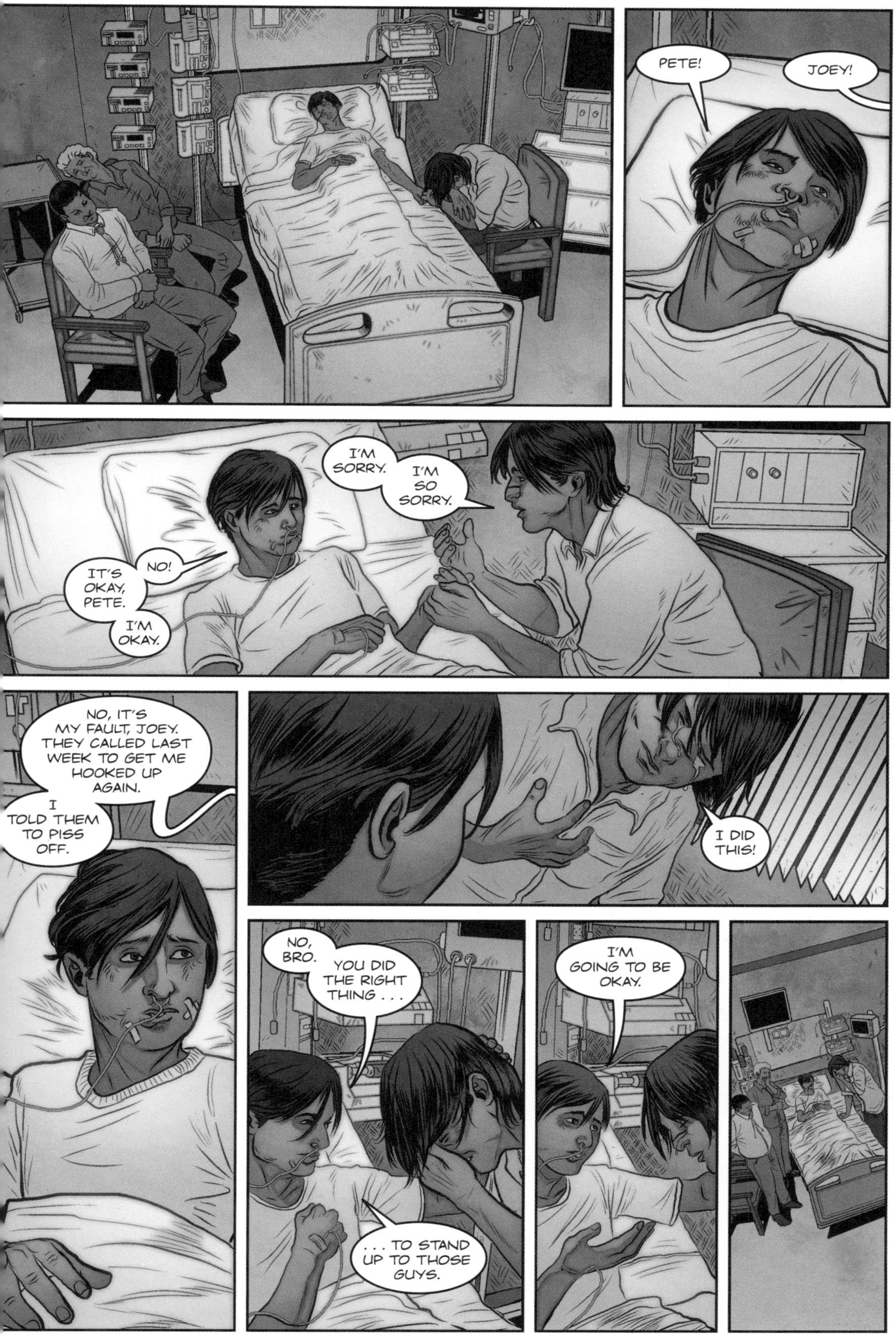
PETE!
JOEY!
I'M SORRY.
I'M SO SORRY.
NO!
IT'S OKAY, PETE.
I'M OKAY.
NO, IT'S MY FAULT, JOEY. THEY CALLED LAST WEEK TO GET ME HOOKED UP AGAIN.
I TOLD THEM TO PISS OFF.
I DID THIS!
NO, BRO.
YOU DID THE RIGHT THING . . .
. . . TO STAND UP TO THOSE GUYS.
I'M GOING TO BE OKAY.

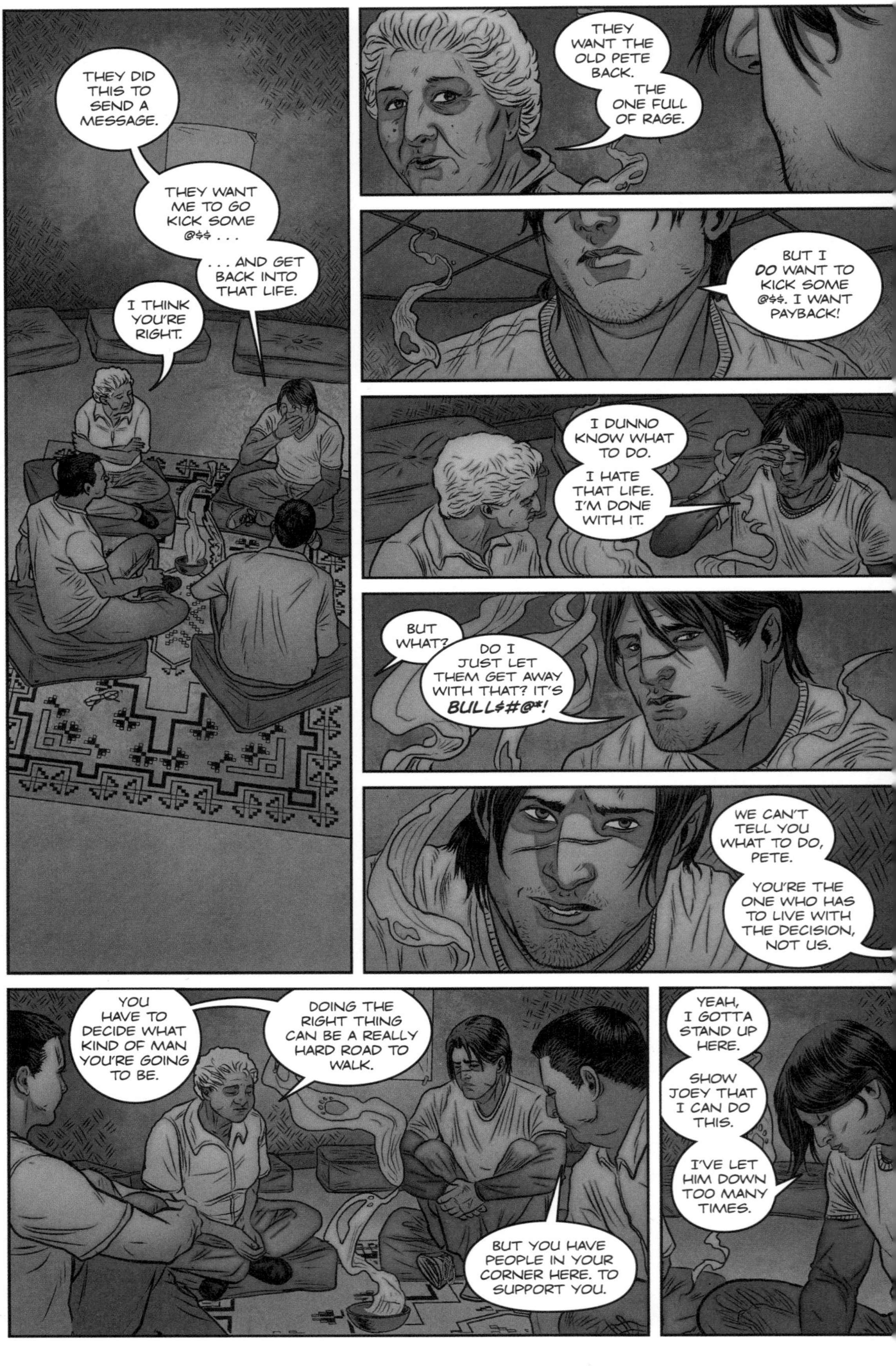
THEY DID THIS TO SEND A MESSAGE.
THEY WANT ME TO GO KICK SOME @$$ . . .
. . . AND GET BACK INTO THAT LIFE.
I THINK YOU'RE RIGHT.
THEY WANT THE OLD PETE BACK.
THE ONE FULL OF RAGE.
BUT I DO WANT TO KICK SOME @$$. I WANT PAYBACK!
I DUNNO KNOW WHAT TO DO.
I HATE THAT LIFE. I'M DONE WITH IT.
BUT WHAT?
DO I JUST LET THEM GET AWAY WITH THAT? IT'S BULL$#@*!
WE CAN'T TELL YOU WHAT TO DO, PETE.
YOU'RE THE ONE WHO HAS TO LIVE WITH THE DECISION, NOT US.
YOU HAVE TO DECIDE WHAT KIND OF MAN YOU'RE GOING TO BE.
DOING THE RIGHT THING CAN BE A REALLY HARD ROAD TO WALK.
BUT YOU HAVE PEOPLE IN YOUR CORNER HERE. TO SUPPORT YOU.
YEAH, I GOTTA STAND UP HERE.
SHOW JOEY THAT I CAN DO THIS.
I'VE LET HIM DOWN TOO MANY TIMES.

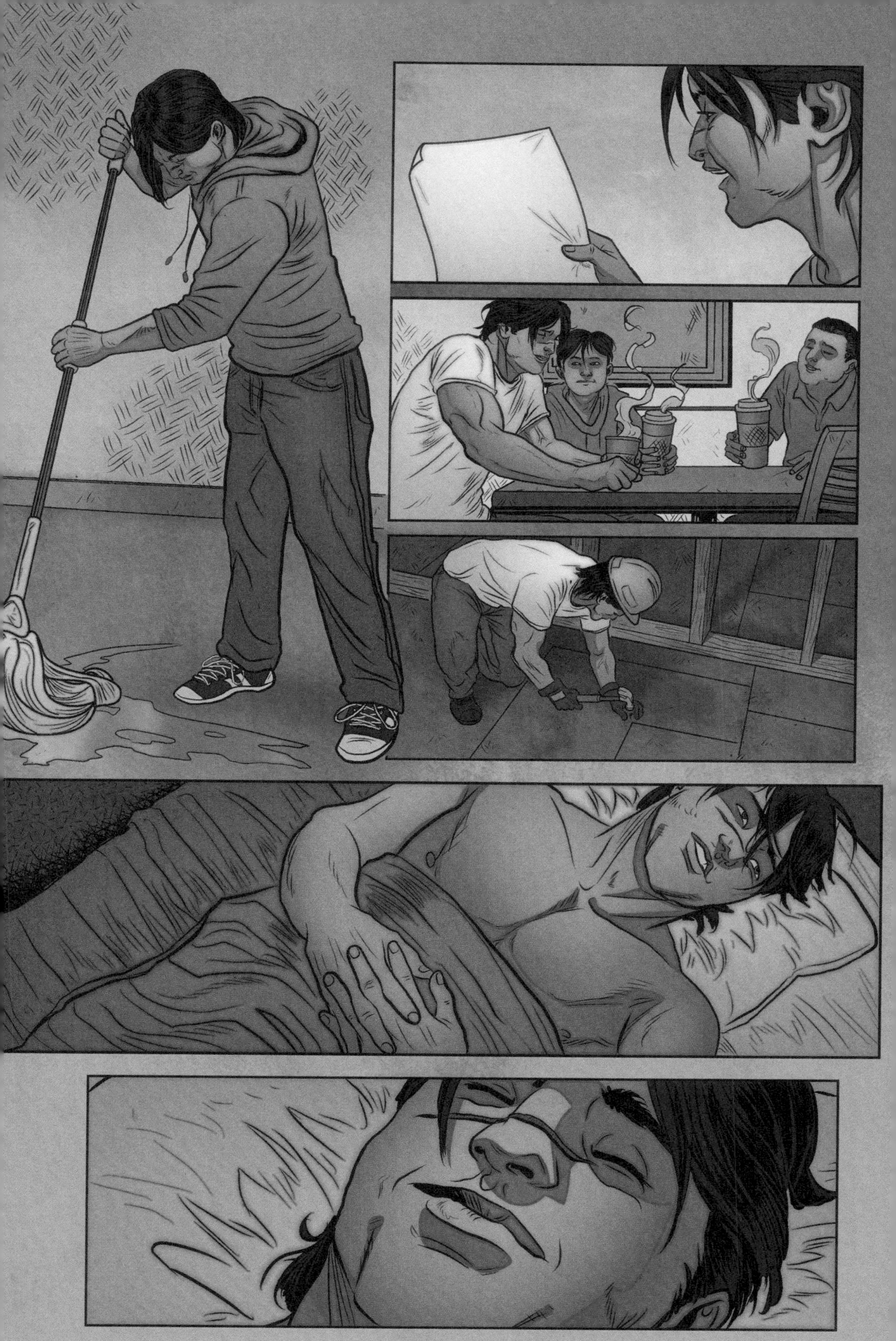

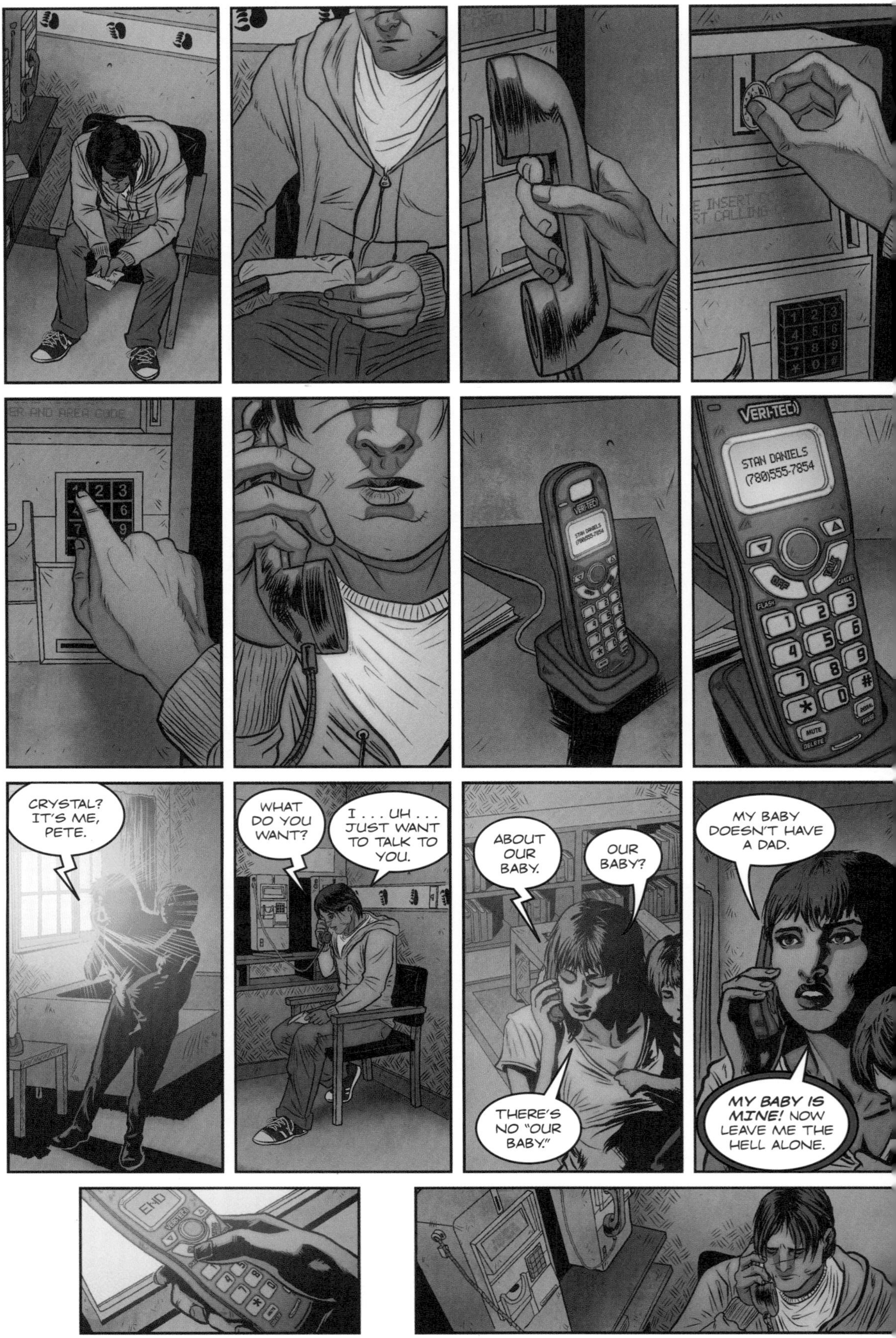
STAN DANIELS
(780)555-7854
CRYSTAL? IT'S ME, PETE.
WHAT DO YOU WANT?
I . . . UH . . . JUST WANT TO TALK TO YOU.
ABOUT OUR BABY.
OUR BABY?
THERE'S NO "OUR BABY."
MY BABY DOESN'T HAVE A DAD.
MY BABY IS MINE! NOW LEAVE ME THE HELL ALONE.
END

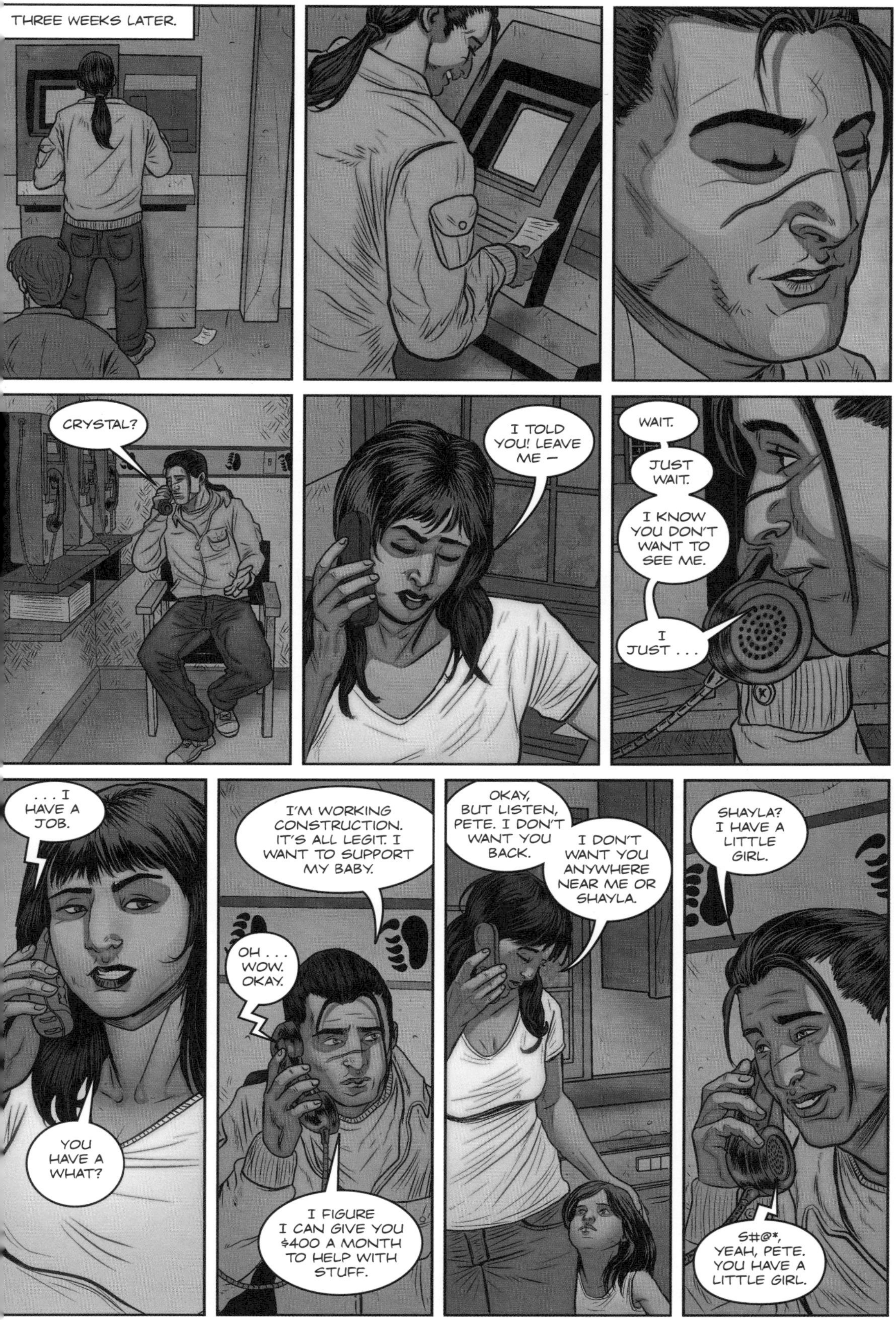
THREE WEEKS LATER.
CRYSTAL?
I TOLD YOU! LEAVE ME —
WAIT.
JUST WAIT.
I KNOW YOU DON'T WANT TO SEE ME.
I JUST . . .
. . . I HAVE A JOB.
YOU HAVE A WHAT?
I'M WORKING CONSTRUCTION. IT'S ALL LEGIT. I WANT TO SUPPORT MY BABY.
OH . . . WOW. OKAY.
I FIGURE I CAN GIVE YOU $400 A MONTH TO HELP WITH STUFF.
OKAY, BUT LISTEN, PETE. I DON'T WANT YOU BACK.
I DON'T WANT YOU ANYWHERE NEAR ME OR SHAYLA.
SHAYLA? I HAVE A LITTLE GIRL.
S#@*, YEAH, PETE. YOU HAVE A LITTLE GIRL.

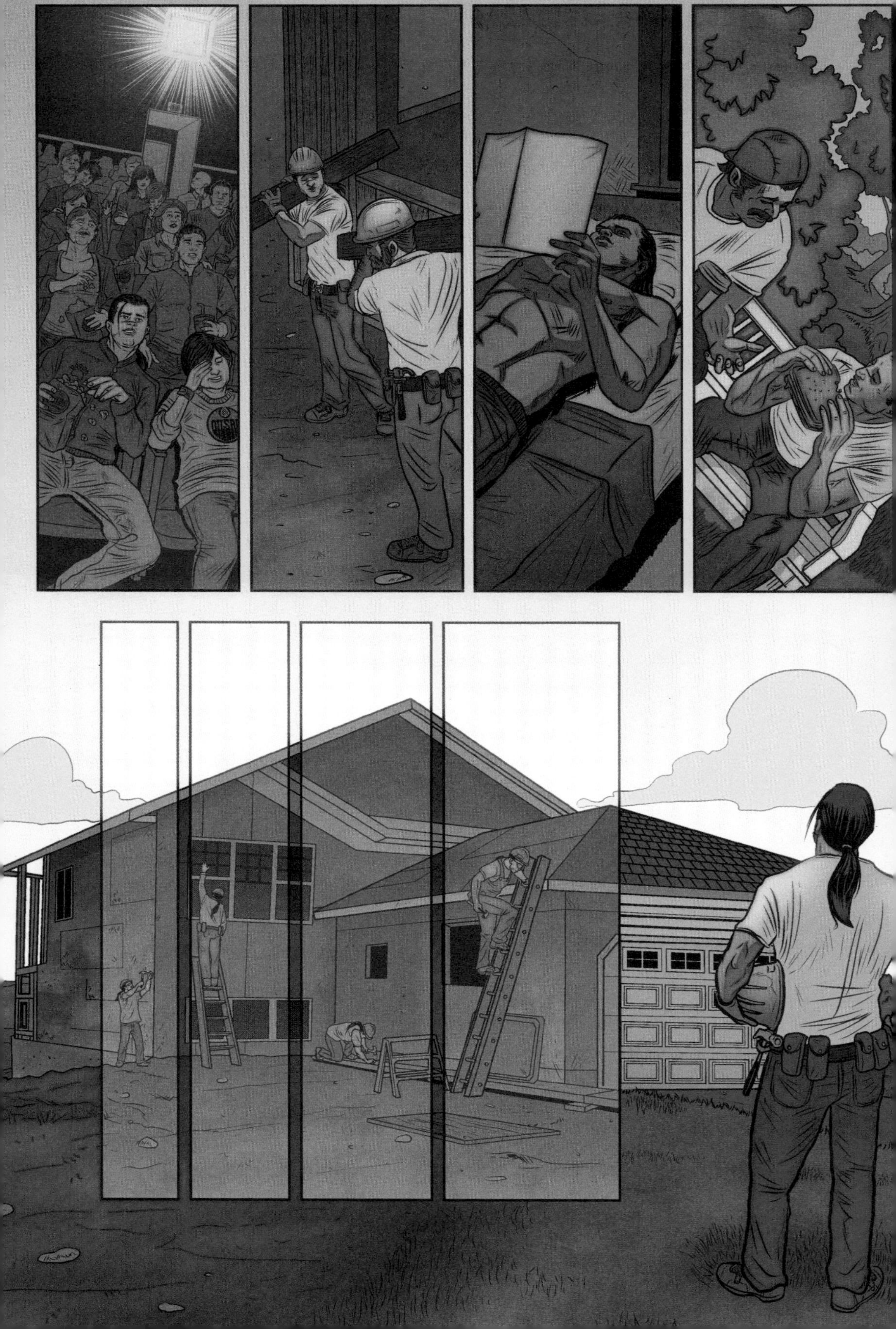

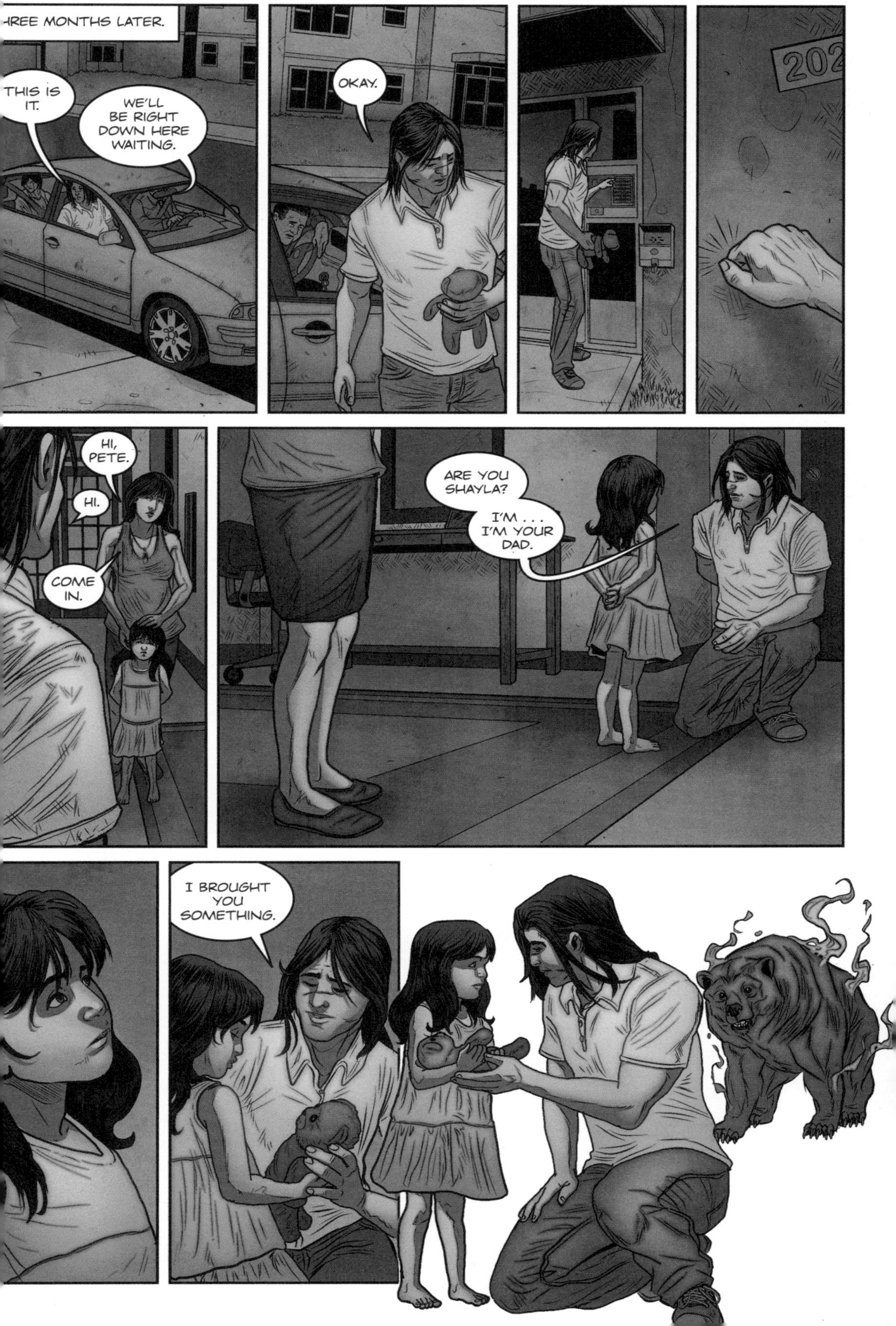
HREE MONTHS LATER.
THIS IS IT.
WE'LL BE RIGHT DOWN HERE WAITING.
OKAY.
202
HI, PETE.
HI.
COME IN.
ARE YOU SHAYLA?
I'M . . . I'M YOUR DAD.
I BROUGHT YOU SOMETHING.

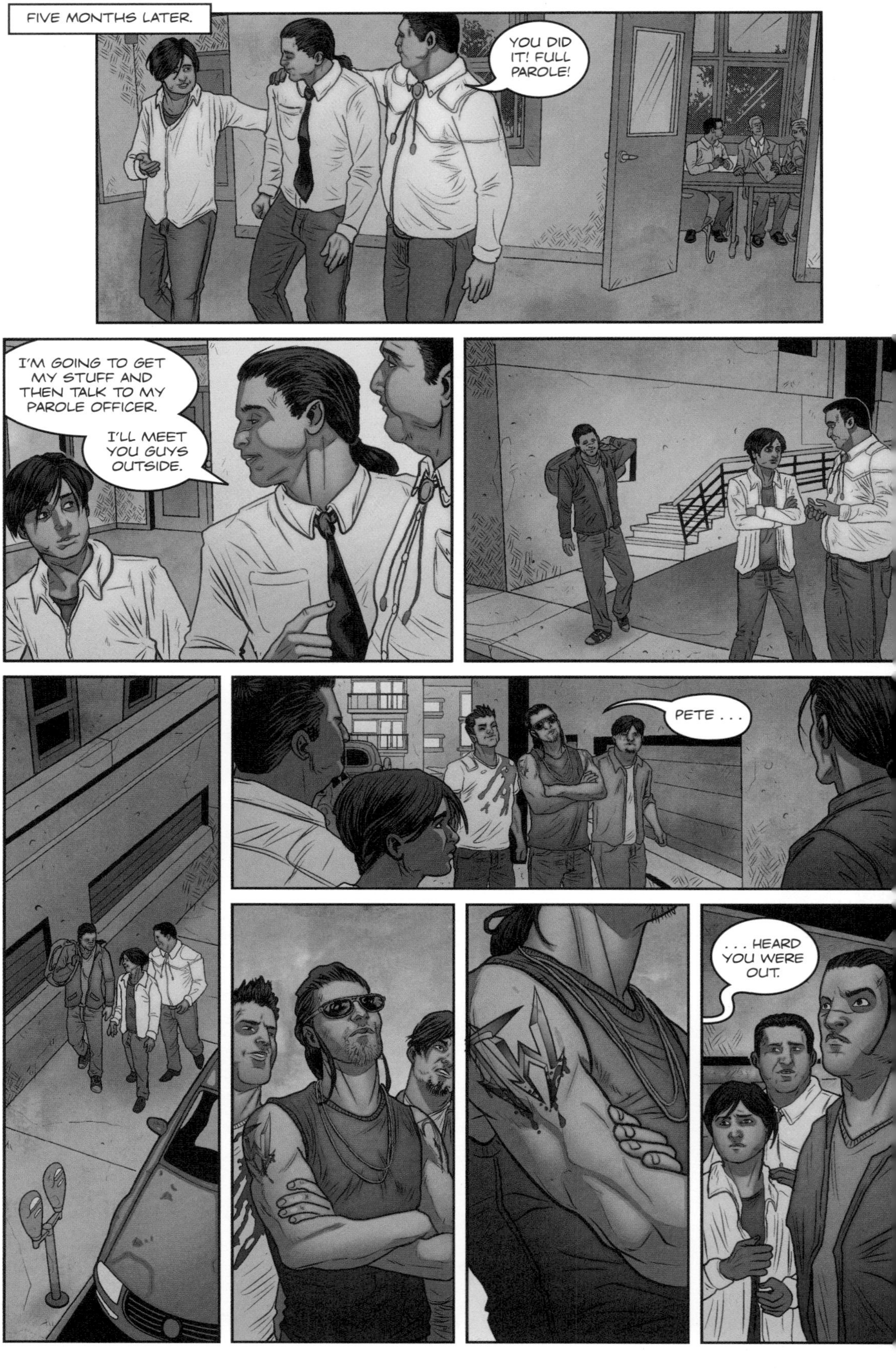
FIVE MONTHS LATER.
YOU DID IT! FULL PAROLE!
I'M GOING TO GET MY STUFF AND THEN TALK TO MY PAROLE OFFICER.
I'LL MEET YOU GUYS OUTSIDE.
PETE . . .
. . . HEARD YOU WERE OUT.

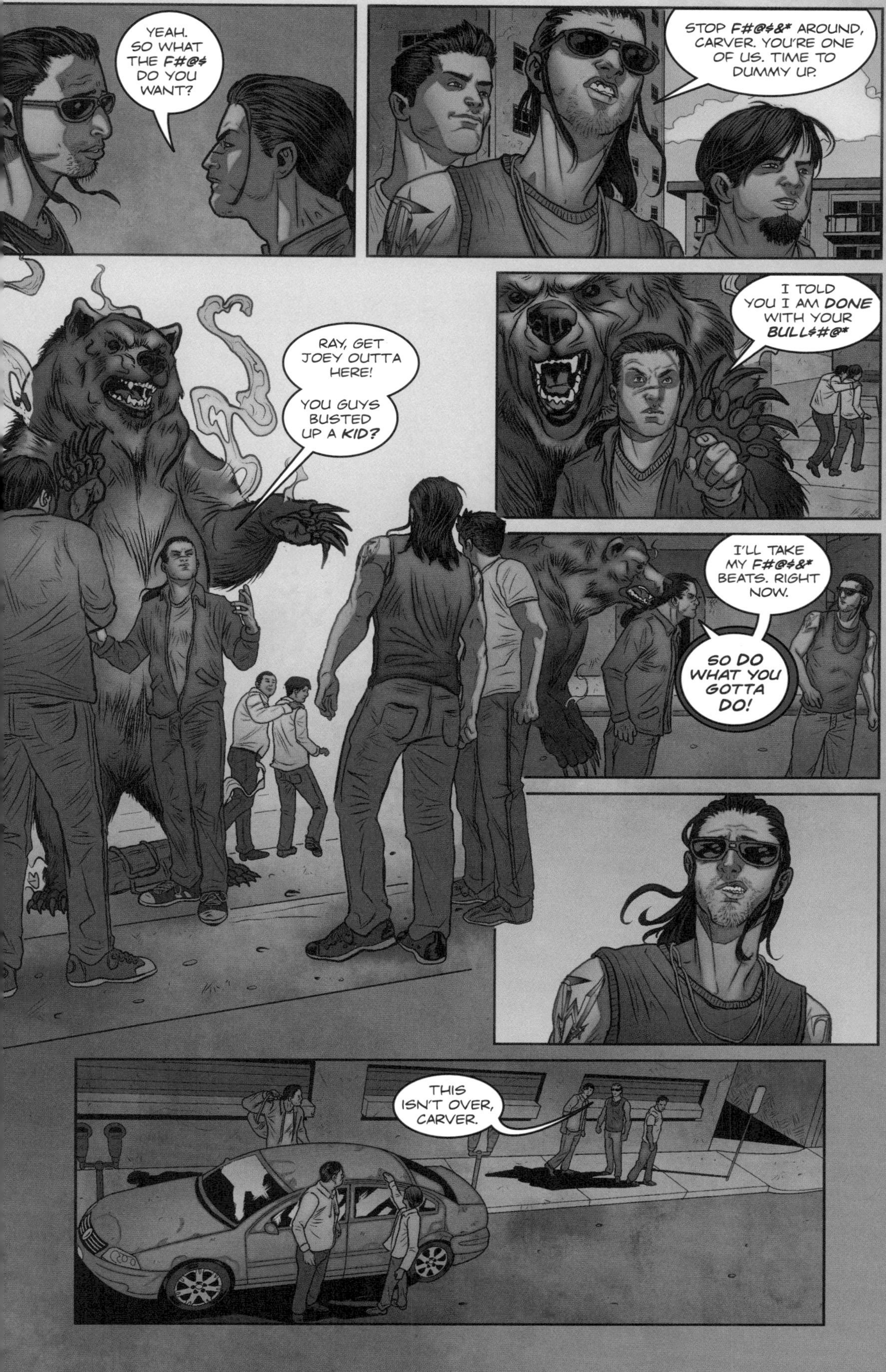
YEAH. SO WHAT THE F#@$ DO YOU WANT?
STOP F#@$&* AROUND, CARVER. YOU'RE ONE OF US. TIME TO DUMMY UP.
RAY, GET JOEY OUTTA HERE!
YOU GUYS BUSTED UP A KID?
I TOLD YOU I AM DONE WITH YOUR BULL$#@*
I'LL TAKE MY F#@$&* BEATS. RIGHT NOW.
SO DO WHAT YOU GOTTA DO!
THIS ISN'T OVER, CARVER.

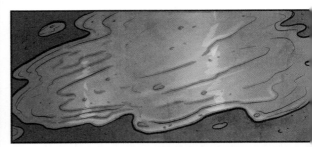

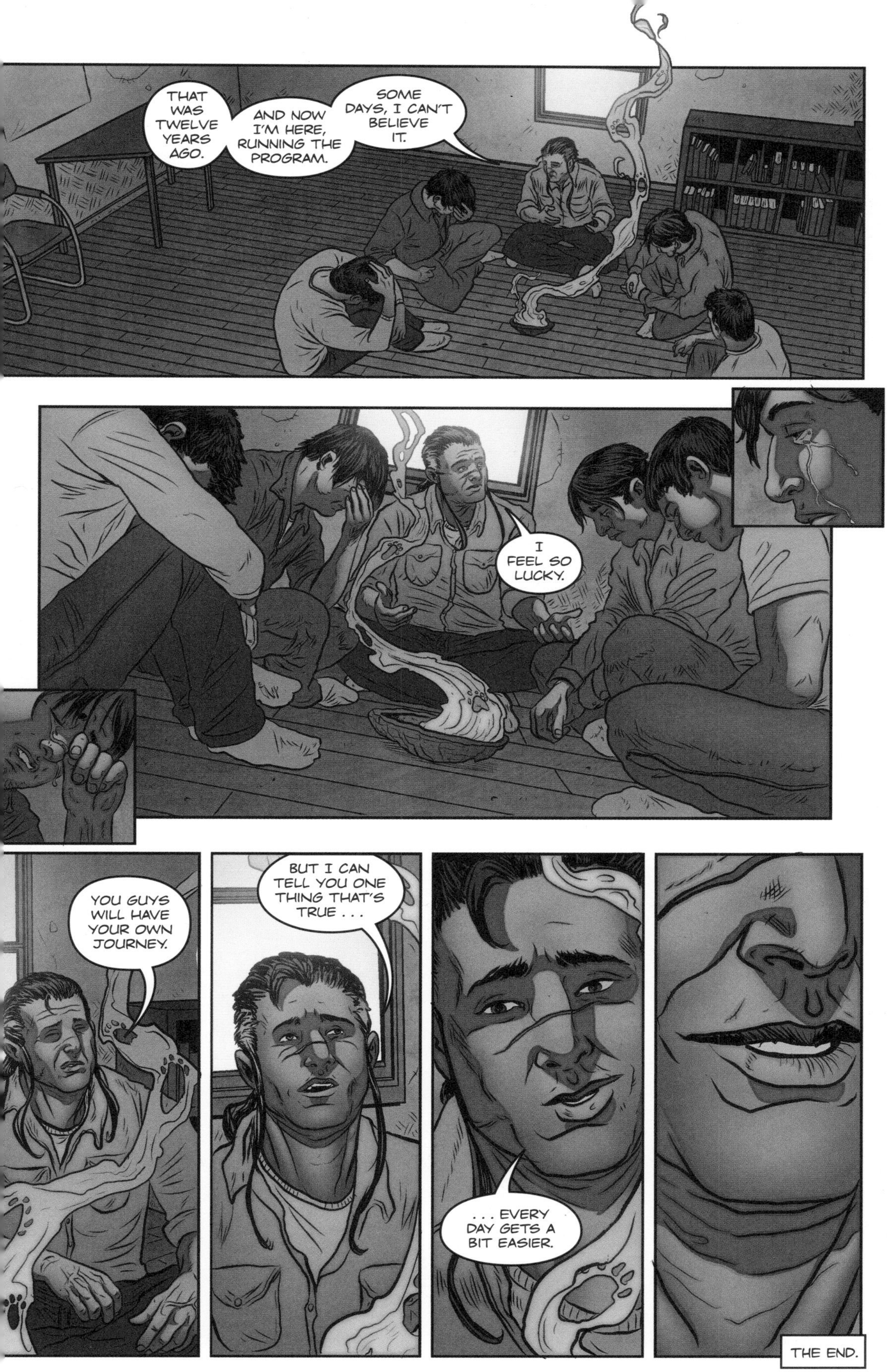
THAT WAS TWELVE YEARS AGO.
AND NOW I'M HERE, RUNNING THE PROGRAM.
SOME DAYS, I CAN'T BELIEVE IT.
I FEEL SO LUCKY.
YOU GUYS WILL HAVE YOUR OWN JOURNEY.
BUT I CAN TELL YOU ONE THING THAT'S TRUE . . .
. . . EVERY DAY GETS A BIT EASIER.
THE END.

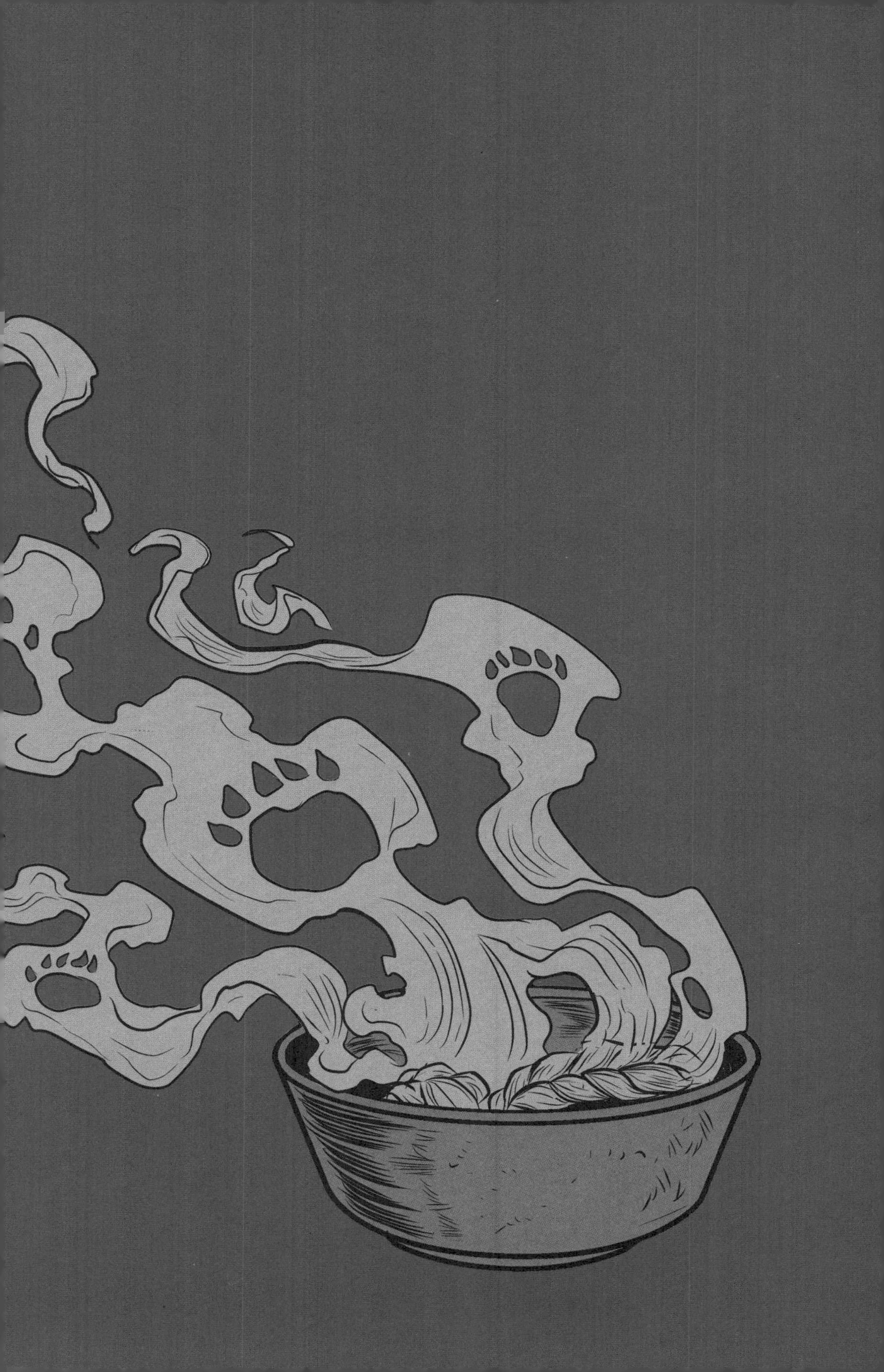

ABOUT THE IN SEARCH OF YOUR WARRIOR PROGRAM

One of the most devastating outcomes of colonial policy in Canada is the overrepresentation of Aboriginal people in the criminal justice system and of Aboriginal children in government care. For many Aboriginal people and families, the legacy of historical trauma has been the intergenerational transmission of hopelessness, helplessness, and powerlessness.

The In Search of Your Warrior program provides an intensive historical-trauma-healing process for incarcerated Aboriginal men. It takes courage, as well as profound emotional and spiritual tenacity, to complete it. It's been one of my most fulfilling and inspiring responsibilities to oversee program facilitator training, curriculum development, and implementation for Native Counselling Services of Alberta (NCSA). Between 2001 and 2009, I completed Ph.D. research that looked at the efforts of NCSA to create the space required to develop the program and how historical trauma healing programs for Aboriginal offenders can build resilience in families and communities.

During that same period of time, I offered protocol to learned Ceremonialists and Elders, and participated in numerous ceremonies and Elder teaching circles. I was (and still am) seeking the original, traditional information given to Cree and Indigenous families. In addition, I sought out Indigenous philosophers and went to ceremonies as a part of my own healing journey.

What I've learned is that colonial policy has caused a great deal of intergenerational pain in many Aboriginal people and is the root cause of many present-day issues that Aboriginal people face. Healing historical trauma is an emotional, physical, psychological, and spiritual process. In the end, I came to underst personally and deeply that the processes of hea and resilience building are one and the same.

In addition, a model emerged that helped m understand what conditions need to exist to b resilience. In 2011 this model of building resilie was formally adopted by the NCSA Board of Direc as well as its managers and field staff; it guides development and delivery of all programs and serv offered by the agency.

Illustrated on the facing page, the model demonstr our interconnectedness with a spiral. The p represent the factors that need to be in place fo to keep that spiral whole, beautiful, and with hea boundaries. First, we have to reclaim a worldview has firm rules and values that makes our relations a priority, and a worldview that has firm rules values that informs our interactions with every o living being. Second, we need to reconcile our bro relationships — with ourselves, our families, community, and our Creator. Finally, we have to ourselves. No one can do it for us — it is our pers and sacred responsibility.

I believe those are the hallmarks of Pete's hea journey: reconciliation with members of his family development of a positive identity as protector provider, and a strong sense of hope and confide that he can be a good man and make good decisi Thank you for taking the time to walk beside Pe his transformation.

— Patti LaBoucane-Benson

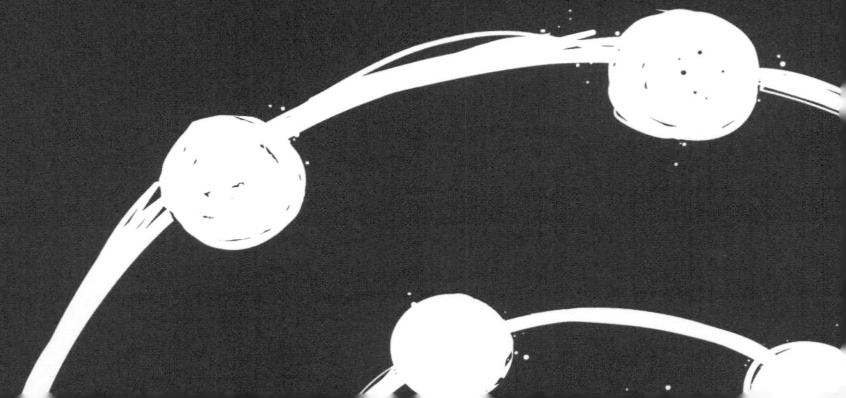

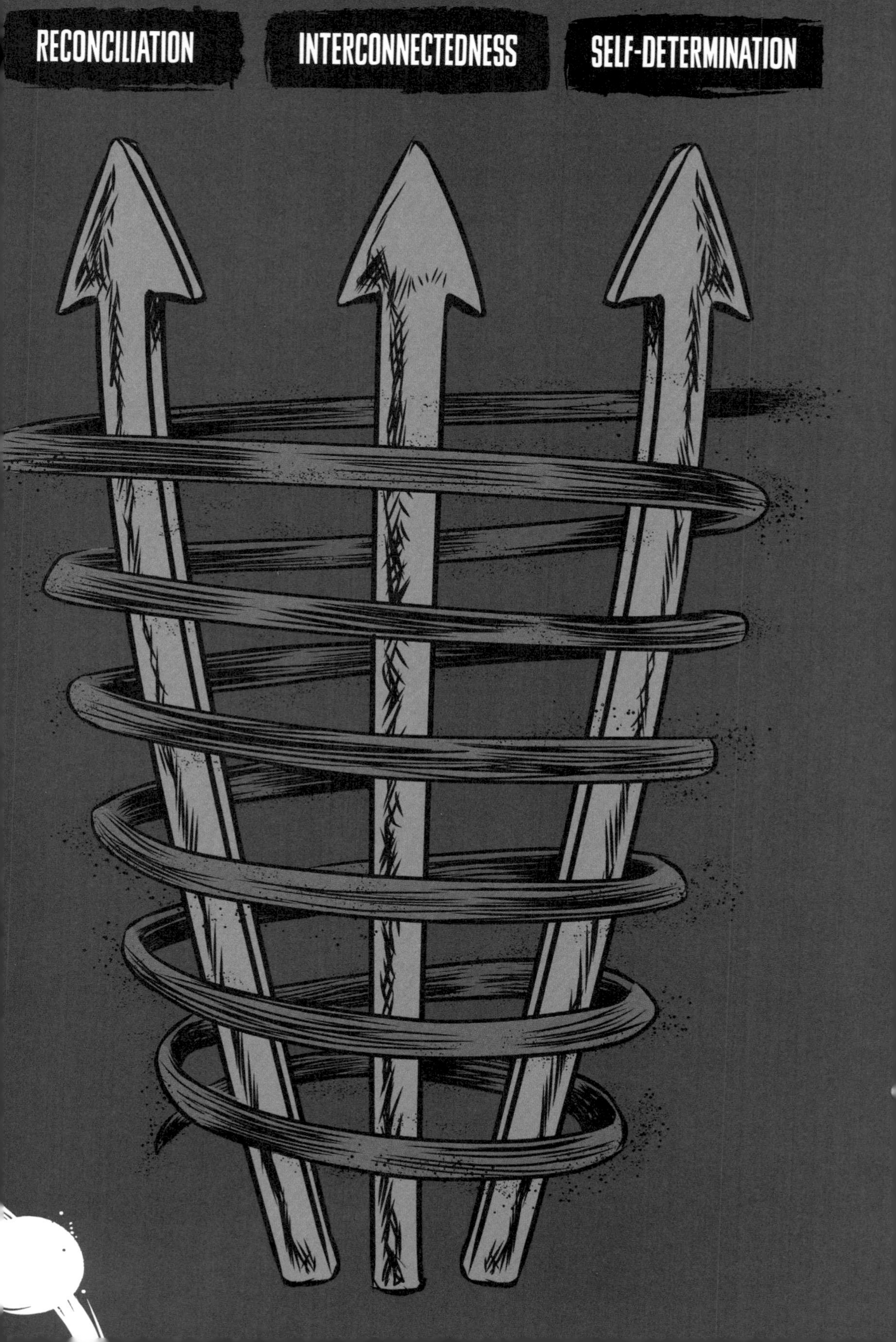
RECONCILIATION
INTERCONNECTEDNESS
SELF-DETERMINATION

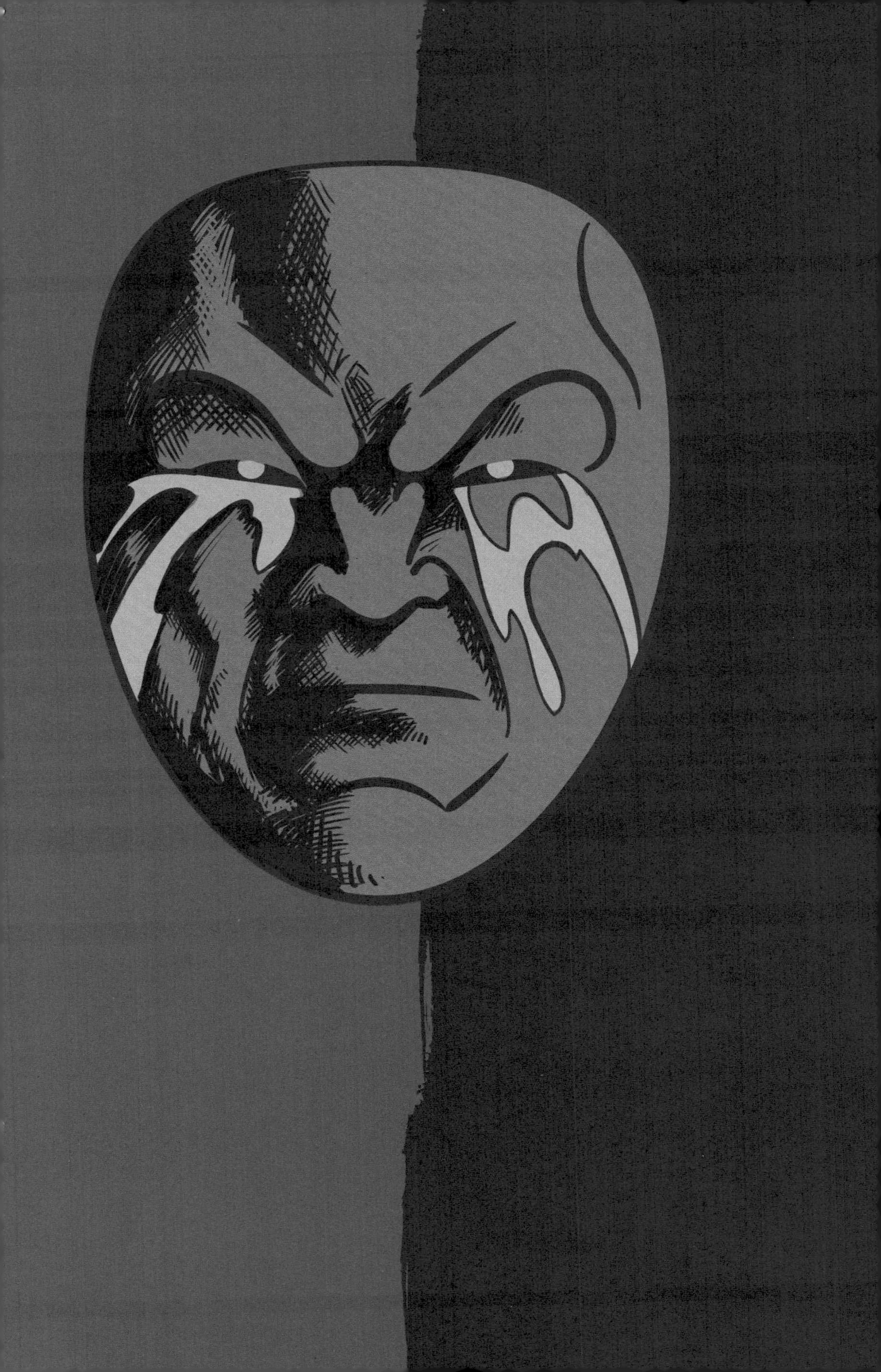

THANK YOU

ant to acknowledge and thank the Board of Directors at Native unselling Services of Alberta for their unwavering support of this earch and their wisdom that guides the agency. Thank you also to management team and field staff who breathe life into the service very model — their compassion and dedication to the people serve inspires me everyday. Special thanks to Victoria Whalen has been my co-keeper of the Warrior programs over the past en years. The character of Violet was inspired by Victoria, who is fted facilitator, trainer, Ceremonialist, and healer. The character of er Roy was inspired by Wil Campbell, another Warrior trainer, who dedicated his life to helping his community. Although Violet's story is npletely fictional, the characters of Violet and Roy are meant to honour Victoria and Wil heir outstanding contribution to the healing of so many men and women. I would also like hank Greg Miller for his assistance, feedback, and management of the book production. I so blessed to work for and with the NCSA team. I also want to acknowledge Kelly Mellings his dedication to the project. He participated in a sweat lodge ceremony, as well as visited aximum security prison, Stan Daniels Healing Centre, and the Blue Quills residential ool, to really understand what he was drawing. His thoroughness, attention to detail, inspired illustrations honour the story. Finally, this book would not exist without the mplary leadership and input of Allen Benson, CEO of NCSA, who walked beside every step of the research project and model implementation. Hi Hi!

atti LaBoucane-Benson

nks to all the people whose stories have inspired this novel. Native Counselling Services of Alberta for opening my s and my heart many, many times. My experiences Elders, residential school survivors, and isolated hern communities, participating in smudges and ats, meeting Warrior graduates and witnessing ceremony have all changed how I think and feel ut First Nations people. I hope my art has shared t I have learned. Thank you to Patti for trusting me such an important story; your strength, knowledge, passion have inspired me. I also want to thank Greg, magically morphs into any role needed, while always aining a true friend. My wife and daughters sacrificed their with me to allow the extra effort that the story demanded. , I love you and owe you a vacation with no work involved. I'm so fortunate my mother and father always encouraged my art, and taught me that anything h doing was worth doing well. I am gratefull for Kelly Goodine and on Mann assisting me with inks and for John Rauch's amazing urs. My business partner Corey Lansdell supported this project, shouldered more responsibilities to give me the time I needed nish it. And finally, thanks to my friends, family, and co-workers were drafted as models to get the right poses, angles, and essions: Christy Dean, Vérité Grey Mellings, Niels Rasmussen, n Halun, Ava and Olivia Delaney, Chontelle Bushore, Jaryn emaker, Meaghen Hicks, Corey Lansdell, Kaillie Burghardt, nda Burghardt, Greg Miller, Allen Benson, Karl Muller, Elder Victoria Whalen.

lly Mellings

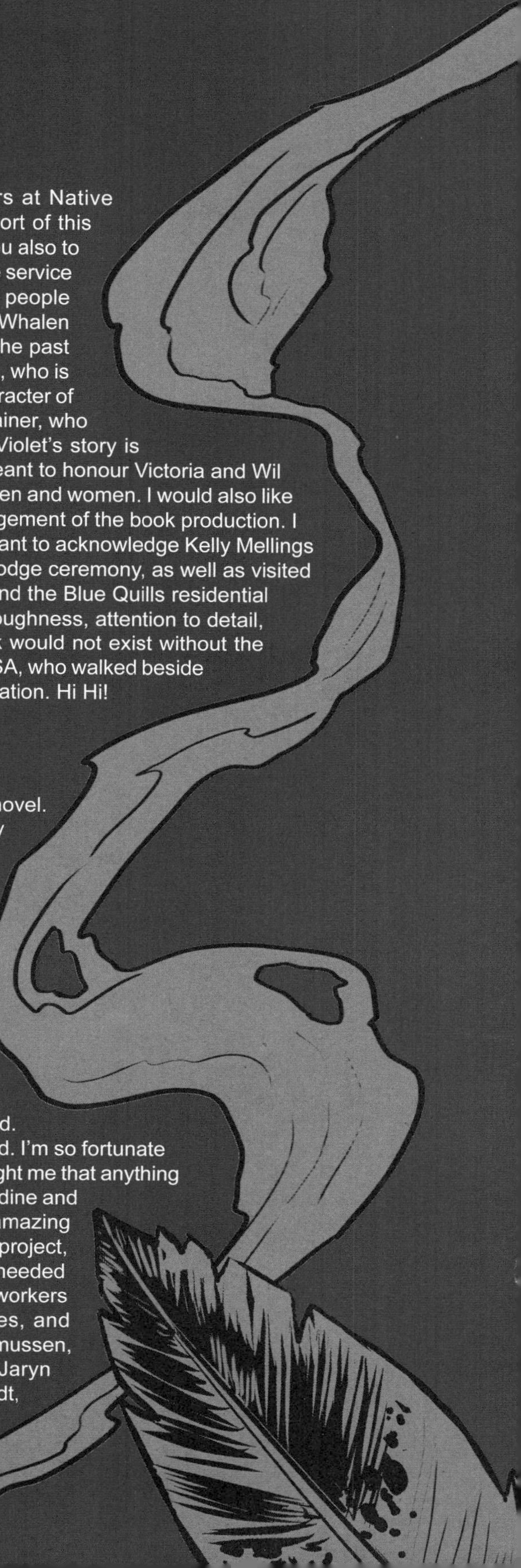

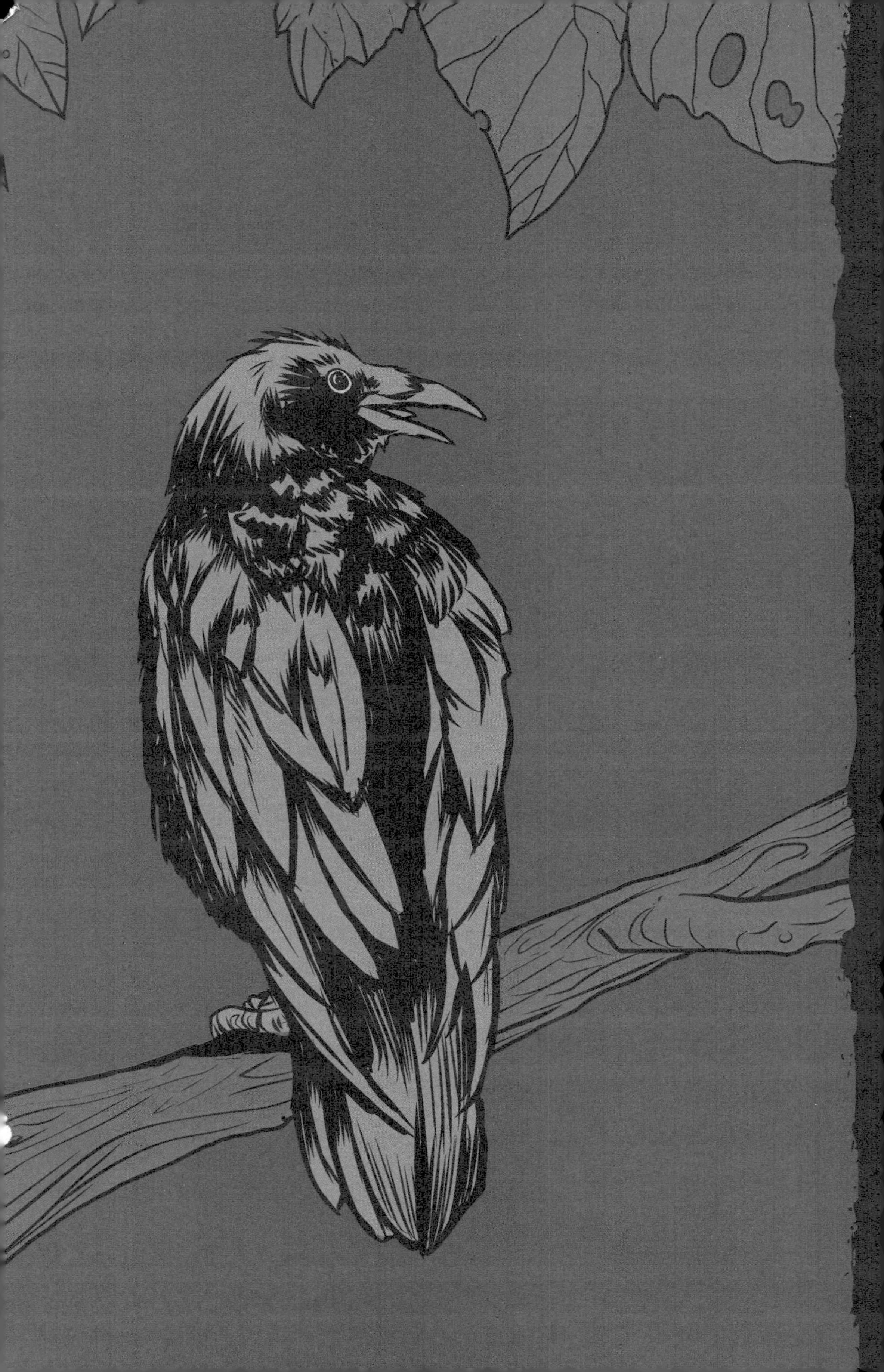